FORBIDDEN DARK VOWS

A FORCED PROXIMITY BILLIONAIRE DARK ROMANCE

VIVY SKYS

Copyright © 2024 by VIVY SKYS

All rights reserved.

No part of this book may be reproduced in any form or by any electronic or mechanical means, including information storage and retrieval systems, without written permission from the author, except for the use of brief quotations in a book review.

FORBIDDEN DARK VOWS

**Ruby and Harry
1987**

She was mine the moment I set eyes on her. ~ Harry.

1

RUBY

RUBY & HARRY 1987

My mom straightens my coat collar, checks me out, eyes narrowed like she's disappointed I left home without applying lipstick, *again*, and says, "Smile, Ruby, for God's sake."

I stretch my lips upwards in a fake smile and roll my eyes at the same time. I can't help it. She clocks the eye-roll, and her mouth pinches into a tight buttonhole shape. "Remember why we're doing this."

We are not doing anything. What she means is, remember why *you're* doing this, Ruby.

"I didn't pay for all those ice skating lessons for nothing," she adds, her voice silky smooth while making sure that I understand we're in this together.

I work at the outdoor skating rink some evenings. I don't mind it. I like being outdoors. I like watching folks landing on their butts on the ice and leaping up again, laughing like they planned it that way. Like they enjoy making a total ass of themselves on a night out.

Sure, the boots stink sometimes, and I have to pinch my nose and hold them at arm's length when I shove them back onto the correct shelf, but it means I get to skate for free whenever I want. The rink gives off holiday vibes anyway, especially when we've had a frosting of snow in Chicago, and people are snuggled up inside their furry hoods and ski gloves.

The fairy lights strung around the rink twinkle behind my mom, highlighting her rosy cheeks and pink-tipped nose. I knew as soon as I saw the VIPs rock up in a black stretch limo that it would only be a matter of time before she showed up. I could've timed it down to the second if I wasn't so busy shoving boots into the hands of celebrities wanting to show off their skills—or lack of—on the ice.

I don't even know how she does it. It's like she has a built-in radar: *money alert, money alert, money alert.*

My dad had a stroke thirteen years ago, shortly after I started middle school. Before he got sick, he'd been a successful businessman. He started his company from the basement of his parents' house when he graduated from university with a master's in computer technology and an idea that he believed would make him a millionaire.

It did. And then some.

And then it almost killed him.

Well, not the business exactly, but the stress of running a company that was evolving faster than he could keep up with. I don't know what happened exactly—my parents don't talk about it—but I do know that a bad deal wiped him out and his business collapsed faster than a house of cards.

I watch my mom fussing over my hair, teasing strands over my shoulders and clicking her tongue like she could do with a can of hairspray right about now. Her hair is immaculate as always, her clothes old but still with designer labels attached to the inside. Her eyes skim my face, noting the state of play of the makeup and nothing else.

"It's fine, Mom," I say. "An extra layer of mascara isn't going to make any difference."

"It makes all the difference, Ruby." Her eyes finally meet mine. "I didn't bring you up to be the kind of girl who forgets to check her teeth in the mirror before she leaves home."

My mom applies two coats of mascara every day, more sometimes, depending on who she wants to impress.

She works in a beauty salon—I guess looking perfect comes with the job title. It's what she did before she met my dad and got swept off her feet and into the parallel universe of exclusive hotels, expensive champagne, and glitzy parties. Between her full-time job and my three part-time jobs, we cover the household bills now that my dad can't work.

She doesn't resent him for it—for better, for worse, until death do us part, right? But she misses the lifestyle they had before the business went bankrupt. She misses the doors money opened for her, the front row seats on Broadway, and the way people looked at her like she was somebody.

That's why she's here now.

She glances over my shoulder, and her eyes widen. "He's even more gorgeous in real life than he is in the movies." I see it in the slant of her eyes and the tilt of her head, flirting without even realizing she's doing it.

I have my back to the rink, but I saw Alessandro Russo arrive with a bunch of his wealthy friends. The boss served them.

Only the best for celebrity guests—I guess he couldn't risk me trying not to gag as I handed over the bladed boots.

Mom thinks they ooze money.

I think they could do with oozing a little less arrogance and a little more authenticity.

So, maybe Alessandro Russo *is* Hollywood's rising star. Maybe his last movie *did* make him a bunch of dollars and first pick of the lead roles in next year's planned productions. But there's also the teensy little advantage in his pocket that his family is wealthy and associated with the Russian Mafia—if the stories are to be believed.

But I bet his shit still stinks.

"Don't look at me like that." Mom stands back and surveys her handiwork. AKA me.

"Like what?" I know that she knows exactly what I'm thinking.

You know how some moms say there's no point lying to them because they'll always catch you out? That's my mom. Celia Jackson. Lie detector extraordinaire. I swear it must've been her party piece when she was younger.

She places her hands on my shoulders, turns me around so that I'm facing the rink, and whispers in my ear, "Go catch yourself a Russo, sweetheart."

My dad used to take me fishing when I was a little girl when he still had time to spend doing family stuff. I never caught a fish because I couldn't sit still for more than a couple of minutes. I couldn't keep quiet either.

But more importantly, I never saw the point of trying to catch a fish using maggots as bait. It felt dishonest; those poor fish in the river never knew that the tasty maggot might be their final meal. They never knew that the meal came with a lethal hook, one that would sink inside their gullet and reel them in before they even knew what hit them.

This feels the same.

There's Alessandro Russo gliding around the ice without a care in the world in his black leather coat and shiny gold scarf. And here's me: the maggot.

The guy can skate, I'll give him that. He turns around so that he's skating backwards, legs crossed, body all sleek angles and swarthy good looks, grinning at his friends before he executes a simple toe loop and whizzes off, a trail of teenaged girls in his wake.

Ugh!

Of course, he's lapping up the attention like the cat that got the cream. He glides towards a couple of teenaged girls who are watching him from the edge of the rink, heads almost touching so that they can whisper about how hot he is, and hisses to a halt in the middle of them. I watch their cheeks turn pink as he offers them a hand each and leads them towards the middle of the ice where everyone will be able to watch the performance.

I don't even know how I'm supposed to get close to him.

A glance at my mom, and she raises her perfectly groomed eyebrows with a nod in the actor's direction.

Deep breath. I do a few laps of the rink, practicing my spins and salchows in time to the music and lose myself to the Friday-night atmosphere and the chill on my face. When I'm skating, I can forget everything else and pretend that I'm an ice princess, the way I used to do when I was younger.

The crowd around Alessandro Russo grows. I can still see his head above the girls trying to smother him with their autograph requests and their eager smiles, but he's obviously basking in their adoration like a lizard in the sunshine.

I skate away from my mom and stop at the edge of the rink, bending to fasten the lace of my left boot which has come undone. As I do, someone knees me in the side and performs a somersault over the top of me, landing on their back on the ice like an upturned beetle. I hear the whump of air whooshing from their lungs and flinch.

It sounded like it hurt. A lot.

"Are you alright?" I move closer and offer the guy a hand, and he takes it with an embarrassed smile. At least he isn't trying to fool me that he did it on purpose.

His hand is warm through his woolen glove, and his grip is firm, although he hauls himself upright and puts no pressure on me to help him.

He has a kind face, that's my first thought. My second thought is that his eyes are the color of the sea on a clear day in fall. Pumpkins pop into my head. Fiery orange leaves, steaming coffee, and log fires.

"Sore," he says, "but I guess that'll teach me to watch where I'm going next time." His gaze drifts towards the actor in the middle of the rink like a candy store owner handing out free sweeties.

"It's what happens when you choose to come skating on the same evening as someone famous." I shrug. "You should come midweek. You can practice falling elegantly as much as you like."

He smiles, and his whole face lights up. "Is that what you do?" Heat floods his cheeks. "I mean, not that I'm suggesting you can't skate. I've been watching you. Not like that, not in a pervy kind of way, just, well... You're good."

I can't help laughing. "My mom made sure I could skate. She said no one wants to be seen flat on their back with their legs up in the air, at least, not when they're wearing skates. She said if I didn't learn, there was always the possibility that someone else's blades would slice my fingers clean off."

He blinks, those cool blue eyes growing even wider. This man doesn't need an extra coat of mascara, that's for sure. "She said that?"

"My mom's full of life's important lessons."

He smiles again, his expression fading rapidly as his skates slide out from under him... While he's standing still.

I offer him another hand, only this time, when he grabs it, I can't help laughing. "On second thought, maybe you should stick to walking, or swimming. Although there's always drowning..."

He's laughing though. Which is a bonus. My mom always says I should try reining in the sarcastic humor when I'm in company because not everyone understands or appreciates it.

"Harry Weiss." He shakes my hand.

"Ruby Jackson."

"Do you want to—"

He doesn't finish because my mom has walked around the outside of the rink and is waving something at me. Harry follows my gaze, and I inhale deeply.

"Gotta go, sorry. Nice meeting you, Harry Weiss."

He nods. "You too, Ruby Jackson."

I feel mean abandoning him, but at least he can hold onto the side and pretend that he's taking a break. My spot beside him is immediately filled by another guy in a smart tweed coat, and I recognize him as one of the men who arrived with Alessandro Russo. Maybe Harry knows him too.

"Ruby!" My mom grabs my attention, and I shove Harry Weiss to the back of my thoughts. Wrong surname. Probably wrong background, too for what my mom has in mind. "What are you doing?"

"Being friendly to the paying customers?" I've spotted my car keys in her hand and try to grab them, but she snatches them away from me.

"Nu-huh. Not until you get out there and get yourself noticed."

"Have you seen how many people have had the same idea?"

She pockets my keys and sets her features into a this-is-me-you're-talking-to expression. "Other people are not you, Ruby. Other people can't skate right over there, grab his goddamn hand, and show him what you can do."

"What makes you think he'll be interested in what I can do?"

"He's a good-looking, hot-blooded young man, and you're a beautiful young woman."

That's it. That's her reasoning, and she doesn't even see anything wrong in the way she presented it like being a female is enough.

I don't tell her that I'm done being a maggot. He'll either notice me or he won't. And even if I reel him in, there's no guarantee that he won't flip straight back into the water to chase the fish already wagging their tails in his face.

"You're not getting your keys back until you do," she says, "so I suggest you start performing now." My mom walks away, her eyes on the prize who is currently autographing the back of someone's hand, a well-practiced smile on his face.

I skate around the group of fans, giving my best impression of someone who doesn't know that she's in the presence of movie royalty. I don't even look in Alessandro Russo's direction. I focus on the blades cutting the surface of the ice, and everything I ever learned when my mom dragged me to the rink as a child.

I sense, rather than see, the shift in the atmosphere. The music grows livelier, cashing in on the Friday night experience, and the crowd starts moving away from the celebrity, giving him space to strut his stuff. Two tunes later, and he's skating alongside me, hands behind his back like this was what he was born to do.

"Do you come here often?" He flashes me his most dazzling smile like that will seal the deal with minor effort on his part.

"Seriously? That's your chat-up line?" Sometimes, I can't help myself.

He laughs out loud. I bet it's won him a few dates before now with that laughter. "Shit. You got me there. You're good." He gestures to the ice.

Here's the point where I should tell him that he's not so bad himself. You know, flirt a bit, bat my eyelashes at him. But then I spot Harry Weiss in my peripheral vision, clinging for dear life to the side of the rink as my mom approaches him, says something, and then waits for him to make his way off the ice.

Whatever she said, it worked. He glances my way, once, but he doesn't smile or wave or even acknowledge that he almost took my fingers off. Nothing.

Then a new track comes through the speakers. 'Love is in the Air'. It's my dad's favorite tune, and it hits me like a jolt straight through my heart that I'm doing this for my dad. For us. To give us all a better life. And I smile at the hot actor.

2

HARRY

It's late by the time I arrive at the InterContinental for Alessandro's birthday party. I didn't even see the others leave the skating rink—I was too busy changing the tire on Ruby's car. Her mom, Celia, told me that she'd noticed her daughter's car had a slow puncture and she didn't want her to be stranded in the city when she finished her shift.

I mean, how could I refuse?

I stumbled right over the goddamn top of her—changing her tire was the least I could do. Not that I was helping as an apology. I'd already made an ass of myself with that one.

If I'm honest, I don't even recall the physical process of the tire change. I guess I was shell shocked, or at least in a bit of a daze, reeling from my brief conversation with Ruby. Something about her...

Anyway, I study my reflection in the elevator mirror and realize that I have grease on my chin. I try scrubbing it off with the sleeve of my sweater and only succeed in spreading it further, so now I look like a kid who's just returned from summer camp. I smooth my hair back with my hands and sigh when it springs straight back up again.

The party is in full swing, buzzing with laughter and loud conversations that will only grow more boisterous as the evening progresses. I'll stay for a couple of drinks and then leave—parties are not really my scene, they're much more Alessandro's thing. I guess if we met now, rather than at Uni, we probably wouldn't be friends, we wouldn't even socialize in the same circles.

Carlos, Alessandro's brother, comes over and grimaces when he notices the smears on my face, and I subconsciously try to wipe them away with the palm of my hand. "What happened to you? Is this supposed to be some kind of camouflage so that no one will notice you? If so, it isn't working."

I check my fingers—they're grubby now too. "Just helping a damsel in distress."

He peers all around, his eyes twinkling. That's the thing about the Russo family—they all have that sparkle, a charisma that people literally find irresistible, and they're genuinely nice people with it. Must be why the universe smiles down on them.

"Where is she then, this damsel in distress?"

I can't help smiling. "She's the one that got away."

Carlos clamps a large warm hand on my shoulder and peers around at the guests.

Alessandro hired a function suite for the party, the ceiling heavy with crystal chandeliers that cast shimmering diamonds across the room. Waiters in crisp white shirts and black bow ties are walking around with trays of champagne. The tables lining the room are laden with platters of food and floral centerpieces.

Not the kind of place I'd ever have envisaged my friend hosting a birthday party, but he's drifting into a new lifestyle, and I wonder how long it will be before he leaves his old friends behind. I recognize a young actress from a recently released movie, wearing a gold dress that looks as if it has been poured over her. She's talking to a movie director who looks remarkably like Martin Scorsese.

I swallow hard, wishing that I'd at least gone back to my room to shower before making an appearance.

"I see Alessandro has finally met his match," Carlos says, dragging me out of my self-indulgent misery.

"Who?" I scan the room for Alessandro—he's taller than most people—and the air seems to leave my lungs for a second time this evening when I spot him across the room with a small group of people I don't recognize. Apart from the young woman standing beside him.

Ruby Jackson.

Do they know each other? Or did Alessandro dish out invitations like autographs at the ice rink? A quick glance around the room tells me that she's the only one here who isn't dressed to impress, so I guess he didn't bring a busload of folks back with him.

She's the only one.

A waiter comes over, and I accept a glass of champagne which I down in one go. And regret it instantly when the bubbles resurface almost instantaneously.

"Have you ever seen him like this?" Carlos nods in their direction.

He doesn't need to elaborate—I know exactly what he means. Alessandro is charming as always, steering the conversation, the wide easy smile a constant, but his eyes keep flicking to the woman at his side, the sparkle unmistakable. His hand snakes around her and settles on her lower back as he lowers his head to whisper in her ear, and she smiles up at him...

I signal for the waiter to bring more champagne and switch my empty glass for a full one. I sip this drink slowly.

I don't know why Alessandro inviting Ruby to his birthday celebration bothers me so much. Scratch that. I know exactly why it bothers me.

We've been friends long enough for me to understand that he'll woo her and then drop her like a lead balloon as soon as he gets bored. Alessandro is the classic chaser. He enjoys the challenge, and if my brief conversation with Ruby is anything to go by, she'll present the kind of challenge he'll be unable to refuse.

And Ruby Jackson deserves better than that.

I swallow another mouthful of bubbly liquid. I need a beer. I'll never get used to drinking champagne and expensive wine that needs time to breathe before you can taste it.

How do I know that she deserves better?

I don't. At least, that's what I tell myself, as I turn away from the sight of my best friend nuzzling her neck while she chews her bottom lip.

"I think I need to meet the woman who has captivated my

little brother." Carlos raises his glass to me in a mock toast and navigates around the guests to go join Alessandro and Ruby.

"Did you get into a scrape or something?" Ronnie comes over with a beer and eyes up my greasy face.

"Long story. Where did you find a beer?"

Ronnie taps the side of his nose. "I brought a secret stash. I can't be drinking that shit."

I follow him to the cloakroom, where he has hidden a crate of beer underneath a rail of glamorous but impractical winter coats. We crack open a couple of cans and follow the steady thrum of voices back to the function room.

Ronnie spots an old friend and leaves me standing next to a table filled with hors d'oeuvres, bite-sized morsels that smell overwhelmingly fishy. I'm so busy studying the swirls of pink mousse and crab claws and tiny mounds of caviar, that I don't notice anyone approaching.

"Have you recovered?"

I spin around to find Ruby standing next to me, a smile tugging her lips up at the corners. "Yes. Thank you. Yes, I always feel safer when my feet are touching the ground."

She nods. Too late, I realize that she has already spotted the black smears on my chin. "Another accident or did you read the newspaper on the way here?"

I can't help chuckling. She seems to have that effect on me, creating laughter that gurgles beneath the surface just waiting to erupt every time she speaks.

"I changed your tire. I should've gone back to my room to shower, but I didn't think, and, well, you're not the first person to have noticed, so it looks like I'm stuck with it now."

She furrows her brow. "My tire?"

"Yes. Your mom said you had a slow puncture. It was flat as a pancake when I got there. She was worried about you getting home."

She nibbles her bottom lip with her front teeth and then says, "May I?" gesturing to my beer. I hand it over and she takes a long swig, wiping her mouth with the back of her hand before handing it back to me. "Thank you. For the beer and the tire."

Ruby moves closer and surveys the guests in their fancy clothes. "Are you and Alessandro friends?"

Alessandro... The name already sounds comfortable on her tongue.

"Known each other since Uni."

"Are you an actor too?"

She studies me intently, and I notice now that her eyes are green. I've never seen green eyes close up before, and I think I understand why cats are so bewitching.

"No. I work in oil. Petroleum. Fuel."

Her laughter caresses my cheek like a chiffon scarf. "So, you're used to getting your hands dirty."

I peer down at my empty hand and ball it into a fist to hide my grimy fingers. "Not quite. At least, not anymore."

Her eyes narrow briefly. "Not anymore?"

"I seem to spend more time in the office these days, managing numbers."

She gives me a curious sideways smile. "So, what, you're an accountant?"

I'm generally uncomfortable discussing what I do—most women turn their nose up at the word fuel—but Ruby isn't like most women. She's still here and she doesn't look like she's trying to escape. Yet.

"Not exactly." I swallow, the back of my throat clicking drily. "I'm the boss. I own my own company. It's still early days. We can't compete with the likes of BP or Chevron, but, well..." I glug a mouthful of beer. There's the dark family business but I'm not involved with it yet, and I don't want to scare my woman away. *My woman?* "What do you do? When you're not skating?"

"I read a lot."

I nod and pray that she doesn't ask me who my favorite author is. I haven't read a book since Uni.

"I studied literature," she continues without waiting for a response. Which is just as well really, as book talk isn't my strongest subject. "It was the only thing that I stood a hope in hell of passing, so I went with it."

She has an air of confidence that allows her to say exactly what she means rather than pussyfooting around. I like that about her.

"Favorite book?" I ask, because damn, I want to know.

"*Wuthering Heights*. I've lost count of the number of times I've read it. Doesn't everyone want to be loved the way Heathcliff loves Catherine Earnshaw?"

I must be gaping at her because the smile is back, but she isn't laughing *at* me.

"I guess," she continues, "if your next question is what I want to do with my life, it would be to write a modern-day

Wuthering Heights. Not because I want to go down in history as the next Emily Bronte, but because if I can write about love with that kind of passion, then I'll be a very happy lady."

"Was Emily Bronte happy?" I ask.

She studies me coolly. "What a question, Harry Weiss."

A shiver travels down my spine at the way she says my name.

"You know, she probably wasn't. She died when she was thirty years old. Can you imagine what she might've gone on to write had she lived a full and healthy life?"

"There you are!" Alessandro is standing in front of us, his eyes sparkling for Ruby. "We're all heading down to the pool before we're too drunk to stay afloat." He entwines his fingers with hers and pulls her away.

"Are you coming, Harry?" Ruby doesn't move; she's waiting for me to answer.

"Course he's coming. Aren't you, Harry?" Alessandro raises his eyebrows at me, telling me to get a move on.

"Sure. I didn't bring swim shorts though."

"Who cares?" Alessandro guides her away from me. "No one did."

IN TYPICAL ALESSANDRO RUSSO FASHION, the party quickly gets messy. Some people climb into the pool in their underwear, while others strip off their clothes and jump in naked, some still clutching glasses of champagne.

I stand back and listen to their voices bouncing off the walls, the smell of chlorine tickling my nostrils and reminding me of childhood swimming lessons. The desire to swim is huge, but the requirement to ditch my clothes first is keeping me immobile.

I search for a glimpse of Ruby amongst the splashes and the beaming faces like a bunch of kids just out of school for the summer. Is that what being naked does to them, sets them free? I'm strangely relieved when I don't spot Ruby's honey-colored hair.

"Not going in?"

I turn around and there she is, fully clothed, and I can't stop my grin from spreading. "Not really my scene."

She smiles back at me. "My mom always says that you should leave something to the imagination."

"Always? Do you often discuss getting naked in public?"

"You haven't met my mom." She goes to say more and then changes her mind.

"I did, briefly, remember? Your tire."

Ruby faces the pool, and I wonder if she's looking for Alessandro. I spot him in the deep end, getting close to the actress who has poured herself out of the slinky gold dress and wrapped her arms around his neck like she's clinging to a lifebelt.

"Do you want to get out of here?" I want to take her away before she notices him too, but mostly because I don't want to see the disappointment in her eyes.

She nods and walks away without waiting for me to catch up with her.

Even though I didn't swim, I feel strangely cleansed as we make our way outside, the cold air stinging our cheeks. I hail a cab and open the door for her, climbing into the back seat next to her. Ruby gives the driver her home address, and we sit in comfortable silence as we drive through the Chicago city streets.

Ruby peers out of the passenger window. I don't know if she expected more from Alessandro or if she's simply tired, but I want to hold her hand and keep her warm, tell her that he might be my friend, but he'll only hurt her, and that seeing her hurt is the last thing I want right now.

But I don't.

When the car stops, I climb out and open the door for her, and we stand on the sidewalk outside her house, the ground glistening with frost, the chill nipping our noses.

"Take care, Ruby Jackson," I say.

Fuck, but I want to kiss her lips so badly.

"You too, Harry Weiss." She reaches up and kisses my cheek, and then she's gone, running up the path to her front door, while I climb back into the cab, the imprint of her lips forever on my skin.

3

RUBY

"When are you seeing him again?" Mom sips her coffee leaning against the kitchen counter the following morning before she goes to work.

"I'm not." I slather butter onto a slice of toast. The world does not think nearly highly enough of toast—it is the food of gods. "What did you think was going to happen? A marriage proposal within an hour of meeting?"

"I thought you would at least have secured a second date, Ruby." Faint lines appear between her eyebrows. She's disappointed, which means that she'll already be scheming to get me back in front of Alessandro Russo.

"To secure a second date, we would need to have enjoyed a first."

"Don't get clever with me, Ruby. No one likes a smartass."

"I do." I munch on my toast and lick dripping butter from my fingers.

I don't tell her that I'm not taking anyone's sloppy seconds. I saw his tongue disappearing into that woman's mouth. It's obvious that Alessandro Russo is never going to be a one-woman man, and I'm worth more than that, even if my mom doesn't believe I am.

"Even if he has no money and no prospects?" Mom finishes her coffee and grabs her purse from the counter.

"I'd rather have an intellectual conversation with a smartass than a bottle of champagne in a snooty restaurant with someone who's eying up the waitresses."

"Oh, sweetie." She comes over and teases the curls out of my ponytail. "All men eye up other women. So long as they don't touch, there's nothing you can do about it."

"Did Dad?"

She hesitates, her spine stiffening, the usual glazed look appearing in her eyes. "Of course he looked at other women. Lucky for me, he realized how good he had it at home."

She leaves the house in a waft of Chanel No. 5, calling out goodbye to my dad as she goes, and poking her head back around the kitchen door to say, "Leave it with me, sweetie. This one's not getting away so easily."

I finish my breakfast, the toast clinging to the roof of my mouth. I try to empty my mind, focusing on my food and coffee instead of my mom's determination to bag me a rich husband, but it doesn't work.

Was Emily Bronte happy?

Why did Harry Weiss of all people pop into my head? It wasn't like I was ever going to see him again, but something about the way he asked the question had stuck with me. He didn't tell me that he knew nothing about the book or that he preferred movies to reading—although he probably did—but instead he'd ingested my comment and gotten straight to the heart of it. What made the author tick.

I swallow another mouthful of toast. Time for work.

I clear my dishes and go into the den where my dad is tucked up on the couch with a Harold Robbins book open on his lap.

"Are you off?" I see the way his expression crumples even though he tries to hide it.

I know he must be bored at home all day on his own, and it breaks my heart to have to leave him, but the bills won't pay themselves. He makes me think of a dog waiting by the front door all day for his humans to come home because that's the best part of the day.

"I'm due in the library in exactly—" I check my watch "—ten minutes." I'm late again, but I sense that he doesn't want me to leave.

"Go. I'll be fine. You love your job at the library."

I do. I enjoy it even more than I enjoy the dog walking I do to earn some extra cash. The library is the only place where I can forget everything else and pretend that I'm in Narnia or Wonderland or the Yorkshire moors. There's no pressure to be me in the beautiful old building.

"See you later." I cross the room and kiss his cheek. "I have a question to ask you when I get back."

He smiles. "I'm intrigued. Can I wait that long?"

"Sorry. You have no choice."

He stops me when I reach the door. "So long as it doesn't involve your mom's determination to clip your wings and tie you down."

I freeze. I've never heard Mom discuss anything like that with him, so I'm surprised to hear him say it out loud. He knows more than he ever lets on, but I guess what else does he have to fill his day with?

"You know me, Dad. I'll fly when I'm ready."

He nods, and I swear there are tears in his eyes. "That's my baby girl."

I spend the rest of the day restocking bookshelves and directing people towards the right aisles. The smell of old books is my comfort zone, especially in winter when the days are short and the early twilight brings a gentle hush to the old building. When the whole world has gone home to put the fire on and shut the curtains, I choose a book and go lose myself in a squashy sofa somewhere quiet.

Today, I choose the same book my dad is reading: *A Stone for Danny Fisher*. It makes me feel close to him, like I can get inside his head and know what he's been thinking all day.

I lose track of time until I hear whispered voices and the gentle click of the front door. I close my book and listen. "Mrs. Bates?" I call out. Mrs. Bates is my boss and although she's easygoing and happy to let me read when my work is done, she'd never go home without checking if the building is empty.

Come to think of it, I haven't seen her in a couple of hours.

I stand up, make my way towards the front desk, and stop when I reach the end of the history section. The ceiling lamps have been switched off, ready to close for the night, but the main entrance is aglow with golden light. Is there an event tonight that I've forgotten about?

"Mrs. Bates, did I forget—"

I round the corner of the bookcase and freeze.

The entire library has been decorated with fairy lights, giving it the appearance of Santa's grotto. Music is playing in the background, an old song by the Carpenters, and Mrs. Bates is nowhere to be seen.

Then Alessandro steps out from behind the romance section and grins at me. "Do you like it?"

I blink like this is a dream and I need to wake up. But no, he's still there.

"I brought champagne." He reaches behind him for a bottle which he pops open, then pours the bubbling liquid into two tall crystal flutes. He hands a glass to me.

I take it in silence, my brain still trying to process what's going on.

"You left so suddenly last night," he says. "I couldn't leave without saying goodbye."

"Goodbye?" I sip the champagne, the bubbles fizzing on my tongue. "Where are you going?"

"LA. Hollywood. We start shooting next week."

Of course he's going to Hollywood. My mom didn't expect him to meet me and stick around in Chicago for a while, did she? Or maybe she hoped he'd take me with him, lavish me with expensive gifts and a new wardrobe befitting the role of an actor's girlfriend, while I proved to him that he couldn't possibly live without me.

"You could've picked up the phone."

His smile is wide, and I remember the woman climbing him in the pool of the InterContinental. He's oblivious. "You didn't give me your number."

"Do you do this for every woman who doesn't give you her number?"

"What do you take me for?" He spreads his arms wide.

"The kind of guy who can snap his fingers and have any woman he wants."

"Ouch." He doesn't look like he's in pain. "You sting me, Ruby. Have dinner with me. Please."

"I don't know."

The image of them naked in the pool isn't going away, and it'll take more than a glass of champagne and some fairy lights to erase it. Even if he is destined to become a household name.

"I brought you a gift." He picks up a small neatly wrapped package from the front desk and holds it out so that I have to step closer.

I put down my glass and take the gift from him, his long, slender fingers caressing mine a beat too long. I pretend not to notice as I unwrap it.

It's a first edition copy of *Wuthering Heights* in mint condition. I run my fingertips across the cover and turn it over to make sure the back is as perfect as the front.

"It's a rare edition," he says. "I couldn't believe my luck when I found it."

I want him to stop talking. I want him to stop making this about him and me, and just let me enjoy it before I give it back to him.

Because I can't keep it. I have no idea how much it would've cost, but it wouldn't have been cheap, and he doesn't even know me.

"It's beautiful." I glance up at him and catch his eager eyes before the smile is back. For a moment, he looks like a little boy surprising his first crush with a present. "But—"

"This is me now, standing in this library with you."

He has adapted a quote from the book and switched the word 'moors' with 'library'.

"Did my—did someone put you up to this?" I'm reluctant to let the book go, but I know I can't keep it.

"I had some help from Harry," he says sheepishly. "Have dinner with me, Ruby."

Harry helped him? I find myself saying yes without even understanding why, but all I do know is that I'm even worse at reading men than I thought I was.

HE HAS ALREADY BOOKED a table for two in a cozy corner of the kind of restaurant I can barely afford to peek through the window of. He tells me to order whatever I want from the menu like I might be swayed to choose something cheap because he's paying. So, I order lobster, the most expensive thing I can find.

He talks about his role in the new movie, and his family, and Italy, which is where he was born and where his parents still own several homes and quite a lot of land.

And I think about how much my mom would love him for a son-in-law.

A man comes over when we've finished our main course and shakes Alessandro's hand, clapping him on the back like they're lifelong buddies. He drags a seat over from a nearby table and sits down, and my breath catches in my throat when I recognize Kurt Russell.

Jesus fucking Christ.

Kurt Russell!

If she could see me now, my mom would have me in the nearest bridal store and trying on wedding gowns before I could blink.

Alessandro introduces me to Kurt Russell, who leans over, takes my warm hand in his, and kisses me on the cheek. I'm never going to wash my face again.

He picks up the book Alessandro bought for me, strokes the cover the way I did when I opened it, and says, "I remember reading this in high school and hating it." My stomach twists, my first crush crumpled like autumn leaves. "But I read it again last year and boy do I get it now."

I'm floating. The waiter will have to grab my feet and drag me back down to earth any moment now.

Then, Alessandro leans closer and places his arm around my shoulder, his thumb stroking my left breast. I sit forward and reach for my wine glass which, I realize too late, is empty. Kurt Russell signals to the waiter to bring another bottle, and they settle into a conversation about upcoming movies and the roles they'd love to audition for, given the opportunity.

I drink my wine, and only half tune into the conversation.

Alessandro's hands are everywhere. He's paying attention to the conversation, but his eyes are everywhere too, and I'd bet my last dollar that he could tell me everyone who has walked in and out of the restaurant, and what they had to eat.

"Great guy," he says about Kurt when we're leaving. "Helped me a lot when I was first starting out."

I keep quiet; he doesn't need an answer. This is his world, and I just want to go home.

A chauffeur-driven limo is waiting outside for us. I give the driver my address and climb in, Alessandro sitting way too close, his thigh pressed up against mine.

I move away from him, and he moves closer. He strokes my cheek with his right hand, but before I can ask him to stop, his fingers are inside my coat, and underneath my sweater.

"What are you—"

His mouth closes on mine, and the image of the woman in the pool with her tongue in his mouth floods my mind again. I try to pull away, but he grips my chin tightly, his fist like warm metal, his fingertips digging into my skin.

I squirm and wriggle, trying to twist my face away from him, but his tongue is probing, filling my mouth, and I can't breathe.

He pulls away long enough to whisper, "God, you're beautiful," like it's the standard compliment that he rolls out for every woman he wants to fuck.

I try pushing him off me, but somehow, he is on top of me, pinning me down, and my senses are filled with one thought: *I need to get away from him*. But his hands are everywhere, inside my sweater and my pants... Something gives—I think it's the zipper of my pants—and I feel so exposed, so vulnerable, and I wonder why the car is still moving... Why hasn't the driver stopped?

"Oh, baby," he murmurs, his breath entering my lungs.

He doesn't even say my name. I'm just 'baby' to him, like every other woman he has ever screwed, and it gives me the shot of rage and energy that I need.

He raises his upper body a fraction to maneuver his hand inside my panties, and I slide my arms between us and thump his chest with both hands, pounding his ribs like I'm battering down a door. He pulls his hands out of my clothes and grips my wrists to stop me.

It's all I need. I raise my knees and shove him off me, rolling out from under him and landing on my knees on the floor of the limo. I drag my coat back around me, and shuffle backwards, putting as much distance between us as possible.

My breaths are coming in short, shallow gasps. And Alessandro is watching me with a look of genuine confusion on his face.

"What's wrong? I thought you wanted this."

I pull the limited-edition *Wuthering Heights* from my purse and throw it at him, flinching when I hear the spine rip. "Stop the car."

"What?" He shakes his head. "What did I do? It's why you came to the party last night, isn't it? I mean, we're both fucking adults here. You didn't grab your skates last night for the sheer fucking fun of it."

He doesn't get it. I guess that's what happens when you're a good-looking movie star. The world is your oyster. Women throw their panties at you, and you take whatever you want, whenever you want it.

"Stop. The. Car."

He scoffs and shakes his head at me like I'm a little girl who just realized she doesn't want to play big-girl games and now shit's getting real. He leans forward, taps on the window separating us from the driver, and asks him to pull over.

I open the door and climb out, as the first snowflakes hit my face and make my eyes water.

"Good luck getting a better offer," he says, before I can slam the door shut.

"I already did, asshole. Kurt Russell gave me his number when you were eying up the woman at the next table." I know I shouldn't lie about Kurt when he's in love with Goldie Hawn, but I hope it infuriates him.

I walk away, my boots crunching on the icy sidewalk, a light frosting of snow collecting on my eyelashes as I tilt my head towards the starry sky.

4

HARRY

I'M towel-drying my hair with a fluffy white hotel towel when someone starts pounding on my door. I grab a bath sheet towel, wrap it around my waist and open the door.

"It's our last day in Chicago." Alessandro pushes past me and flops backwards onto my unmade bed, arms and legs spread eagled like a starfish. "I want to go to the amusement park."

I close the door and wrap the towel around my neck. "Right now?"

"Why not?" He props himself up on his elbows and eyes up my bare chest like he's comparing our physiques and congratulating himself on still being the hottest member of the group.

"I've just got out of the shower." As if this isn't obvious.

Alessandro crosses the room to the mini bar and fixes himself a drink. JD and Coke. It's barely mid-morning.

The curtains are open, but the world outside seems white and muffled like we're nestling in the middle of a bank of clouds.

When I peer outside, I understand why. It must've been snowing all night—the plows have cleared tracks along the street , and the sidewalks are lined on both sides by ridges of slushy snow.

"Have you looked outside?" I turn to face Alessandro who's peering into his empty glass tumbler. "We could go to the museum instead or, I don't know, somewhere inside ... and warm."

"Where's your sense of adventure? Or are you worried that I'll make you ride the Ferris Wheel?"

"Seriously, man?"

"It's settled anyway. Call it research."

"Research? An amusement park?"

"Sure. There's a movie my agent wants me to audition for. I've never been on a rollercoaster before. If it's going to make me throw up, I'd rather know about it now."

Alessandro has always had more energy than the rest of us put together. He's always the last one to leave a nightclub and the first one out of bed the morning after, even with a hangover. It's almost as if his blood fizzes through his veins like soda, making him chase the next thing and the next until he finally crashes.

This morning is no exception.

"How did the date go?" I blurt it out before I can talk myself out of it.

He came to me yesterday morning and begged me to help him find Ruby, said that she was the most extraordinary woman he'd ever met, said that he couldn't leave Chicago without seeing her again.

And, like an idiot, I agreed to help him.

I told myself that if Ruby was the woman for my best friend, then who was I to stand in the way of true love? And if she wasn't...

Ruby Jackson wasn't hard to find, especially when we dangled the name Alessandro Russo in front of the manager of the skating rink. He told us about Ruby's other jobs, and when we learned that she worked in the library, the rest was easy. Alessandro wanted to barge straight in there, bribe the manager to let her off her shift and impress her with a trip to the Skydeck Chicago Willis Tower and dinner.

The limited-edition book was my idea. If anything was going to speak to Ruby Jackson's heart it was her favorite love story.

"Great. Yeah, fantastic." He downs his second drink.

"What did she say about the book?"

He grins at me. "Gotta give it to you, man, that was ace. She was ... lost for words."

My stomach twists. It's what I wanted to hear, right? I wanted her to like the book. In fact, I want her to treasure it for the rest of her days, pulling it off the bookshelf and rereading it over and over until she's old and gray. I want to be old and gray myself with that image still fresh in my mind.

I can't quite put my finger on it, though, but something about his attitude this morning feels a little off, and my hackles are up.

"Where did you take her?"

"We had dinner at the new restaurant on State Street. You'll never guess who was there. Kurt Russell." He doesn't wait for me to guess. "He came over and spoke to me like I'd known him all my life."

Me. I. My.

This is Alessandro all over. But I'm noticing it more now, and I don't know if that's my bad or his.

He sets the empty tumbler down on the desk and goes to the door. "I'll round up the others and wait in the lobby for you." Then he's gone.

SURPRISINGLY, Great America is busy with people who want to experience the thrill of the world's tallest carousel and the three-armed Ferris Wheel in the snow. The aromas of hot dogs, barely fried onions, and cotton candy follow us around along with the klaxons and tinny tunes of the rides in motion.

Alessandro wants to ride everything. He's wearing his trademark leather coat and a Russian hat that only he could pull off, lapping up the appreciative stares of everyone who recognizes him.

We ride the rollercoaster, but once isn't enough for him today. He lines up behind a young couple who are holding hands and huddling together for warmth, stomping their feet to stop their toes from freezing.

"What's he doing?" Ronnie elbows me in the ribs through my coat.

When I check out the line, Alessandro has sidled in between the couple, turned his back on the man and is stepping forward with the young woman to share a car with her. He sits a little too close, his arm pressed up against hers. I think I must be the only one who has noticed, but then the woman's boyfriend walks away, head down, hands stuffed deep inside his pockets.

I want to go after him, tell him that it doesn't mean anything, that Alessandro will go find someone else to ride with next time, but they're futile excuses. She chose him. She chose Alessandro because he didn't give her the choice.

I ball my gloved hands into fists and walk off to grab a hamburger and a coffee.

He did the same to Ruby. He didn't give her a choice, and now that he has no doubt spent the night with her, he's out here looking for the next thrill.

Ruby Jackson isn't anyone's next thrill.

But I have the strongest suspicion that Alessandro hasn't been entirely honest with me. He hasn't gloated about how many times they fucked when he took her back to his room or elaborated on what position she liked best or how loudly she screamed when she had an orgasm. By the time I've finished my hamburger and tossed the wrapper into the trash can, I've convinced myself that Ruby turned him down, and the klaxon blaring from the bumper cars nearby doesn't even rattle my nerves and make me jump.

While I've been eating, the snow has started falling in thick fluffy clumps, settling on my overcoat and turning the park into a winter wonderland. I tilt my face towards the sky and wonder if Ruby is doing the same. Or perhaps she's curled up in an armchair in front of a roaring fire with her rare edition of *Wuthering Heights*.

Ronnie comes running over and almost lands on his ass when his feet slide out from under him. "Alessandro got into a fight. He's leaving."

"A fight?" Maybe that guy didn't walk off and forget about his girlfriend after all.

"Yeah. It's nothing. He knocked the guy over, but he says he's getting out of here." Ronnie is already backing away, and I follow him towards the entrance.

Alessandro is outside, making footprints in the settling snow. I call out to him, but he doesn't break stride or glance over his shoulder.

"Let the others know that we're leaving," I say to Ronnie. "I'll go after Alessandro."

I run to catch up with him. He gives me a sideways glance, but he doesn't stop, doesn't even acknowledge my presence. Once he gets to the main road, he hails a cab, barely waiting for me to climb in next to him.

"What happened?" I ask.

He slides a silver hip flask from his pocket and glugs whatever liquor he filled it with earlier. His right eye looks puffy, gray-mauve bruising already seeping through the delicate skin. "Nothing I couldn't handle. You should see the other guy." He gives me a lopsided grin and offers me the hip flask.

I shake my head. "You wanna talk about it?"

"Nope."

"We'll go back to the hotel, warm up, and take a look at your eye."

"I'm not sticking around." He tips the flask into his mouth again, only this time he gets the dregs.

I sit back. "I checked the weather forecast. This is only the start of it. They're expecting a blizzard overnight."

"I'll be in St. Louis by then."

"What's in St. Louis?"

"My cousin's throwing a party. I was going to bail, but I think I'm done here." He keeps his eyes fixed on the passenger window, peering through the slushy ice trickling down the glass and forming a narrow ridge at the bottom.

It's early afternoon, but the world is already preparing for sleep, twilight taking over before its time. The streets are not as busy as usual. Folks are staying inside, cranking up the heating, and making hot chocolate. No one in their right mind would travel in this.

"The flights will probably be cancelled."

"Who said anything about flying?" He looks at me then for the first time, his eyebrows dancing independently.

"Buses too."

He shakes his head. "Don't worry about me, Harry. I'll get there."

My pulse is racing. I don't know what was in that hip flask, but he already had a couple of drinks in my hotel room before we left, so he can't be considering driving to St. Louis. Or can he? He's no longer buzzing with energy, but his mood is scratchy now, jerky, like there's a rope fastened around his neck, and someone is tugging on the other end.

I pay the driver when the cab stops outside the hotel.

Alessandro is already out of the vehicle and heading straight for his neat blue Porsche parked out in the front. He opens the driver's door and climbs in.

"Hey! What are you doing?" I barely manage to jump in and close the passenger door behind me before he starts the engine.

The wipers drag a mini mountain of snow across the windshield. He ramps up the heating to full capacity and throws the car into gear. I peer through the snow-streaked glass at the ominously gray sky, heavy with the blizzard to come. The streetlamps are on, casting puddles of eerie yellow light across the slippery sidewalks, a few people dipping in and out of the glow with their heads down.

I fasten my seatbelt as the rear wheels lose their purchase on the street. Alessandro turns the steering wheel into the spin and straightens the car inches away from careening into a lamppost.

"You can't drive to St. Louis in this." I'd hoped that he was joking in the cab, but my thumping heartbeat and his white knuckles on the steering wheel are telling me I was wrong. He's doing this.

"No one asked you to come." He hunches forward in his seat and wipes the inside of the windshield with the sleeve of his coat to clear the steam that's forming with the heat inside the car.

I ignore his comment. "You've been drinking. The roads are already treacherous, and the blizzard hasn't even started yet."

"Anytime you want to get out, you just say the word."

I study his profile which looks gaunt in the flickering lights trying to reach us from the storefronts and streetlamps. I wish I knew what he was thinking. He has always been the adventurous one, the guy who'd sign up to freefall from an airplane or climb a mountain or go diving with sharks. But driving from Chicago to St. Louis in a blizzard to attend a party...

There's a huge difference between being adventurous and being reckless, and I find myself gripping the sides of the passenger seat like my life depends on it.

"If I say the word, will you stop the car and walk back to the hotel with me?" He hasn't even gone back for his clothes.

The traffic signals turn red, the glow turning the dashboard rosy, and Alessandro hits the brakes, the car spinning out of control across the road. I hear a strange guttural sound that might be me, and then the car jerks to a stop. I don't know how.

I can't think straight. My head is pounding with the blood pumping around my heart, but Alessandro laughs out loud.

"Woohoo!" He doesn't waste a beat. He hits the accelerator and speeds off again towards the Interstate out of town.

I don't speak. My mouth is dry, and all I can taste is the hamburger I ate at the amusement park. I don't want to be in the car, but I can't let him do this alone.

By the time we reach the highway, the blizzard is in full swing, the heavy flakes hitting the windshield with a series of dull whumps. The wipers try to keep up with the snowfall, but I can barely see the road through a couple of inches of smeared glass.

"We could find a roadside motel and pull over for the night," I suggest.

Alessandro either doesn't hear me, or he's choosing to ignore me because he doesn't want to admit defeat.

Bright lights make me squint and turn my eyes away. A truck is coming towards us on the other side of the road. That's why I don't see it happening.

I feel the rear tires skidding across the icy slush, the sensation inside my stomach a little like being on the Ferris Wheel when it tilts sideways. My fingertips grip the seat more tightly. My head moves in slow motion to watch Alessandro turning the wheel back and forth, the car lurching into a spin that makes the bile rise in my throat.

And that's when I realize that he isn't wearing his seatbelt.

5

RUBY

"Have you heard the news?"

Mom is making ham omelets. Her cooking repertoire literally consists of omelets and grilled cheese, anything else is down to me. Dad did most of the cooking before his stroke, so Mom didn't have to, and she conveniently forgot everything she'd ever learned while she had someone else to do it for her.

Dad peers at me over the top of his book, and I mouth, "She's talking to you."

"What news?" he asks.

"Alessandro Russo died in a car crash on the Interstate out of town." She doesn't even look up from what she's doing, grating cheese over the top of the omelet in the pan.

My heart constricts like someone is squeezing the life out of it. I think of him on top of me in the back of the limo, his hands inside my pants, his breathy words, "God you're so beautiful," and my pulse is racing a marathon. I can still taste him. Still smell his cologne and his leather coat. I can still remember wondering why the driver didn't stop the car when he saw what was happening in the rearview mirror.

The images in my head make me feel nauseous, but I can't seem to understand that he's dead. A life snuffed out, just like that. How is that even possible?

"Who, sweetheart?" Dad asks, and I want to throw my arms around his neck and sit on his lap the way I used to do when I was a little girl.

I want him to smooth my hair and tell me everything will be okay. Only, that promise isn't his to make anymore.

"He's an actor." Mom uses present tense, and I don't correct her. "Ruby met him at the ice rink the other night."

I swallow and force myself to make eye contact. I give my dad a smile. "He was surrounded by fans," I say as if that explains everything.

"Do we know what happened?" This is typical of my dad—he cares about everyone and everything that's going on in the world, even though his world has practically shrunk to the size of our house.

"He was driving in the blizzard, in a Porsche. God knows why he didn't wait for the weather to clear." Mom slides the first omelet onto a plate and sticks it in front of my dad. "More money than sense," she adds, turning back to the grill.

My thoughts are scrambling headfirst down a rabbit hole. What if our date hadn't gone the way it did? What if he'd asked me to skip town with him? I might've been in that wreckage.

"There was a passenger in the car with him," Mom continues the personal news report. "A friend. Guy named Harry Weiss."

Harry Weiss.

The name gets stuck in my throat, and all that comes out is a feeble squeak.

"Okay, sweetheart?" Dad is waiting for Mom to sit down before he tucks into his meal.

"Did-did he die too?" I'm numb.

I shared Harry's beer at the party. He tripped over me at the ice rink. He told me that he worked in oil, and somehow that is a hundred times more personal than having Alessandro Russo's tongue in my mouth.

"Apparently he's in a critical but stable condition in the hospital."

I'm already on my feet. I hear Mom say, "Where are you going? Your omelet's ready," as I dash into the den and switch the TV on.

The news reporter is standing outside the University of Chicago Hospital, a scarf tucked inside her coat and pulled up to her chin, her shoulders hunched up around her neck. It's still snowing, and she looks as if she would rather be anywhere else than outside in the middle of the worst blizzard since 1979.

"All we know so far," she says, "is that Alessandro Russo was pronounced dead at the scene of the accident. His brother, Carlos Russo, was seen arriving at the hospital a short while ago but declined to comment."

"What about Harry?" I gravitate towards the screen and zone in on the reporter, willing her to mention the passenger in the car.

"The passenger, wealthy oil tycoon, Harry Weiss, is said to be in a critical condition. The eligible bachelors were travelling south on I-55 when the Porsche driven by Mr. Russo hit a patch of ice and skidded across the central median and into the path of an oncoming vehicle."

I mute the sound, the reporter's mouth still moving, and her eyes staring directly at me, leaving me alone with the silence.

Wealthy oil tycoon, Harry Weiss.

Eligible bachelors.

Harry told me that he was the boss, that it was early days for his business. He played it down like it was nothing to brag about, like the words 'oil tycoon' applied to other people who were not Harry Weiss. And she called him an eligible bachelor...

I pace the den. She made Harry sound like a player, another Alessandro Russo using women because he knew he could have anyone he wanted. Because every woman wants to hook an eligible bachelor, right? But that's not the Harry Weiss I met at the rink. That Harry wanted to know if Emily Bronte was happy.

That Harry wouldn't have touched me up in front of Kurt Russell as if I was his personal property.

But lurking beneath my thoughts and battling frantically to be heard is the reminder that his condition is critical. Harry Weiss might die too.

I slump onto the floor and hit the mute button to get the sound back on the TV. If I have to sit here all night waiting for an update, I will.

The footage has switched to images of Alessandro Russo from his latest movie. Images of him with a beautiful model on his arm on the red carpet. Images of him as a little boy in Italy. Right at the end of the report, they produce a photograph of Harry attending an event with a stunning blond—his face is turned away from the camera, but it is unmistakably him, his friends from the rink in the background.

Why do they have to focus on their lifestyle? A man is dead, and another is seriously hurt; isn't it enough to report the facts without having to glam it up with pictures of red carpets, movie premieres, and models?

The door opens and my mom peeps into the room. "Your food is getting cold." Her eyes drift to the TV screen. "Such a waste of a young life. Don't be sad, darling. It obviously wasn't meant to be."

I can't even look at her. How can she be so callous? So coldhearted? So fucking calculating?

The snow is still falling heavily. Our backyard is pure white, apart from the tiny fragile claw prints of the birds that have been searching for food. I feel like I should do something, only I'm not sure what, and just looking at the snow is giving me shivers.

I know which hospital Harry is in. I could go visit him myself instead of relying on the news reporters to spice up the facts to make them a little more appetizing for the viewers. I reach the door and stop.

What if his model girlfriend is there at his bedside? How would I explain that he fell over me on the ice and now I'm invested in his well being? God, I already know what she would think, that I'm just another gold-digger after his money, now that I know he has some.

I go back to the news report which has now moved onto the blizzard.

I'll wait here. His family will be with him, if they can get to Chicago from wherever they are. He might not even be allowed visitors, and even if he is, he probably won't remember me.

But what if he dies from his injuries? Will I regret not making the effort to see him when he's so close? What would my dad do?

That settles it. I sneak out of the den, grab my purse from my room, and tiptoe to the front door, my heart hammering against my ribs. I'm not telling my parents. My dad won't question me wanting to visit a friend in hospital, but if my mom hears the words eligible bachelor associated with Harry, she'll be sharpening her own talons and chaining me to his bedside.

I don't even put my boots on inside the house. I open the door just enough for me to step outside onto the porch, hopping while I slide my feet into them and my arms into my coat, zipping it right up to my neck. Then I narrow my eyes against the bitter wind and walk towards the main road where I am able to get a cab.

The traffic is crawling.

The cab driver drops me as close to the hospital as he can get. I ignore the camera crew loitering outside the main entrance and am greeted by a blast of warm air when I step inside. The man on the front desk tells me where to find Harry when I claim to be his girlfriend, and I take the stairs slowly, wondering what on earth I'm doing here.

What if he doesn't recognize me? What if he thinks I'm a crazy stalker trying to get my five minutes of fame because I happened to bump into him and Alessandro Russo by chance? I shouldn't have come. What was I thinking?

But my legs still keep moving until I'm sitting beside his bed. Harry's eyes are closed and he looks like he maybe shouldn't have survived.

I sit on the uncomfortable plastic seat and study his face. His eyes are swollen and bruised. There's a shelter over one of his arms, and a tube inserted into the back of his hand. But I still can't help smiling at him even though he's asleep.

The nurse told me that he was lucky, but they had to perform emergency surgery to correct a brain hemorrhage following trauma to his skull. I take off my coat, sit back and watch the monitor beeping regularly beside the bed. I wonder how much he remembers of the accident or if he even knows that he's in hospital.

Now that I'm here, it feels like it was the right thing to do, which is strange considering I hardly even know Harry. But I make myself comfortable and settle in for the long haul. I've already made up my mind that I'm not going anywhere until I know that he's alright.

I must close my eyes and doze off because when I open them again, Harry is watching me from the pillows, his expression unreadable. "You're awake." I stretch my arms above my head and yawn.

"Ruby?" His voice is hoarse. "What are you doing here?"

"Someone had to come and talk some sense into you." I sit on the edge of the bed.

Then it hits me that he probably doesn't even know that Alessandro is dead, and I pray that he doesn't ask me.

"How are you feeling?"

"Like I got hit by a truck."

I can't help smiling. At least he still has a sense of humor. "Do you want some water?"

He nods with his eyes, and I fill a plastic cup with tepid water from the jug on the bedside cabinet and hold it to his lips. There's nothing awkward about being here with him like this. I can't explain it, but it feels like I've always known him, well, known him a lot longer than a couple of days anyway.

He slumps back against the pillows like it hurts too much to hold his head up.

"Do you remember what happened?"

"Vaguely. The snow... St. Louis..."

"St. Louis?"

But Harry is lost inside his memories, and I wonder if he'll ever be able to erase them. "I tried to stop him. Bright lights..."

He closes his eyes again, and looks so peaceful, I hope that he'll drift off to sleep.

"I thought I was going to die..." Tears well in his eyes and trickle down the side of his face.

"It's okay," I murmur. "You don't have to talk about it."

"What do you think happens to people when they die, Ruby?" he says, and my heart skips— that, after everything—he remembers my name.

"I've never really thought about it." It's a lie. I thought about it a lot when my dad had his stroke, but all I knew was that if he died, he wouldn't still be here.

"I think our souls go someplace else." He's still watching me with huge watery eyes. "I saw it..."

"Harry." I reach for his hand and squeeze it. "I'm glad you're still here."

"I saw her... My mom."

I swallow. You hear stories about people having near-death experiences, but how can anyone prove or disprove them? But, I believe him. I believe that's what he thinks he saw anyway, and if that's going to help him recover, there's no way I'm questioning it.

"She was only forty when she died. Too young."

I nod. My dad was younger than that when he had his stroke.

"I sometimes think..." More tears spill. "...that I'll be the same. I'll die young."

"I don't think that's how it works."

I mean, what do I say to that? I can't exactly tell him that it's not going to happen to him too, and if he's always had it in his head. *Shit!* Maybe he'll manifest it with his gloomy thoughts.

"You mustn't think like this. You're still here, Harry."

"Marry me, Ruby Jackson."

I release his hand without thinking, and stand up, turning my back to him. He's delirious. He must be. He thinks he saw his mom, and that he's going to die when he's forty, and this is the medication talking.

"I'll go down on one knee when I get out of here. Do it properly."

I force a smile and turn back around. "You won't even remember this." Thank God, I think.

"If I forget... I want you to remind me."

Yeah, that's not happening. "Okay."

"Promise me, Ruby."

"I promise, but you don't even know me."

"I'll learn." He closes his eyes, and I watch him until his breathing grows shallow, his chest rising and dipping, the blip-blip of the monitor steady and even.

I make up my mind that I can never tell him about Alessandro Russo and what happened in the back of the limo.

6

HARRY

She doesn't keep her promise. She thinks that I don't remember my spontaneous proposal, that I was high on whatever drugs they're pumping into my veins. But I've never been more serious about anything in my life.

I *am* going to marry Ruby Jackson.

Whether Alessandro beat me to it and proposed to her on their date or not. It wouldn't be the first time he was one step ahead of me in something that was important to me.

There was the little matter of the front row tickets to the most important Knicks game of 1980. Ronnie was giving them away since he couldn't make it. He'd already promised me that my name was on them, until Alessandro told him that his brother was sick, and the Knicks game would cheer him up. He took those tickets and didn't even use them.

She looks so cozy with her legs curled under her on the plastic seat that I'm almost grateful to be here so that I can have her all to myself for a short while.

She stretches like a cat, and I wonder if she has any idea how graceful and sexy she is, all at the same time. "How long have you been awake?" I can tell when her cheeks grow even rosier than they already are that she's waiting for me to mention the proposal.

"Not long. Do you have to get home?" Please say no, I think. I shouldn't have asked. Now, I've given her the perfect excuse to get up, grab her coat, and walk straight out of my life.

"Are you trying to get rid of me?"

Fuck no, that's the last thing I want. "No, but I'm not exactly great company."

She gets up and comes and sits on the side of the bed, so close that I can feel her warmth through the covers. "Tell me about your mom."

I tell her about how I never once heard my mom raise her voice. She worked with vulnerable people, helping them integrate and cope with real life, as well as raising two kids practically single handedly. My mom always said there were two sides to every story and that no one else had the right to claim they knew both of them.

"You must miss her." Ruby's green eyes study mine intently. I can't imagine how bad I look, but she doesn't flinch or turn away or stare at the bandage around my head.

"Every day of my life."

"Do you want me to let your dad know that you're here?"

"No," I say a little too quickly. "I don't want to worry him."

"He will have seen it on the news." She freezes, chewing on her bottom lip as if it might take the words back.

"I made the news?"

"Two eligible bachelors involved in a car wreck." She keeps her tone light-hearted. Doesn't mention Alessandro.

I try to see what's going on inside her head, but I already know. My friend didn't make it. My heart starts racing, the tears hot and stinging.

"You never told me you were—" Her expression crumples as the monitor starts beeping erratically. "Harry?" She's on her feet. "Harry, what's wrong? Do I need to fetch the nurse?"

She doesn't wait around. I hear the door shush open softly, hear Ruby calling out, "Nurse, we need help in here!" Footsteps and voices, and then everything goes black.

"CAN you at least give me some warning before you do that again?"

I don't know how long I've been out, but Ruby is still here when I regain consciousness. My head feels like it has been cleaved in two, and my entire body is trembling. I don't ask what happened, and Ruby doesn't tell me.

"Sorry." It comes out as a rasp.

She holds the cup of water to my lips and waits for me to swallow before putting it back on the bedside cabinet. "Do you always apologize for things that are not your fault?"

"Bad habit, I know."

"My dad did that when he first got sick. He would follow me around the room with his eyes and keep saying 'sorry' for needing my help. Like I should be off doing other things, you know."

I do know, but I want to listen to Ruby talking about what makes her happy so that I can forget I'm lying in a hospital bed and my best friend is dead.

"What would you be doing right now? If you weren't here trying to make me feel better."

She gives me a mischievous grin, and I can't help thinking that I want to spend the rest of my life making her smile this way.

"Firstly, I need to make it quite clear that I can't take any credit for keeping you alive. And secondly..." She hesitates. "I'd be watching the news report for updates on your 'critical but stable' condition."

"Thank God it's not unstable."

I try to prop myself up, and she rushes over, sliding an arm behind my shoulders and plumping the pillows with her free hand. I breathe in the honey smell of her shampoo and settle back again, praying that I never forget that scent.

"You'll be back out there doing whatever it is eligible bachelors do in no time." Her eyes meet mine and then she looks away. "Do you dance, Harry?"

"Badly. My feet never quite seem to do what my brain is telling them to do. I'll never be John Travolta."

"Goddammit!" Ruby grins at me. "I thought I could see you in a white three-piece."

She tugs her hands inside the sleeves of her sweater as if she's cold and checks out the window. The sky behind the glass is black. The nighttime hush has settled over the hospital, and the lights have been dimmed, but even so, the world still feels as if it has been packed out with cotton wool.

"My dad trained in ballroom dancing when he was younger," she says. "He used to compete professionally until he went to college, then I guess, other things took over. It makes me sad that I'll never get to see him dance."

"Did he teach you before… Before his stroke?"

She nods her head. "He would always waltz around the kitchen with me when his favorite tunes came on the radio. He made it look so easy. So effortless."

"Does your mom dance?"

Her mouth twists to one side, and she sucks in a deep breath. "Not in the house."

I guess she must feel bad about dancing in front of Ruby's dad when it was such a huge part of his early life, but before I can say anything, the door opens, and the nurse comes in to record my vital signs.

"You're still here," she says to Ruby while taking my temperature and checking my pulse. "I thought you'd gone home while you still could." Pause. "You haven't looked out the window in a while, huh?"

Ruby gets up, crosses the room and peers outside, her hands cupped around her face.

"I'll fetch you a couple of blankets," the nurse says. "They've closed the roads in and out of the city. I don't think you'll be going anywhere in a hurry."

"Do you need to call your mom?" I ask her. "Let her know that you're okay?"

She nods. "I'll go call her now." She sounds as if there's nothing she would rather do less, but I guess I'm imagining it.

Ruby opens the door, and Ronnie bounds in bringing with him a sprinkling of snow as he removes his hat and shakes his head. "It's Baltic out there." His gaze flits between me and Ruby, and he says, "Fuck, man, look at the state of you."

"Great to see you, too."

I'm glad he's here, even if it does mean that I have to share Ruby with him. Ronnie is a reminder that the world still exists outside this hospital room, even if it will never be the same again. He takes off his coat and drapes it over the back of one of the visitor chairs.

"I'll leave you to it." The nurse completes the chart at the foot of the bed and leaves, warning Ronnie that I still need rest and no excitement.

"How did you get here?" I ask him when we're alone.

"Sled." His expression is deadpan, and then his face breaks into a grin. "Seriously, man, how are you feeling? I'd have come sooner, but..." He puffs up his cheeks and wipes his forehead with the sleeve of his sweater.

"Ask me again when I get out of here."

"Have they said how long you'll have to stay?"

"I haven't asked."

I don't want to talk about me. I don't want to tell him that every single bone in my body feels as if it has been broken in two and glued back together again, and that my head feels like a bowling ball. I want to talk about Ruby because this might be the worst thing that has ever happened to me, but it has bizarrely thrown us together. Which also makes it the best thing that has ever happened to me.

As if reading my mind, he glances at the door. "Who was that woman I passed in the doorway? She looks familiar."

"Her name is Ruby Jackson. She's the woman I'm going to marry."

Ronnie is silent for a moment and then he starts chuckling. "Okay. What drugs have they been giving you? For a moment there, it sounded like you said you're going to marry her."

"I am. I've already proposed."

"And?"

"And... She said the same as you. She thinks I've already forgotten about it."

Ronnie sits heavily in the chair and rests his elbows on his knees. "That's not quite the conversation I expected to have when I came in."

"She'll be back soon. I want you to help me show her that I'm serious."

He studies me for several moments, trying to work out if I'm high or delirious or both. "Ask her again. Keep asking her until she says yes."

"I don't want to ... bully her into accepting."

Ronnie rubs his chin with his hand. "You're actually serious about this." I nod, and he adds, "I'm not sure I'm the best person to give advice on marriage proposals. I still haven't plucked up the courage to ask Sumaira."

"But you will."

Frown lines crease his forehead. "How long have you two known each other?"

"Two days. Maybe more, depending on how long I've been in here." I swallow, my throat feeling like sandpaper. "We met at the skating rink on Friday."

Ronnie blinks. "She was at the party with—" He freezes, the color draining from his face. "Why don't you give yourself time to heal, see how you feel when this is over and you're back in New York."

"It won't change my mind."

"You're sure about this?"

"I'm sure."

Ronnie grins at me. "This will be a story to tell the grandkids in years to come."

"Now she just needs to say yes."

7

RUBY

"...AND she thought I was joking when I said I'd be back the next day for breakfast. And lunch. And then again for dinner."

Ronnie's laughter is easy, spontaneous. He is talking about his girlfriend, Sumaira. They met at a roadside diner when she poured his coffee and served extra maple syrup with his pancakes, and blushed when he asked if he could take her out on a date.

"She obviously said yes."

Ronnie is easy to get on with, and the boy can talk. Harry hasn't said much, but I can tell that he's comfortable just listening to the conversation play out around him. He looks tired, the flesh around his eyes growing shinier and blacker by the moment, but he's fighting it to stay awake in case he misses something.

Outside our bubble, the world has grown dark and silent, smothered by a blanket of snow. And still, it keeps falling, as if the sky can no longer contain it.

The nurse fetches blankets for me and Ronnie. "This goes against hospital regulations, but these are not regular circumstances, and I can hardly turf you out in this weather, can I? Besides—" she gives Harry a half-smile, and I realize that he has drifted off to sleep "—after what he's been through, your company is probably the best medicine we can give him."

I curl up on the seat with my legs under me and pull the blanket up to my chin. On the other side of the bed, Ronnie takes the other seat, stretches out his legs and crosses them at the ankles, the blanket barely covering his knees. He'll ache all over by morning if he tries to sleep in that position. We both will.

But neither of us are going to complain.

"It's not exactly the Hilton," the nurse says before she leaves, "but at least you'll be warm and dry."

I should feel awkward sharing a room with two guys I hardly know, but I don't. It's cozy. The gentle blip-blip of the equipment wired up to Harry is soothing, like a child listening to its mom's heartbeat, and it doesn't matter how uncomfortable the shiny plastic seats are, I feel protected. Safe.

We both watch Harry sleeping for a while, and then Ronnie's eyes meet mine. "He likes you; you know."

I smile. Was this what I wanted to hear? Was this the reason I rushed here the instant I heard that he was involved in the car crash?

That's not how it works, is it? Love at first sight is for fairy tales and Disney movies, not real life. So, why do I close my eyes with a warm tingling feeling in my gut and a smile on my face?

. . .

During the night, I open my eyes and glimpse the nurse standing beside Harry's bed. The lights are dimmed, the room is enjoying its own company in familiar silence, and Ronnie is snoring gently from the other seat. My eyelids flicker shut almost instantaneously despite the discomfort of being curled up like a hedgehog in a peanut shell.

When I finally unfurl myself and stretch my legs, a dull burning ache spreads up my spine and across my shoulders, it is morning, and Ronnie is missing.

It takes me several moments to get my bearings, by which point, Harry is watching me from the bed, propped up against the pillows. I rub the sleep from my eyes and arch my back, suddenly self-conscious with his eyes on me.

"Morning," he says, like getting snowed in at the hospital and crashing on a visitor's seat happens every day.

"How are you feeling?"

"Like the truck came back in the night to finish me off."

"Ouch." I glance across the room at the empty seat. "Where's Ronnie?"

"He's probably having a coffee down at the nurse's station." Harry smiles, and his face appears shadowy with the bruising spreading beneath his eyes.

Right on cue, the door opens, and Ronnie enters backwards carrying a tray, the aroma of freshly cooked toast and coffee wafting in with him. He sets breakfast down on the mobile tray and pushes it across the bed, motioning for me to join them. He has somehow sourced a mountain of toast, sachets of butter, marmalade, and jelly, and three cups of steaming coffee.

"Where did you get this?" I help myself to a slice and spread it thickly with butter and marmalade, shreds of orange peel glistening in the glow of the stark overhead lights. I'm suddenly ravenous.

"The woman in the cafeteria was most helpful when I explained that we're snowed in with our reckless friend here. Told her I'm stranded until they thaw out the wings of the next flight back to New York." He slathers honey on a slice, takes a bite, and then fills his mouth with coffee at the same time.

"You'll have to excuse him." Harry shakes his head. "Old habits die hard."

"What?" Ronnie studies his toast, eyebrows lowered, as if Harry just suggested a spider was crawling across it. "I'm washing it down. Nothing wrong with that."

I don't always eat breakfast. Most days, I'm running late for work, and I'll either skip the meal completely or grab a cookie from the biscuit barrel in the kitchen on my way out, much to my dad's dismay. But sitting on the side of Harry's bed, licking jelly from my fingers and wishing the coffee cup was three times bigger than it actually is, this is the most delicious meal I've ever eaten.

When only a few crumbs remain on the plate, Ronnie reaches into his pocket and produces a pack of cards. "Picked these up too from the shop on the first floor. Thought it would help pass the time."

"Anything else we should know about?" Harry's smile is a hundred times brighter than it was when I arrived the day before, and I wonder if it's because he's feeling a little better or if it's all down to the company.

"It's still snowing." Ronnie shrugs and clears a space on the tray for us to play a game. "The weather reports say this will make the blizzard of '79 look like a flurry." He sounds unfazed by the news.

Harry looks at me. "If you need to get home, we'll help."

Ronnie arches an eyebrow while he shuffles the deck of cards like a professional, ruffling them between his hands and making them dance. "You're going nowhere, and I'm not letting her step foot outside this building. I'm sure she'd rather keep all her fingers and toes. Wouldn't you?" He winks at me.

"Yes." I rub my hands together. "Harry is only worried that I'll beat him at Rummy."

"Harry probably doesn't even know how to play Rummy."

"Don't you?" I ask him, and he shakes his head. Or rather he moves his eyes from side to side, his head still too delicate to roll across the pillow. "We're going to need more coffee then because I learned from the best: my dad."

We play Rummy until the porters come to take Harry for a brain scan.

While he's gone, Ronnie gets more food from the cafeteria, and we sit and talk about Sumaira. It's obvious how much he loves her—it shines through his eyes and his voice turns to runny honey whenever he talks about her.

"I wish she were here," he says like we're on vacation in a log cabin somewhere in the snowy mountains. "She'll be gutted that she missed this."

We don't mention Alessandro Russo. It's an unspoken agreement between us when Harry isn't in the room, that we're here for him, and we'll deal with the difficult stuff once he's feeling stronger.

That afternoon, we play Crazy Eights and Go Fish, the two men frustrated that I won every round of Rummy. The nurses come and go. They take Harry's vitals, the assistants bring his food, the cleaners clean around us, but mostly they leave us alone.

The day barely makes an appearance before night waves hello again. The world outside the hospital feels like someone built an igloo around us, and we must wait for it to melt before we can leave. The window is half covered by snow, and we leave the blinds drawn, making us feel even more like caterpillars inside a chrysalis.

Day two degenerates into boisterous games of Hearts and Snap. Even Harry manages a chuckle when Ronnie slams his hand down hard on the tray and yells, "Snap!" for the tenth time in a row.

"I think you're cheating." I watch his pile of cards growing while I only have a handful left, and Harry is down to his last three cards.

"I think you're a sore loser." Ronnie flips over the Ace of Hearts and sets it down on the mobile tray. "Come on. If you win this game, I'll buy you all the chocolate in the shop downstairs."

I place my card, the Ace of Diamonds, on top of his and shout, "Snap!" before he can react. "Challenge accepted."

Ron wins the next three games, but he goes to the shop nonetheless, and returns with a carrier bag filled with chocolate. I eat so much that I'm buzzing with the sugar rush, and we move onto Charades instead.

I'm miming dipping my head underwater and opening my mouth to scream when the nurse walks in and says, "*Jaws.*"

"Where was the shark?" Ronnie shakes his head, but his smile is wide. "We'd have gotten it right away if you'd tried eating the end of the bed."

THAT NIGHT, I sleep fitfully. I must sense that our bubble is about to burst. The snow has finally stopped, and even though the temperature inside the building has been constant, the sky is a shade lighter, and I don't shiver whenever I glance at it.

I wake up a couple of times to find the same night nurse standing beside Harry's bed. Later, I'm jolted from a bizarre dream in which Harry is trying to scale the John Hancock Tower in his hospital gown while Ronnie zooms around him in a hot air balloon. I suddenly realize that Harry is awake and trying to sit up in his bed.

I'm out of the seat in a heartbeat. "What are you doing?" I keep my voice low so that I don't wake Ronnie.

I go to cover Harry's chest with the blanket, but he grips my wrist gently. "Get in with me, Ruby."

I instinctively glance at the door. "I can't. What if the nurse comes in?"

"She won't be back around until morning." His eyes are like huge dark stones in the dim glow of the night lights. "Please."

He must sense it too, that this is coming to an end. This has all been so surreal that it can't possibly continue for much longer.

It isn't real life, and right now, Harry's reality is brain scans, a fractured arm, and grieving for a friend who died in the same wreck that put him in hospital.

"What will Ronnie say?"

"He'll say that I finally got lucky."

I can hear the pleading in his voice. He's worried that when the snow clears, I'll walk out of here, and he'll never see me again. He's worried that, in time, this will become a distant memory, something to be confused with a dream he had one night induced by the strong pain relief administered to him by the medical team after the accident.

It's just one night, I tell myself.

What harm can it do?

When he's fully recovered, he'll go back to New York, and I'll stay in Chicago where my mom will continue trying to push me into the arms of another eligible bachelor, to make our life easier.

Before I can talk myself out of it, I climb onto the bed, slide my legs under the covers, and snuggle up against Harry.

His warmth heats my skin instantly, like someone set a fire blazing underneath the bed. He wraps his good arm around my shoulders, and I rest my head on his chest. I never thought about how it would feel to be in his arms, but now that I'm there, I realize that it feels like the most natural thing on earth. Like there's a dip in his chest beneath his collarbone that was made for my head.

"You will keep your promise, Ruby," he whispers, stroking my arm with his thumb.

I freeze. "My promise?"

"I asked you a question when you first got here."

Shit! I thought he'd forgotten about that.

Propping myself on an elbow, I rest my chin on his chest and study his face. "Ask me again when you know me a little better."

It's a cop out, but I know he'll thank me for it when he's back in New York, and his life settles back to normal. I'm saving him the hassle of finding a plausible excuse for calling it all off when he comes to his senses.

"I know all I need to know. The rest will be a bonus."

Then his lips are on mine, and even though I'm scared I'm going to hurt him, or raise his blood pressure, or give him another panic attack like he had when I first arrived, I kiss him back.

His hand is in my hair, gripping it tightly so that it's pulling on my scalp. I straddle him on the hospital bed, my tongue probing his mouth because suddenly, inexplicably, the bubble is just for the two of us, and nothing else exists.

I want Harry Weiss.

There, I've allowed the thought to take form and grow wings. There was no bolt of lightning when he bumped into me—literally—at the skating rink. He didn't make me go weak at the knees, or blush, or giggle like a sixteen-year-old schoolgirl, but Harry Weiss has gotten under my skin anyway. My pulse races. Between my legs tightens and tingles, and my nipples harden as he crushes my breast with his hand.

"Ruby..." His breath is warm on my face. "Marry me."

"You don't mean that." I kiss him harder.

I can't believe I'm doing this. He almost died a few days ago. His arm is broken, his face is covered in bruises, but I want to feel him inside me just like in all the historical romances I've ever read. He isn't Heathcliff. He isn't a swashbuckling pirate with long hair, a gold tooth, and a way of undressing women with his eyes.

He's just Harry.

But just Harry has made me feel things I've never felt before.

I pull away from him and tug my sweater over my head, tossing it onto the floor beside the bed while Harry studies my breasts as if it's his first time too.

"You're so beautiful, Ruby" he whispers.

I feel beautiful. I'm not wearing any makeup, my hair is greasy, I haven't changed my panties in three days, but Harry makes me feel like I'm the most gorgeous woman on the planet.

His eyes devour me as he squeezes my nipples, pulling me down to him so that his lips can close around them. He nibbles them between his teeth, his tongue circling, licking, sucking. Every part of me is tingling, and my breaths come in short, ragged gasps.

Harry shifts his hips, pain flaring behind his eyes and then disappearing, but I've already felt it. His cock is hard beneath me and I raise my butt so that I can slide my hand between my legs and feel it. It takes my breath away. But at the same time, it excites me in a way that no one else has ever made me feel.

"Not like this," Harry murmurs, his voice husky.

I lean closer, kissing his lips, his eyes, his face, tiny butterfly kisses, my lips barely touching his skin. "Why not?" If we don't do this now, it will never happen. We'll both go home, carry on with our lives, and this will forever be the moment that almost was.

What if no one else ever makes me feel this way again?

"No." His eyes flash in the comforting twilight of the hospital room. "I want to do it right, Ruby. I want to ... make you happy."

He pulls me back into his arms, my head resting on his chest, my naked breasts squashed up against him under the covers, and I close my eyes. We stay that way until the nurses' footsteps along the corridor as they start their early morning rounds jolt me awake.

I'm sitting in my seat, fully clothed, my lips and nipples still tingling from Harry's kisses when the door opens, and the nurse comes in.

8

HARRY

I'M FLOATING the next morning, and it has nothing to do with the meds they're pumping into me. I wanted Ruby so badly, but there was no way I was screwing up our first time by making her do all the work ... in a cramped hospital bed ... with my friend snoring in the visitor's seat.

I miss her presence beside me in bed the way I would miss my right arm. She has left a gaping hole through which I feel my essence gravitating towards her like bees to pollen. My eyes keep drifting to hers, the two of us exchanging glances that no one else would understand, and I already know that this is going to be our thing for the rest of our lives. We'll be in our seventies and still messaging each other with our eyes.

Something has shifted between us overnight. Until now, the three of us have been a little family, bonding over silly games and telling stories, but now there's me and Ruby, and Ronnie is like the distant cousin who's trying to rediscover his niche. If he notices the change, he keeps it quiet.

The nurse comes in with her practical shoes, her ready smile, and her efficient bedside manner. "Morning, did you sleep well?" She aims the question at me, and heat instantly rises in my face. I hope it isn't going to affect my temperature.

"I did, thank you." I flash another glance at Ruby, whose expression is completely neutral.

The nurse unwraps the cuff to go around my arm. "The snow is already starting to thaw out there." She doesn't say the words out loud, but she means that when the roads clear, Ruby and Ronnie can go home.

"Much longer, and my socks would've been walking out of here by themselves." Ronnie cricks his neck from side to side.

"How long do you think Harry will be kept in?" Ruby asks.

"A few more days." The nurse records my blood pressure on the chart at the end of the bed and removes the thermometer from under my tongue. "You're welcome to come back and visit him."

It's their dismissal.

The bubble has been popped, and I already feel the pang of loss inside my chest. It won't be the same without Ruby and Ronnie. I'll be left alone with my thoughts and my bruises while they go back to their regular routines, and their worlds return to normal.

My world will never be normal again, not now that Ruby Jackson is in it.

The conversation over breakfast is more subdued than it has been the past couple of days. The card games are quiet, and Ronnie doesn't even cheat at Snap.

So, our ears all prick up when we hear the raised voice from the corridor.

"Where is my daughter? I've come to take her home."

Ruby's shoulders are hunched up around her neck like she's already preempting leaving the tropical ambience behind and stepping into the sub-zero temperatures outside the building. I don't recognize the voice, but it's obvious this is aimed at Ruby.

The voice comes closer.

"I'll be having words with whoever runs this place. My daughter has been missing for three days, and where do I find her?"

Ruby stands up, the chair legs scraping across the floor behind her. She doesn't say a word. She doesn't need to—the crumpled expression on her face is enough.

"Ruby..." I reach for her hand, but she doesn't take it.

"Are you leaving?" Ronnie stands too, and I feel so useless stuck in this damned hospital bed with my arm in plaster and a tube inserted into the back of my hand.

I don't know what's going on, or what has prompted her mom's anger—Ruby called home on the first day to let her know that she was safe—but my veins are already pumping with anxiety.

The door bursts open, and Ruby's mom stops on the threshold, surveying the room with eyes like bullets. She's wearing a heavy navy-blue coat and an ivory woolen scarf that almost covers her chin.

Her eyes settle on Ruby, and a shudder of something,

disappointment maybe, passes behind her eyes. "Get your coat. You're coming home," she says.

"Mom, I told you—"

"Now, Ruby!"

"Mrs. Jackson, ma'am." I try to sit up, and Ronnie rushes over to help me, one arm supporting my shoulders and hauling me higher up onto the pillows. "It wasn't Ruby's fault. She had no choice with the snow—"

"I don't want to hear another word from you." Mrs. Jackson narrows her eyes and jabs a finger in my direction. "If I find out that either of you two have touched my daughter—"

"Mom!" Ruby grabs her coat from the back of the seat, and marches towards the door. "Let's go."

"Ruby, will you be back?" I hear the pleading in my own voice and pray that Mrs. Jackson is too irate to notice.

"Not if I can help it." I sense her mom's eyes linger on me a beat too long, like she's trying to figure out exactly what has been going on while the three of us have been holed up in a hospital room.

Then she follows Ruby outside to the corridor and closes the door behind her.

Ronnie and I both stare at the door as if waiting for Ruby to come back and tell us that she has changed her mind. She doesn't.

The silence is tangible, taut, and Ronnie breaks it first. "What happened last night?"

I slump back against the pillows and swallow hard. Did he

hear us? Was he awake the whole time and only pretending to be asleep? "What do you mean?" I choose the innocent route.

"This is me you're talking to, H. You can't fool me. I saw the way you two were looking at each other this morning."

I suck in a deep breath and puff up my cheeks, releasing the air slowly. "Nothing happened. It almost did," I quickly add, "but it wouldn't have been right. Not here. Not like this."

"Thank fuck for that." Ronnie scratches behind his left ear and scrunches up his face. "I love you, man, but I don't want to be around when you screw the missus."

"The missus?" I can't help grinning at him, partly with relief that he didn't see anything in the night, and partly to distract myself from Ruby's absence.

"Don't tell me you've changed your mind now that you've met the mother-in-law."

"It'll take more than an angry mom to keep me away from Ruby." I get the impression that Mrs. Jackson is used to getting her own way, but Ruby knows her own mind, and won't let anyone stand in the way of what she wants. I hope.

"So, what are we going to do about it?"

"We're going to show her that I'm serious. That I meant every word I said."

Ronnie grins at me. "I like her, even if she did accuse me of cheating at cards."

"You always cheat at cards."

"Shh." Ronnie raises a finger to his lips. "Don't give all my secrets away."

. . .

WITH RONNIE'S HELP, I send a van load of flowers to the library where Ruby works. I know where she lives—I dropped her home in the taxi after the birthday party—but I don't want her mom to get in her two cents' worth of negativity. I understand that she was concerned about Ruby's safety during the blizzard, but I'm still reeling from her reaction to me and Ronnie.

I mean, is there a safer place to be holed up than a hospital?

I don't know what I expect Ruby to do when she receives the flowers, but I'm disappointed when she doesn't even call the hospital to say thank you.

The following day, I request that the local radio station plays 'Wuthering Heights' by Kate Bush and dedicate the song to Ruby Jackson.

And nothing.

"Maybe she didn't hear it," Ronnie suggests. He's playing Solitaire, alone, the cards spread across the mobile table in my room. "It was a long shot."

He's right. The thump-thump of the headache that has been my constant companion since the accident has ebbed away, and although my eyes are still heavy, and I'm sleeping twelve hours a day, when it comes to Ruby, I've never been able to think more clearly.

"What about theater tickets?" Ronnie peers up from the card game. He doesn't seem in any hurry to go back to New York, and for that I'm grateful.

It's a great idea ... for anyone else. But not for Ruby. I haven't known her for long, but I think that Ruby will be more impressed by thoughtful gestures than by grand expensive ones. Then it comes to me, and I know what to do.

With the help of several nurses, one of whom is the sister of a publisher, we locate a local author who has been compared to a modern-day Emily Bronte, and I arrange for her to visit the library and discuss books with Ruby.

I've never been so nervous in my life. I spend the rest of the day eying the door to my hospital room, waiting for it to open and for Ruby to fling her arms around me and tell me that no one has ever made her feel so special.

But she doesn't come.

We shared something special. I will never be able to erase the memory of Ruby straddling me with her breasts exposed, her hair cascading over her shoulders, the way she kissed me back with such passion.

I didn't misread it. I know I didn't.

So, why the silence?

"Do you want me to go and find her?"

Ronnie has been back to the hotel to shower, change his clothes, and get a decent night's sleep, but he has still been arriving shortly after breakfast with a basket filled with sweet pastries and fruit, and staying until lights out. Flights out of Chicago are still canceled, and he said he has nothing better to do, but I think he's secretly worried how I'll react to the news of Alessandro's death.

And, whether he wants to admit it or not, he's already invested in me and Ruby too.

I shake my head. I don't want to hear that she isn't interested in me. I don't want her to ask Ronnie to make me stop. I'm not ready for disappointment, not on top of everything else.

When the nurse pokes her head around the door later that same day, my heart almost leaps out of my chest. "Telephone call." She comes in, pulls the covers back, and helps me onto my feet.

"Who is it?"

My heart is pounding so loudly, I think I've misheard her when she says, "Your father."

I glance at Ronnie who keeps his head down, his face scrunched up in disappointment. He's nowhere near as disappointed as I am; I can barely drag my feet along the corridor to the phone in the nurse's station.

The nurse leaves me to take the call in private, and I raise the phone to my ear, my heart skipping erratically with the fading adrenaline rush. "Dad?"

His clipped voice drums home the aching disappointment: Ruby isn't going to call. "You're still alive then?"

I don't respond.

"I couldn't get a flight. The blizzard," he continues. "Lizzie and I, we've tried to keep things straight in the office, but there are some ... issues that require your attention."

"Okay. Thanks, Dad." That's all I can manage.

"How are you? When are they sending you home?"

"Soon. I'll be home soon, Dad."

I end the call. Back in my room, I climb into bed and roll onto my side with the covers pulled up to my chin—I can't deal with Ronnie's questions.

I'm still waiting to hear from Ruby the next day when the doctor announces that I'm ready to be discharged. I want to ask the nurses if they've received any telephone messages, but I don't want to sound desperate. Needy. Pathetic.

Ronnie fetches clean clothes from my hotel room and helps me dress. I take one last look at the room where I first kissed Ruby Jackson and make my way through the hospital to the waiting cab outside.

I'm quiet in the car on the way to the airport. Ronnie has taken care of the tickets and settled my hotel bill, and he doesn't press me for conversation.

So, I'm caught off-guard when the cab stops outside the library where Ruby works.

"Why have we stopped here?"

"I'm not traveling back to New York with you moping like a kid who lost his favorite ball." Ronnie leans across me and opens the passenger door. "Go speak to her. I'll wait here." When I don't move, he says, "Go get the girl for chrissakes."

My legs are trembling as I climb out of the taxi and make my way into the library. This is Ruby's natural habitat, I tell myself— a backdrop of bookcases overflowing with other universes and magic and adventure. I feel as close to her here as I did in the hospital, because I'm breathing the same air as her, I'm walking in her footsteps, I'm seeing what she sees when she's working.

At the front desk, I ask the manager if I can speak to Ruby Jackson.

Her eyes twitch behind her spectacles. "I'm sorry, Ruby isn't here. Can I help?"

My stomach is lurching. This is it. This is goodbye, and I don't know if I can face not seeing her again.

"No... Thank you."

"Would you like to leave a message?"

I peer around the library and realize that there are no flowers. Not a single bloom. Not a rose petal under a bookcase, not a lily spreading its pollen like fairy dust across the reading carrels, not even a whiff of their scent.

"No, it's okay." I turn around and start walking away.

"Who shall I say was looking for her?" the woman calls out.

"No one." I salute her on my way out.

9

RUBY

"Harry Weiss was discharged yesterday."

I stare at a patch on the hallway carpet and chew my bottom lip. "Thank you," I mumble into the telephone handset before replacing it on the stand.

So, that's it. Harry has gone back to New York, and I'll never see him again. The blizzard of 1987 will fade into a distant memory, ragged around the edges like a worn photograph, and one day, I probably won't even remember his name.

I wander back into the kitchen on numb legs, going through the motions of this thing called life without the one person in it who gave me a light to follow.

"Where are you going?" Mom eyes up my jeans, jersey sweater, and flannel shirt, like she's measuring me for a costume.

I switch the kettle on to boil, spoon coffee into a mug, and find the cream in the refrigerator. "Work. You know that thing we both do when we're out of the house."

This is how it has been between us since that embarrassing episode in the hospital. I still can't believe that she threatened Harry and Ronnie if they'd touched me, like I'm some sweet sixteen who has never been kissed. What was she thinking?

I'm not sure that she even knows what she was thinking. She has refused to explain why she behaved the way she did, putting it down to going stir crazy from being snowed in with Dad at home.

I don't believe a word of it.

My mom can make her own entertainment with a few glossy magazines and lengthy telephone conversations with her friends. She's the gossip queen—she thrives on gossip—and the only inconvenience the blizzard would've caused her was not being able to see her friends in person at the wine bar after work.

Her beef is with Harry Weiss.

He might have been friends with Alessandro Russo, but he doesn't quite come with the same celebrity status, and my mom has set her sights high. It wouldn't surprise me if her next target was the prince of some random European microstate—she's always banging on about Grace Kelly, the actress who bagged herself a prince.

In the eyes of the media, Harry Weiss is an eligible bachelor, a rising star, an entrepreneur destined for greatness. But in the eyes of Celia Jackson, he's a guy from New York City who has yet to prove himself. And my mom isn't prepared to wait around.

"We've already spoken about this, Ruby." She eyes up the amount of cream I add to my coffee—about a third of the mug—and purses her glossy red lips. "You can stay home until that man has left town. I'm not having him tracking you down at work."

"*That man* almost died in a car crash." I add an extra spoonful of sugar. I need it. We've been going around in circles for days.

I never told her about the flowers that were delivered to the library. Mrs. Bates took some home and delivered the rest to a nearby nursing home to bring some joy to the residents. All except for some white tulips which are still in a vase in my bedroom; when they die, I'm going to press them and keep them forever. A reminder of Harry and the snow blizzard.

I didn't tell her about the radio dedication either. Or the local author who came to the library while I was at home with Dad.

I wanted to visit Harry again. I wanted to perch on the edge of his bed and play cards while snacking on chocolate and potato chips. I wanted to laugh at Ronnie when he lied about cheating.

More than anything, though, I wanted to feel Harry's hands on me. I wanted to kiss him and hear him whisper, "You're so beautiful, Ruby," and soak up his warmth beneath the hospital covers.

But I knew I couldn't. If he found out about my mom's grand designs to marry me off to someone wealthy, or famous, or preferably both, he'd never believe that I like him for who he is. That I like him because he's funny, sweet, and kind. That I like him because he's the only man I've ever met who listens to what I have to say.

And I couldn't bear it if he accused me of being a gold digger.

So, I stayed away. I feel bad because I didn't even thank him for the romantic gestures, but I told myself it was for the best. I called the hospital every day to check up on his progress and asked the nurse not to tell him that I'd called, and now... Now I've lost even that final connection to him.

So, I'm free again.

Only I feel like one of those birds Dad warned me about with their clipped wings. Because this kind of freedom comes with its own gilded cage.

"Oh, sweetie, we've already been over this a hundred times."

More than a hundred, I think as she crosses the room and strokes my cheek.

"You can do so much better than Harry Weiss, and I'm not going to let you throw your life away on a guy you feel sorry for."

"I don't feel sorry for him." I already know I'm wasting my breath. "And what if I don't want to do better?"

"Trust me, Ruby. You'll regret it when you're older and your best days are behind you."

Jeez, thanks for the advice, Mom.

"Don't forget to stop off at the grocery store on your way home." She air-kisses me before she leaves—heaven forbid she should go to work with smudged lipstick.

I go through to the den and sit with my dad, eating toast and strawberry jelly. It doesn't taste the way it did in the hospital. Nothing will ever taste as good again, because nothing will ever live up to the surreal bubble we were stranded in for those few days.

"Back to work today?"

The left side of Dad's face droops slightly since his stroke. He has very little appetite and has lost weight, which makes his face look gaunt and his neck scrawny, and he walks with the aid of a cane, but his voice hasn't changed at all. The voice still belongs to my dad, the man who used to hoist me onto his shoulders when I was little and didn't want to walk; the man who gave me a patch in the garden to grow my own vegetables; the man who took me to the library every couple of weeks for as long as I can remember and encouraged me to read whatever I wanted.

I wish this hadn't happened to him. He has so much kindness in his heart, so much to give, and it seems that it wasn't enough for the universe that swallowed it whole and spat it back in his face.

I flop into an armchair with my legs draped over the arm and try to swallow my toast which has suddenly lost its appeal. "He was discharged yesterday."

My dad knows all about Harry's romantic gestures. He doesn't understand why I haven't contacted him, and I can't tell him that Mom has other ideas. He has enough shit going on in his life without discovering that his own wife is looking for a millionaire to pave her future path with golden cobblestones.

"Call him, Ruby. What have you got to lose, eh?"

Tears sting behind my eyes. How can I tell him that I feel as if I've already lost everything? I don't want to sound so ungrateful and melodramatic when my dad can't even work due to his medical condition.

He can't even dance now for fuck's sake. The one thing that made him happy, forever denied to him because his blood stopped flowing to his brain for a few moments one day.

"Long distance relationships are a recipe for disaster." I turn away from him and wipe my eyes with the back of my hand.

"Sounds like the kind of comment your mom would come out with." When I face him again, he's looking at me with a wistful smile on his face. "Don't ever let anyone else tell you what to think, Ruby. You're too brilliant for that."

My dad should've had lots of kids. He's the kind of man who would sit in a rocking chair in front of a log fire when he's old, reading books to all his grandkids, making them laugh with his funny voices.

Perhaps it's because Harry's discharge from the hospital has made it so final, but I blurt out, "He asked me to marry him."

My dad blinks. "Harry did? What did you say?"

"He was on medication, Dad. He was drugged up to his eyeballs and in pain. He didn't know what he was saying."

But I can still hear Harry as clearly as if he is sitting right next to me, saying, *"If I forget... I want you to remind me. Promise me, Ruby."*

"You don't ask a question like that without knowing exactly what you're saying." He pauses. "How did it make you feel?"

"Special?" I shrug. I don't tell him that Harry proposed again on our last night together in the hospital. "Anyway, it wasn't real life. He'll go back to New York and he'll have forgotten all about me this time next year."

"I wouldn't be so sure of that." Dad leans closer when I kiss his cheek goodbye, his eyes boring into mine as if he is trying to see right through to my soul.

. . .

ALESSANDRO RUSSO'S funeral is a huge glittering affair—the young actor is as large in death as he was in life. There has been no news of Harry since he left Chicago and returned to New York, and I sit down in the den with my dad one afternoon between walking a Great Dane for a client and my shift at the ice rink, to watch the funeral coverage on TV.

I don't feel any sense of morbid curiosity for the actor's family. I can't even begin to imagine the extent of their grief, and besides, it's a private thing, even though they agreed to the funeral being televised. I'm simply hoping for a glimpse of Harry.

Kurt Russell is there with Goldie Hawn. I try to picture meeting him in the restaurant with Alessandro the night before he died, and the memory is hazy, like a pencil sketch splashed with water. So much has happened since then that it's almost as if I pressed the reset button on my life when I walked into the hospital room to see Harry. Everything before is a blur.

"They make a handsome couple," Dad says, pointing at Kurt Russell and Goldie Hawn. "That's a match made in heaven if ever I saw one."

"You say that about everyone, Dad."

"Not everyone. See the way they look at each other?" He gestures for me to pay attention with a nod at the TV screen. "That's the kind of love everyone wants."

I laugh. "You've been watching too many Disney movies while I'm at work. Maybe I'll start taking you out on dog walks with me. Just with the slow movers."

"If you're talking about Peggy the Dachshund, I'm in. I think even I can walk faster than she does."

I return my attention to the TV. The Russo family arrive in a gauze of black, heads down, escorted directly into the church by bodyguards wearing black suits and black wraparound shades. I recognize Tom Cruise as he enters without stopping to pose for the cameras. It hits home that Alessandro Russo had a starry future ahead of him, cut short by an accident that should never have happened.

Then I spot Harry and Ronnie, both dressed in smart black suits, Harry's arm in a sling. My pulse races, my heart performs somersaults, and I feel like I'm going to be sick.

What is wrong with me? This is the funeral of the last man I went on a date with, and here I am acting like the heroine from an old historical romance, going weak at the knees over the sight of his friend.

Harry isn't striking in the way Alessandro was, but there is something about him that makes him stand out on TV as he follows the guests inside the church. Is it the way he carries himself with his head held high and his chin jutting? Or is it those clear blue eyes, even though he didn't look directly at the camera?

"Was that him?" Dad asks.

I suck in a deep breath and try to hold it in my lungs. "Was it that obvious?"

"Only to me, sweetheart." He watches me closely. "You know, it wouldn't hurt to call him and ask how he's feeling after the funeral."

I stand up; I've seen enough. "Don't ever apply for a job as a matchmaker, Dad. You'd be terrible at it."

"Aw, shucks. Just when I thought I was winning."

Laughing to myself, I go to the kitchen and make hot chocolate—it feels like it's going to be a long winter even if the thaw is almost complete—and come back with a plate of cookies. Just in time to watch the footage cut to the funeral party leaving the church.

There's Harry standing beside Ronnie and another guy I vaguely recall from the ice rink, staring straight at the cameras. I freeze, cup of hot chocolate in one hand and cookies in the other. It's as if Harry can see me watching him, and I instinctively step backwards, trying to avoid his line of vision.

But I don't move far enough. My eyes are still glued to the screen when a young woman in a short black coat, six-inch heels, and legs that would reach the moon, squashes herself in between him and Ronnie and kisses Harry full on the lips.

10

HARRY

I watch the footage again later that evening on the news report.

I'm alone in my apartment, still wearing my suit pants, white shirt, no tie, with my feet up on the glass-topped coffee table, and a brandy and soda in my hand. It has been a strange day. One of tears and laughter, of stories—old and new—and memories shared of Alessandro.

Carlos Russo hardly left my side. He was like the big brother I never had, my shadow, keeping an eye on me to make sure that I didn't overdo it. I'd spoken to the family about the accident. I didn't need to tell them that Alessandro had been drinking before he climbed into the driver's seat of his car—it had shown up in the postmortem results. But rather than guilt-tripping me over allowing him to drive, they said that I shouldn't have gotten in the car with him.

I wish I had answers for them. I wish I could tell them what had triggered his strange mood that day, but we'll never know, and it will always come back to haunt me because I was the one who encouraged him to take Ruby out for dinner.

I sip my brandy—my first drink since I was discharged from hospital—and feel the burn as it travels down inside my body. Today, the ache of loss for my friend has overtaken the ache I feel in my chest for Ruby, but already her image is sneaking back into the spotlight. Her smile. Her huge green eyes. The way she looked with her hair tousled around her face when she straddled me on the hospital bed.

The stirring inside me isn't purely sexual. It goes way deeper than that, although I want Ruby more than I've ever wanted any other woman. It's a connection that refuses to be severed.

In Greek mythology, humans originally had four arms, four legs, and two faces—two people in one human form. Zeus, out of either fear or rage, split humans into two, and tasked them with spending their lifetime trying to find their other half. It's a bizarre story, one that I would've scoffed at in the past, only now I can believe it.

Because I believe that I have found my other half.

On the TV screen, I leave the church with Ronnie and Pete. Camera crews and reporters line the street, hoping to capture the Russo family's grief and enough celebrity images to sell a few magazines. I watch myself blinking at the cameras, overwhelmed by the insensitivity of it all, and then Alessandro's younger sister Alicia appears from nowhere and kisses me on the lips.

I sit forward, sloshing brandy over my wrist and onto the floor.

That wasn't how it happened.

I know what I've just witnessed, but that wasn't what happened outside the church. Alicia came over to ask me if I was okay. There was too much going on, too many people in the crowd calling out and jostling to get close to Tom Cruise, no doubt in the hopes of getting his autograph. Alicia leaned closer and murmured into my ear so that I would hear her.

But the press made it look as if she kissed me. A full-on, lip-tingling, knee-jerking kiss on the lips. Why did they even need to show this shit? Someone fucking died, and there they are cashing in on people's tears.

Anger pulses through me, and I down the brandy, the burn no longer touching the sides. I know that this is what sells stories, but jeez, not at the expense of someone's funeral.

I stand up too quickly, my head swimming from the alcohol, and pour myself another shot. No soda.

I'm still trying to figure out how they managed to make it look like a kiss, when I've known Alicia since she was a little girl. It's quite a skill. Then it dawns on me like a blow to the gut, that Ruby might've been watching the same news report.

Shit!

What if she thinks that there's something going on between me and Alicia? What if Ruby thinks that I was messing around when I asked her to marry me? She'll have seen this footage and convinced herself that I was lying in the heat of the moment and now that I'm home, I'm relieved that she didn't take me up on my proposal.

I down my brandy and almost choke on it, coughing and spluttering, my head suddenly pounding with a combination of stress and booze.

What should I do now?

Ruby obviously didn't want to see me again after she left the hospital, but I can't sit back and let this ride. I don't want her to think that I lied. I don't want her to think that I'm like every other guy she's probably met before, sweet-talking her to get what I want.

But more importantly, I still want to marry her.

I'm *determined* to marry her.

There's only one thing I can do, I quickly realize. Tell her the truth, face-to-face, tell her how I feel, and remind her of her promise.

In my bedroom, I chuck some clothes into a small suitcase, grab my jacket and my wallet, and switch off the lights as I leave my apartment.

I'm going to Chicago.

I DIDN'T THINK this through.

There are no flights until the following morning. So, I spend the night hugging my jacket around my chest, curled up on a row of seats in the first-class lounge area, with a travel pillow under my head, wondering why I was so adamant that a private jet was an extravagance I could do without.

I don't sleep. I don't know what Ruby will say, or if she'll even want to see me.

And I can't blame her. I wouldn't want to see me either.

Five minutes. That's all I want: five minutes to explain my version of events and tell her that I can't stop thinking about her, that I wish I was still in hospital, in the middle of the worst blizzard in a decade, with her easy smile and her insatiable appetite for chocolate.

I REMEMBER WHERE RUBY LIVES. The cab drops me off outside her house, and I drag my suitcase along the front path, my heart hammering against my ribcage.

Everything I've thought about during the flight, all the opening conversation lines I've rehearsed, trying to preempt her responses, vanish the closer I get to Ruby's front door. My palms are sweating despite the bitter chill in the air. My mouth is dry.

I knock on the door and wait, peering around at the neighboring houses.

Eventually, the door is opened by a man wearing loose khaki pants and a Fair Isle sweater, leaning heavily on a cane. Recognition dances behind his eyes, and he reaches out a hand to shake mine. "Harry?"

"Yes." His handshake is still firm, and for some reason, this makes me happy. "Is Ruby home?"

"She's working at the library today." He stands aside and opens the door wider. "Come in. She never said that you were coming."

I step inside and the nerves seem to drain away as he closes the door behind me. "She doesn't know. It was a spur-of-the-moment thing."

"Sometimes, it's the only way to go about things. Don't give yourself a chance to change your mind."

He leads the way along the corridor to the kitchen that's painted in bold shades of ochre and sunflower yellow. The room is bright, vibrant, and warm, and I imagine that, in the summer, it's on fire with the sunlight streaming through the windows. I notice a gold-tasseled cushion on one of the windowsills and immediately picture Ruby sitting there reading a book in the winter when the oven is on and the room is cozy.

Ruby's dad fills the kettle and switches it on to boil. "I'm Graham," he says, and his smile is Ruby's. "How do you take your coffee?"

I tell him I take it with a dash of cream and three spoons of sugar, and he gestures for me to take a seat at the worn pine table in the middle of the room.

I already like Graham. He hasn't asked why I'm here. He isn't probing for my intentions regarding his daughter, and he didn't slam the door in my face. The anger must belong solely to his wife.

He carries our coffees to the table, one at a time, and sits facing me, propping his walking stick up against the edge. The house is cozy, comfortable, a home that has soaked up the personalities of the inhabitants.

"I'm glad you're here," he says, finally. "Maybe now, Ruby will start smiling again." He doesn't seem to expect a response, so I keep quiet. "She likes you; you know."

I can't contain my own smile. A wave of emotions battles with the tiredness crashing through my head, and I choke back tears. I didn't know what to think when I didn't hear from Ruby again. My thoughts scrambled between thinking that I'd pushed her too far and fearing that her mom had convinced her to stay away from me.

Standing outside the house, I'd fought the overwhelming urge to turn around and head straight back to the airport, but I understand now that this was my only option. This is me trying to win the girl I love. And now that I'm here...

"I'm going to marry Ruby."

Graham doesn't even seem surprised. "I'd have been more concerned if you'd said you *wanted* to marry her. Wanting to marry her would've implied that there's a chance it might not happen."

"I've already proposed to her. Twice. She thinks it was the pain meds talking."

Again, no shock registers on Graham's face. "Are you sure about that?"

My brain takes a couple of beats to process his question. "I scared her off, didn't I? It was too much, too soon. I should've given her time to—"

Graham makes a wave motion with his hands for me to stop panicking. "You did what felt right at the time—it's all any of us can do. Have you ever heard the saying, *what's for you won't go by you*?" I shake my head. "I think you have to trust that fate knows what it's doing."

Ruby talked about her dad a lot when we were snowed in at the hospital, but nothing she said could ever have done this man justice. Life served him a bum deal, but it hasn't kept him down. It hasn't destroyed his spirit, the same fighting spirit that I see in his daughter.

We're sitting in the cozy den with the huge window overlooking the backyard where the trees are still wearing their Christmas-card-worthy snow hats when Ruby comes home.

She freezes when she sees me sitting in the armchair with a mug of coffee in my hands. "Harry? How did you...? What are you doing here?"

Her eyes widen with surprise and then narrow like she has been pranked, and I know that she saw the kiss on national TV.

"I wanted to explain... In person." I stand up, set the cup down on the coffee table, and try to take her hands, but she pulls away and turns an accusatory glare on her dad.

"Did you organize this?"

Graham raises both hands, palms facing outwards, in a gesture of surrender. "Nothing to do with me. I'm just the doorman."

Ruby swallows. "I think you should leave."

"Not until I've had a chance to explain."

"Hear the man out, Ruby," Graham says.

She goes to leave the room, a sigh of exasperation escaping her lips, and this time I don't let her snatch her hands away.

"What you saw on TV—that isn't what happened. I've known Alicia since she was at school. The crowd was loud. She wanted to ask me if I was okay, but I couldn't hear her. I know how it looked, Ruby, but I promise you that there isn't, and never has been, anything between me and Alessandro's little sister." I pause. "That's why I'm here. I caught the first flight out of New York this morning."

I'm running out of steam, a night spent in an airport catching up on me. But at least I've said what I came to say. If it isn't enough...

She turns around to face me. "That's what you came to tell me?" I can't read her tone, but I'm certain that I can see amusement in her eyes, and my pulse picks up speed.

"When I watched the news report last night, I saw how it looked and I... Well, I panicked."

A smile tugs her lips upwards, and her entire face lights up, skittering butterflies around inside my chest at the same time. Ruby moves closer. She stands on tiptoes and kisses my cheek, her lips barely graze my skin, and I'm immediately transported back to the hospital room.

I wonder if this is how it's always going to be. If every kiss, every touch, every conversation is going to whizz me back to where it all began. If so, I can live with that.

"Don't they have phones in New York?"

I can't help returning her smile. "Who needs phones when you can catch a plane?"

"Are you hungry? Has my dad fed you?"

"Of course I have," Graham says.

Ruby hesitates, and I sense every nuance of her mood, the uncertainty, the frisson of delight, the anticipation of what's to come next. She believes me. She is happy that I came. But something is still bothering her.

"Maybe we should go into town and grab a pizza or something." She widens her eyes briefly in her dad's direction.

Graham nods. "I'll tell your mom that you met up with an old friend."

That's what's worrying her. She doesn't want her mom to find me here.

Before either of us can move, the front door opens, and Celia Jackson comes in, stomping her feet on the mat in the hallway, keys jangling, and perfume heralding her arrival.

Too late.

"Ruby, why haven't you started dinner? I finished early. The salon was dead again today." Celia enters the den and freezes when her gaze drifts from her daughter to me. "What's he doing here?" Her tone is like ice.

"He came to see Ruby." Graham grabs his cane and stands awkwardly, knuckles white around the handle. "They're just on their way out."

"Oh no." Celia shakes her head. "Ruby is going nowhere with him. Get out." This is aimed at me.

"Ma'am, I came to talk to Ruby." I don't understand what I've done wrong, but I'm not leaving until it's sorted. I don't want to make an enemy of my future mother-in-law, but if that's the way she wants to play this, I can guarantee that it will be her loss.

Celia folds her arms across her chest. "I said get out. I don't want you in my house. I don't want you anywhere near my daughter."

"Ma'am, I promise you that nothing happened—"

Ruby stands in front of me, forming a barrier between me and her mom. "If he leaves, Mom, I'm going with him."

"Don't be ridiculous, Ruby. You're going nowhere."

"I'm sorry you feel I'm being ridiculous, Mom," Ruby's voice is calm and steady, "but I mean it. I'm going to get my bag, and I'm leaving with Harry. I'll come back when you're ready to accept that I'm twenty-one. I'm old enough to make my own decisions."

"I-I..." Celia splutters. "You're making a huge mistake, Ruby."

"Then I'll hold my hands up and own my mistakes." Ruby entwines her fingers with mine. "Ready?"

"Don't you dare walk away from me!" Celia snaps.

Ruby tugs me out of the den and doesn't even glance over her shoulder. She grabs a backpack from her room, and heads toward the front door.

Before we leave, I hear Graham say, "Let them go. This is her life, Celia. Let her go live it."

11

RUBY

My hand feels like it belongs in Harry's.

When I first saw him in the den with my dad, the image of him kissing the beautiful woman on TV came flooding back, making me feel queasy and broken inside. But then he told me that he'd flown from New York to Chicago to tell me there was nothing going on, and everything else seemed to evaporate like morning dew in the summer sun.

Even my mom.

She can't tell me what to do. She can't tell me what to do. She can't!

It goes round and around inside my head like a mantra. I'm an adult. I have to find my own path even if it is a bit windy and hilly sometimes, and I know my dad needs me, but it isn't like I've left for good. Is it?

Harry hails a cab and I climb into the back seat while he gives the driver directions. He stows his suitcase in the trunk and sits beside me, his fingers instinctively seeking mine.

"Are you sure about this, Ruby? We can turn around, go back and speak to your mom. I don't want to be on bad terms with her from the outset."

The bruises around his eyes and temples are still yellowy-green. His arm is still in a cast, the pouches under his eyes are puffy, but he is still the same Harry who tripped over me on the skating rink a few weeks ago. I don't know anything about him, not really, but that first day on the ice added the prefix 'my' to his name without me even realizing.

My Harry.

No fighting it. No turning back. No regrets.

I shake my head. "I'm sure about this."

"If you change your mind—"

"I won't. No one has ever traveled across the country for me."

No one has ever traveled anywhere for me, but I have the weirdest sensation that our journey has only just begun.

"Okay. I just want you to know that we'll do whatever you want, Ruby."

I can't help laughing. "Next you'll be telling me that I have three wishes."

"Oh no." Harry's tone is serious. "You have far more than three wishes." His eyes crinkle at the corners. "And you still have a promise to keep too."

I barely register the city passing us by. For the first time in my life, it feels as if the world is a giant shell that is slowly opening to reveal the purest pearl inside. It doesn't even matter where we're going, and I'm not surprised when the taxi slows to a halt at the airport drop-off point.

I'm not leaving Chicago behind.

I'm taking the first step over the side of a precipice, and I'm not the slightest bit afraid because I know that Harry is waiting there to catch me.

Inside the terminal, the airport is buzzing with excitement.

Harry squeezes my hand, his body communicating with mine. He checks out the departures screen, his eyes scanning the destinations and flight times.

Finally, he says, "Do you trust me?"

"It's a bit late to ask me that now."

Leaning closer, he kisses the tip of my nose and sends a whisper of anticipation down my spine. "Wait here. I'll be right back."

I'm starving, so I make my way to one of the airport cafés and order pepperoni pizza slices to go and a couple of sodas. When Harry finally returns waving tickets in front of my face, his eyes are glittering.

"I hope you packed your passport."

I hand him a slice of pizza. "I packed it last night. I was going to give you twenty-four hours, and then I was coming for you, Harry Weiss."

He blinks. A slow smile spreads across his face, lighting him up from the inside. He takes the pizza, his fingers stroking mine and sending sparks of electricity through me. "I wish you'd said, you'd have saved me a journey."

He bites the end of the pizza slice as I punch him playfully on the arm.

. . .

HARRY DOESN'T TELL me where we're traveling to until we're boarding the British Airways flight to Edinburgh.

It's crazy. I've never been further than Mexico and I have no idea what to expect. But the word Edinburgh clings to my tongue like peanut butter, nesting there as if it was always waiting for Harry to introduce us to each other.

We fly overnight. First class. We're greeted by stewards wearing suits and ushered into our sleeper seats like plush armchairs, with fresh flowers on tables and heavy purple drapes separating us from the rest of the aircraft.

"It's like going to the cinema." I fasten my seatbelt and lean across to kiss Harry. "Only bigger."

Harry inclines his head. "And don't forget the minor detail that we'll be flying above the clouds."

I laugh. It's an intoxicating, heady experience. The curtains, the plaid blankets, the glass of champagne—*in a real glass*—that the steward serves when we're comfortable. I sip the bubbles and wait for them to go straight to my head.

What am I doing?

"Harry, pinch me."

He obliges, and I squeal like a child.

We eat a full-blown three-course meal washed down with wine, play Rummy for a while with the complimentary playing cards, and when the lights inside the aircraft are dimmed, I rest my head on Harry's shoulder and fall asleep instantly to the low purr of the engines. By the time we reach our stopover at London Heathrow, it feels as if we have known each other forever.

I know nothing about Harry's childhood, his family, his life in New York, but it's unimportant because I know Harry. The rest will come. It will seep into our life through shared experiences and snippets of conversation, and there's no rush.

Edinburgh is like no city I have ever experienced before.

We check into the George Hotel, a grand old building that seems to span an entire block with wide arches and tall stately columns giving it a regal appearance. Stepping inside is like stepping back in time to an early twentieth-century colonial mansion, with parquet flooring, wood paneling, huge gilt-framed paintings and plush sofas. The reception is framed by more columns and heavy white drapes, buttoned armchairs strategically placed around small round tables.

While Harry checks in, I turn three-sixty, soaking up the genteel atmosphere and hushed whispers of guests passing through on their way out to explore the city.

How is this even happening to me, I think.

Yesterday I was in Chicago and today... Today, I'm in *Edinburgh*!

Our suite overlooks George Street with its ancient buildings and trams trundling along the middle of the road. I can see the castle in the distance at the top of a hill. An actual castle. An actual castle that was once inhabited by real live monarchs.

I drag myself away from the view to freshen up before we go and explore. There's a walk-in shower in the marble-tiled bathroom, complimentary robes and slippers, and towels so thick and heavy that I don't want to get dry.

Dressed, I take a shortbread and then we step outside into George Street with its restaurants, wine bars, and modern stores set inside magnificent aging buildings. Following the map of the city we found in the room, we make our way towards the old town where cobbled streets wind up and down steep hills, and in and out of buildings that are centuries old. The imposing castle sits sentinel at the top of the hill as if protecting its people.

We explore the Royal Mile, the streets lined with towering tenement buildings, cafés, souvenir shops, and museums. We sit inside St. Giles Cathedral for a while, soaking up the solemnity and splendor of its architecture. We visit the graveyards, known as kirks, and study the names on the ancient headstones. We see the statue of Greyfriars Bobby, the dog who, according to legend, guarded the grave of his owner for fourteen years.

We eat haggis in a breakfast bun with square sausage. It's spicy, the texture rough on my tongue, and I like it until Harry says, "Try not to think about what it's made from."

"What?" I freeze, the haggis halfway to my mouth. "Now you have to tell me what it's made from."

"You really want to know?"

"Of course I do. You can't throw a curveball like that at me without following it through."

"It'll put you off." Harry obviously has no such qualms as he chews and swallows another mouthful of haggis.

"Tell me! Or I'll..." I peer all around searching for something to threaten him with.

"You'll...?" Eyebrows raised.

"I'll buy you a kilt and make you wear it with nothing underneath."

Harry laughs. "Don't say I didn't warn you."

"Harry…" I start walking towards the kilt shop.

"Okay, it's made from sheep offal and—"

"Enough!" I open my mouth and stick my tongue out to catch the chill and blow away the taste of the haggis.

Still laughing, Harry takes another mouthful and grabs me so that I can't escape.

After, when I've washed away the tang of sheep offal with a bottle of water, we stand in the cold listening to a man in a kilt playing the bagpipes. The sound is so unlike any other musical instrument, so gut-wrenching and pitiful, that I lose track of how long we stand there in the cold, our noses turning pink, Harry's arm draped over me. He buys huge tartan shawls to wrap around our shoulders, pulling mine around my shoulders and kissing the tip of my cold nose.

We tour Mary King's Close, the underground city, wide-eyed and open-mouthed at the sight of the narrow dingy streets that housed so many people centuries ago. "People actually lived down here?" I huddle against Harry, soaking up his natural protection and warmth.

As the starry, velvet night sinks overhead, our footsteps slow down.

We haven't discussed our plans beyond going back to the hotel after dinner. Tomorrow doesn't exist. Neither does the day after tomorrow, or the day after that. All we have is this moment in this beautiful city, and nothing else matters right now.

Walking along the cobbled streets, Harry suddenly takes my hand and drags me into a tight alleyway between buildings. Narrow stone steps lead down to dense darkness, and he grips me tightly, leading the way until we reach a tiny square courtyard surrounded by dozing buildings.

Harry leans against the wall and hugs my head against his chest. I can hear his heartbeat, da-dum, da-dum, da-dum, through his coat, and I close my eyes, soaking up his warmth while his arms shield me from the chill.

When he tilts my head back and kisses me, heat floods through my veins. I don't want it to end. We could stay here forever, I think, walking the bumpy streets, discovering hidden alleyways that lead to real homes inhabited by real people. This is a city of secrets, so what harm will one more do?

I explore Harry's mouth with my tongue, my nipples hardening beneath my clothes. Freeing my arms, I wrap them around his neck and run my fingers through his hair, our kisses growing harder, more demanding.

His lips travel down my neck, his fingers fumbling with my coat zipper. When he tugs it down, the chill spreading through my sweater and raising goosebumps on my flesh, I shiver. But it isn't just from the cold.

He reaches underneath my clothes with his good hand and squeezes my nipple, forcing a groan from my lips. "How does that feel, Ruby?"

"Good..."

"It's going to feel better than good."

If this isn't right, then nothing else ever will be.

"Harry..."

The sound of his name is all he needs.

Spinning me around, he pushes me up against the stone wall and lifts my coat and sweater to expose my breasts. Then his lips are there, and his tongue is chasing circles around my nipple, the tingling spreading between my legs.

His mouth is hot on my nipples, the cold winter air caressing my bare stomach. I arch my spine, pushing my nipples into his mouth, wanting him to be greedy, to devour them with his tongue.

Harry kneels. He tries to unfasten my jeans, but is struggling with one hand, so I undo them for him. I'm already wet. My pussy is clenching and unclenching uncontrollably before he has even touched me. So, when he slides the tight denim over my hips and drags his moist tongue across my skin, I tilt my head backwards and stare up into the darkness at the millions of brilliant stars twinkling overhead.

He said he wanted to do this right. I only hope he understands that, for us, this is perfect.

"Talk to me, Ruby." His voice sounds far away.

"I..." I can't talk. I can't think of anything but his tongue between my legs.

His fingers are on my thighs, spreading them apart, and I gasp at the chill between my legs. I don't know if it's the cold, the impossibility of finding ourselves in another country, in a city steeped in history, or the thrill of danger that someone else might walk down those stone steps and find us here, but my entire body is thrumming for Harry to fuck me.

His tongue flicks between my legs and I must groan out loud because the sound hovers in front of me. I want to bat it away, but I can't move. All my concentration is being used up by the feel of Harry's tongue, licking, flicking, gently parting my pussy, teasing me before he goes in.

I want this sensation to last forever.

I want it to be over.

My mind no longer belongs to me. It belongs wholeheartedly to Harry's tongue, dragging across my clit, back and forth, until my orgasm explodes out of me. I can't think. Even the stars are blinking in and out of existence as my body shudders, my breath lost somewhere in the courtyard until I can think clearly enough to rescue it.

Harry rises. "You taste so fucking good, Ruby."

His tongue fills my mouth, and I can taste me, my orgasm, mingled with the taste of him. He presses his body against mine, pinning me to the wall. I try to explore his body with both hands, to keep this going, to make sure that he doesn't stop, but he grabs my wrists with his good hand and raises my arms above my head.

"Not here." His voice is husky. "This is only the beginning, Ruby."

Reluctantly, I allow him to pull away from me. I tug my jeans back up, fasten the zipper, my pussy still throbbing. I straighten my sweater and pull down my coat as if I'm snuggling back inside my cocoon, armoring myself against the outside world.

His face is in shadow in the unlit courtyard, but I could recreate it with my eyes closed. It's as if I have always known this man. As if our paths were simply biding their time until they crossed.

We mount the narrow stone staircase and emerge back into the busy city like moles crawling out of our burrow. Then we walk back to the hotel in comfortable silence, fingers entwined, sparks flying between us while adrenaline pumps through my veins.

12

HARRY

The taste of Ruby is on my lips all the way back to the hotel. I don't make eye contact with anyone; I don't want them to suspect that I've had my face buried between her legs. I have never tasted anything so sweet, and rather than shying away from it, Ruby couldn't get enough of the taste of her on my tongue. Which only makes me want her more.

It's hard to walk. My legs feel weak, and my cock is throbbing for her.

But there was no way I was going to fuck her quickly in a hidden courtyard, so that we didn't get caught. I allowed myself to get caught up in the moment—Ruby's moment—but now we're going to finish this my way.

At the hotel reception, I ask the concierge to send a bottle of champagne up to our room. Ruby's lips are swollen, her cheeks flushed, frost clinging to her hair. And she is even more beautiful than she was the first time I met her.

When we reach our hotel room, I start filling the bathtub and drizzle passion fruit scented bath oil into the steaming water.

Without a word, I lead Ruby into the bathroom and slowly undress her, one item of clothing at a time, until she is standing in front of me naked. I've imagined this moment many times since the accident, but none of my dreams ever came close to the reality of Ruby Jackson. Her skin is creamy smooth, unblemished apart from a tiny, perfect birthmark on her inner thigh.

Ruby isn't shy. She watches me studying her the way she might watch a gangly-legged fawn learning to stand for the first time, a faint smile playing on her lips.

I undress myself, wishing that my arm wasn't in plaster. I want to be as perfect for her as she is for me, but this can't wait. Not now. Not when I have already tasted her, and I need her like a drug.

I offer Ruby my hand and help her into the tub, then I climb in and sit facing her, the bubbles bobbing against her naked breasts. She doesn't try to cover herself but watches me with wide, eager eyes, lips parted expectantly.

I pour soap onto the sponge and take her left hand—starting with her fingertips, I smooth it the length of her arm, across her shoulders, and down her right arm, goosebumps popping gently on her skin and tracking my journey. And Ruby watches me the whole time. I wash her legs, raising them one at a time above the tub, and tracing the glistening skin with my eyes. I wash her breasts, resisting the urge to suck her nipples, then her stomach and her back, Ruby arching her spine to accommodate me, a faint smile tugging at her lips.

Still, she doesn't take her eyes off me, like she's relishing every single moment.

At some point, room service knocks and leaves the bottle of

champagne I requested in the room, departing again like a whisper.

Rinsing Ruby off, I offer her my hand and help her out of the bath, our wet bodies sliding against each other and making my hard cock throb.

I could take her here. I feel every inch of her against me. Wet and slippery. I picture hoisting her up onto me, damp legs wrapped around my waist, my cock teasing her moist slit, as I slam her against the wall and fuck her 'till she begs me to stop.

It would satisfy the ache building up inside me. Fuck, it would satisfy both of us, but Ruby deserves better than a messy, frantic fuck in a hotel bathroom.

"Harry," she murmurs and I press my finger to her lips. We're doing this my way.

Reaching blindly for a fluffy white towel, I wrap it around her shoulders, drinking in the curve of her collarbone, the dip at the base of her throat, the swell of her breasts. The ache in my balls swells to bursting point. All in white, she's even more perfect to me.

When I pick her up, Ruby instinctively slides her arms around my neck, legs swinging over my arm like a bride being carried over the threshold. This... This is everything I wanted and more as I lay her down gently on the king-size bed.

Her lips part.

I've kept her waiting long enough.

I pop the cork from the champagne bottle, fill two crystal flutes, the bubbles simmering towards the rim and then settling down again, and hand a glass to Ruby.

"Cheers." I clink my glass against hers and take a sip, the bubbles fizzing on my gums.

I take another mouthful and don't swallow. Instead, I set our drinks aside, lean over Ruby, our lips touching, and drizzle the liquid into her mouth. Her arms wrap around my neck, and she pulls me down on top of her. Her kisses are passionate, demanding, greedy. Ruby's lips cling to mine until I remove her arms from my neck and pull away from her.

"I want to look at you, Ruby." Unwrapping her from the towel like a Christmas gift, I kiss her neck, her earlobes, her throat, tracing her contours with my lips. "You're so beautiful. I want to spend the rest of my life looking at you."

My cock is painfully hard, but I need to taste every inch of Ruby before I enter her. I want to leave no part of her unsampled. No part of her untouched.

I sip my champagne and, this time, dribble it into her belly button, enjoying the way she wriggles her hips beneath me. I suck the liquid from her and, holding it in my mouth, I force her legs apart, inserting my tongue into her and filling her with champagne.

Ruby gasps. Her back arches, and she instinctively grips the headboard with both hands. I nibble her clit between my teeth, sucking and licking and nibbling some more, discovering her body and what I can do to it.

"Tell me how it feels."

"I... It feels..."

"It feels?" I pull away and insert a finger in place of my tongue, wanting to keep her there on the brink.

She pants. "It feels like nothing on earth." The words spill out of her.

"Do you want more?"

"Yes."

"Say it, Ruby. Say, I want more."

"I want more, Harry."

I slide my finger out slowly, studying her wetness on my skin, and push my tongue back in. She's dripping. Ready for me. I find the spot and lick her hard, her shallow breathing urging me to lick faster. Just as she's about to come, her gasps become louder, with an animal-like quality.

I stop and kiss her roughly, hungrily, my own lust fueled by her demanding tongue.

I slide myself inside her slowly, relishing the tightness, the way her pussy closes around me, hugging me tightly like she's never going to let me go. Ruby gasps. Her eyes widen. She pants hard, her fingertips closing around my arms, clinging to me like she's afraid she'll fall if I move another muscle.

"Ruby...?" I whisper. "Am I hurting you?"

She shakes her head, a smile forming on her lips and lighting up her face. "No, it's... I've never..."

Realization dawns on me, sending a thrill down my spine and straight into my cock. I throb inside her, and she gasps again, only this time, she's clinging to me because she's waiting for more. She wants to experience it all.

I stay there for a while, my length throbbing inside her like a heartbeat, her tongue still chasing mine. I kiss every part of her face, her ears, her throat, teasing her with my tongue, feeling her erect nipples, and her wetness oozing around me.

Unable to wait any longer, I raise my hips, sliding my cock back out of her again, all the way out, until the very tip is stroking her clit. I watch her reaction, the wide-eyed surprise as I pull out, and the back-arching groan of pleasure as I push it back in. All the way in. Her enjoyment is everything, like watching a perfect picture come to life.

Ruby instinctively moves with me, matching my thrusts with her own, forcing herself onto me, begging me to fill her up. Something gives inside her, and I hear the groan escape from my own lips. "I need to come, Ruby," I murmur, my lips pressed against her neck.

"Do it." Her lips find mine.

She's holding me so tightly, I can't breathe. Our oxygen is combined. Our bodies glued together with love, lust, sweat, and when I come, my entire body shudders on top of her until all that is left of me is her heartbeat drumming in synch with mine.

I WAKE up early the following morning. We fucked more times than I can remember in the night, dozing in between. Each time I awoke and saw Ruby's contented face next to mine, I was instantly hard again. I snuck under the sheet and aroused her with my tongue, and she responded by spreading her legs wide and letting me in, until finally, we both fell into a deep, dreamless sleep.

I don't know where I'm going, but I know what I need to do. I think I've needed to do this since the first moment I set eyes on Ruby Jackson, but it feels as if Edinburgh is our city. It's where dreams are made and wishes come true, and the frost sparkling across the cobbled streets when I leave the hotel is only more proof that this was meant to be.

Everyone wishes me a good morning as they walk by.

Everyone is smiling.

The sun is low in the wintry sky, winking at me from behind the gothic buildings, setting the windows aglow and sprinkling diamonds across my path.

Another omen.

I find the jewelers I want, or rather the jewelry store finds me, its small-paned windows blinking in the weak sunshine, letting me know that it's there. I step inside and breathe in the musty air of a building that has seen far more than anyone else on this planet.

The manager, an old man with silver hair, wearing a red bowtie with a tartan waistcoat and white frilled shirt, peers up at me from polishing a gold pendant and slides his spectacles back up his nose. "Good morning, sir," he says with a smooth Scottish accent. "How are you enjoying our fine city?"

"I'm enjoying it greatly. Thank you." It must show.

"Ah, an American accent. Let me guess." His eyes roam my clothes, my face, the cast on my arm. "You're a New Yorker."

"How did you know? Is it that obvious?"

"I've spent my life studying people." He reaches under the counter and pulls out a velvet pad filled with diamond rings. "And diamonds. Now, if I might take the liberty of making a suggestion, I do believe that this is the ring you are looking for."

I peer down at the ring he is offering to me. It's a heart-shaped diamond, the facets like tiny, magnificent icicles trapped inside the huge sparkling heart. I had no idea what I was looking for, or the kind of engagement ring that Ruby would like before I stepped inside the shop. But now that I've seen it, I'm absolutely certain that this ring was meant for Ruby Jackson.

I hold it tentatively, marveling at the way the diamond catches the light as I turn it around. It's mesmerizing and made even more so when I imagine it on Ruby's finger.

"Beautiful, isn't it?" The man finds a small velvet lined box in a drawer and leaves it open on the counter. "I can make the ring larger or smaller if the fit isn't quite right."

"I'll take it." I didn't expect it to be this easy, but I'm learning. Everything is easy where Ruby is concerned because we're cut from the same mold.

With the engagement ring ensconced safely in its box in my pocket, I find a tiny café on a narrow side street and order breakfast bagels and coffees to go. I'm literally floating down the streets, hovering above the frosty ground like I'm riding a magic carpet. I've not slept more than a couple of hours, and yet I feel as if I could run a marathon today with the heart-shaped diamond close to my chest.

I'm riding so high on excitement and adrenaline that I don't even notice the cop car parked outside the hotel entrance.

Carrying our breakfast, I walk into the lobby, my stomach rocking when I spot two policemen, their backs to me, speaking to the concierge at the front desk. It's okay, I tell myself. They could be here for any number of reasons, and Ruby and I have done nothing wrong.

Still, I don't wait for the elevator but take the stairs up to our room, not waiting around to be noticed. My heart is thumping. Why would the cops be looking for us? The concierge has my credit card details; we've not broken any regulations; we both have valid passports. It's irrational, but I can't shake the notion that they're looking for us.

I hear the phone in the room ringing as I let myself back in.

Ruby rolls over in bed, a bare arm snaking out from under the covers to answer the call before I can stop her. I hear her say, "Hello," into the mouthpiece, and I put our breakfast down, sitting on the edge of the bed, still in my coat.

Ruby smiles at me, affection gleaming in her eyes. But the smile fades as rapidly as it appeared, confusion knitting her brows together. "Okay, sure," she says to the concierge. "Let me get dressed, and then we'll be down."

She replaces the handset and sits up in bed, clutching the sheet to her breasts. "That was the concierge. The police are looking for me."

I blink, trying to process this information. "For you, or for both of us?"

"Just me. He said my name, Ruby Jackson. He wants me to go down and speak to them." Her voice is dull as if a single phone call has sucked the life out of it.

This is wrong. All wrong. I have a diamond ring in my pocket. I was going to give it to her while we ate breakfast in bed. This was supposed to be the happiest day of our lives, so why do I suddenly feel as if the universe has other plans for us?

"Did he say what they want?"

Ruby pushes back the covers and slides her legs over the side of the bed. The clothes she wore yesterday are still strewn across the bathroom floor where we left them last night, but she grabs some panties from her backpack and drags them on followed by clean jeans and a sweater.

Her movements are urgent. Hurried. She grabs her stuff, whatever she can find, and shoves it into her backpack, and I wonder if this is the reason she didn't hang her clothes in the wardrobe and make herself at home. She was waiting for this to happen.

"Ruby, what's going on?" I haven't moved. I'm still clutching our breakfast, the engagement ring burning a hole in my side through my pocket.

"We need to leave." She darts into the bathroom and collects her discarded clothes. "Now."

She scans the room to see what she has forgotten, and when I still don't move, she drags my suitcase out of the wardrobe, unzips it, and starts tossing my clothes in, hangers clattering onto the floor.

I empty the drawers with one hand, sweeping them clear, and depositing my belongings into my luggage. Her sense of urgency is contagious. "Do you want to tell me why we're leaving?"

"My mom. She must've put the police up to this."

I straighten, a rolled-up tie in my hand. *Why did I pack a tie for chrissakes!*

"But you told her you were leaving. It's not like you ran away."

"I don't think that matters."

"I don't understand." I rumple my hair with my hand. This can't be happening. Celia wouldn't go to such extreme lengths to keep Ruby away from me, would she?

In my head, I replay her reaction when she came to the hospital, and again when she came home and discovered me in their den. She was undeniably angry. But I don't understand why. I don't understand what I have done to deserve her obvious dislike and mistrust.

She hasn't even bothered to ask me how I feel about her daughter.

"It isn't you." Ruby shrugs her arms into her coat, hoists her backpack over her shoulders, and turns to face me.

"It sure feels like it is."

"She's..." Ruby hesitates, choosing her words carefully. "I don't know, overprotective since my dad had his stroke."

I nod. There's something she isn't telling me, but I'm not going to press it now.

Leaving the key on the desk in the room, I take one final look around, not to check we've left nothing behind, but to imprint the memories of our first night together on my brain.

In the corridor, Ruby heads in the opposite direction to the elevators and through a door marked STAFF ONLY. We take the stairs down to the ground floor and find ourselves in a large room lined with laundry bins. Through the wide fire exit door, and we're at the back of the hotel, in a small yard with sodden weeds and mini mountains of mulch and trash collecting in the corners.

I hold Ruby's hand, and we lose ourselves in the narrow, cobbled alleyways of Edinburgh once more.

13

RUBY

WE CLIMB to the top of Arthur's Seat, an extinct volcano in Holyrood Park, and eat breakfast sitting on the frosty grass overlooking the city. The climb allows me to forget about my mom for a while. Harry doesn't believe that she would report me as a missing person to the police, but he doesn't understand the lengths she would go to, to get what she wants.

I didn't truly understand either, until now.

What other explanation is there for the cops turning up at our hotel in another country and asking to speak to me?

I know that I must go home eventually and tell her how I feel about Harry, but not yet. I'm not ready to face her yet. I'm only sorry that my dad will be on the receiving end of her anger until I return. I'd bet every cent I've ever earned that she hasn't told him she has involved the cops.

"Is this how it feels to be a fugitive?" Harry scrunches up the brown paper bag our breakfast came in and stuffs it into the side flap of his suitcase.

"It's an adventure." I shrug. "If she thinks I'm going to come running home with my tail between my legs, and tell her that she was right all along, she's got another thing coming."

Harry laughs and kisses me with his icy lips. Strange how kissing him already feels as natural as drawing breath. Walking away from him now would be like forgetting every book I've ever read. It would be like stepping onto the moon without an oxygen tank.

"She was right all along?" Harry furrows his brow.

"About me and you." Guilt swirls around inside my stomach, and I wish I hadn't drunk the cold coffee.

One day I'll tell him about my mom's plans for her only daughter, but not yet. Not here. Edinburgh has brought us together in a way that Chicago never could have. I feel like this will always be our city, the place where happy memories were given life, the city where we lost ourselves and found each other.

"She'll understand when she sees how good we are together." Harry peers out across the city.

In his eyes, it's that simple. Two people fall in love, and the whole world claps as they set off into the sunset holding hands. He doesn't know my mom.

"I'm not going back. Not yet."

His smile lights up his face despite the bitterly cold wind at the top of the hill turning his lips blue. "Phew. I was sitting here trying to figure out how I could abduct you for real without getting caught."

It's my turn to laugh. "You only had to say. I'd have bought some rope and a blindfold myself."

"Now there's a thought." His eyebrows dance comically. "Time to go. I can't even feel my butt anymore."

"Where to?"

"We'll find the railway station and get on the first train out of the city, see where it takes us."

It takes us to Glasgow.

This city is louder, brasher, livelier, like Edinburgh's gin-swilling, opinionated great-aunt. We wander out of the grand, high-ceilinged station, grab a kebab and sodas from a takeout, and wander along Sauchiehall Street, where the air feels charged with something I can't quite put my finger on.

Anticipation. Tension. Confidence.

We pass a couple of uniformed cops and Harry squeezes my hand tightly, trying to tug me to the other side of the street. But I carry on walking, my head held high, making eye contact as they come closer.

"We can't stay here," Harry says as soon as they're out of earshot. "They tracked us down in Edinburgh. They'll do the same here if we check into a hotel."

"No hotel then."

He gives me the side eye. "I'm not sleeping on a park bench."

"And I thought you were enjoying being on the run."

He stops on the sidewalk and wraps his arms around me, his chin resting on the top of my head. He's warm, and I stop shivering, just for a moment. "I'd enjoy being anywhere with you. But I draw the line at benches and doorways."

A bus approaches us, and I realize that we're standing next to a bus stop. Pulling out of his embrace, I join the line, dragging Harry along with me. We hop onto the bus and find a seat right at the back where the windows are steamed up, and the seats are cozy.

"Where are we going?" Harry clears a patch on the window with his sleeve and presses his forehead against the glass.

"No idea."

"I like the sound of that."

The bus heads out of the city, leaving the gray buildings and the colorful murals behind, and I rest my head on Harry's shoulder, my eyes feeling heavy. The terrain becomes greener, the roads winding around turns, the bus picking up speed and slowing down at regular intervals, rocky streams following us and disappearing, only to rejoin us further down the route.

The clouds dissipate, allowing the sun to smile down upon us like ants hitching a lift on the back of a many-legged beetle.

Harry and I move closer to the window, soaking up the view, alert again.

I've never seen green so vibrant and glossy and glorious. The hills roll away in the distance, some growing into snow-capped mountains, others supporting wind turbines and the occasional, lonely Gothic mansion.

"That house has turrets." Harry points to a tall, narrow house set back from the road in the middle of nowhere, the long driveway guarded by stone lions. "Must belong to a princess."

"Or a witch."

We pass stone huts and drywalls that crisscross the land like a patchwork quilt and fat-bellied sheep munching on lush grass in every direction.

And then the sea comes into view.

We both gape at it, wide-eyed. The sun casts a zigzag pattern straight down the middle of the gray-blue sea, sparkling like diamonds, so bright it hurts our eyes. There's a gigantic rock in the distance, just sitting in the water, majestically, a perch for the seagulls and puffins.

We get off at the next stop, an unspoken agreement. It's a tiny village nestled between granite mountains and the sea, the land in between filled with sheep. Even from the bus stop, we can hear the sea crashing against the shore, and my body is filled with a sense of peace that I don't believe I've ever felt before, like the wilder the terrain, the calmer I feel inside.

There's a pub in the village, a small, single-fronted grocery store, and a curiosity shop with marionettes watching passersby from behind dusty windows. The cottages are low-built and weather-worn. The wind whips across the village from the sea, tugging our hair around our faces, and making us snuggle deeper into the shawls Harry bought in Edinburgh., our fingers belonging to each other now.

Passing by the grocery store, I spot a card in the window announcing that a local farmhouse is operating as a B&B. It would mean no checking in using a credit card that the cops can trace back to us.

"We can use fake names," Harry suggests. "What do you want to be called?"

I grin at him. "How about Mr. and Mrs. Heathcliff?"

The farmhouse is just outside the village. The sheep eye us up suspiciously as we trudge along the gravel path between fields to the large stone cottage situated at the bottom of a hill.

We knock on the bright red door and are greeted by a ginger-haired woman wearing a faded apron and a wide smile. Her cheeks are mottled pink, no doubt from the biting wind, but her eyes are bright blue, smile lines fanning from the corners and around her mouth.

"Can I help ye?"

"We're looking for a room." Harry gestures to his suitcase. "We noticed the card in the grocery store window."

"Come a long way?" She peers behind us as if we might be carrying a sign announcing that we're from the States.

"Chicago," Harry says at the same time as I say, "New York."

The woman's smile grows wider. "Come in. It's blowing a hoolie out there." She opens the door wide and gestures us through to the kitchen.

The room is warm and filled with the aroma of baking bread. The table in the middle of the room is rich pine, a vase of heather sitting in the center. The work surfaces are scrubbed clean, and I notice freshly washed towels flapping on the washing line outside the window.

It's cozy, and it feels instantly like home.

"How long are ye wanting to stay?" The woman fills a kettle with water and switches it on to boil. Then she takes three large mugs from a wooden stand and drops a tea bag into each.

"We're not sure," Harry says. "A few days maybe. Is that going to be a problem?"

"Ach, not this time of year. Sit yourselves down while I make ye some tea, and then I'll show you to your room."

We both do as we're told.

The woman tells us that her name is Eileen. She and her husband, Alastair, manage the farm and take in guests to make a bit of extra money.

"The pub in the village does great food if ye're wanting to eat out in the evenings. I'll provide a full Scottish breakfast—do ye like haggis? But ye're welcome to use the kitchen in the meantime. I want ye to treat it like home while ye're here."

She smiles at us and slurps her tea while it's still scalding hot.

"Alastair will show ye round the farm if ye're interested."

I wonder if she's starved of company while Alastair is out on the farm all day because she barely stops to draw breath while she's talking.

The bedroom is just as clean and cozy as the kitchen. The bed has a floral comforter, and a faux fur throw on top, with plumped up pillows and cushions, and fluffy white towels folded to resemble swans. It's hard to believe that this woman has welcomed us into her home as if she has known us all our lives, and I hope that we can find a way to repay her kindness.

"Settle in," Eileen says, from the threshold. "There'll be fruit cake in the kitchen whenever you're ready."

She closes the door behind her, and I flop backwards onto the bed. My muscles ache. My brain is scrambled from traveling and running from the police, and all I want to do is sleep, but Harry lays down beside me, his hand slipping underneath my sweater.

"Are you ready for fruit cake, Mrs. Heathcliff?" His fingertips find my nipple and his tongue pushes its way between my lips. "Or...?" He leaves the sentence hanging.

"Or...?" I can't help smiling at his use of the fake name.

"Or shall we work up an appetite first?"

"Hmm, what do you suggest, Mr. Heathcliff?"

His hand snakes a path down to the waistband of my jeans, and he opens the button easily with a flick of his thumb. My body is instantaneously throbbing.

"I'm sure I'll think of something." He kisses the tip of my nose before sliding my jeans over my hips and spreading my legs wide.

His fingers stroke between my legs, sending a shiver down my spine, and I grab his arm, guiding him inside me. "Can you think about it down there?"

"Hmm...I'll try." He kisses my lips while he slides two fingers inside me, opening me up. My body is instantly wired, my sex already wet.

I nibble his bottom lip, catching it between my front teeth. "Harder, Harry."

"Harder ... Heathcliff. Say it, Ruby."

A gasp escapes my lips as my favorite quote slides into my mind of its own accord: *Whatever our souls are made of, his and mine are the same.*

"Harder, Heathcliff."

"Harder?" His breath mingles with mine. "You mean like this?" He rams his fingers inside me, and I pant. My spine automatically arches, pushing my pussy onto him.

"Yes."

Harry leaves my side, and I muffle my moans of pleasure with my fist when I feel his tongue between my legs. His fingers drag back and forth, rubbing my clit before his tongue is right there, licking slowly, hitting the spot with each stroke. He slides a hand up to my breasts, pinching my nipple between his fingers.

"I can't see you, Ruby."

I raise my head from the pillow and peer down at him, his tongue inside me, his eyes watching me hungrily. He starts sucking then, holding my gaze, his eyes lighting up when he sees what effect he's having on me.

I can't control my orgasm. I bite down hard on my knuckles, feeling the explosion everywhere.

Harry doesn't waste a beat. Before I've caught my breath, he's inside me. He pushes my thighs backwards, and drapes my feet over his shoulders, my knees almost touching my ears. He's in so deep, I swear I can feel the end of his cock hitting my spine.

"Hard enough for you?" His face is so close, I can see the faint red lines crisscrossing the whites of his eyes.

"Yes." It comes out breathily, mingled with my shallow breaths.

"Sure?" He grips my hair tightly, arching my neck backwards and exposing my throat to his kisses. "I think you can take more, Ruby."

On his knees, he slides his cock all the way out, its absence leaving me breathless, then rams himself back inside me. So deep it forces the air from my lungs.

"How about that?" He smothers my mouth, his teeth biting into the soft flesh around my lips and making my brain cells swim.

I entwine my fingers with his hair, holding onto him, his kisses as hot and hard as his thrusts. I've never wanted him so badly. He fills my mouth with his tongue, and I suck on it, desperate to keep him inside me. To feel him filling me up. I hold him tightly until he reaches his own orgasm, his wetness exploding inside me, his body juddering in a reaction that is already so familiar, I can't help smiling to myself.

This is Harry.

My Harry.

14

HARRY

The wind howls around the cottage all night, battering the windows, and flinging rain at the glass as if it's trying to get inside. We snuggle under the fur throw, creating a tent over our heads, and we talk. We talk about whatever pops into our heads.

Ruby talks about her favorite books aside from *Wuthering Heights*. "*Forever Amber*. It was banned when it was first written, although God knows why. There's nothing risqué about it now. And *The Other Side of Midnight* by Sidney Sheldon. This book literally left me speechless for days after I finished it."

"I find that hard to believe."

"Hey." She punches me playfully on the arm. "I can be quiet... When I want to be."

I tell her about my sister Melanie.

"She and my mom were really close. When my mom got sick, Melanie looked after her. She washed her, and fed her, and brushed her hair. I'd come home from work and find her sitting in the rocking chair beside my mom's bed, reading books to her, while my mom simply faded away."

Ruby proves to me that she can be quiet. She holds me in her arms and transfers her warmth to me beneath the furry blanket, and I doze off, dreaming that Melanie, dressed as a British cop, comes to find us here in this remote farmhouse.

THE FOLLOWING MORNING, we're woken by the aroma of sizzling bacon and fresh coffee. I slide my arms out from under the blanket and immediately regret it as the chill raises goosebumps on my flesh. We dress quickly and head to the kitchen where Eileen is humming while she fries eggs in a pan on the stove.

"Morning," she tosses over her shoulder with her usual wide smile. "I hope you're both hungry."

"Ravenous." Ruby sits down at the table. She's wearing a baggy sweater and clean jeans, and I don't think that I could find a more perfect setting for her, despite knowing that she's a city girl. "Can we explore the farm after breakfast, Eileen?"

"Aye, but don't get too close to the cows. They're in the shed up the hill for the winter. You'll find Alastair up there."

She places in front of us plates heaped with food and goes back to the counter where she slices homemade bread into thick pieces and spreads them thickly with butter.

I've never considered myself a foodie. I can cook—my mom made sure to teach me the basics—but I can't remember a meal that I've enjoyed more than this breakfast. Perhaps it's the wind still howling around the cottage, or the sea stretching endlessly towards the horizon, or perhaps it's simply because I'm here with Ruby, somewhere where no one will ever think of looking for us.

Eileen refills our coffee cups and tells us to take some wellies from the front porch when we wander around the farm.

The wellies are splattered with dried mud, but Eileen has provided thick woolen socks to keep our feet warm. Ruby giggles when she realizes that they reach over her knees. "How am I supposed to walk in these?"

A faint tang of manure assaults my nostrils as I step into another pair. "Are you sure you want to do this?"

"Sure, I'm sure. You can't pull the New Yorker act on me now, Harry. We're in this together, remember."

I kiss her forehead. "And you've never looked sexier."

"Maybe I'll bring the wellies to bed with us later."

Alastair is a sandy-haired man with ruddy, weather-stained cheeks and a wiry beard. He introduces us to the cow shed, where the animal smell is quite overwhelming.

Ruby, unfazed by the farm odors, asks, "Do the cows have names?"

The farmer shakes his head. "Forming a personal attachment to the animals will only make my life more difficult."

Ruby's expression crumples when she understands the meaning behind his words. "Well, I'm going to name them."

We wander around the shed, Ruby choosing names and stroking their foreheads, trying to ignore the plastic tags attached to their ears.

"This one is Daisy." The honey-colored cow stops munching, hay and grass spilling from her mouth, and watches us with obvious mistrust. "Hello, Daisy. My name is Ruby, and the city boy here is called Harry. Don't mind him. I'll make sure he doesn't touch your food."

The sheep are even less friendly, running away the instant they spot us walking down the path. We go to the rocky beach and spend the rest of the day collecting pebbles and hunting in the rockpools for crabs. My foot slides off a mossy rock and I land on my back in the icy sea, gasping for air as the shock of the chill sucks the oxygen from my lungs.

Ruby offers me a hand, chewing her bottom lip to stop herself from laughing. I grip it tightly, but she loses her balance too and lands on top of me, drenching her knees and splashing both our faces.

"Oh ... my ... God... That's so cold." Her teeth are chattering, her lips turning blue.

Laughing, we run back up the beach towards the cliffs where we've spotted a narrow gap between rocks. Squeezing through the gap and into a cave barely large enough for both of us to sit, I'm surprised at how warm it is when we're out of the wind.

Ruby shivers against me, and I pull her closer, our cheeks colliding in the cramped space. "I'm ... so ... cold." Even inside the gloomy cave, I can see that her face is turning blue, her jaw clenched.

I unzip my jacket to share my body heat with her, and she dips inside it, while I wrap it around her. "Better?"

"A bit."

I hug her tightly, rubbing her arm to keep her circulation going when I feel her icy hand slide inside my pants. I jump involuntarily.

"Sorry," she murmurs against my chest. But she doesn't stop. She frees my cock, a gentle groan escaping her lips before her warm mouth closes around it.

It's my turn to groan. I hadn't realized how cold I was until the heat from her mouth transfers to my throbbing cock. I lean back against the walls of the cave and listen to the hiss and shuffle of the waves outside competing with the thumping of my heart.

The cold. The cave. The cozy room waiting for us back in Eileen's farmhouse all contribute to the blood pumping around my veins and into my cock. I can't hold back.

I feel blindly inside my jacket and wind her hair around my fingers, holding her mouth on me, not letting her go. She instinctively resists, but I'm already ejaculating into her mouth, my cock pulsing, my cum shooting down her throat.

Moments pass. My brain is still recovering from the intensity of the moment, and I can't speak.

Then Ruby's face appears in front of me, and she kisses me on the lips. I taste myself, sour, salty, surreal. "That's one way to warm up."

We stay inside the cave until our clothes are turning stiff with the salt before making our way back into the village. We buy a peculiar marionette with a face that could be either male or female dressed in a frilly white shirt and red corduroy dungarees, and a Noughts and Crosses board game with tiny figurines cloaked in red and black robes for pieces.

That evening we eat steak and ale pie in the local pub and wash it down with a pint of Guinness which the landlord assures us is good for our blood. We listen to the gentle accent of the locals, play pool with two silver-haired fishermen who beat us easily, and dance around the bar tables to Roxy Music's 'Avalon', me twirling Ruby around with one arm above her head and trying not to fall over.

Then we wander back to the farmhouse in the dark, our hearts filled with new memories.

And at night, in the safety of our furry makeshift tent, I take my time exploring Ruby's body.

Spooning her from behind, I kiss the back of her neck and stick my tongue in her ear, something that makes her arch her back and breathe heavily. I cup her breasts and tease her nipples between my fingertips, shifting her hair aside and tracing her neck and shoulders with my tongue until she grabs my hand and places it between her legs.

Ruby is always wet. She's like a flower that opens up whenever we are together. Lying on her side, she raises one knee to her chest giving me access to penetrate her with two fingers, stroking her clit until her lips find mine greedily.

I pull my fingers out and roll her onto her back, spreading her legs wide. But this isn't enough for Ruby. Gripping the headboard, she brings both knees up almost to her shoulders, tilting her pelvis upwards, her glistening pussy ripe for me.

"Lick me, Harry," she murmurs.

"Very bossy." I drag my tongue along her pussy. "Try again."

"Lick me, Harry. Please..."

I lick her again, this time making sure my tongue gets right inside her.

"Again."

Panting now. "Please lick me, Harry."

I hold back, watching her, my mouth close enough to touch her sexy wetness. "Better."

"Please, Harry. I want you to lick me."

Smiling, I cup her butt with my hands and lick her gently, tasting her, teasing her with my tongue until she groans out loud. Then I push the tip inside her, find what I'm looking for, and drag it back and forth, feeling her wetness oozing into my mouth.

When she is still in the throes of her orgasm, I slide my cock into her, taking it slowly, filling her with my length. She thrusts against me, our hips pounding together, my mouth smothering hers to stop her from crying out and disturbing the sleep of the farmer and his wife.

I start to wonder if our life together will become a series of bubbles. Each one bigger and brighter than the one before, places in which to lose and discover ourselves at the same time. I don't think about work. I know I must at some point, but right now, Ruby is the most important thing in my life.

The engagement ring is still in its tiny velvet box in my coat pocket. Just as the jeweler knew which ring I was looking for, I tell myself that I'll know when the right moment presents itself. No rush. We have our whole lives ahead of us.

On the third day, when the wind drops and the setting sun is still warming our faces, we stroll along the beach towards the village pub, eager to sample the local fishermen's catch of the day and try to beat our new friends at a repeat game of pool. They've whipped our butts twice, but Ruby promised them that we were merely warming up, lulling them into a false sense of security.

Up the slope from the beach and onto the road that leads to the pub, we both spot the police car outside the establishment at the same time.

"No." Ruby shakes her head. "They can't have found us here. They can't have."

I hear the incredulity in her voice above the drumming of my heartbeat.

"Maybe they're inquiring about something else. Something local." My words are swallowed by the sea shushing across the pebbly shore. "Maybe they're here for dinner."

Ruby's shoulders slump inside her coat. "You don't believe that do you?"

She's right. I want to believe it, but it's too much of a coincidence, the cops turning up again where we're staying. Whatever problem Celia has with me, she's not going to back down until I take Ruby home.

"Maybe it's time." I place my hands on Ruby's shoulders and turn her around to face me.

Her eyes are large with tears. "I'm not going back, Harry." Her voice is as determined as ever, and I feel a rush of pride in my chest for this beautiful woman. "I'm not letting her win."

"Okay." Deep breath. The cops only have to mention that they're looking for an American couple and the landlord will know exactly which direction to point them in. "What do you want to do?"

"There's no time to grab our stuff from the B&B."

She squeezes her eyes shut, a tear spilling over her bottom lashes. Clothes are not important to Ruby, but I know that the marionette is. It's a souvenir of our time here, a reminder of the precious time we've stored up inside our minds, snapshots of perfect moments to be brought out later and reminisced over.

Do you remember when we stayed in that tiny fishing village on the west coast of Scotland?

I pat my pocket with my hand. The ring is still there. I'm not going anywhere without it.

Two cops walk out of the pub, peering left and right along the street, eyes narrowed. That settles it. They're not here to sample the beer-battered haddock fillets. They climb back into the vehicle, the headlamps throwing golden beams along the road towards us, and we both instinctively duck behind a moored rowing boat.

I wait for them to drive away before I stand up, helping Ruby onto her feet. "We'll stay here until the next bus pulls in, then we'll run for it. They'll probably wait at the farmhouse for us to come back."

Ruby nods. "Eileen will keep them talking." She chews her bottom lip. "I hope she doesn't think badly of us when we don't come back for our stuff. It makes us look guilty."

"I don't think Eileen will jump to conclusions without hearing all the facts." I don't know how I know this, but I'm certain I'm right. Eileen is the kind of woman who tells it like it is and pays no attention to idle gossip. "Besides, I think she liked having us around."

Ruby rests her head against my chest, and I hold her tightly.

I don't say it out loud, but I was starting to feel like we could stick around for a while too.

Day has melted into twilight when the bus pulls around the corner heading towards the bus stop. The sign on the front, in bold black letters, reads: GRETNA GREEN.

15

RUBY

It's disappointing how quickly the fun has been sucked out of running from the police. I don't say anything to Harry, but I was starting to grow roots in the charming little fishing village. Not because I wanted to spend the rest of my life there, but simply because everyone had opened their arms and welcomed us into their fold.

They thought of us as Mr. and Mrs. Heathcliff, and that's who we were. Without even trying.

In Gretna, we find a guest house, a rambling whitewashed building surrounded by heather-filled flowerbeds. We check in under a different name: Earnshaw. And sleep in each other's arms, our tummies rumbling because we haven't eaten since Eileen's cooked breakfast the morning before.

Gretna is quirky. Busier than the fishing village, it doesn't take us long to figure out that it's the Scottish version of Vegas: people elope to Gretna Green to get married. Or at least they used to, before legal requirements got in the way.

We wander around the pretty wedding venues, reading various plaques and notices about the village's history. It seems that Gretna became a popular runaway wedding destination when the law in England and Wales prevented people under the age of 21 from marrying without parental permission. The same law didn't apply in Scotland, and with Gretna being just across the border, word quickly got around.

"I knew there was a reason we caught that bus." Harry tries out a Scottish accent and fails epically.

I laugh at him. "Ach, get away with ye."

He shakes his head. "How have you picked it up so quickly?"

"I pay attention."

We're strolling past the wedding anvil outside the old Blacksmiths Shop, when a woman wearing an ivory lace-trimmed dress and carrying a petite posy of pink flowers comes over to us. Her partner is wearing a traditional kilt complete with furry sporran, white shirt and black jacket.

"Hello," the woman says. "This might be a bit of a strange request, but would you be our witnesses? You see, we're getting married today, now actually, and well, we didn't want to tell anyone, and now we need someone to sign the marriage certificate."

I glance at Harry, and he is beaming at the couple and shaking the man's hand. "We'd love to be your witnesses. Wouldn't we, Ruby?"

Their happiness is infectious.

We follow them into the old smithy where the registrar is waiting to complete the simple ceremony. I thought I would feel awkward encroaching on the wedding of two complete strangers, but it feels strangely intimate, and I realize that it's an honor to be invited to share their special moment with them.

I lean against Harry and wonder if this will be us one day. How will it feel to marry Harry? "You should get married in a kilt," I whisper in his ear. "They're sexy."

"Only if we get married in the summer."

When the registrar completes the ceremony by announcing, "I now pronounce you husband and wife," tears well in my eyes.

I can't look at Harry. I know that he asked me to marry him in the hospital after his accident, and I've refused to acknowledge that he was serious, but knowing what I know now about him, I understand that he meant every word. He wants to marry me ... now... But he'll change his mind when we get back to Chicago and he speaks to my mom.

The couple kiss. I can see it in their eyes: this is their happy-ever-after moment.

I envy them this quiet wedding, their vows witnessed by two people they met on the street outside. I envy them for the freedom to fall in love and plan a future together, no running away, no fights, no secrets. I wonder if they realize how lucky they are.

They ask us to have a celebratory drink with them, and we accept. I wish I'd had time to buy some clean clothes, but they're so wrapped up in their own little wedding bubble that they don't even seem to realize that my jeans have grubby patches on the knees and my sweater has been worn three days in a row.

The pub is old-fashioned with dimmed lights, red velvet cushions on the seats, and a selection of desiccated bouquets strung around the walls, obviously donated by people who have gotten married here.

The newlyweds order champagne and Harry refuses to let them pay, saying that it's his treat. He's wired, buzzing with happiness, and I wonder how excited he'll be on his own wedding day. I feel a stab of sadness in my chest—he'll make someone an amazing husband one day.

We learn that their names are Donna and Bill. They met in a cinema. They were watching a gory horror movie when Donna's best friend puked over Bill's then girlfriend—sitting in the row in front—during a particularly gruesome scene.

I cringe. "That's the weirdest meet cute I've ever heard."

"How did you two meet?" Donna sips her champagne, her eyes sparkling.

Harry inhales deeply. "I fell over her at an ice-skating rink. Literally."

"Ouch." Bill chuckles. "Lucky you didn't slice her fingers off with the blades."

"Thank you!" I raise my champagne flute to toast him. "My mom always claimed that was a thing when I was younger. She believed that fear was the best way to teach me to skate."

Everyone who enters the pub comes over to congratulate the couple. Weddings have this effect on people. It's a celebration of love and happiness and the future, and I find myself smiling so much that my cheeks are sore.

Between pats on the back, kisses, and handshakes, the discussion turns around to the kind of wedding Harry and I would like.

"I want to get married in a forest or a field. Somewhere outside." Inexplicably, my cheeks grow hot as Harry stares at me intently, like he's taking notes in case I test him on my preferences later. "You know, in a long floaty dress, something ethereal, with flowers in my hair."

"Sounds lovely," Donna says. "What about your wedding reception? Would you have that in the forest too?"

I never thought that far ahead. I've only ever envisaged the ceremony, something informal, where my husband and I read out our own vows and people throw wildflowers over our heads.

"Donna is thinking about the great British weather," Bill adds. "Raincoats, umbrellas, wellie boots getting stuck in the mud."

"Would kind of ruin the dress." Donna shrugs.

"Or add to the adventure." I sip my champagne, and my mind immediately flits to Harry dribbling bubbles into my belly button. "Depending on which way you look at it. It's the person you're marrying that's important, right?"

"Cheers to that." Bill clinks his glass against hers.

"What about you, Harry?" Donna asks. "Ever thought about your wedding?"

Harry sets his drink down on the table and catches the condensation on the side of the glass with his thumb. "I always thought I'd have a big wedding. You know, the kind of event that the paparazzi are clamoring to get exclusive pictures of. Hundreds of guests. My wife-to-be in a huge, sparkling white gown."

"Princess Diana style." Donna smiles at the image.

I can't tell if he's serious or not, so I keep quiet.

Harry reaches for my hand underneath the table. "I want everyone to see my future wife. I want to show her off, let them see how beautiful she is, and how happy she makes me." He pauses. "But I can do that in a forest if that's what makes her happy too."

Donna dabs her eyes with a tissue. "Stop. You're going to make me cry."

"Well said, mate." Bill claps Harry on the back. "Maybe we can repay the favor, come along and be your witnesses one day."

"I'd like that."

Harry is all sunshine smiles and fluid edges. He's living his dream, only he's confusing it with reality, and this isn't real. None of it is real.

I stand abruptly and make an excuse about needing the restroom, stumbling blindly towards the rear of the pub, my thoughts swimming frantically against the tide.

All this talk about weddings and forests and sparkling dresses has brought me down to earth with a thundering jolt. This isn't our life. One day we'll have to go home, and then it will all come crashing down around us and this ... adventure ... will end up being nothing more than a moment of madness that we'll look back on with much eye rolling and shaking of our heads.

In the restroom, I splash cold water on my face and stare at my reflection in the mirror above the basin. I look pale, tired, with dark smudges under my eyes. But my cheeks are rosy, and my lips still bear the imprint of Harry's kisses.

My stomach twists when I think of our naked bodies entwined beneath the fur blanket at Eileen's B&B. If only we could somehow make it real, stay here forever, make a new life, one in which dreams do come true.

Donna and Bill have made it happen. But even as I think this, I know that their situation is nothing like ours, and the dark cloud that I've been ignoring since we landed in Edinburgh settles above my head again, threatening and ominous.

I breathe deeply, trying to calm the insects crawling around inside my chest.

Walking back to the bar, I can hear Donna's laughter, loud and dirty, the kind of laugh that hints at sexual innuendos every time and makes people smile.

I've only walked a few steps when the front door to the pub opens, and two policemen walk in, their eyes scanning the patrons. I freeze. I'm guessing they've been given photographs of us, which means there's no point trying to pretend we're the Earnshaws if they spot us.

I need to warn Harry. They're closer to him than they are to me, but if I go back to the table and tell him that we should leave, Donna and Bill will require an explanation, and it will only draw attention to us. Running away has confirmed our guilt enough already.

Harry's face lights up when he sees me, a wide smile stretching his lips. He hasn't noticed the cops. Yet.

I know what I must do. He didn't force me to come here with him against my will. It was my idea to pack a bag and leave home with him, and it was my idea to run from the hotel in Edinburgh when the cops first caught up with us. He said that he would do whatever I wanted, and I—with my head filled with books—wanted an adventure.

I can't look at him.

Navigating my way around the tables filled with people enjoying a drink with their friends, I approach the policemen, my pulse racing.

One, a tall lanky guy with a protruding Adam's apple glances at me, looks away, and then immediately returns his gaze to me.

"Hi." My voice is filled with confidence I don't feel inside. "I'm Ruby Jackson. I believe you're looking for me."

For one awful moment that seems to last an hour, he blinks, frown lines appearing between his eyebrows. His colleague stares at me slack-jawed, and I wonder if I've misread the situation completely. Maybe they're not looking for me after all. Maybe my mom didn't file a missing person report.

"Ruby Jackson?" the first officer says.

My heart is thumping. This is a mistake, a huge silly mistake prompted by my own insecurities.

But before I can smile and back away, pretend that I've drunk too much champagne and have no clue what I'm talking about, Harry is standing next to me, his fingers entwined with mine. I feel something hard and cold sliding onto my ring finger, and Harry's eyes meet mine. We exchange the briefest glance, but it's enough for me to know that he has everything under control.

I raise my hand. It feels heavier, somehow, weighted down, and my eyes bulge when I see the huge, heart-shaped diamond set into a neat white-gold band.

It's ... beautiful. Breathtakingly beautiful. I instinctively twist my hand back and forth and follow the shimmering patterns dancing across the room and causing the officers' buttons to glint like the sea when the sun is shining.

"Hello, officers." Harry shakes their hands warmly. "My name is Harry Weiss. I'm afraid you've been sent on a wild goose chase. You see, my beautiful fiancée and I have eloped. We've come to Gretna Green to get married."

His smile is easy, his tone is self-assured. This is a side of Harry that I haven't seen before, the side that he no doubt adopts when he's discussing business with potential clients.

The policemen both stare at the ring and then at me. I want to smile. I want to be as confident as Harry, but my facial muscles are refusing to cooperate.

"Getting married?" The first officer nods. "I assume all the necessary paperwork is in place."

"Yes, sir." Harry inclines his head, his voice still strong.

The policeman turns his attention to me. "We will have to report back to confirm that we've spoken to you."

"Yes," I say. "Thank you."

"Well, good luck then." The officer smiles for the first time, and I realize that he's a lot younger than I first thought.

All eyes follow them out the door, and then Donna is hugging me tightly, and Bill is shaking Harry's hand vigorously, and the ring on my finger is lighting up the room with dancing patterns.

16

HARRY

My head, my chest, the blood gushing around my veins ... everything is scrambled. It wasn't the proposal I'd planned, but I'm starting to worry that nothing will ever go to plan with me and Ruby.

Is that a bad thing?

I haven't got as far as working that out yet.

Bill claps my shoulder, shakes my hand, and his congratulations are lost in the rising sound of voices all around us. Donna is hugging Ruby tightly, examining the ring, holding it up to the light so that she can get a better look.

And suddenly everyone in the pub congratulates us. So many faces. So many handshakes and hugs. And the landlord cracks open another bottle of champagne—on the house.

Ruby is surrounded by women all oohing and aahing over the engagement ring, and she goes with them, moving with the crowd, a glazed look in her eyes whenever I get the chance to look at her. It seems everyone wants to celebrate our engagement; everyone wants to share our excitement; everyone has already dismissed the brief appearance of the cops as nothing.

Apart from the one person who matters.

I'm gutted. I'm disappointed that I didn't give Ruby the special proposal that she deserved, but like a fish swimming against the tide, I'm starting to believe that it was always destined to be this way. No point fighting it now. I did what I had to do, and although it's a relief to get the ring out of my pocket and onto her finger, I have no idea how she feels about it.

"I feel like we've stolen your thunder today."

Bill stands next to me, a glass of champagne in his hand, and watches the group of women congregated around Ruby all raising their own drinks in a toast. Donna's voice is the loudest, and no mistaking the raucous laughter.

"Not at all. If anything, I should apologize to you—this is your wedding day."

A silver-haired man wearing a tweed jacket over a claret-colored waistcoat comes over with another bottle of champagne. "I hear congratulations are in order. Oh, how I envy you having the rest of your life together ahead of you." He winks at us and walks away.

"I hope you and Ruby didn't have any other plans for today," Bill says. "It's party time." He rejoins his new wife, slipping a hand around her waist and kissing her on the lips.

Each time I try to get close to Ruby, to get a moment alone with her, it seems that the rest of the world has other ideas. The music gets louder. People are dancing. Champagne and beer and spirits mixed with soda keep appearing in my hand.

And my brain gets foggier and foggier, the niggling feeling still there, but clawing now at the fuzzy surface of my liquor-soaked brain cells.

I need to talk to Ruby...

Suddenly, I'm seated back at our table. I don't even know how I got here, but the room is starting to sway a little, and I have the overwhelming urge to go outside, breathe in the cold air, and down a bottle of water.

"Here." Ruby puts a pint glass of clear liquid in front of me. "Water. You look as if you could use it."

"Ruby?" I guzzle half the water without coming up for air.

"Wow, you're drunker than I thought you were." She's smiling, so I know she isn't angry with me.

"I'm so sorry, Ruby." My voice hitches in my throat.

She blinks, her expression unreadable, or maybe it would be if I hadn't drunk so much champagne. "Sorry for what?"

"For not proposing to you properly. I wanted to get down on one knee..."

My stomach lurches, and I pause, waiting for the water to settle. I should go back to our room, sleep it off, attempt this conversation with a clear head in the morning, but it can't wait. I have to let her know how I feel.

"I didn't want to just spring it on you like that."

"It wasn't your fault, Harry."

The water is already working its magic, reviving, reenergizing, clearing some of the cotton candy from my head. "I didn't know what else to do. I didn't want them to take you home, take you away from me."

She narrows her eyes and gives me a sideways smile. "Is that the only reason you proposed?"

"No!" I say too quickly. "No, I meant it the first time I asked you, in the hospital. I'll mean it every time I ask you, Ruby, until you say yes." Because it suddenly occurs to me that she hasn't accepted ... yet.

"How long have you had the ring?"

"I bought it in Edinburgh. With breakfast. I mean, I didn't buy it with breakfast, I bought it that morning. Then, the cops arrived at the hotel, and the moment was gone, and, well, I was waiting for the right moment."

She chews her bottom lip and raises her hand in front of her face to study the diamond.

"Do you like it?"

Her smile is gentle, genuine. "It's beautiful, Harry. I couldn't have chosen a more perfect ring myself."

I wait for her to say more. When she doesn't, I say, "But...?"

It takes her a beat too long to answer, giving my heart enough time to start tearing in two. She's going to hand the ring back to me, I think. This is the part where she says it's been fun, but she doesn't want to get married.

"There's no but." She shrugs. "I don't care about you going down on one knee, Harry. That's not our story. This is."

"It is?"

I'm still trying to process what she's saying. She doesn't want me to take the ring back. I glance at her finger, and it's still there, and she hasn't said yes, but it doesn't matter because we're not like anyone else, and this isn't a fairytale.

I lean closer. Our lips meet, and the room spins when I close my eyes, but Ruby is right here, keeping me grounded.

"We do need to figure out where we go from here," she says, when I pull away.

I nod. We can't keep running forever, and besides, we don't need to run now. Celia will know that we're engaged to be married, and there's nothing she can do to stop us. But I want to give Ruby the best of everything, which means that I need to go home at some point and start paving our future path with gold.

"Come with me to New York. Not right now. When we're ready to leave. I want you to come back with me to New York, Ruby."

Her gaze drops to the empty champagne bottles on the table. "I want to tell my dad. I don't want him to hear it from the cops. I... I know that he'll be happy for me. For us." Her eyes widen as the word 'us' lingers in the air.

"We'll go see your parents first." I check out the time on my wristwatch. "Or we could call him now. Chicago is six hours behind the UK."

"How do you know that?"

"From business meetings with British clients."

I shake my head to clear it, grateful the room has stopped spinning so violently thanks to the half pint of water I downed. I'm not in the right headspace to think about work, so for the moment, it's staying outside of our bubble.

"Okay." Ruby is even more beautiful when she smiles. "Let's call him."

I take her hand and ask the landlord if we can use his telephone to call home and give our folks the good news. I'll pay for the calls, of course. He points us in the direction of the phone out the back, in the dingy hallway between the bar and the kitchen, and we make an international call to Ruby's dad.

He picks up on the first ring.

"Dad? It's me, Ruby." She grins at me, her eyes dancing. I know her smile is really for her dad, and that's okay.

I hear the gentle buzz of his voice from the handset although I can't decipher what he's saying.

"We're in Scotland, Dad. A place called Gretna Green." There's a pause during which Graham must ask what we're doing here. "We got engaged, Dad. We're going to get married."

There's a brief silence followed by Graham's excited congratulations. Ruby covers the mouthpiece with her hand and grins at me. "I think he's excited."

I wonder if he knows that his wife has had us tracked down by the police.

"Dad," Ruby says, "don't say anything to Mom. I'll tell her when I get back."

She'll know soon enough anyway, but I guess if Graham knows nothing about her reporting Ruby missing, she'll either have to explain the whole story or keep quiet about it when she finds out.

"No, Dad." Ruby's smile is still wide—her dad's approval obviously means a lot to her. "No, we haven't thought about where we'll get married yet, but I promise I won't do it without you. You're walking me down the aisle, remember?"

Graham must ask about me then.

"Harry's fine. He sends his love, Dad."

She ends the call and throws her arms around my neck. I know how she feels. It's as if inviting Graham into our secret has made it finally feel real for us both, and now she's ready to tell the whole world.

Minus her mom.

It's something that they will have to work out between them, but I already know Celia will have to work hard to regain her daughter's trust after this.

I call my dad next. He's in the office and comes to the phone holding a second conversation with someone only he can see.

"... until Harry gets back. Karl Weiss speaking," he says into the phone.

"Dad?" Pause.

Why is my heart skipping right now? I hear the muffled sound of him covering the phone, his voice sounding as if it's underwater, and then he says, "Where the fuck are you, Harry? I've not heard from you since the funeral."

"I know, sorry, Dad. Something really important came up, and I had to get away fast." Another pause. "I'm in Scotland."

"Fuck!" I can picture his shoulders slumping as he turns away from the desk to face the window. "When are you coming back?"

"Soon. I don't know." I sense Ruby's eyes on me, curious, waiting for me to tell him, and I can't look at her. "Dad, I—"

"I don't know isn't good enough, Harry. You go off gallivanting around the world and leave me here to deal with this shit. You're needed here, unless you want this business to—"

"What do you mean?" The words stick in my dry mouth. I knew I should've finished that pint of water. "What's going on?"

"I'm not telling you over the phone. Let me know when your flight gets in and I'll arrange for the car to pick you up from the airport."

"I wish you would tell me."

It's a lie. I wish I hadn't called him, saved our news for when we got back, because I'm sober now, and this feels like the end of our adventure and our first steps into God only knows what.

"I've got to go, Harry. Someone has to keep this business afloat."

"Dad, wait a sec. I have news."

The line clicks and I'm left with the buzzing sound of a dead conversation and a swirling sensation in my gut.

"What is it?" Ruby's eyes are wide. "What's wrong?"

"I don't know." I don't want to spoil our time here talking about my business.

"We have to go home, don't we?"

I nod. The party is over.

17

RUBY

It feels even more surreal to be traveling home again.

The mind adapts to its new surroundings, survival instinct, I guess, making it the new normal and replacing the old. We're quiet during the flight, each lost in our own thoughts. When we were flying to the UK, we had the unknown on our side, like going on vacation and not knowing what to expect when you arrive. But now...

I know that Harry is worried about his business. He wouldn't tell me what his dad said, but it clearly wasn't good news. I feel guilty for keeping him away for so long, but whenever I mention it, he tells me he wouldn't have swapped this trip for the world. And I know that he means it.

I only hope that he won't regret putting this ring on my finger.

We go directly to Harry's place, a sleek, one bedroom apartment in a building on East 54th Street. It's decorated in neutral colors with bold patterned rugs on the wooden floors, abstract paintings on the walls, and ivory cabinets in the open-plan kitchen. It's bright and spacious. And it tells me nothing about Harry Weiss.

We both shower and Harry orders takeout noodles which we eat sitting on chrome stools at the breakfast bar. Neither of us has said the words out loud, but staying here together is going to be a whole different ball game to staying in Eileen's B&B.

This whole new persona seems to have dropped onto Harry's shoulders, one that I didn't even see when he was in the hospital, a sharp-pronged reminder that we know so little about each other.

While Harry gets dressed in the bedroom, I call home. I can't put off speaking to my mom forever.

"Hello?" The greeting is more like a growl than a welcome.

"Mom." I swallow hard.

"Ruby! Where are you? What's going on?" The second question is more hushed than the first, and I hear the rustle of her moving about in our home.

A pang of homesickness swells inside my chest. "I'm in New York."

"What are you doing in New York? When are you coming home? What has that man done to—"

"Mom!" I'm too tired to fight with her. That will have to wait for another day. "That man has a name. Harry. His name is Harry, and I'm going to marry him."

"Like hell you are, Ruby. Not if I have anything to do with it." The growl has transformed into a hiss, like a serpent slithering down the telephone line searching for its prey.

"Why? Why are you being like this, Mom? We love each other. I thought you'd be happy for me, or doesn't love count for anything anymore?"

"You don't know the first thing about him. What are you going to do when you realize that he isn't the man you think he is, huh?"

"What's that supposed to mean?"

"It means that he turned your head at a fancy party and now you think you're going to spend the rest of your lives together."

Deep breath. "The fancy party that you wanted me to attend."

Harry walks through to the living room of his apartment, and I almost don't recognize him in a smart gray suit, crisp white shirt and silver tie. His hair is slicked back, and his chin is smooth. I swear he looks ten years younger.

'Your mom?' he mouths, and I nod, covering the mouthpiece with my hand.

"Don't go yet," I whisper to him before going back to the telephone conversation. "Mom, I've got to go. I'll call you again tomorrow."

"Ruby, wait. Don't you dare hang up—"

I end the call and cross the room to Harry, breathing in the smell of his aftershave. "So, this is how Harry Weiss looks when he's in the office?"

He wrinkles his nose. "I'm glad I got that ring on your finger before you saw me in a suit."

"Hmm." I tap my top lip with my fingertip and walk a circle around him, eyeing him up from all angles. "I don't know. I think I'll enjoy undressing you when you get back from the office."

Harry laughs and pulls me in for a hug, wrapping his arms around me, his plaster cast resting on my shoulder. "How did your mom take the news that you're in New York?"

"As expected, she was thrilled to bits, and says she can't wait to celebrate with us when we're next in Chicago."

He pulls away, holds me at arm's length, and studies me intently. "We can go as soon as I've sorted out whatever's going on in the office. Or would you rather go without me? Speak to her alone first?"

"No. I'm in no hurry to see her." I chew my bottom lip when concern flashes behind Harry's eyes, guilt rearing its head inside my chest. "What time will you be back?"

"Missing me already?" His smile is wide. "I don't know, sorry. I don't want to leave you here alone, but I-I've been away too long..." He leaves the sentence hanging, torn between needing to resolve whatever is going on, and not wanting me to feel bad for keeping him away.

"Can I come with you?"

He blinks furiously—he obviously hasn't considered this as an option.

"Please? I want to know everything about you, Harry. Who knows, perhaps your secretary will let me in on a few of your secrets."

"If I had any secrets, I'm certain that Lizzie would be only too happy to sit you down and reveal them over a bottle of wine."

"You're worried now though, aren't you?" I tease. "Now I simply must come. And I'm not taking no for an answer." I peer down at my travel-stained clothes. "I don't have anything to wear though."

"I tell you what," Harry relents. "I'll take you into the office, introduce you to my father."

"And Lizzie."

"And Lizzie. And then you can take my credit card and go shopping for some new clothes. Deal?"

The words 'I love you' are on the tip of my tongue, but I hold them back. Maybe I'm being silly or over-cautious or paranoid, but they're not ready to come out yet. We still have to break down the Celia barrier first.

"Deal."

Harry's company—Weiss Petroleum—takes up one level in a Manhattan skyscraper owned by the Russo family. When we leave the elevator, the office is bright and busy, and it seems immediately apparent that Harry is ready to expand.

Despite the 'eligible bachelor' title bestowed upon him by the news reporter, I hadn't given much thought to Harry's company until now, and my chest swells with pride. Harry did this. He built this business, he gave it wings, and now he's the man in the saddle, steering it onward to greatness. But no one would ever know, because he's just Harry when he isn't wearing a suit.

I'm introduced to Lizzie, a woman in her mid- to late-forties, with a blond 70s perm, glossy lips, and wearing a dress with shoulder pads.She smiles with her teeth and blushes slightly when her gaze flits between me and Harry.

"Oh, honey, I can't tell you how long I've waited for this moment."

She hugs me, squeezing my arms against my sides. As she releases me, her hands drift down to mine, her fingers settling on the diamond. She raises my hand and studies it closely, her mouth opening and closing like a goldfish bobbing to the water's surface for food.

"Is this...?" Her eyes narrow.

"It is," Harry answers for me.

Her cheeks turn even rosier, and she squeals with delight. "Oh my God, why didn't you warn me?"

"I'm sorry, I didn't realize you needed a warning." Harry succumbs to his secretary's hug with a chuckle. "We wanted to surprise you."

"Surprise me? You've almost given me a heart attack. Does your father know?" Her eyebrows lower briefly. "No, of course he doesn't. He wouldn't have complained..." She clamps her lips together, eyes darting around the office and settling on a door with Harry's name printed on a neat gold sign.

"Is he through there?" Harry gestures at the door.

"He is." Lizzie takes my hands in hers again. "Good luck, honey. I promise you his bark is worse than his bite."

I glance at Harry, but he isn't listening. He has already opened the door to his office and is waiting for me to join him.

"Dad, I want you to meet—"

"When did you get back?" His dad cuts him off. "I said I'd have organized the car."

"I wanted to go home first, Dad. We were traveling almost twenty-four hours."

"Well, you're here now." Pause. "We?"

Harry stands aside, and I join him just across the threshold of his office to meet my future father-in-law for the first time. "Dad, this is Ruby Jackson, my fiancée."

Karl Weiss is nothing like his son. Taller, stockier, darker, I can instantly tell that Harry's looks were softened by his mom's genes. He must've inherited the blue eyes from his mom too.

"Hello, Mr. Weiss."

I cross the room and reach out to shake his hand, but he turns away from the desk, walking around it instead, with his head lowered.

A glance at Harry, and he is watching his father's reaction with furrowed brows. "Dad?" he prompts him.

Mr. Weiss freezes, his spine stiff. "Your fiancée?" he mutters without looking at either of us.

"Yes." Harry is undeterred. "Ruby Jackson."

"I heard you the first time."

Harry faces me, and I can see anger sparking behind his eyes and in the set of his thin lips. "I apologize for my father's rudeness, Ruby. I can only assume that he left his manners at home this morning. I'll ask Lizzie to come shopping with you, and we'll try again another time."

I don't understand what's going on, but now's the time when Karl Weiss should relax his shoulders, smile at us apologetically, and begin the conversation over. Only, he doesn't. He keeps his back turned as if he can't bear to look at me, and tears well in my eyes for Harry because he doesn't deserve this inexplicable reaction.

I follow Harry back to Lizzie's desk in a daze. Lizzie doesn't even question Harry but grabs her purse and ushers me back through the office to the elevators keeping up a steady stream of chatter that I barely even register.

Outside, I can't help comparing the busy city streets with the tranquility of the farm by the sea, the water lapping the shore and the sheep bleating as they run away. There are too many sounds, too many people, too many cars.

Lizzie takes me into a small café, sits me down at a table-for-two by the window, and orders two espressos. "You look a bit shell-shocked, Ruby," she says with a motherly smile. "He can come across as a bit of a tyrant at first, but he's lovely when you get to know him."

I only have her word for it, and from what I've seen so far, I'm not sure that I believe her.

I BUY some clothes to get me through the next few days: jeans, sweaters, and a couple of shirts. I still feel unsettled after the introduction-from-hell to Harry's father, and spending Harry's money doesn't sit well with me. I need to sort my life out and think about getting a new job if I'm going to stay in New York.

I'm so lost in thought that my brain takes a couple of beats to recognize my mom waiting for me inside the lobby of the Russo tower when we get back, she's so out of context.

"Mom?"

"You wouldn't come to me, so I came to you." Her gaze skims Lizzie, but she doesn't acknowledge the other woman with a greeting. Her lips form a tight O of disappointment.

"Not here, Mom." I close my eyes briefly, tiredness crashing through me and sending my brain cells reeling. I don't understand why everyone is trying to keep me and Harry apart. "Not now."

"Yes now." She hoists her purse higher onto her shoulder like she's arming herself for battle.

"Ma'am," Lizzie interjects, "perhaps you'd like to come up to the office and talk to Ruby in private."

"No." Mom turns her steely glare on Lizzie. "I'd like my daughter to come home with me, that's what I'd like."

"Mom, I'm not coming home." I stand my ground.

"Okay, have it your way, Ruby."

Mom's voice is cold, laced with something sharp, and I realize too late that I should've taken her outside. Whatever is going on, she intends to do this right here in the foyer of Harry's place of work.

"Let's go grab a coffee," I say.

"I don't want coffee. I want my daughter to call off this ridiculous fiasco and come home."

"*Ridiculous fiasco?*" My voice is shrill. "Is that what Grandma said when you fell in love with Dad?"

Mom blinks at me furiously, eyelash extensions creating shadows on her cheeks. "You're not in love with Harry Weiss. You're playing a foolish game to get back at me for something, and it ends now."

My chest is heaving with the effort of containing my temper. "That's where you're wrong, *Mom*. It's only just beginning."

"You leave me no choice then, Ruby. I didn't want to tell you, but I don't know how else to get you to see sense. Karl Weiss is the reason your father's company went bankrupt. Because of that man, your father had a stroke and has never worked since."

18

HARRY

I KNOW the instant Ruby walks back into my office that something is wrong. She doesn't make eye contact, instead, her eyes seek out and follow my father's stiff back as he rises, grabs his suit jacket from the coat stand in the corner of the room, and goes to leave. We haven't known each other long, but our bonds are deeper than conversation and amazing sex.

"Ruby?" I rise too, walking around the desk to stand in front of her, forcing her to look at me. "What's happened?" I reach for her hands, but she pulls away.

"Did you know about my dad's business?" There's a tremor in her voice that makes my skin prickle.

"What do you mean? About it folding shortly before he had his stroke?"

"No, I mean about *your* dad being the reason *my* dad lost his business."

I shoot a glance at my father who has frozen by the door, head lowered, his back still facing us. He doesn't look around.

Doesn't even move, although he clearly heard Ruby's accusation.

"What are you talking about?" It's a feeble response, but I'm frantically trying to piece together how a simple shopping spree has degenerated into this crazy idea that my dad ruined Graham Jackson's life.

"Why don't you ask him?"

There's unmistakable animosity in her tone as she stares at my dad's back, and it feels as if we're voodoo dolls having needles stuck in us from all angles.

"Dad?"

He turns around slowly, and he doesn't need to speak for me to understand that it is true. "That's business, son. Shit happens. If you can't handle the stress, you should get yourself a regular nine-to-five job that you can leave behind on a Friday evening."

Ruby shakes her head, her eyes growing huge with tears. "It wasn't just a case of shit happens though, was it? You sold him out, got him involved in a contract that you knew would ruin him, and then you stepped in and bought up the shares of his business for a fraction of what they were worth."

"Hang on a minute," Dad says, his eyes narrowed. "How dare you come in here and accuse me of something of which you have no knowledge. You should get your facts straight before you start throwing accusations around—"

"Whoa, Dad!" I raise my hands in mock surrender, one aimed at him and the other at Ruby like I'm the referee in a boxing ring. "I'm not going to stand here and listen to you speaking to my fiancée this way."

"Your fiancée!" A sardonic grin twists his mouth into an unpleasant grimace. "Of all the women in the city you could've had your pick of, and you chose a Jackson."

"Okay, Dad." I move closer to Ruby, choosing my side. "I don't know what happened back then—perhaps you'll explain it to me later when you've had a chance to calm down—"

"Calm fucking down? Don't tell me to calm down, son, when *she* came in here all guns blazing, trying to stir the pot."

I ignore him and turn to Ruby who still hasn't moved. "Ruby, I don't know what's going on, or how you heard about this, but can we talk about it later? Please?"

I want to get her away from my dad. I want to go back to when it was just the two of us in our cozy Scottish bubble, walking along the shore with the gulls circling overhead. When we had a fur blanket to snuggle under at night and no one trying to tell us that we were crazy to think that we were in love.

"I don't know, Harry."

She spins the engagement ring round her finger, and I think that if she takes it off right now and hands it back to me, I'll never forgive my father for destroying the best thing that has ever happened to me.

"I need some time..."

My pulse quickens. "You believe me though, don't you? You believe I knew nothing about this until you mentioned it."

"I-I don't know what to believe." She deliberately refuses to look at my father. "I don't know if this is such a good idea. The ring. The wedding. Us."

"Don't say that." I take her hand in mine, my fingers trapping hers, so that the diamond is digging into my flesh. "We're not our parents, Ruby. Their mistakes don't have to be ours."

"Let her go," Dad barks. "Save yourself the hassle and let her go before you're in too deep."

I ignore him. I'm already in too deep.

"Ruby, please. I'll come home with you now. We'll go back to Chicago if that's what you want. Right now. Me and you. We'll walk away from here and have a fresh start. We'll go back to Edinburgh if you tell me that's where you want to be. I'll go anywhere in the world with you, you must believe me."

My dad scoffs from the doorway, and it's the fingertip that pushes me over the edge of the precipice.

"Stay the fuck out of this, Dad. This is between me and Ruby."

"If that's the way you want it. You can walk out of here with her right now, but don't expect me to keep your company running. In fact, you can kiss goodbye to any help from me ever again."

"I don't need your help, Dad. Not if it's going to cost me the woman I love."

"Love!" His face grows dark with rage. "You think you can run a fucking business on love. Oh boy, have you got a lot to learn. Love is what will fucking destroy you and everything we've worked so hard for."

I turn on him. "You're a fucking coldhearted bastard, Dad, do you know that? You're not content with pushing Mel away, you want to lose me too."

His expression crumples, but it's too late. I have no sympathy for him. All these years since Mom died, listening to him complain about the injustice of life and how hard he had it when he first came to the States, like he's the only person in the world with problems. I've finally realized that he wants to ruin my life the way he ruined my sister Melanie's because he doesn't know how to be happy.

"Yeah, well, good luck with trying to keep this business afloat without my connections."

"I don't want your connections, and I don't want your help," I say, surprised at the coldness in my tone. "I want you to leave. Now."

"Harry..." His mouth opens and closes, but no words come out. Then he opens the door and walks away, slamming it shut behind him.

Ruby jumps. She hasn't looked me in the eye since she came in, and I can't bear for her to think that I knew about this and kept it a secret from her.

"I mean it, Ruby, we can go anywhere in the world. Say the word, and I'll make it happen."

She shakes her head, and the tears finally spill. "I can't..." her voice breaks.

"You can't what? Please, Ruby."

I'm still squeezing her hand, the heart-shaped diamond growing warm against my skin. "I don't care about any of that. My dad. Your mom." Deep ragged breath. "Whatever happened with your dad... I'll get to the bottom of it, and I'll do whatever it takes to put it right. I'll spend the rest of my life making it right."

"You can't, don't you understand?" She still can't look at me. "You can't make him better."

"You don't know that. I'll..." I shake my head, raking my minimal medical knowledge for a plausible argument. "I don't know, find a neurologist who specializes in aftercare for stroke patients. I'll arrange for him to see the best physiotherapists in the country. I'll—"

"Harry," she interrupts my rambling. "You don't have to make promises you can't keep."

"You have to trust me, Ruby. I mean every goddamned word, and I won't ever stop trying to prove it to you."

"I believe that you mean it, but don't you see? Everyone is opposed to us being together. How will it ever work if everyone around us is trying to split us up?"

"Your dad isn't." I recall our conversation in their den while Ruby was at work. "He knows who I am, and he didn't warn me to stay away from you."

She stares out the window without really seeing the outside world. "I never told him your name. He only knows you as Harry."

I shake my head. That can't be true. I'm trying to remember if either of us mentioned my surname, but I can't.

Before I can speak, raised voices reach us from outside the door, and I'm flooded with the overwhelming sensation of Deja-vu. I'd recognize Celia Jackson's voice anywhere.

The door bursts open, and Lizzie appears, her face flushed. "Sorry, Harry, I tried to stop her—"

Celia pushes past Lizzie and walks into my office, her gaze skimming me and settling on Ruby. "We're leaving, Ruby."

"Mom, can you just give me a little while to—"

"It's your father," Celia says, cutting her off. "He's had another stroke."

The color drains from Ruby's face, and I instinctively reach out to stop her from collapsing, but she pulls away from me a second time, and it's like a stab wound straight through my chest.

"I'm coming back to Chicago with you." I don't wait for Ruby to respond but turn to Lizzie. "Can you book us on the next flight out of New York?" Fuck the extravagance. I'm making a private jet my priority the instant the dust settles on this shit.

"No, Harry." Ruby shakes her head. When she speaks, her voice is dull, lifeless. "You should stay. You have a business that needs you."

Lizzie hesitates in the doorway, and I give her a nod. Discreetly, as ever, she closes the door behind her.

"The business isn't important." Ignoring Celia, I move closer to Ruby and this time I don't allow her to snatch her hand away. "Nothing else matters, Ruby. I want to come with you. Please, don't shut me out. Not now."

"I..." She shoots a glance at her mom. "I'm not shutting you out."

I'd feel better if she wasn't so distracted, but I understand it's the best I can hope for with Celia's presence in the room, and her dad's stroke looming over her head.

"Thank you." I don't know what else to say.

Ruby's eyes finally meet mine, and I can see the torment behind them. She wants to believe me, but she needs time to process the information, and she can't do that until she knows that her dad is going to be okay.

Her gaze drops to the diamond ring on her wedding finger. I pray that when she looks at it, she remembers our time in Scotland, the cobbled streets and narrow alleyways of Edinburgh, the fur blanket in Eileen's B&B and the cave on the stony beach. It's all part of our story, and I refuse to accept that it ends here. Not like this. And certainly not because of our parents.

Ruby leans closer and kisses my cheek. Then with another glance in her mom's direction, she turns around and walks away.

My heart is soaring. It was an 'I love you' kiss, different to any other kiss we've shared, and I know that we'll get through this. It's only a hiccup. Graham will get better, we'll plan our wedding, and one day soon, we will be Mr. and Mrs. Weiss.

Following Ruby with my gaze, I barely even register that Celia is still hanging around until she stands in front of me, her expression unfathomable. "I wouldn't count on Ruby sticking around." She keeps her voice low, for my ears only. "She only wanted you for your money and, well, that's not going so great now, is it?"

19

RUBY

The flight back to Chicago is nothing like the flights with Harry.

I take the window seat, and Mom doesn't object. Instead, she flicks through the magazines in the pouch attached to the back of the seat in front of her, keeping up a steady stream of chatter about perfume and makeup and exotic vacations.

"I always wanted to go to Fiji. Sounds so ... I don't know—" she peers up from the glossy pages on her lap "—glamorously tropical, doesn't it? Your dad and I went to Puerto Vallarta once, before you were born. It was so colorful and vibrant and loud, but it doesn't quite have the same ring to it as Fiji."

I don't even know how she can concentrate on the pictures in the magazine, let alone think about going on vacation. Is she so hardened by Dad's first stroke that news of the second one has barely registered with her? Or is this all a façade, her brain incapable of dealing with the consequences of Dad getting sick again, incapable of considering our new reality?

She hasn't even asked me about our trip to Scotland. It's almost as if she has convinced herself that I've left Harry behind, and now she can keep it that way.

I study her profile, her eyelids fluttering across the pages of the magazine, her glossy lips smiling whenever she spots something that my future husband's money will buy for her. She smiles sweetly at the stewardess, orders a gin and tonic, and pops the can with a soft hiss.

"Don't look at me like that, Ruby," she says, tipping the soda into a plastic cup. "It'll calm my nerves."

I turn back to the window and press my forehead against the cool glass. I watch the land below us fading in and out of view through the dense clouds and remember sleeping with my head on Harry's chest when we flew to the UK.

We were humming with anticipation and excitement, riding high on the buzz of what we'd done, leaving the country without telling anyone, just the two of us. We were trying to figure out what the word 'us' would mean. How we would slot into each other's lives, like two puzzle pieces finally coming together.

But more than anything, we were just enjoying that first-date feeling. I smile to myself, my breath creating a steamy donut on the window. Has there ever been a first date quite like ours in the history of time? What would Emily Brontë have to say about it?

My mom leans across me with a waft of Chanel No. 5 and peers out the window. "There wasn't much to see on the way here. Honestly, I didn't think I'd be flying back so soon."

Because she thought she would have a fight on her hands to get me away from Harry?

I would give anything not to be traveling back home because of my dad. Maybe this is why I can't look at her right now. She seems smug, like she won the fight and now she can sit back and reap the rewards of cutting short my little escapade.

When I think of Harry, I feel numb.

I believe him, I think. He couldn't have faked the shock of finding out what his dad did to my dad, he's not that good an actor. But I don't know how we can ever make this relationship work, not when our families have such awful connections.

Why did it have to be Karl Weiss? Why couldn't it have been someone else? Anyone else. Seven million people live in New York City, and our fathers had to go and find each other. Worse than that, they had to go and do fucking business together. I wish I knew what had happened between them, but wishing isn't going to make it better.

"Stop grinding your teeth, it's not a good look." My mom shoots me a sideways glance and digs into a packet of peanuts with her scarlet talons.

My mom and Karl Weiss are never going to sit together at our wedding rehearsal dinner. They're never going to join us in our first dance, or throw confetti, or smile at the camera for the obligatory wedding photos. Or if they do, they're literally going to be stabbing each other with their pointed looks and jutting chins.

A sudden thought pops into my head, and I groan out loud, masking the sound with a fake cough so that I don't disturb my mom's enjoyment of her second gin and tonic, mostly gin.

I already know the extreme lengths my mom will go to in her misguided attempts to keep me away from Harry. I admit that

I know nothing about Karl Weiss—Harry has barely spoken about him in the short time I've known him—but what if... And here is where my pulse gathers speed like a snowball rolling down a hill. What if they join forces to keep us apart?

I swallow hard, stare at my mom as if I can read what's going on inside her head, until she turns to me with her perfectly manicured brows furrowed. "What is it? Do you want me to move?"

"No. It's nothing." I turn back to the window.

My mom wouldn't do that, would she? From the way she spoke Karl Weiss's name out loud, she hates the man. Losing the business affected her too, not just my dad, and I have to believe that she wouldn't stoop that low.

I steer my thoughts back to my dad. I don't know how serious this stroke has been or what side effects he might have to live with after, but guilt floods my chest in icy waves: what if this was all my fault? He told me to go with Harry, but that doesn't mean that he wasn't worried about me, and I wonder how much of my mom's rage he had to deal with while we were gone.

Guilt doesn't seem to be affecting her though. She's now sniffing perfume samples and discussing the merits of YSL's Obsession and Estee Lauder's Beautiful with the passenger across the aisle.

I stare at the window without seeing anything beyond the glass. How can I tell my dad who Harry is now? What if he finds out and has another—potentially fatal—stroke? How could I ever live with myself?

By the time we disembark the aircraft, the stewardess aiming her wide well-practiced smile our way, I feel as if I left my future behind in New York City. Perhaps it was never my future to snatch hold of. Perhaps my time spent with Harry was nothing more than a pleasant interlude, something for me to look back on when I'm older with a wistful smile and a sad shake of my head.

I take a deep breath and try to arm myself to see my dad again.

DAD SMILES at us with half his face, the other half drooping lazily like plastic warmed too long in the sun. He is sitting up in the hospital bed, looking frail and vulnerable in the cotton hospital gown.

"Hello, Dad." I deliberately refuse to acknowledge the wires attaching him to the monitors beside the bed.

Last time I was here, I was playing cards with Harry and Ronnie, the imprint of Harry's lips lingering on mine. Now... Now, I'm worried that my dad will not be my dad anymore, that we won't sit in the den in the evenings chatting about our favorite sitcoms, *The Cosby Show* and *Cheers*, dunking cookies in hot chocolate while he talks about the birds he spotted in the backyard during the day.

I lean across the bed and kiss his cheek. It feels cold and clammy, not like my dad's cheek at all as if the hospital has given him a mask to wear and told him not to remove it until they send him home.

"How are you feeling?" I keep my smile in place, just like the airline stewardess, and remind myself not to judge them next time I fly. They're only doing their job.

"Never better." The words sneak out of the corner of his mouth, sounding clumsy, strained.

"Glad to hear it." I perch on the edge of the bed—just like I did in Harry's room—while my mom air-kisses his other cheek.

"We came as soon as I got the call." She sits on the visitor's seat and crosses her legs neatly at the ankle. "You gave us quite a scare. Terrible timing."

Like there's ever a good time to suffer a stroke.

"Harry wanted to come," I blurt out before I can stop myself. "But he had work issues to resolve, so I told him to stay."

The atmosphere has altered with the mention of Harry, like my mom has sucked all the goodness out of it and replaced it with something stiff and toxic, and I feel like I need to get it back on track.

"Sokay." Dad smiles at me with one eye. "Don't wanna ... cause trouble." His words don't sound right, slurring into one another as if he's drunk.

"Oh, Dad, you could never cause us any trouble."

I throw my arms around him, telling myself that he won't be wired up to these machines like a laboratory experiment forever. He'll get better. He will.

He rubs my back, clings to me like he's afraid I'll disappear again if he lets me go, and another wave of guilt explodes inside me.

"Where have you ... been?" he asks when he pulls away.

"We don't need to talk about that right now, Graham." Mom's voice reaches us from the plastic seat. "She's back now. That's all that matters."

She says it like she knows she's the one at the steering wheel again, telling me what to do, where to go, how to be.

"I want to know." Dad's eyes are on me, and I see a glimmer of the man who has always spent hours talking to me about his favorite books and movies and food. He's still there. He hasn't gone away and left me behind and the rush of love in my chest goes partway to easing the guilt.

I tell him about Edinburgh. "It was like we'd traveled back in time, Dad, the streets were so old and narrow and winding. We saw someone playing bagpipes on the sidewalk wearing a kilt, and we explored the underground city, and climbed Arthur's Seat."

The more I talk, the deeper the barrier between us and my mom seems to grow. It's as if the room is expanding, her seat sliding away from us, while the bond between Dad and I strengthens, solidifies, knots my heart to his, excluding her from this part of my life in which she has no interest. She hasn't even asked where we've been, like she can pretend it didn't happen if she knows nothing about it.

"Sounds ... great." Dad's half-smile is back, trying so desperately to lift the side of his face that's still functioning as it should.

"It was, Dad." I instinctively rub my fingers across the diamond on my left hand.

"Ruby!" The word snaps me back to reality like a firecracker being set off. My mom is trying to close the distance, trying to rein me in before I slip so far away from her that she can't reach me. "Do we have to do this now?"

Dad's eyebrow rises and drops again like the movement has sapped the last of his strength. He doesn't react, but I know that he's waiting to hear from me whether we should do this now or not.

I know my mom thinks that she has won but, for me at least, this isn't over. I could hide the ring, say no more about it, call Harry when I get home and tell him that it's over. Or I could show my dad the diamond, tell him that Harry chose it himself, that he wants to spend the rest of his life with me, and hear what he has to say.

There's no contest. My dad's opinion means the world to me.

I raise my hand so that he doesn't have to move. His eyes flicker between me and the engagement ring, back and forth, like he has no control over them until finally, his smile shines from them, lighting up his sickly gray face.

"You-you're getting married."

What do I say? I would be getting married if my future father-in-law didn't destroy you thirteen years ago, and my mom hadn't already made it perfectly clear that she isn't happy about it?

"She doesn't have to go through with it." I bristle at my mom's words, my spine stiffening. "They'll realize what a huge mistake it would be now that they've come back to reality."

Dad's eyes twitch. "Let Ruby speak."

My shoulders slump. When I think about being alone with Harry on our trip, my entire body comes alive, tingling with desire, like a hunger that has to be satiated now that I've tasted it. But more than that, far more than the physical attraction, I yearn to be with him. I miss him. Without him, I feel incomplete.

Hot stinging tears fill my eyes. I can't even blink them away because my dad has already spotted them. Is this love or am I still caught up in the whirlwind trip like a sixteen-year-old experiencing a vacation romance and convincing herself that it's real?

"Ruby?" Dad prompts. "Do you ... love him?"

"How can she possibly be in love when she barely knows him?" Mom gets up and stands on the other side of the bed. "It's a recipe for disaster. Long distance relationships never work and—"

"Celia." Dad trembles, but it's enough to cut her off, her voice skittering through the cracks in the room like a frightened mouse. "This is Ruby's life. She must ... make up her own mind."

I hadn't thought about our relationship being long distance. Until Mom said the words out loud, I'd assumed that Harry and I would live in New York when we were married because of his business and because ... well ... I don't exactly have a career to cling onto. But now, I realize that I can't go to New York, not while my dad is sick. I'd never forgive myself if he needed me, and I wasn't there.

"It's okay, Dad. I'm not going anywhere."

"You-you're not staying here because of me." Dad's face crumples, his mouth contorting as if he's about to cry.

"No. It's not that." I chew my bottom lip. I can't lie to him, but I'm not going to tell him who Harry is, not like this.

"What then? I... Did I do ... something wrong?"

Tears spill down my cheeks and I wipe them with my

fingertips. The ache in my chest feels like it is here to stay. I can keep Harry's secret if it means my dad will be okay.

But my mom has no such qualms. "His name is Harry Weiss. He is Karl Weiss's son, Graham. That's why she can't marry him."

Dad's eyes drift shut, and he is perfectly motionless for so long that my heart races, afraid that he is slipping away. Then, he opens his eyes and looks at me through fat tears. "Marry him, Ruby. Marry this Harry ... and be happy."

20

HARRY

I sit at my desk for hours after Ruby and Celia have left, staring at the window without seeing anything. Celia is simply trying to cause trouble, for whatever reasons she has for keeping us apart. That's what I tell myself, but now that the seed has been sown, I can't help replaying every moment since I met Ruby over and over in my head.

The ice rink. When I catapulted myself over the top of her, she wasn't skating, but she was watching Alessandro on the ice surrounded by his adoring fans. She left with him too, accepting his impromptu invitation to his birthday party, while I was changing her tire.

It means nothing though. It doesn't make her a gold digger.

When Alessandro came to me and said that he wanted to impress her, I helped him set up the library, and even chose the rare first edition *Wuthering Heights*. If it was money Ruby was after, she'd have sunk her claws into Hollywood's rising star and never let go. Wouldn't she?

Ruby didn't even know that I'd already made my first million a couple of years ago. She came to the hospital because she was worried about me and stayed until her mom came and dragged her away.

During our trip, she never asked me for anything. *I* booked the first-class tickets; *I* chose the George Hotel in Edinburgh; *I* chose the diamond ring. An image of Ruby's face when she was naming the cows on Alastair's farm pops into my head—if I'd suggested that we stay in Scotland, buy a cottage by the sea and live the rural life, she would've been happy. She wants to get married in a forest for fuck's sake.

So, why am I allowing Celia's comment to get under my skin?

The woman is clearly manipulative and controlling.

But then I recall Ruby's comment about the news report that brought her to the hospital when I was injured: *"Two eligible bachelors involved in a car wreck."*

She knew who I was before she came, arriving just as the blizzard got hold of Chicago. Had she planned it that way, hoping the staff would suggest that she stay? Was Ronnie's arrival a spanner in the works, throwing her plan askew? Was it part of Ruby's game to play it coy, pretend my first proposal was the medication talking, keep me dangling until I couldn't wait any longer?

Oh God... Was Celia in on the whole thing?

My brain is scrambled, my pulse racing as I relive the special moments from our trip again, only this time, putting the gold digger slant on them. How a different perspective can alter things! I imagine Ruby calculating the cost of the trip, watching me, waiting for the right time to take things further, teasing me until she knew I was fit to burst.

She even made me believe that it was her first time.

Heat floods my face and cheeks. Did she really take me for a fool all along? Did she help me back onto my feet on the ice, thinking that I was a suitably gullible target?

Was that planned too? Ruby just happened to fix her laces as I was skating past—now it seems too much of a coincidence to be true.

My office door opens, and Lizzie's face appears. "Harry, Carlos Russo is asking to see you. Shall I show him in?"

I inhale deeply. "Please do."

"How are you feeling?" Carlos asks as he fills the space in my office with his booming voice and that huge Russo charm. "When did you get back?" He shakes my hand and pulls me into a warm bearhug.

"This morning." It feels like it was an age ago.

"Where were you? You disappeared after the funeral. I've been worried about you." He sits in the seat across my desk and folds one leg over the other, comfortable in his own skin.

It occurs to me then that my own father wasn't worried about me, but here is Carlos Russo checking up on me when he is still grieving for his younger brother, and my heart reaches out to him.

"The UK. Scotland. I... It's a long story."

"Does it begin with a girl?" The smile is so wide that I can see a gold filling in one of his back teeth.

I can't help returning the smile. "It does."

I haven't even told Ronnie that I'm engaged to be married to

Ruby Jackson, but the urge to speak to someone who will be rooting for us right now is too strong to resist.

"I bought her a ring. I want to spend the rest of my life with her. She's the one, Carlos. She's the one."

He is on his feet, marching around my desk and hugging me so tightly I fear for my ribs. "Congratulations, Harry. I am so happy for you. It is about time you found a good woman to complete your life."

He sits back down, leaving me reeling and my ribs crushed by his exuberance. It is more than I could've hoped for after what he and his family have just been through.

"You will realize that your life is only just beginning and all this—" he waves a hand around my office "—is nothing without her. We are all simply playing along until we find our soulmates, do you know that?"

I nod, grinning, my earlier insecurities still nudging at the corners of my mind but suppressed for now. "Thank you, Carlos. It means the world to me."

"Hey!" He narrows his eyes briefly. "I know what you are thinking, but you must not feel guilty for living your life. You are still here for a reason. Don't ever forget it." He pauses. "Who is she, this woman who has claimed your heart for her own? And why did you never mention her before?"

"Her name is Ruby Jackson. I-We met at the skating rink on Alessandro's birthday."

I swallow. Carlos thought that his little brother had met his match in Ruby, and I've realized too late that he might not be quite so free with his blessings when he discovers who my fiancée is.

"Ruby Jackson." He rolls the name across his tongue with his soft lilting accent. Then understanding creeps in. "Did Alessandro have dinner with her the night before...?" His voice breaks, his emotions playing out behind his eyes.

"Yes." I shouldn't have mentioned it.

I had no idea that Alessandro had spoken to anyone about his date with Ruby—he hadn't mentioned it to me, Ronnie, or the rest of our group. Again, I'm stabbed in the gut by my conscience. Alessandro seemed off the following morning, and I'd let it pass without trying to find out what was bothering him. If I'd only tried harder, he might still be here...

Carlos turns his attention to the window. "Alessandro came to my room after his date with Ruby." He speaks slowly, without looking at me. "He... He was worried that he had crossed a line."

"Crossed a line?"

Still, Carlos keeps his eyes fixated on the world outside the window. "He liked the girl. He thought she liked him too, but it seemed that he had misread the situation. Alessandro never struggled to find women. He must've assumed that Ruby was like all the others, looking for a good time, no strings attached."

He turns to face me then, and he appears to have aged visibly since stepping into my office.

"It's okay, Carlos. I don't need to know what happened." My fist is clenching and unclenching along with my heartbeat, trying to prevent an image of Alessandro 'crossing a line' with Ruby.

He rubs his face with both hands as if checking the length of his stubble. "I am not making allowances for him," he continues, regardless. "He should've had more respect for women. Perhaps this is something he would have learned in time. But my concern was that he was afraid she might leak her story to the press and ruin his career. Do you understand what I am saying?" His brown eyes hold mine, not letting go.

I nod. It explains everything. Alessandro's strange mood the day he died. His drinking. The fight at the amusement park.

It dawns on me then... Ruby didn't say a word about the date.

"So, if you and Ruby have found love, you have more than my blessing, Harry."

Now I understand Carlos's mixed emotions. He is embarrassed by his brother's behavior but cannot say the words out loud because it is wrong to speak ill of the dead. Instead, he is giving us his best wishes in the hope that it will atone for Alessandro's actions.

"Ruby never spoke about it." One blessing deserves another, and I hope that it will help Carlos to remember the best of his brother.

"Thank you, my friend." A gentle smile this time, no teeth. "I am glad to see that life is working out for you. And now, I hear through the grapevine that you need some assistance."

There is no fooling Carlos. He is devoted to his family, but he is also an astute businessman with contacts around the globe.

"Talk to me, Harry."

"I appreciate your concern, Carlos, but it is nothing I can't resolve."

He inclines his head, a low chuckle rumbling in his throat. "I do not doubt it for a moment. But I am here, and I want to help."

I tell him that my largest debtor is experiencing problems with a new venture that isn't performing as well as they'd hoped. "They're using me to bankroll their own company."

"How much?"

"Twenty million."

Carlos doesn't flinch. "Is that it?" He already knows there's more.

"Looks like I just missed the boat on two takeover bids that should've been done deals."

I haven't looked into this yet, but I'm trying to ignore the niggling feeling that my dad allowed them to slip through his fingers. Everything was in place before the car crash. The sellers had agreed to hand over once the creditors had been informed. The problem is, I'd poured a lot of money into keeping them afloat until we'd signed on the dotted line.

Carlos stands up and offers me his hand to shake. "Leave it with me."

"I-No, Carlos, I can't possibly accept—"

"Consider it an early wedding gift." He doesn't let go. "Deal?"

I smile as the weak winter sun casts a gentle glow across the room. "Deal."

He leaves, and Lizzie brings in a pot of coffee and some cream. "You look like you could do with some caffeine." She doesn't wait around.

I sip my coffee, sit back in my seat, and try to piece together what happened between Alessandro and Ruby. Whatever it was, she doesn't want me to know, and I wonder how much of this is out of respect for my friend.

The longer I dwell on it though, the more certain I am that Celia was lying about her own daughter. Ruby had the perfect opportunity to either take things further with Alessandro or to blackmail him with spilling the beans about his behavior. And she chose neither.

The actions of a woman who was out to make some easy cash? I don't think so.

By the time I'm staring at the bottom of an empty cup, I've also realized that it was Celia who asked me to replace Ruby's tire at the skating rink, almost as if she saw me as an obstacle to be removed.

I pick up the phone and buzz through to Lizzie. "Can you get me the number of the finest neurologist in Chicago?"

I STAY in the office until late, the city streets coming alive with the nighttime ritual of people flocking to wine bars, nightclubs, and strip joints for their next fix, sexual or otherwise. With Carlos taking care of the bigger issues, I've managed to trawl through the rest of the paperwork that was sitting on my desk, and now, with the lonely night ahead of me, I don't want to be here without Ruby.

I don't *need* to be here without Ruby.

I could take the next flight out of New York City and be in Chicago by midnight. I won't disturb Ruby after the day she has had, but at least we will be in the same city, breathing the same air, and gazing up at the same stars.

Before I can stand up and grab my suit jacket, the phone rings. It's a direct call, bypassing Lizzie. I pick it up and swivel my chair around to face the window.

"Mr. Weiss. I have some information that might interest you."

I'm on my feet, dragging the telephone cable with me, my pulse thrumming as I eagerly anticipate this new information that I requested. "Have you found her?"

"I have a lead that checks out so far. I'll fax some images through to you now."

"Where is she?"

"Diablo Lake, Washington State."

"Diablo Lake? What is she doing there?"

I had instructed a Private Investigator to locate my sister when I made my first million. A gift to myself. After years of not knowing what happened to her, I hoped that if we couldn't be reunited, it would at least bring me closure.

It was three months before he caught his first lead in a medical clinic in Florida. My sister was working there as a nurse under an alias with a fake ID. By the time my flight landed the following day, the woman had disappeared, leaving behind no forwarding address.

That was the first lead.

Every other lead has been the same—my sister always one step ahead of me— like she's paying the same PI to tip her off each time he gives me a lead to follow.

"She's working at the North Cascades Environmental Learning Center."

The fax machine trundles to life, and I wait for the images to print off. Blurry, they are of a woman who vaguely resembles my sister, with hair cut into a short bob and dyed blond. I often wonder if I would even recognize her after all these years, and studying the photographs now, I can't be certain that I would.

I thank the PI and end the call, staring at the vague images. I hold the same debate in my head every time: do I follow it up, chasing the illusion of my sister Melanie around the country, or do I ignore it? I already know the answer.

I have enough guilt to live with.

I make another call first though. I get put through to the ward where Graham Jackson is currently being treated and ask to speak to his daughter.

It's several long minutes before Ruby comes to the phone, and when she does, her voice makes my heart jump. "Hello, Harry." How has her voice become as familiar as my own in such a short space of time?

"How is your dad?"

"He's ... okay. Paralyzed down one side, but the consultant said he's lucky." Her voice dips like she doesn't believe it. "Thank you. I don't know how we'll ever repay you."

"Repay me for what?" I'm smiling at the ceiling, eyes closed, picturing myself standing right next to her.

"You know what."

My heart knocks to tell me that she's still there. *My* Ruby.

"What did the neurologist say?"

"That he can get him walking again."

My shoulders slump with relief. "I'm glad." As I pause, I'm certain that I can feel her breath on my cheek. "I miss you."

"I've only been gone a few hours."

"Are you counting?"

It's Ruby's turn to pause. "No."

I don't believe her. "I was going to catch the next flight into Chicago, and before you say that I don't have to, I'm doing it because I want to, so humor me."

"Are you always so bossy when you're in the office? Or has the suit gone to your head?"

I chuckle. It sounds way more nervous than I intended. "Always. Do you like it?"

"Hmm, I guess I could get used to it."

Yes! I punch the air with my fist.

"Harry…"

"Ruby…" We both speak at the same time.

"Your turn." Ruby gets in first.

"Okay. I've had a lead on Melanie. She might be in Washington State."

"You must go. Call me when you get there." Ruby ends the call before I can object.

21

RUBY

THE THERAPIST IS WORKING with Dad when I go back to the hospital the next morning, getting him to clench and unclench his fist. Dad's face is screwed up in concentration like his whole life depends on him balling that hand.

I wait for the therapist to leave before I sit on the side of the bed and show him the pile of books I picked up from the library.

His lopsided smile falters. "I'm not sure ... I can read them."

Shit! My stomach churns. Why didn't I think of that?

"My sight is ... not so great in my left eye." The eye that's drooping. "Give it time though..."

The neurologist retained by Harry said that he can help my dad get the movement back in his left leg. "I can't promise that we'll get you fully mobile, but you'll be walking with a stick. You got lucky, Mr. Jackson."

Lucky. That word again. Depends which way you're looking at it.

At least he's still upbeat. It'll take more than a stroke to keep my dad down.

"I think ... my dancing days were already over." Dad doesn't look at me.

I've seen photographs of my dad competing at ballroom dancing when he was a kid. He wore smart black suits and shiny shoes, and his hair was immaculate, the perfect complement to his dance partners in their floaty gowns with their hair scraped back into severe buns. It's a part of him that existed before I knew him, a part of him that he'll never get back now, but strangely, whenever I'm with him, I still try to imagine him swishing his partner around a ballroom floor.

"I should learn to dance."

It's completely out of the blue. I never wanted to have dance lessons when I was younger—I was always the girl who wanted to be out racing my bike against the boys, climbing trees, and finding the strongest buckeyes. But now... I'll do anything to put that glint back in my dad's eyes.

"I could..." His mouth works hard to find the right words, and my heart breaks a little bit more when he concedes defeat.

"Teach me?"

"If I can ... remember how..."

"You never forget, Dad. It's like breathing." I might be making this up, but I don't care when I see hope dancing around the corners of his eyes.

We have a long way to go, endless visits to the neurologist and physio sessions to get his mobility back, but if I've given him an end goal, something to aim for, then I have to believe that we'll get there.

"You know I have two left feet though, right?" I knock his elbow softly with mine.

"Never... I've seen you ... on ice."

"Damn! You caught me out again."

We're doing what we always do, keeping it normal so that we can stop the darkness from creeping in. We'll do this forever if we must. Whatever it takes to stop the image of Karl Weiss with his mouth turned down at the corners from taking root inside my head. Karl Weiss who can still walk unaided, still work, still dance if he ever wanted to while my dad has to learn to walk all over again.

"Where's ... your mom?"

And there it is, the question I was dreading.

How can I tell him that I don't know where she is? That I heard her pottering around the house in the night like a thief, her footsteps careful, the house holding its breath in case she created a din. Then, when I woke up this morning, she was gone.

"She went out to run some errands." Smile, Ruby, act like you mean it. "She'll be here later."

His eyes settle on me while still zipping about like a fly caught inside a window. "She ... means well. She ... loves you, Ruby."

I could say that if he needs to tell me this, there's something not quite right.

I don't need to hear my dad say the words out loud. I know that he loves me; it's like there's something inside my heart that gets tugged towards him wherever we are, but there's an invisible barrier between me and my mom, and I don't even know how it got there, or who built it in the first place.

She reported me missing to the police.

She told me to go catch an actor, never realizing that I might catch a Weiss instead.

She brings me lip gloss and eyeliner and beauty magazines when all I really want is books.

Everything she does has an ulterior motive that will benefit Celia Jackson, and I often think that she doesn't know me at all.

"I know." I force a smile, my eyes drifting to the pile of books I brought in for my dad. "Shall I read to you?"

He settles back against the pillow and flashes me that clumsy lopsided smile. "You're a ... good girl, Ruby."

I pick up *The Piranhas* by Harold Robbins—my dad loves his books—and open it at the first page. This feels wrong somehow. Our roles have been reversed too soon. It feels like only yesterday that my dad was reading to me in bed, the comforter pulled up to my chin, my eyes closing to the sound of his voice, and I'm not prepared for this.

Concentrate, Ruby, for fuck's sake. If he can hold it together, still smile after what he's been through, the least I can do is read a book to him like I'm enjoying it.

I start reading, consciously injecting some life into my voice. It's all I can do to stop the words from vanishing beneath a wall of tears, and they slip out of my head the instant they leave my tongue. I almost cry out with relief when the door opens, until I realize that it isn't the nurse.

It's my mom.

Her gaze glides around the room, barely noticing the open

novel on my lap. "You didn't wait for me." Her glare is accusing.

She doesn't want to do this now, I think. Not in front of Dad.

"I didn't know when you'd be back."

Her eyelids flicker—she knows she's been caught out—quickly replaced by her usual expression. "I went for bagels."

"Bagels?"

Really, that's what she's going with? She could at least have come up with a plausible excuse.

She slides a brown paper bag onto the mobile tray, and I get a waft of herby cream cheese and smoked salmon. "Your favorite." She kisses my dad, cheek-to-cheek, and takes my usual spot on the side of the bed. "From the little corner bakery near City Hall."

Dad's face turns pink and blotchy, his mouth twitching as he struggles to express his gratitude. "The-the bakery?"

"Uh-huh. The food here is shit. I thought it would bring back memories of early morning breakfasts when Ruby was a baby."

He looks at me, his eyes wet and full. "Best bagels in town..."

Mom opens the bag and shifts a bagel closer to his good arm. Smug. It's like a game of chess, the first one to catch the king unguarded, wins. Only she has forgotten one very important rule: it takes two to play chess, and I'm not getting sucked into her little game, whatever it is. She didn't leave home at silly o'clock to pick up bagels.

I'm not having this conversation in front of my dad though.

Closing the book softly, I stand up and look away as he struggles to get the food between his lips.

"Where are you going?" Mom narrows her eyes at me.

"To call Harry." I don't wait around for her to object.

I use the payphone in the hospital foyer to call the number of the hotel just outside of Diablo Lake that Harry was checking into.

He sounds distracted when he picks up, like he's rearranging the furniture in the room. "How's your dad?"

"He's eating bagels." I don't want to talk about anything else.

But Harry must understand. "Are you okay, Ruby? Do you want me to come to Chicago?"

"I'm fine." I've managed to hold the tears at bay so far, but one look at Harry and I'll melt into a sloppy puddle. "Did you find your sister?"

I hear the deep inhale. "No, whoever the lead thinks they saw, she moved on a couple of days ago. There's been another potential sighting in Washington, but I'm not sure I'll even bother checking it out."

"You must, Harry." Even though the phone has given his voice a tinny edge, I'm getting tiny shivers of excitement running up and down my spine. "You can't ignore it."

"I'd rather be with you."

My pulse quickens. "Go to Washington. I'll still be here." Pause. I can hear rustling from the other end of the line. "Are you packing?"

"Ruby, I've got to go." There's a bluntness to his tone that I haven't heard before, and the excitement of hearing his voice is replaced by something cold and slimy.

"What's wrong, Harry? What's happen—"

"It's nothing. I'll call you when I get to Washington." The line goes dead, leaving the buzz of the dialing tone in my ear.

I'm still thinking about Harry when I get back to my dad's room. *It's nothing.* That's what people say when there's a whole load of something going on, and they don't want anyone else involved. I know he's trying to protect me, but there's only so many secrets a relationship can handle.

My dad has barely nibbled the edge of the bagel. His eyes are closed, his lips slack, saliva creating a slick trail down his chin. I wipe it with a towel while my mom wraps the bagels back up. Dad doesn't move, and I stare at his chest waiting for the rise and fall of his breaths to still my skipping heart.

Mom grabs her purse and heads to the door.

"Where are you going?" She just got here.

"I have to run some errands." Mom-speak for she's going to get her hair done or get a manicure or there's a new dress she spotted in a boutique in the mall. "I'll have to take some time off when your dad comes home, and the cupboards won't stock themselves."

"I'll come with you."

She furrows her brow. "Funny, I thought you were going out of your way to avoid me."

She has a point, but I'm not going to admit it. "I've been worried about Dad." I grab my coat off the back of the chair and follow her to the door. The sooner we have this discussion the better.

"I'm perfectly capable of running errands alone, you know." She stands in front of the door like she might bolt the instant I look away.

She'll never buy it if I say that I want to spend some time with her, so instead, I shrug. "I need stuff too."

Her gaze lingers on my dad who looks peaceful in slumber. I wish I knew what she was thinking, but she paints on this tough exterior like battle armor every morning, and the only person who gets to see her without it is my dad.

We don't speak until we're outside. The streets are still wet from last night's frost, and car tires swish past, occasionally sending a ripple of water across the sidewalk.

There's no point pussyfooting around her, so I just come out with it. "Mom, what happened between Dad and Karl Weiss?"

Her eyes dart towards me without reaching my face, and she sidesteps around a man trying to offer her a leaflet. "I'm not dragging this up again now, Ruby," she says when our steps fall into sync again.

"When then? I need to know, so that I can fix it."

"Fix it?" Her voice rises a notch. "This isn't something you can patch up with a spot of glue and some sticky tape. Don't you think your father has suffered enough?"

It's a low blow that catches me straight in the gut, winding me momentarily. But if Harry and I are going to stand a chance of making this work, I can't leave it. "I want to resolve it for his sake. It was a long while ago. Why can't we all move on? Maybe Harry was meant to come into my life for a reason."

"Ha! Don't you dare pretend that you're doing this for your

father. There's only one person you're thinking of, and that's Ruby Jackson."

I could bite. I could remind her that she was only thinking of herself when she tried to set me up with Alessandro Russo. But that's not going to achieve anything, and there's too much at stake here for us to start hurling insults at one another like teenagers.

"Please, Mom. I only want to understand what happened. You and Dad never speak about it, and it shouldn't be this taboo subject that everyone is too scared to mention."

"There's a reason for that, Ruby, and he's lying in a hospital bed again." She stands on the curb, waiting for the traffic signals to change.

"Fine." I stand next to her. "If you won't tell me, I'll ask Karl Weiss to give me his version of events."

Her cheeks grow hot and pink despite the icy chill in the air. "You wouldn't dare."

"Try me." After this reaction, I'm even more determined to find out what happened. She should know by now that I can never refuse a challenge like this.

The pedestrian light turns green, the signal to walk beeping above our heads, but we don't move. People crossing in the opposite direction skirt around us, huffing because we're blocking the sidewalk. The light turns red again, and still, I'm waiting for my mom to speak to me.

"Go right ahead, Ruby. Good luck with getting him to tell you the truth." She carries on walking and doesn't wait for me to follow.

I walk around the city, the conversation with my mom churning around inside my head. It's obvious that she isn't going to tell me, but I don't understand why, unless she's trying to protect my dad. Did he do something to Karl Weiss that caused him to retaliate? It's hard to connect my dad to that kind of ruthless businessman, but perhaps the first stroke changed him, softened him around the edges, made him the man I've always looked up to. Perhaps it took the stress of losing his company to make him realize what was important.

It would explain Karl's reaction when he discovered who I was.

Lizzie warned me that his bark was worse than his bite though. I'd caught him unawares. Perhaps now that he's had time to calm down and think about it, he'll be willing to talk.

I've made up my mind. I'm going to invite Karl Weiss and my mom to dinner with me and Harry, and the four of us are going to resolve this like mature adults.

I go home and call Lizzie before my mom comes home. She gives me Karl's number and, heart thumping, I tap it into the phone before I can talk myself out of it.

"Karl Weiss." He still sounds like a thick-necked dog wearing a studded collar.

My heart lurches. What if Lizzie is wrong and his bite is way worse than his bark?

"Mr. Weiss, this is Ruby Jackson. We met in Harry's office a couple of days ago."

Silence.

"I wanted to invite you to dinner with me, my mom, and Harry when he's back."

"Back?"

Shit! He doesn't know that Harry is trying to find his sister.

My cheeks grow inflamed, and I'm so glad that he can't see me. "I'll get Harry to arrange the flights. I think it will be good for us to all sit down over dinner and clear the air."

I can hear him breathing, but he's milking the grumpy father-in-law role.

"I'd really like it if we could all get along. I'm going to marry your son, Mr. Weiss."

Silence.

I shouldn't have called him. Will he blame Harry for putting me up to this? Right now, I think that anything is possible.

Finally, he says, "I can't stop him from marrying you, but don't expect me to pretend I'm happy about it."

"Even for Harry's sake?"

"He's old enough to make his own mistakes."

"I'm not a mistake, Mr. Weiss." Anger is burning inside my chest and looking for a way to escape. My mom is stubborn, but this man is an asshole, and I can't believe he's Harry's dad.

"That's what they all say." Then he hangs up.

22

HARRY

I STEP OUTSIDE the clinic in Washington city center, and my hackles are raised. I stare across the wide street, at the glass storefronts reflecting the low winter sun, and scan for movement in my peripheral vision. There are too many pedestrians walking with their heads down and their collars turned up for me to notice anything out of the ordinary, but I can't shake the same eerie sensation I had in Diablo Lake.

Someone is following me.

I turn left, and head back towards my hotel. Another dead end. Another false lead that built up my hopes of finding my sister and dashed them to pieces again. Enough, I tell myself. If Melanie wanted to be found, we'd have been reunited long ago, and I need to start looking forward instead of keeping one eye on the past.

I spot a chestnut-brown dress in the window of a vintage boutique and stop to admire it, thinking of Ruby. She would look stunning in it. Fitted in all the right places, it's floor length with a fishtail and a row of neat ivory pearls around the neck.

I'm about to go inside and buy it for her, when my gut tells me to look left as a man wearing a long black overcoat steps inside a café a couple of doors along. I might be wrong. It might be someone meeting a friend or picking up a coffee to go, but I don't waste a beat.

I hurry back the way I came, open the door, and scan the occupied booths. Three women are in the booth closest to me, cheeks rosy with the heat inside the café. Two older women are seated in the booth behind them, reading books in comfortable silence. There's a family of four in another, two teenagers, and a couple who appear to be around my age, sitting close together, their smiles wide and their eyes bright.

I check out their coats draped across the back of their seats. None of them are black.

I go to the service area and scan the walls for the restroom sign, realizing that I'm now following a complete stranger, but I tell myself that if they're washing their hands, I'll turn around, go back to my hotel, and forget all about it. Chalk it up to being paranoid because I'm no closer to finding my sister.

Opening the door tentatively, I already know that the restroom is empty. Was I mistaken? Did they enter one of the stores on either side of the café?

But even as I think this, I know that they came here. I check out the narrow corridor leading past another door that says STAFF ONLY to the fire exit at the end. I'm about to open the external door when a woman comes out of the staffroom and falters when she spots me. "Are you lost?"

"Sorry." I smile and back away from the door. "Have I gone the wrong way?"

I don't wait around for her to respond.

Outside, I hail a cab back to the hotel and replay what I saw in my head. I wasn't certain before, but now I am—someone has followed me from New York to Diablo Lake, and now they're here in Washington. I don't know who, or why, but I am going to find out.

I call Ruby from my hotel room and tell her that I've had no luck in Washington. I know from 'Hello' that something is wrong.

"Is it your dad? What's happened?"

"No." In the silence, I picture her chewing her bottom lip, my mind automatically flitting to the conclusion that if it isn't her dad, there's a problem with us. "It's *your* dad."

"My dad?"

"I called him earlier. I got his number from Lizzie, I'm so sorry. I didn't want to worry you, and after what happened in New York, I wanted to get the situation resolved before we..." Pause. "Well, before we get married, and I think I've made things a hundred times worse than they already were, and I wish I'd left it alone."

I know that I should focus on what she's saying about my dad, but all I can hear are the words 'before we get married', playing through my head like ticker tape, and already I have a mental image of Ruby, barefoot, in a gauzy floral dress with flowers threaded through her hair.

"Ruby, you couldn't possibly make things worse."

She chuckles into the phone and sniffs back tears at the same time. "You don't know what happened yet."

I can imagine, but I wait for her to elaborate.

"He said you're making a mistake marrying me." The words hang between us as though waiting to choose sides. *Will they, won't they?*

But, for me, there is no question to be answered. "We'll be the ones laughing when we prove him wrong, Ruby."

"But he's your dad, Harry."

"Yes, and you're going to be my wife. You're the woman I want to spend the rest of my life with, and if he doesn't like it, he can make his own mistakes."

"I don't want to come between you."

"Trust me, you won't. You do trust me, don't you?"

"Yes."

"I'm coming to Chicago. I'll meet you at the hospital."

RUBY IS WAITING for me outside the hospital when I arrive in a taxi directly from the airport. Before I climb out of the cab, she joins me in the back seat and kisses me on the lips, a peck, the kind of kiss friends would greet each other with.

My head is reeling from all the traveling I've done since Alessandro's funeral, so I shift over without saying that I was hoping to visit her dad first. My brain is not so fuzzy that I've missed the intention—Ruby is keeping me away from the hospital. She's keeping me at arm's length, and it's not how I envisioned this trip going.

I ask the driver to take us to the Drake Hotel and sit back, grateful for the espresso I picked up en route from the airport.

"How's he doing?" My fingers instinctively cross the seat to entwine with hers.

Ruby pulls her hand away and rubs her face. "He's tired. Like this stroke has sapped the lifeforce out of him."

"He'll need time to heal, but he'll get there."

"You don't know that." She turns her face to the window, but not before I spot the tears spilling down her face.

"Hey." I tilt her chin back towards me and lean closer so that the driver doesn't hear. "I'm not a doctor, but anyone can see that he lives for you, Ruby." She closes her eyes, and I kiss her wet eyelashes. "We're not getting married without him, I promise you."

It's the wrong thing to say, tiredness clouding my brain and allowing me to spew promises that are beyond my control like I'm some kind of superhero or demi-god. Way to go, Harry. But I want to protect Ruby with every fiber of my being; I want to make life perfect for her.

She attempts a smile that doesn't fully materialize. "At this rate, he might be the only guest there."

"You can leave my father to me. He'll calm down and see sense in time."

"I don't think he will, Harry. I don't know what happened thirteen years ago, but it feels like America's most guarded secret. No one wants to talk about it."

I recall the times I've tried talking to my dad about Melanie over the years, and the way he shut me down, made me feel guilty for mentioning it like it was my fault she disappeared. My dad has always been a closed shop, barriers in place and secured with a padlock. He isn't going to change now, for anyone, and if this were only about me, I'd leave him to wallow in his own misery, but I know how much it means to Ruby to get his blessing for the wedding.

"I thought it would be good to organize a meal and invite my mom and your dad." Ruby's face glows intermittently with the streetlamps as we make our way through the city, highlighting the dark circles under her eyes. "But now..." She shakes her head.

I pull her against my chest and hug her close. "Let's do it. If they won't speak to us, or each other about what happened, there isn't much we can do, but at least we'll have tried."

She nods against my chest. "How long are you staying?"

"A couple of days... Unless I happen to get snowed in, or the airlines stop flying between here and New York, or someone makes it worth my while to stay longer."

"Someone?" She tilts her head backwards, her breath warming my cheek. "You mean a business associate?"

"Hmm I'm open to suggestions."

"How open?" Her tongue finds my earlobe, and jeez, I never knew such a tiny part of the body could cause so many shivers to pulse through me.

"Wide, wide open." I slide her hand onto my lap, and she smiles when she feels my erection.

"Challenge accepted."

We don't speak the rest of the journey.

I follow Ruby's expression as we enter the hotel, through the grand entrance, up the plush carpeted staircase to the main lobby, where the chandeliers are the size of trees, and there's a kind of library hush that accompanies the wide-eyed admiration of the guests. I check us in as Mr. and Mrs. Weiss, trying it out and liking the way it sounds, and we take the elevator up to the Executive Suite.

It's airy and spacious, the heavy gold curtains pulled wide to reveal the view from the lounge area across the city. I've lived in New York all my life and hardly notice the skyline when I'm in my apartment, but now, with Ruby's eager smile, I feel as though I'm experiencing the excitement of blinking lights and glowing towers for the first time.

"Why don't you jump in the shower?" Ruby nudges me in the direction of the bathroom. "I'll order room service."

I'd planned on dining out with Ruby, our first date, which seems utterly crazy since we've flown to the UK and back again together and she's wearing the heart-shaped diamond on her finger. But now that I'm not in a moving vehicle with the hum of an engine beneath me, the tiredness feels like trying to battle my way, blindfolded, out of a giant spider web.

In the bathroom, I step into the walk-in shower and stand under the hot water with my eyes closed, waiting for it to cleanse the disappointment of my trip to Washington State from me. I lose track of time, my brain sliding back and forth between constantly being one step behind my sister and trying to figure out who is having me followed. During the flight, I'd made up my mind not to mention this to Ruby, but now that I'm here, I don't want to go any further with secrets between us.

Clean, I blast cold water over me, trying to shake the fug from my brain. It helps a little. When I emerge from the bathroom in a cloud of steam, Ruby has created a picnic on the rug in front of the floor-to-ceiling window and is waiting for me, cross-legged, a robe wrapped around her, and her hair loose over her shoulders.

"Something smells good." I fasten my fluffy white robe around my waist and sit opposite her, eying up the food. "Pizza?" I can't help smiling at Ruby's menu choice.

"Comfort food." She picks up a slice of pepperoni pizza, strands of melted mozzarella sticking to her chin and trailing down her neck as she tilts her head back to catch them on her tongue and misses.

There are sticky chicken wings, spicy fries, sweet chili and garlic mayo dips, apple pie and cream, all to be washed down with a couple of cold beers. I help myself to a slice of pizza, realizing that it's exactly what I needed. "Heaven on a plate."

"Or a takeout box." Ruby pops open her can of beer and taps it against mine. "Thought we'd do Chicago my way."

"I'm glad we did."

"You're not disappointed I didn't order champagne?"

I dip my pizza in mayo and take a huge bite, the spicy meat and fragrant tomato sauce exploding on my tongue. "It's an acquired taste."

"Like oysters."

I can't help grinning at her. "Never could get to grips with oysters."

She chooses a chicken wing and licks sauce from her fingers and wrist. "Have you noticed how sauce gets literally everywhere even though you only move your hand from the plate directly to your mouth?"

"The manufacturers are in cahoots with the laundry detergent companies."

She laughs. "Favorite pizza? And please don't say Hawaiian."

"What happens if I say Hawaiian?" I swallow a mouthful of beer. The pizza and shower combined have reenergized me, the blood pumping around my body and reminding me how good it will feel to be inside Ruby Jackson.

She peers at me mischievously over the top of a chicken wing and licks her lips. "I might have to think of a suitable punishment. Pineapple on pizza is just wrong."

I get up, stroll casually to the bedside table, and pick up the phone. "Hello?" I pretend to call room service. "Can I get a large Hawaiian pizza with extra pineapple?"

Laughing, Ruby waits for me to sit down before she tosses a pizza crust at me. It bounces off my nose and lands inside the mayo dip like it was a trick shot she perfected while I was showering.

"You are not the man I thought you were, Mr. Weiss. I might just have to call the whole wedding thing off."

"Shucks. And here I was hoping we could set the date."

Ruby stuffs some fries into her mouth and chews, still watching me with that playful glint in her eye. "What date did you have in mind, Mr. Weiss?"

Now that I've sowed the seed, what the hell have I got to lose? This has nothing to do with anyone else apart from me and Ruby, and I want to marry her now more than ever.

"Six weeks' time."

She almost chokes on a mouthful of beer, liquid spluttering from her mouth, her eyes watering. She swallows. "For a moment there, I thought you said six weeks' time."

"I did."

"Why? I mean, why six weeks?"

"Why not?"

She licks her fingers and wipes her hands on a napkin. She's stalling, and my gut churns with the awful premonition that she has changed her mind. I've gotten caught up in the moment, the swanky hotel room, the Chicago skyline, the pizza, and pushed her too far.

A smile dances from her lips to her eyes. "Right now, I can't think of a reason why not."

I blink, processing her words. "Does that mean yes?"

She sucks her bottom lip. "I think it does."

I clean my hands, wipe my mouth on a napkin, and crawl across the floor to her. Ruby lays back on the rug and pulls me on top of her. "In six weeks, you'll be a married man. You know what that means?"

"What does that mean?"

"You'll suddenly get boring in bed."

It takes a couple of beats for me to realize that she's joking. "Is that right? Best we screw like rabbits while we still can."

"I thought you'd never ask."

I kiss Ruby slow and deep, my tongue exploring her mouth, the Chicago lights blinking in the background. She's warm and soft beneath me, and when she parts my robe, sliding her hand between us and tracking a line down to my cock, I'm already throbbing.

We roll over together, our minds and bodies thinking alike, and Ruby straddles me, shrugging the robe over her shoulders, leaving her naked. I cup her breasts with both hands, and tease her nipples towards my mouth, squeezing them together, flicking both nipples with my tongue. She leans closer, ass thrust upwards, and rubs her pussy up and down my cock, her wetness staying on me.

She waits for me to close my eyes before she climbs off me and takes my cock in her hand. Gripping it loosely, she takes the end in her mouth, licking all around the rim, tasting and teasing, inserting the tip of her tongue in the slit of my cock.

I groan out loud. "Suck me, Ruby."

Ruby does as she's told and starts sucking, gently at first, gradually growing more insistent, more demanding, her grip tightening. I feel my pre-ejaculation rising, my cock twitching in her hand.

"Ruby, I'm going to come." I'm panting, trying hard to hold it back, but she feels so damned good…

Ruby stops sucking. Before she can move, I grab her hands and pull her towards me.

She shuffles forward along my body, straddling me, her knees over my shoulders, her pussy in my face. I lick her slowly, dragging my tongue back and forth, watching her watching me as she grows wetter. Her legs start to tremble, and she arches her back, tipping her head so that she's staring at the stars outside the window.

I open her up with my fingers, force my tongue in as far as it will go, finding the spot and licking her hard. Her body writhes, torn between wanting to reach orgasm and wanting to prolong it, so I push harder. Further.

"Tell me when you're ready to come, Ruby."

I can tell by the way her legs tremble that she's close.

"Ruby?" I withdraw my tongue, holding her to ransom.

"I'm ready," she gasps.

"How ready?" I slide two fingers inside her. She's dripping.

"Ready ... as I'll ever be."

"I'm coming for you, Ruby." I open her wider.

She instinctively leans forward, supporting her upper body with both hands and lowering her pussy onto my tongue. Three licks, and she explodes in my mouth, her body convulsing, her face twisted away from me.

But I'm only just finding my rhythm. Gripping her upper thighs, I keep right on licking, bringing her to orgasm again. And again. Until she's practically lying on my face. Then I hold her hips and slide her down my body.

Ruby kisses me slowly as if waking from a deep slumber and lowers herself onto me, leaning forward, her upper body pinning me down. We kiss as she rides me, her movements slow, measured, feeling my length gliding fully in and out until I squeeze her butt and hold her on me, my hips thrusting against her, needing to fill her up when I come.

It doesn't take long. My cock and I have missed her.

We stay like that for a while, Ruby lying next to me on the rug, our faces pressed together, breathing each other's oxygen. Completely at peace.

Finally, she rests her chin on my chest and peers into my eyes. "So, what is your favorite pizza?"

I smile at her, my fingers entwined in her hair. "Hawaiian."

23

RUBY

I don't know how Harry convinces his dad to fly into Chicago the following day, but after a whirlwind twenty-four hours I find myself walking into a new restaurant called Charlie Trotter's, my hand folded into Harry's, and nerves making my mouth dry.

Harry insisted on buying me a new outfit: a burgundy-colored dress that clings in all the right places with a Bardot neckline exposing my shoulders. I've never felt so unlike me, but neither have I ever felt so sexy, which might have something to do with Harry whispering in my ear that I look beautiful. I caught a glimpse of the price tag before Harry paid for the dress—it was more than I earn in a week—and wanted to cry at the extravagance. But he has style, I'll give him that.

He is looking debonair—as my dad would say—in a silver suit with a faint burgundy pinstripe, pink shirt, and burgundy tie. Coordinated. Knotting us together as a couple.

People stare at us as the maître d' guides us to our table, and I gasp when I realize that my mom and Harry's dad are already seated.

I blink the restaurant back into focus. But no, they're still there. For a few brief moments, I have them all to myself, as they sit there staring into their drinks, blissfully unaware that they are being watched, and I can't help thinking that something has already passed between them before we arrived.

A conspiracy to keep me and Harry apart?

Something that they can agree on after thirteen years of despising each other from a distance. A common ground. Perhaps they've even stumbled into a silent agreement to leave the past behind … for their sakes, not ours.

Then, my mom looks up, checks out my outfit, calculating how much it must've cost before a tentative smile appears and vanishes in a heartbeat. It was for my eyes only. She never intended Harry to claim it for himself.

Karl's gaze doesn't quite reach me, and my stomach lists sideways as if I'm walking on a boat. I sway, my head spinning, and Harry grips my hand tightly.

"Are you alright?" He stops a short distance from the table, giving me a moment. Breathing space. He sensed it too: the battle to come.

"I'm fine." I force a smile.

It must be the stress of my dad being sick and not knowing how tonight is going to go. I realize that all I've eaten today is half a cheese and ham croissant that my mom brought into the hospital for me, and now it's threatening to come back up.

I need to sit down.

I need to eat.

I need tonight to be over so that we can get on with the rest of our lives.

The maître d' helps me into my seat and says that he'll allow us some time to look at the wine list. Karl still hasn't looked at me, and from my mom's rosy cheeks, I'm guessing that her almost empty glass isn't her first drink of the evening.

"Hello, Celia." Harry offers her a warm smile that isn't reciprocated. "Thank you for coming."

"Aren't you being a little presumptuous? You haven't even ordered the wine yet."

"Mom." I try to keep my voice low and my eyes down, but I don't miss Karl's smirk. Now, I'm almost certain that they arranged to meet here early to discuss tactics.

"You're here, aren't you?" Harry doesn't look away. It's another glimpse of the man who sits in a boardroom with clients, knowing what he wants from the outset and determined to win.

"You gave us no choice." Karl picks up his glass and downs the dregs, staring at it as if he doesn't know where it went.

"Wow." Harry shakes his head. "Are we really doing this? The man who told me we always have a choice when I was growing up?"

"That was when I thought you had the sense to make the correct choices." Karl signals the waiter to the table and orders another vodka soda for himself.

The waiter glances around the table, and Harry compensates for his father's rudeness by ordering a bottle of Dom Perignon and a carafe of water.

Harry waits for the waiter to walk away before he says, "Correct choices as in *your* choices."

"In this, I know I'm right." Karl Weiss sits back in his seat like a man who has already had the final word.

I bristle. Who does this man think he is to choose who his son can or cannot marry? My mom hasn't moved, elbows on the table, stroking the outside of her glass like alcohol is going to make this whole situation go away.

"You obviously have your reasons," I say.

I have no desire to speak to the man, but I can't even begin to look at the menu with my stomach roiling like someone cranked up the heat inside me.

"So perhaps, rather than coming at Harry like a bulldozer, it might be better if you explain them, so that he can make a decision armed with all the facts."

Karl shakes his head, his eyes fixated on the slim vase and single white daisy in the center of the table. He avoids eye contact with everyone, but watching him closely, I'm almost certain that he hasn't looked at me once. Not tonight, or the first time I met him in Harry's office.

Eventually, he says, "There's nothing to tell. Business is business. Your father couldn't hack it."

A flush creeps up my mom's neck and into her cheeks. "Where's the water when you need it?" she mutters under her breath.

On cue, the waiter returns with the water and four tall glass tumblers. The atmosphere at the table must be tangible, because he keeps his eyes on the tray, his body poised to make a hasty retreat should we start slinging insults at one another in his presence.

Harry pours. He slides the first glass in my mom's direction. She swallows a huge mouthful without thanking him.

"My dad has given us his blessing," I say.

Something is niggling away at the back of my mind. He told me to go with Harry before he knew that he was a Weiss, but even after he knew the truth, after his second stroke, he was still adamant that I should marry Harry. That's what he said: *Go marry Harry.*

Or was it?

I sip my water. My mom is unnaturally quiet, and that worries me more than if she was her usual vocal self. Why isn't she defending Dad? Is she scared of this man?

Like all bullies, I get the impression that he's a coward underneath the bravado.

A sinister smile twists the corners of Karl's mouth. He raises his hands and claps them slowly, three times, the sound dropping onto the table like dead flies. "Very gracious of him. So, what, you thought you could invite me to dinner and change my mind? Convince me to see things your way? You have a lot to learn, girlie."

"Dad!" Harry's eyes have darkened as if a thundercloud has settled above his head, throwing him into shade. "That's my fiancée you're talking to. I am going to marry her, with or without your blessing, so you either accept it and we all learn to get along, or you walk away now."

"I haven't eaten yet." Karl picks up the menu and raises it in front of his face. "I'm not traveling all this way without being fed."

Harry clenches his fist on the table, and I place my hand over it, surprised to find him trembling. This was a mistake. I don't even know why they came when neither of them has anything constructive to say.

But seeing the disappointment etched on Harry's face, I give it one last shot. "Please, Mr. Weiss. It would mean the world to both of us if you would leave the past in the past and allow us all to move forward."

He lowers the menu, his eyes finally grazing mine. Briefly. As though he's staring directly into the sunshine and is afraid of being blinded. "What makes you think that I haven't already left the past in the past?"

"I-I don't know. Why are you so opposed to us getting married then?"

"The answer is simple. I don't want anything more to do with your family."

"But..." This all happened so long ago, and he wasn't even the loser. "Why do you hate us so much?"

He scoffs, and the mirthless smile is back. "I don't hate you."

I'm confused. "Then why...? Why can't you just be happy for us?"

"It's okay," Harry murmurs, entwining his fingers with mine. "He isn't going to listen to you."

"On the contrary." Karl sets the menu down in front of him. "I'm listening to every word." He turns to me. "So, you want me to be happy? Correct?"

It wasn't exactly what I said, but I'm not prepared to play word games with him. I won't give him the satisfaction.

"What will make me happy is for you and your family to stay in Chicago where you belong and let me get on with my life."

Tears well in my eyes, and I blink them back. I won't cry in front of him either. I don't understand his hatred, and if he isn't prepared to talk about it, Harry and I will just have to get married without him. Only, I don't want to start our lives knowing that I came between him and his dad.

"Okay, Dad." Harry squeezes my fingers, letting me know that he's alright. "You've had your say. Now, I'm going to have mine. I love Ruby. I know that she's the one for me, and nothing you can say will ever change that."

"Are you done?" Karl's eyebrows slide upwards, the smirk still in place as if he finds the entire conversation amusing.

"No." Harry's expression is unreadable. "I came here tonight hoping that you would be willing to discuss what happened before. I thought that we might at least clear the air between you and Celia because we want you both at our wedding without the need for bulletproof vests and plexiglass shields. Or should I say *wanted*."

Harry glances at me, and I understand that he doesn't want to proceed without my agreement. I nod with my eyes. Anxiety is still coursing through my veins, and I don't like the fact that it's because of my future father-in-law.

"Don't come to the wedding." Harry shrugs. "It's your choice, and you're the one who will have to live with the decision. Your absence will not spoil our day because I intend to give Ruby the wedding of her dreams. I've already made it my life's mission to make her the happiest woman on the planet."

I can't help smiling. No one has ever made me feel as special as Harry does, and I wouldn't even care if he suggested that we leave everything behind and make a home on a remote island. My only regret would be leaving my dad behind.

"You're quiet." Karl aims this at my mom. "Think you can sit there and let me take the blame for all this, do you?"

"No one is blaming anyone, Dad." Harry shakes his head, incredulous.

"Not how it sounds to me, son." Eyes still locked on my mom Karl continues, "You must have something to add, some input to the preposterous notion of these two living happily ever after."

"Ruby knows how I feel." I sense my mom is clamming up like an oyster.

"Ha!" Karl inhales deeply and returns his attention to the menu. "Just as I thought. You had no balls then, and you still haven't grown any."

"Okay, I've heard enough." Harry stands abruptly, and the waiter rushes over to save the chair from toppling backwards. Harry gives him a curt nod of gratitude, and the man slinks away again. "We're leaving. Enjoy your meal. I'll settle the bill before I go."

I stand too. "Mom?" I don't want to leave her here with this insufferable man, but she doesn't move.

"Go, Ruby." Her voice is laced with defeat, and I wonder if that's why she hasn't put up a fight. She knew it was game over when she was doing her makeup and getting ready to meet us here. "You got what you wanted. You always do in the end."

"What's that supposed to mean?" I always thought people were supposed to learn from their mistakes, but our parents have clearly learned nothing over the years.

Harry's hand finds mine, his warmth spreading through me, although it does nothing to settle my nerves. I can't wait to get out of here, breathe in the cool night air, and think about something else other than family.

"In case you're interested," Harry says, "we've set the date. We're getting married in six weeks' time." He turns to lead me away as the waiter arrives with the bottle of Dom Perignon. "They'll only be needing two glasses."

"Sir?" The waiter's eyes dart back and forth between us and the table. "Is everything okay, sir?"

"Everything is fine." Harry salutes him as we find the maître d' on our way out and settle the bill. "I think that went rather well." Harry injects some humor into his tone as he helps me into my coat, and we step outside.

We grab hotdogs from a stand and eat them walking through the city, the aroma of fried onions and mustard following us around.

"Let's not talk about it." I need time to process the things that were said. The hotdog has satiated my hunger a little, but I still can't shake the uneasiness that has lodged itself inside my chest all day.

Harry must sense it too. Back in our suite, he leads me by the hand into the bedroom and undresses me tenderly, sliding the dress over my shoulders and raising one foot at a time to help me out of it. When I'm naked, he whispers, "Lay down, Ruby," and I do. I don't have the energy to give anything back.

Starting with my eyelids, Harry kisses me all over, his tongue trailing to my earlobes, my neck, my nipples. My body responds instinctively, my skin coming alive to his touch. I close my eyes and savor every moment.

Harry licks his way down to my pussy, the tip of his tongue finding its way inside me and then quickly moving on, down the inside of my thighs, behind my knees, and onward to my toes. He massages my instep and sucks on my toes, one at a time, separating them, licking in between them, sending shivers down my spine. How can it possibly feel this good?

Without warning, when my brain is still consumed by the strange sensation of having my toes sucked, Harry spreads my legs and finds me again with his tongue. He inserts a finger, probing me while his tongue hits the spot and hesitates, listening for the sound of my shallow panting. He inserts a second finger and licks harder.

"You are so fucking beautiful, Ruby Jackson. I am never going to stop telling you this for as long as I live."

I grab the pillow under my head with both hands and cling onto it tightly. Just as I'm about to explode, Harry stops. He kisses the inside of my thighs tenderly, his fingers still resting inside me.

"Want more?" His voice is husky.

"Yes," I pant.

"I can't hear you."

"Yes!" I'm clinging onto my orgasm, waiting for him to finish what he started, and my voice is shrill.

His tongue is back. Harry doesn't stop until he has tasted every drop of my wetness, then he comes back to me, gently removing the pillow that I covered my face with to stop myself from screaming.

He rolls me onto my side, his hand cupping my breast, and enters me from behind, pushing my left knee up towards my chest and spreading my butt cheeks. He moves slowly, his hips finding their rhythm while he kisses my neck, my ears, and my throat, his fingers stroking my clit and making my body convulse.

"I'm going to come, Ruby," he whispers into my ear. "Do you want me to?"

"Yes." I twist my face around and kiss him hard, curling his hair around my fingers and holding on tightly as he thrusts inside me, his legs vibrating until finally, we both slump onto the pillows.

24

HARRY

Ruby tosses and turns all night, and only settles when I spoon her from behind and stroke her hair away from her clammy face, whispering to her that she doesn't need to worry about anything. That's what I'm here for.

The temperature in the room is comfortable, not too hot and not too cold, but despite the sweat beading on her forehead, she is shivering. I cover her with the comforter and call Lizzie.

"How did it go?" She's talking about the trip to Diablo Lake, but I can't stop the image of my father from popping into my head.

"Another dead end."

"Oh, I'm so sorry, Harry. I hoped this one was going to bring you some closure."

"Me too." I glance at Ruby in the bed, her face pale against the pillow, her eyelids fluttering. "Any messages for me from Carlos Russo?"

"Yes. He said good news and bad news, but he has a proposition for you."

"Did he say what it is?" I already know that Carlos will want to tell me himself.

"No, but he's eager to see you today. I get the impression that if you don't act quickly, it will be too late."

"Can you book me on the next flight back to New York?"

"Just one ticket?" I can hear Lizzie's smile.

"Yes. For now."

Ruby stirs. Kneeling beside her, I study her face. Her cheeks are warm and rosy. "How do you feel?"

She swallows hard and rotates her shoulders. "Fine. Who were you talking to?"

"Lizzie. Alessandro's brother, Carlos, has a business proposition for me."

"You're flying back to New York today?"

"I don't have to. Carlos can wait, Ruby. You're way more important to me than any business proposition."

Her eyelids flicker as she shifts her gaze from me to the telephone like she might be able to erase the call with the power of her mind. "Of course, you must go." She smiles.

But I'm not convinced. I thought she had a temperature in the night, and I don't ever want her to think that she comes second to my work.

"Harry, I'm fine."

Clutching the comforter to her naked breasts, she rises onto her knees and kisses me on the lips. Before I can tug the covers away from her, my erection is already growing, she seems to fold in on herself, like a flower curling up for the night.

The pain passes, and she gives me a weak smile. "Period pains, that's all." She twists her mouth into a lopsided grin. "I don't want you to think that I'm a wimp."

"What can I get you? Do you need anything?"

"Tylenol. I have some in my purse."

I fetch the packet and the glass of water on the nightstand and pop the tablets into the palm of her hand. I wait for her to swallow. "Better?"

"Better. I'll be fine by tonight." She sits back on the bed, the comforter bunched up around her. "You don't have to worry about me, Harry. I'm a big girl now."

"But I do worry about you, Ruby, and the sooner you get used to it, the better."

She nods. "I knew you were only staying a couple of days. I-I just wish last night hadn't been such a disaster."

"Last night was last night, and today is today. Whatever they think, I'm going to marry you in six weeks, Ruby, and I'm going to make you the happiest woman alive. Promise." Because that's one I can keep. I stand up and retrieve my carry-on from the closet. "You have a wedding to plan, don't forget."

"How could I forget?"

By the time I've showered, dressed, and repacked my clothes, Ruby is asleep. Her eyelids flicker open when I lean over her and kiss her goodbye.

"Promise me you'll call if you don't feel well."

"I'm fine, Harry. I'm just going to doze a little longer."

"Promise me, Ruby, or I'll have to fuck you again before I go."

"Hmm... How can I resist an offer like that?" She smiles mischievously, her eyes slanting sideways. I grab the comforter to pull it off her, and she grips it tightly. "Okay, okay, I promise."

Her eyes follow me to the door, and I can't wait for us to live together so that I don't have to do this anymore.

CARLOS IS WAITING for me in the office.

"I'm not sure we can recover all the money owed to you," he says, adding cream to the cup of coffee Lizzie has placed in front of him, "but I have a joint venture that I think might interest you."

I sit down. I haven't stopped thinking about Ruby since I left the Drake Hotel, and I need to get my head into gear and pay attention. This is *our* future now, mine and Ruby's, I'm not just doing this for me.

"I have a contact in Saudi," Carlos continues. "He is looking to expand his income from the States, and I think that a deal will be mutually beneficial to everyone concerned."

He runs through what the joint venture would mean to his company and Weiss Petroleum and shakes my hand before he leaves. "We are like brothers, you and I. We look after each other."

I don't know how I'll ever repay him for his generosity, or even express how grateful I am that he has taken me under his wing when I need him most.

As if reading my mind, he says, "One day, I might not be in such a fortunate position, and then you will have your chance." His booming voice follows him from the office and past Lizzie's desk to the elevator.

I stand, remove my jacket, and walk to the window. Ruby and I haven't even discussed where we'll live once we're married, but I realize that I'd just assumed that she would come here. My office is here. My family—what's left of it. I would say my life too, but, apart from Ronnie, my friends are scattered around the country now like dandelion seeds.

And Ruby won't want to be far from her dad.

"I swear I can still hear him talking outside the building." Lizzie is standing in the doorway, and I didn't even hear it open. "Can I send out for some lunch for you?"

"Please, Lizzie."

I turn back to the window, searching for Carlos Russo outside, as my gaze settles on a man in a black coat standing on the other side of the street, staring up at my window. Our eyes meet, and he doesn't look away.

The hairs on the back of my neck stand to attention. I grab my jacket off the back of my chair and make my way outside. "I've changed my mind," I tell Lizzie. "I'll grab my own lunch."

The man is gone by the time I walk out of the lobby. I scan the street, left and right, for a glimpse of a black coat and find that everyone in the damned city is wearing black today. Everyone is drab, wearing their gray winter faces along with their hats and scarves.

I turn left. I figure it's fifty-fifty whether I've chosen the right way but pointing him out in a sea filled with moving black overcoats will be like finding the ant that stole your last crumb.

Because now, every face I see appears to be looking at me. Eyes following me everywhere, and I wonder again if I have imagined the whole thing.

Only I know what I saw in Chicago, and people generally don't vanish in restrooms.

I grab a salted pretzel from a street seller and make my way back to the office, my thoughts drifting back to Ruby. Carlos may have set us up to rise above our competitors, but he's been making waves on my behalf, and it's entirely possible that he has upset a few folks along the way. If someone is having me followed, they will already know about Ruby, and the last thing she needs right now is a stranger gatecrashing her life because they have a beef with me.

Back in the office, I ask Lizzie to hold my calls. I contact the PI who has been trying to track down my sister.

"I was about to call you." His voice is naturally cautious as if he has spent too much time investigating shady characters and has lost faith in his fellow man. "I have a lead on Melanie. A potential sighting in Hawaii."

Hawaii?

Before she disappeared, my sister never travelled outside the city unless it was to visit our grandparents and cousins. This doesn't sit right with me now. I couldn't overlook Washington State, but I draw the line at Hawaii. It's almost as if someone doesn't want me here in New York City, someone perhaps, who can't afford to settle their invoices.

"I'm calling off the search."

Pause. "I know we've had a few bum leads, but I think we're closing in on her," he says, still in that same monotone.

"I've changed my mind." I don't want his excuses in exchange for the money I transfer into his bank account every month. "Send me your final invoice, and then we're done."

"Wait, is that—"

I cut him off. Ronnie gave me the number for another PI, and I dial it now. It rings and rings, and a woman finally answers as I'm about to hang up.

"Pagan PI." She has a faint accent, one that I can't quite place. I ask to speak to Mr. Pagan and am rewarded with a sigh. "You're speaking to Ms. Pagan. I'm all you're going to get, so if it's a man you're after, maybe try one of the shysters who operate out of Brooklyn."

I sense the phone being replaced and blurt out, "No, wait. I'm sorry. I need someone to keep an eye on my fiancée in Chicago."

Pause. "I cut my PI teeth on cheating partners; it's not something I want to get involved in again."

"She isn't cheating on me." I like this woman already, and I have a feeling that Ruby would like her to. "I think she might be in danger."

"Okay, now you're talking."

My next call is to Ruby's home.

Celia answers. She and my father might've tried intimidating me and Ruby into calling off the engagement, but she doesn't scare me.

"Ruby isn't feeling great," she says when I ask to speak to her.

"What's wrong? Is she sick? Has she seen a doctor?" I fucking knew I shouldn't have left her this morning.

"She's sleeping right now, Harry. I don't want to disturb her." Her tone is almost pleasant like she can switch it on and off when it suits her, and I can't help thinking that my father would've met his match in Celia Jackson.

"No, I understand. What did the doctor say?"

"I haven't called the doctor. It's just stomach cramps, Ruby always suffers with them. And anyway, she has me to look after her."

"Will you tell her I called?"

"Sure. Any message?"

"No... Just tell her that I'm worried about her."

"No need to worry. It's just Ruby being overdramatic. Luckily she was at home when it happened and not in a strange country where she would've had no one to look after her."

There was no mistaking that this was a dig at me.

"I would've looked after her."

"Hmm, didn't you cut and run back to New York this morning?"

"I had a meeting I couldn't get out of." I can't even think why I said that, but I do believe that the less Celia Jackson knows about my affairs the better. "Ruby told me it was nothing."

"And you believed her, of course you did."

"I'd have stayed if she wanted me to." I'm disappointed at the pleading tone in my own voice. I shouldn't have to justify my actions to this woman who has made it quite clear that she doesn't want me in her daughter's life. "Please tell her I'll call again later."

The line goes dead, and I'm left staring at the silent handset.

Sitting at my desk, I replay the conversation in my head. I can't help thinking that this has played straight into Celia's hands. I'm here, and Ruby is there, exactly where she wants her.

The meal that never happened has left a sour taste in my mouth. My dad's behavior was appalling, like a child who didn't get a shot at the ball because the other kids were faster than him, but he's still my dad, and if I don't try to clear the air one last time, I know it will always be hanging over my head.

I call home. No answer.

I try the hotel in Chicago where he was staying, and the receptionist tells me that he checked out earlier today. I even try calling his cleaning lady, who tells me that he fired her a couple of days ago.

So, where the fuck has he gone?

25

RUBY

I HEAR my mom talking to someone and I throw back the covers on my bed. Goosebumps immediately pop on my bare arms and legs, and the room sways out from under me like I'm drunk. I didn't even have a drink last night. At least, I don't think I did. It's all a bit vague, but I'm still left with the lingering sense of uneasiness that I haven't been able to shake since I first called Karl Weiss.

I wait for the dizziness to pass. My heart is racing, and I can't seem to slow it down, even when I take deep breaths.

It must be stress related. I remember my roommate in college talking about an auntie who lost all her hair when she discovered that her husband had been cheating on her for years, had a whole other family in a different state. She ended up with heart problems and had to have a triple bypass before she was forty-five.

I've been so worried about my dad, and everything with Mom and Karl Weiss, that it's obviously starting to affect me. I need some downtime, but I can't bear to think of my dad in the hospital waiting for me to visit. He needs me. I can't let him down, not when he has always been there for me, no matter how sick he was. Even when he could barely speak after his first stroke, he was still the one who wanted to hear everything about my school day.

I open my bedroom door. The house is quiet again now. "Mom?"

Nothing.

I go back for my robe, my teeth chattering. The heating must not have clicked on yet. I have no idea what time it is, or how long I've been asleep, but the house has settled into its own version of twilight, so I'm guessing that it must be late afternoon or evening.

"Mom?"

Sounds reach me from the kitchen, and I walk along the hallway, surprised when my shoulder keeps brushing the wall like I can't even walk a straight line. I open the kitchen door, and she's staring out the window, a cup of coffee in one hand, and the house phone in the other.

"You're awake." She puts them down on the counter and rushes over to me, her expression faltering. "Why are you out of bed? You should've called me."

She eases me into a seat at the table and flicks the kettle on to boil, dropping a teabag into my favorite cup.

"I'll make you a green tea. It'll flush this virus or whatever it is out of you."

"You think it's a virus?" My head feels heavy like a bowling ball, and I cup my chin in both hands to hold it upright.

"Of course, sweetie. You look dreadful, and you're still shivering, look at you." She pulls a blanket out of the storage cupboard and places it over my shoulders. "You've been running a temperature all day too."

She fills the mug with boiling water and places it on the table in front of me. The smell makes me feel nauseous. I try sliding it away from me and manage to spill some across the table.

"I'll get it!" Mom grabs a kitchen towel and mops up the spill, her mouth set into a narrow line. "There's only half a cup left now, but it will have to do."

I shake my head. "I can't drink it, Mom. The smell..."

"Hold your nose. It's good for you."

She keeps moving around the kitchen, opening cupboard doors and straightening appliances. I can't keep up with her, so I stare into the cup at the teabag that's bleeding green water and try to focus on what I wanted to ask her. Something woke me up. My mom was talking to someone, only now I know she must've been on the phone.

"Who was that?" It's an effort just to speak.

"Who was what, sweetie?" Mom's gaze drifts around the room and settles on the phone. "Oh, I called the hospital to let your dad know why we've not visited today."

I swallow a mouthful of green tea and grimace, hiding my tears behind the cup. "Has Harry called?"

"No, sweetie." She stops fidgeting with her hands and turns around to face me, her smile fading when she notices my damp eyes. "He must be busy. That's what it's like when you marry a businessman. You end up playing second fiddle to the company, and even lower down the scale when you have kids."

The tears start flowing and I can't stop them. I down the rest of the drink, spluttering when pain crashes through my abdomen again and makes me choke. The empty cup rolls out of my hand and across the table as I bend down and double over.

"Ruby!" Mom is on her knees in front of me, stroking my hair away from my face. "What is it? Where does it hurt?"

I cradle my stomach with both arms, rocking back and forth, afraid that the green tea will come back up and my mom will force me to drink another one. "Cramps," I manage to gasp out between shallow breaths.

Her eyes narrow. "Are you bleeding?"

"No." I squeeze my eyes shut, but it only makes the pain flare cold and white behind my eyelids.

"Ruby." Her voice is firm, and I open my eyes again. "You're not pregnant, are you?"

Heat floods my cheeks, and suddenly I'm too hot. I stand up too quickly, tiny stars spiraling in front of my eyes, and try to yank my robe off, but I lose my balance and hurtle forward, unable to stop myself.

My mom catches me before I hit the floor. "It's okay, Ruby, I've got you." She wraps her arms around me and helps me back onto my feet, and I can't remember the last time I was this close to my mom. "Let's get you back into bed, and I'll call the doctor."

"No." I grip her hand tightly. "No, I don't want to see the doctor. It's nothing."

"It is not nothing, Ruby. Look at you." Like I even want to see my reflection in the mirror right now.

She supports me all the way to my room, holds my hand when she sits me on the bed, takes off my robe, and slides my legs under the covers, tucking them under my chin.

I watch her closely, wishing I got to see this side of her more often.

"Mom." I grip her hand, binding her to me. "Don't call the doctor."

She holds my gaze, stares right through me as if trying to see what's going on inside my head. "You would tell me if you were pregnant, wouldn't you?"

I nod, not trusting myself to speak.

"Do you want me to get you a test?"

"No." I can't concentrate. I can't remember if I'm late or when I'm due, but the cramps in my stomach are worse than usual. "Mom?" I sound so puny, so feeble, like a little girl again, scared to ask when Daddy is coming home from the office.

Is this what she meant? Did she feel shunted aside when I came along, and my dad spent every waking hour in the office? I never realized before that she might've felt like an outsider because me and my dad were so close.

I need her now though, and she's here for me, stepping in to fill my dad's shoes.

"It hurts."

"I know, sweetie. Close your eyes, and I'll go get some painkillers from the pharmacy."

I must drift off to sleep, my brain switching off and giving me a chance to heal, because I don't even hear the door close behind her.

I'M in the bridal store, trying on a wedding gown, while my mom waits in the fitting room for me to come out and show her. The dress has a tight bodice covered in diamantes that catch the overhead light and cast sparkling patterns across the mirror in front of me. The skirt is full, layers and layers of frothy lace bulking it out, and I don't even know how I'll get through the door wearing it.

"Harry will love this dress," I say to the assistant who is behind me, lacing up the bodice.

"Is Harry your fiancé?" Her face appears over my shoulder in the reflection.

I smile back at her. "Yes. He always wanted a big white wedding; it's his dream."

"Yours, too." The assistant is in front of me now, straightening the neckline and teasing my hair over my shoulders.

I hesitate. Is it my dream too? I stare at her makeup which is too thick and breathe in her perfume which she must have bathed in. It's so cloying.

I can't remember. Why can't I remember? Why am I going along with what Harry wants if this isn't what I want too?

"You look beautiful." She stands aside and gestures for me to look in the mirror, and I think she must say that to all the brides. It's part of the job—she won't get her commission if I don't buy the dress.

I force myself to stare at my reflection, starting from the floor and working my way upwards. The dress is stunning. It's like something from a fairytale, you know, the one where the poor servant girl wins the heart of the prince, and they live happily ever after.

But when I reach my face, it doesn't look like me.

Who is this woman staring back at me, her face pale, her eyes wide, and her lips parted like she's about to scream? I turn away from those dark eyes. "I have to go."

I push my way out of the fitting room, the dress squashed in at the sides to accommodate the doorway, and stumble into the waiting room where my mom is on her feet. She gasps, hands clamped over her mouth at the first glimpse of her daughter in a wedding dress.

I stop dead. I can't tell if she loves it or hates it, but I realize that I want her to love it. I want her to cry real tears and tell me that I'll be the most beautiful bride ever. But instead, she says, "Oh my God, Ruby, what have you done?"

Huh?

I peer down at the dress as I hear a rip from the waistline. "No," I mutter under my breath. "What's happening?"

I'm frozen, my feet taking root through the floor, growing stringy tendrils and keeping me here to witness what's unfolding. My belly is swelling, growing larger by the second, stretching the heavy fabric, diamantes pinging everywhere. One hits me in the eye, and I try to bat it away, but the dress is so tight that I can't move my arms.

Then there is a horrendous rip, and the dress gapes open to reveal my swollen tummy. Pain tears through me, dragging me onto my knees.

"Mom, help me." I'm sobbing. The baby is forcing its way out of me, tearing my body in two, and I don't even know how I got here, how any of this happened. "Mom, make it stop."

"It's okay, sweetie, I'm here."

"Mom?" She sounds far away, and I can hear her, but I can't see her. "Mom? Where are you?"

"I'm right here. It's okay, Ruby, I'm not going anywhere."

A cool hand strokes my forehead, and I lean into it, trying to find her, waiting for her to make it stop.

"You've been dreaming, Ruby. The fever is making you delirious. Wake up, and I'll give you some painkillers to bring your temperature down. That's it, sweetie."

I follow the familiar sound of her voice out of the bridal store, which disintegrates around me, and back into my bedroom. When I open my eyes, it's dark. My bedside lamp is on, making a golden puddle of light on the floor, and the curtains are closed, making the room appear half the size.

"It was only a dream, Ruby." Mom's face appears above me. "You gave me quite a fright. Sounded like you were fighting off a monster."

The dream—*nightmare*—breaks into tiny, jagged fragments that fall away as I focus on my mom's soothing voice. My pulse slowly regulates, my breathing becoming more normal. I can only remember snippets, the torn wedding dress, the assistant's heavy beige makeup, the pain tearing me apart.

I blink. I dreamed that I was pregnant. No, not just pregnant, I was giving birth right there in the bridal store wearing the dress fit for a princess.

Pain rises in my stomach again, and I roll onto my side retching into a bowl that has somehow materialized next to the bed while I've been sleeping. I grip my mom's hand and close my eyes waiting for it to pass.

"Mom, what's wrong with me?"

"I don't know, honey. I'm going to call the doctor."

I nod, clinging onto her with my eyes. "Did Harry call?"

She blinks, her expression faltering. "He did."

"What did you tell him?"

"I told him that you were sick."

There's more, but she's holding it close to her chest.

"What? What is it?"

"I begged him to come, Ruby, but he said... He said that he's too busy right now."

26

HARRY

I HARDLY SLEEP a wink worrying about Ruby.

Celia told me to call back in the morning, that she got Ruby some medication from the pharmacy and was hopeful she'd be on the mend after a good night's sleep. But now, she isn't answering my calls.

I shower and dress and go into the office early when the night is still stretching its arms and yawning in the face of the day. The city is sleepy, hushed, but a strange sense of foreboding is sneaking around inside my gut and yelling at me to do something. I've never really thought about sixth sense and premonition, but all I do know is that this doesn't feel right.

I call Ruby's house again from the office. Still no answer.

I call my dad's house and the phone rings until the sound is imprinted in my brain. He doesn't pick up. I speak to the night security guard in the lobby, and he tells me he has no record of my dad entering the building over the last twenty-four hours.

I know it's a long shot, but I call the airline and ask them to check if my dad caught his flight back to New York. By this point, I'm not even surprised to hear that he didn't. So, he either stayed in Chicago, or he caught a flight elsewhere; one thing is for certain: he didn't come home.

After making myself a coffee, I sit at my desk and study the investment risks and profit forecasts of the joint venture with Russo Corporation, but the figures bounce about in front of my eyes like fleas on a dog. I usually enjoy the peace of the early morning office before the building fills with people and telephone calls and the hum of electrical equipment, but today, I just feel alone. Like I've somehow been stranded in a parallel universe where no one else exists and, any moment now, I'll realize that I'm the last man standing.

I don't understand how lost I feel until there's a knock on the door, and Lizzie bounds into the room, her smile fading when she sees me with my head in my hands, the desk strewn with paper. "You look like you could do with a coffee."

I peer at her, lack of sleep slowly catching up with me. "The first two didn't touch the sides."

"That bad, huh?" She shakes her head. "Lucky I came in when I did then."

She disappears and returns a couple minutes later with a cup of steaming coffee and some pastries.

"When's the lovely Ruby going to come and take care of you then?" She stands back, arms folded across her chest.

"We've set the date for the wedding. It's six weeks away..."

"But?" She narrows her eyes; Lizzie misses nothing.

"But she isn't well, and her mom isn't picking up the phone this morning."

Saying it out loud seems to ram it home to me. I don't know what's wrong with Ruby, I'm relying on her mom—who hates me—to keep me updated, and I'm eight hundred miles away, staring at a bunch of numbers that will mean nothing to me if I don't have Ruby in my life.

"Not well as in...?" This is Lizzie's organizational skills breaking down the information and sorting it into bite-sized manageable pieces.

"That's just it." I shrug. "I don't know. Ruby said it was nothing, and when I spoke to her mom last night, she told me not to worry—" Lizzie rolls her eyes at this bit "—and she would probably be feeling better this morning."

"But you want to hear it for yourself." It's a statement rather than a question. She studies me carefully, weighing up her options, then says, "Look, if you're really worried, why not call the hospital, and before you start panicking, if she has been admitted, you'll know she's in the best place. Then you'll know what to do instead of sitting here wasting your time on an upside-down spreadsheet."

I follow her gaze and realize that one of the spreadsheets I opened earlier is facing Lizzie. "Damn! You caught me out."

"Harry Weiss, your face has always been an open book ... unlike your father." She mutters the last bit under her breath.

At the doorway between my office and her desk, Lizzie hesitates. "Call the hospitals now and let me know if I need to book a flight."

She winks at me and disappears, but before I can pick up the handset, she buzzes back through. "Carlos Russo to see you. I'll send him through."

The big man appears shortly after, filling the space the way he always does. His gaze skims the graphs, spreadsheets, and documents on my desk, but he doesn't sit down.

"My contact flew in from Saudi last night. He has asked me to schedule a meeting for midday, so I'll ask Lizzie to add it to your diary."

"Today?" I haven't even looked at the five-year forecast yet.

"What can I say?" Carlos shrugs and spreads his hands wide. "He's a busy man, and when he wants to hold a meeting, everyone else jumps." He pauses, studying me carefully. "This is not the face of a man who is preparing to close on the deal of a lifetime. What's up, my friend?"

I sigh. "Nothing."

I force a smile. For all I know, Ruby had some kind of twenty-four-hour bug and is visiting her dad in the hospital right now, oblivious to my churning gut and overactive imagination. If I back out of this venture now, there won't be a second chance.

"Midday. I'll be there."

I wait for Carlos to leave before calling the hospital in Chicago where Graham is currently being treated. I get transferred to his ward and speak to the duty nurse.

"He's responding well to treatment." It's the standard response to an inquiry by someone other than a close relative.

"Is his daughter with him right now?" My heart flutters, eager to settle down as soon as I hear that Ruby is fine.

"No, he's alone right now, sir."

My stomach twists sickeningly. No one is with him. Celia and Ruby are not there, but they're not answering the house phone, so where the hell are they?

My fingers hover over the buttons on the telephone. Call the hospital again and find out that Ruby's condition is worse than Celia let on, or sit here and worry about her until one of them calls me back? Celia's comment replays inside my head. *"I'm taking care of her."*

I hit redial before I can talk myself out of it.

When I get through to the switchboard, I ask if Ruby Jackson has been admitted during the last twenty-four hours.

"Can you please tell me her date-of-birth, sir?"

Shit! My brain scrabbles around trying to figure out Ruby's year of birth on the spot. "Twenty-fourth December 1965." Praying that's correct.

The seconds tick by.

"Yes, Ms. Jackson was admitted via ER last night."

My heart is pounding so violently I think I'm going to be sick. "What's wrong with her?"

"I'm afraid I don't have access to medical information, sir."

"Can you put me through to the ward?"

"Transferring you now."

I tap the desk with my thumb, my body a bundle of nervous energy. Why didn't Celia let me know? Why did she play it down when Ruby's condition had obviously deteriorated after I left Chicago?

The ward takes an eternity to pick up the phone. When they do, I introduce myself as Ruby's fiancé. "How is she?"

"Ruby's condition is stable at the moment."

"Can you tell me what's wrong with her?" Her condition is stable means nothing to me if I don't know what's going on.

"The doctors are still carrying out tests, sir."

"Tests? What kind of tests? What does this mean?"

"I'm sorry I can't give you any more information until we have the results, but she's responding well to pain relief."

Is this supposed to make me feel better? I feel so helpless. I shouldn't have left Chicago yesterday morning. I should've taken care of her myself. We're not even married yet, and I've already let her down.

"Can you please tell her I called. Harry Weiss. My name is Harry Weiss."

THE MEETING TAKES place in a private suite of the Plaza Hotel. Carlos's contact is tall, dark-skinned, with the classic looks of a Hollywood movie star. A young Omar Sharif. He gets straight down to business, talking us through his vision for the project, and shaking our hands warmly when we agree to proceed in just under an hour.

Then, we're invited to dine with him. Four gourmet courses that we eat in his dining area, each course accompanied by the appropriate wine. Carlos already warned me that it would be offensive to refuse the meal, but I'm trying hard not to keep checking the time on my wristwatch.

When our client leaves the room briefly, Carlos's eyes narrow in my direction. "Something is wrong. You've been like a deer in the headlights all afternoon. Is it the contract?"

"No." Lizzie booked me a seat on the 4 p.m. flight to Chicago. It's 3 p.m., and we're still waiting for dessert to be served. "Ruby is sick. I'm supposed to be flying to Chicago to be with her, but I'm going to miss my flight."

Carlos grins. "Today is your lucky day, Harry. My private jet is at your disposal. Once we've signed on the dotted line, I suggest you invest in one too." His booming laughter fills the room.

I force myself to follow the conversation, to express interest in the guy's new purebred stallion, and the home he is having built for his wife, but when we finally shake hands and say our goodbyes, I almost sprint out of the Plaza and into a waiting taxi.

Back in my apartment, I chuck clothes into my carry-on, and hurriedly listen to my messages.

"This is Talia Pagan. Nothing to report on your fiancée Ruby since she was admitted to the hospital last night, but I thought you might be interested in her mother's movements. Seems Mrs. Jackson might be suffering from a touch of insomnia. Either that, or she was enjoying a secret rendezvous with her lover. And before you remind me that I don't do cheating partners, this one is different. I'll keep you posted."

I stare at the phone. Celia Jackson has a lover?

No. I shake my head. Jumping to conclusions will achieve nothing, and I have more pressing concerns right now, like catching the Russo private jet and making sure for myself that Ruby is okay.

The second message is brief. "Mr. Weiss, I can accommodate you on Saturday morning at 10 a.m."

I park this one for now. It's important, but it can be rescheduled if I'm not back.

I HEAD STRAIGHT to the hospital when I reach Chicago. The receptionist points me in the direction of Ruby's ward, and I take the stairs, wishing that I'd picked up some flowers en route. Too late now though.

Walking along the sterile white corridors, I'm reminded of my time spent in the same hospital. First me, then Graham, and now Ruby. It's almost as if the building is playing its own role in our relationship, and while those few surreal days when we were snowed in will always hold a special place in my heart, I'll be glad to move on from it.

My heart is thumping when I approach Ruby's room. I don't know what to expect. My mom had severe abdominal pains when she first got sick, and I don't like that my brain is making me feel the way I did then, like a scared boy watching my mom deteriorate with every visit, getting sicker, frailer, weaker.

Stop it, I tell myself. Ruby is going to get better.

My fingers almost close around the handle when the door opens, and Celia steps out. She blinks, her gaze hardening when she sees me.

"What are you doing here?"

"I've come to see Ruby."

She blocks the door with her petite frame. "She's sleeping. They've sedated her."

"It's okay. I'm happy to sit with her if you're leaving."

Whatever game she's still playing, I'm catching onto the rules. She clearly doesn't want to let me in, and I'm not leaving until I've seen Ruby.

"Visiting time is over." She glances in the direction of the nurse's station as if she might find a sign to back her up.

I smile. "I've cleared it with the staff."

I reach around her for the handle, and she moves in front of it, showing her intention. "She's been restless with all the tests. She needs to be left alone. I'm sorry you've had a wasted journey."

"Oh, but I haven't. I'll stay in Chicago until Ruby is discharged, and then I'm taking her home with me."

I don't want to sink to Celia's level, sniping at each other. But I'm not a child, and I will not let her stand in my way. She might have controlled her daughter's life in the past, but I'm here now, and it has to end.

"We'll see what Ruby has to say about that when she wakes up." She stands her ground, her voice rising a notch.

"Will you step aside and let me in, or do I have to involve the staff?"

"What is going on here?" A nurse approaches us on silent, efficient footsteps and is watching us both, arms folded across her ample chest, as if she caught us squabbling on the school playground. "The patients are trying to sleep."

"I just got in from New York," I say before Celia can respond. "I'm here to see my fiancée, Ruby Jackson."

The nurse's eyes slide from me to Celia.

"I'm her mom. I tried telling him that she's asleep." Celia arches an eyebrow like she was trying to do the staff a favor by keeping me out.

"You just got in?" The nurse has kind eyes, huge and brown, and smooth dark skin. "Does she know you're coming?"

"I left a message when I called earlier."

Celia's eyes widen momentarily, her chest rising and falling with the effort of trying to control her temper.

The nurse inclines her head towards Ruby's door. "Five minutes. I'll be back to throw you out myself if you're still here." She waits for Celia to move before heading back to the nurse's station.

I enter Ruby's room.

Her hair is fanned across the pillow, her eyes are closed, her skin pale and still clammy. I approach the bed, holding my breath so as not to wake her and incur the wrath of the nurse who was kind enough to let me in. Ruby's hands are resting on top of the covers, and I smother them with mine, flinching when I feel how cold they are.

She looks peaceful—must be the sedatives they've given her. Still my Ruby despite the pale skin and the dark circles under her eyes.

"It's okay, I'm here now," I whisper. "I'm not going anywhere without you, I promise."

I kiss her forehead, rest my head beside her on the pillow for five minutes and then let myself out without making a sound, telling myself that she'll know I was here.

27

RUBY

I'm in a building that's like a maze. White walls. White floors. Everything is white, even the doors. I think I must be in the hospital, but there are no signs on the doors or the walls, and I've not even seen any staff. No one to show me the way, not that I can remember where I'm going or why I'm here.

"Help!" I call out, my voice swallowed by the whiteness all around me. "Where am I?"

It hurts my eyes, this dazzling whiteness, like I've been staring at the sun for too long. Where has all the color gone? I peer down at my clothes, and I realize with a jolt, that I'm wearing a white all-in-one, my legs blending in with my surroundings so that it looks as if I'm hovering in midair.

I turn left and start running. There are no footsteps following me around; I can't even hear myself breathing. It's disorienting, the relentless white silence.

At the end of the corridor, I turn left again. The doors are all the same, nameless, closed, silent. It doesn't matter which way

I turn, I'm alone. I stop, holding my side, a sharp stinging pain brewing behind my hip.

"Help!" I cry out again.

Tears flow down my cheeks, but when I raise my fingers to my face, they come away dry. Then lava-hot pain inside my gut sends me crashing sideways into the wall, and I sink to the floor, gasping, clutching my belly as if I can push it back where it came from.

I roll onto my knees, retching onto the floor, only nothing comes out.

I don't know how long I stay like this, but when it passes, I can hear a voice somewhere in the distance. So faint, I strain to find it above the thump-thump of my heartbeat.

"It's okay, Ruby..."

The voice whispers my name, calling to me, showing me the way because now I know what I was searching for. Home.

"Where are you?" I close my eyes, listen harder. "Come back. Don't leave me."

"I'm not going anywhere without you, I promise..."

I follow the whispers, trusting my ears rather than my eyes. Down one empty corridor and then another, clinging to the sound like a lifeline.

I turn a blind corner, and the world turns multicolor again, comes to life, like a color-by-numbers painting slowly being filled in. I close my eyes, squeezing them shut, adjusting to this new reality.

Voices.

Whispers still, but now there's more than one.

Doctors? I vaguely recall being in a hospital. A bed with cellular covers. Monitors beeping in that steady rhythm the way they do. The sterile tang of antiseptic and bleach and ... something else.

What is it? Sickness? Worse?

My dad!

Panic fills my chest making it hard to breathe. I need to find him, I need to get him away from this place before I lose him forever. But there's no oxygen, and I feel my lungs bursting like when I used to try holding my breath at the bottom of the pool when I was younger, trying to beat an imaginary world record.

Then suddenly, I'm bursting through the water's surface, mouth open, sucking in deep gulps of air. My heart is pounding as blood starts pumping around my veins again. My head is reeling.

I don't move, waiting for my brain cells to settle, trying to get my bearings with my eyes closed. Starting with my toes, I wriggle them, noting that they're bare. My legs are covered by a sheet. I'm warm. I tap my fingers and feel a scratchy blanket beneath them.

Wait. Sharp pain in the back of my hand. Something is stuck in it; I can feel it moving against my skin when I flex my fingers.

"*You know I can't...*" A woman's voice, clearer now, closer. A whisper. She's trying not to wake me up.

"What's changed?" A man speaks now. "I don't understand."

Pause.

"You know what's changed. It's just not the right time."

"It never will be, will it?" The man is speaking in low tones, but I can still hear the despair like an undercurrent running through his words.

The pain is coming back. "*Oh no, please no, not now.*"

I'm afraid that I'm going to lose them, that they'll get swept away on the tidal wave of agony wracking my stomach. I'm afraid that, when it's done, I'll open my eyes and I'll be alone in the white maze again, that I'll never find my way out.

It leaves me panting and utterly drained, my heartbeat fluttering like a baby bird. I listen to the silence ringing in my ears and fresh tears spill from my eyes. I've lost them. I've lost them, and they didn't even know that I was here.

"*I never planned for it to happen this way.*"

They're back.

I open my eyes and wait for them to adjust to the muted colors surrounding me. It's dark. There's a soft glow coming from somewhere overhead allowing me to see the room in twilight tones and eerie shadows.

Beep... Beep... Beep...

It's a hospital room. I'm here with Harry and Ronnie; we're snowed in, and Ronnie bought a pack of cards, and he keeps cheating.

I glance towards the bed to see if Harry is awake, but instead, I find two people talking in front of the window, heads together, their backs to me. I swallow, clear my throat, try to get their attention.

"Where's Harry?" I need to know where they've taken him, only they don't look around, and when I try to reach them, I realize that I'm in the bed.

Not Harry.

Me.

"Thirteen years I've been waiting." The man's voice is gruff. He isn't happy. I recognize it, but I can't remember where from. "Thirteen fucking years. How much longer do you think I can wait?"

"Keep your voice down. I don't want to wake Ruby up."

Mom? I stare at her, waiting for her to turn around and notice that I'm awake. She half-turns, enough for me to see her profile, but she only has eyes for the man.

"It isn't going to work this time." The man shoots a glance my way, and my breath hitches in my throat. Even though his face is shadowed, I know who he is.

Karl Weiss.

"What are you talking about?" Mom looks around at me too, but she must not see that my eyes are open, because she turns her attention straight back to Karl.

"You can't keep stringing me along with your fake promises. I'm done waiting around, Celia."

"Please, Karl. Just give me a little longer."

I don't know what they're talking about. I can barely even keep my eyes open, but the memory of the restaurant comes flooding back, and I think I know what they're doing. They're plotting to keep me and Harry apart.

"Ha!" Karl scoffs. "I can still remember the first time you said that. What a fucking idiot I was to believe you."

"No, I meant every word." Mom reaches for his hands, but he snatches them away. "I still do. You know how I feel, Karl, I just never thought... Well, I just never thought it would be so hard with Graham, you know, after the stroke."

Karl rubs his chin with his hand, the scritch-scratch of his stubble rising above the gentle beeping of the monitor. "So, what, you think it'll be easier this time around?"

"No!" Mom shakes her head. "No, but once I've persuaded Ruby to call off this wedding, she'll be free to look after him. I'll tell him then. No looking back."

"What will you tell him?" The question slices the air and sends my pulse racing again.

"Everything. I'll tell him everything."

"Forgive me if I don't believe it's ever going to happen. You don't have the fucking balls. I thought you did back then, but now..." Karl shakes his head. "Now, I'm not so sure."

"I've already got the ball rolling, haven't I?"

"Have you?"

Karl stares straight at me, his dark eyes like bullets, and I close mine quickly, pretending to be asleep. Please don't let him think I'm awake, I repeat inside my head like a mantra. *Please don't let him think I'm awake.* My heart is racing, and it's hard to control my breathing, but something is telling me they mustn't know that I can hear them.

I need time to process what I've overheard. None of it makes sense. Even seeing Karl and my mom in my hospital room makes no sense, and I realize with a heady sigh of relief that I must be hallucinating. The white corridors. The whispers. The maze. It's all just a nightmare prompted by the meds they're pumping into me through the IV in my hand.

I'll laugh about this in the morning. I'll tell Harry, and he'll tease me about all the books I read. "See what happens when you live in fantasy worlds?" I can already hear him chuckling over it.

"What do you think this is then?" My mom snaps.

"I don't know, Celia. You forget that while I've been on my own waiting for you, you've been playing happy family."

"I couldn't leave Ruby. She needed me. It wouldn't have been fair."

"What about me then? Did you care about me at all?"

My breathing is growing shallow again, and I open my eyes. Blink three times. Bring the room back into focus.

They're still there, still standing in front of the window, still speaking in private hushed tones as if no one else exists in the world. I'm not imagining it. This is real, and the jolt of shock as I piece together what I've heard so far, pierces my chest and pins me to the bed.

"I can't believe you're even asking me this. What more can I do to prove it to you?"

"Leave him." A bark more than a growl. "Leave him and be with me like we planned all those years ago. If you love me, you'll do it."

Love? They're talking about love, but it's all out of context. Karl Weiss and my mom. The word doesn't even belong in the same sentence with their names, and no matter how I twist the conversation around in my fuzzy head, I can't seem to make it fit.

"Are you giving me an ultimatum?" Mom's voice is cold.

Karl shrugs. "Sure, why not? I'll give you until Graham is discharged to tell him and then, if you still haven't found the balls, you let me go."

A sound like a sob escapes my mom's mouth. "I'll tell him."

"No, promise me, Celia. You tell him or you let me go and then you'll never hear from me again."

"It doesn't have to be like this, Karl."

"It does." Karl's voice is gentle now. "It just does. I can't spend the rest of my life waiting for you."

He goes to walk away, but my mom grabs his hand, holding onto him for as long as possible. "I need you to promise me something too," she says, and Karl nods. "Ruby must never know that I married the wrong man. She must never find out that you're the man I love."

"She won't hear it from me."

"Thank you." This time, Mom stands on tiptoes and kisses Karl's cheek. "Because she'll never forgive me if she finds out that Graham had his first stroke because of me."

28

HARRY

CELIA ISN'T difficult to follow. Her overwhelming desire to keep me away from her daughter keeps her hanging around the hospital to be sure that I've left. She thinks that I don't spot her with her back to me, talking to a janitor outside the elevator as I pass by.

She could've called me when Ruby was admitted to the hospital. She found us in Scotland for fuck's sake. She turned up at my office in New York. So, I'm pretty damned certain that she could've found a telephone number and let me know, even if she just left a message with Lizzie.

She knew that I'd catch the first available flight out of New York. Hell, she knew that I'd drive if it got me here quicker. Which means that she didn't want me here in Chicago.

But why?

Does she want Ruby to be dependent on her again, to make her realize that all she needs is her mom? If she really loves her daughter, wouldn't she want her to be happy, even if it means swallowing her own pride and sucking up to my father?

I'll deal with my father later but, for now, I follow Celia, hugging the shadows of the buildings and keeping my distance. She doesn't go far. She doesn't even glance over her shoulder as she steps inside the telephone booth and lifts the receiver, head down, punching in the number from a slip of paper she pulls from her pocket.

I stand just inside an alleyway. It has started to drizzle, the kind of icy rain that hardly splashes the puddles on the sidewalk but drenches you without you even realizing. I pull my collar up around my neck, and peer out from behind the wall.

She glances my way, and I duck my head back inside the alley. Count to ten. Look again as she replaces the handset.

Stepping out of the booth, she pulls an umbrella from her purse, unfolds it above her head, and dashes across the road, dodging the sparse evening traffic easily. I wait for a bus to pass by and follow.

Heading back towards the hospital, Celia dashes inside a late-night diner, shaking water from the umbrella and folding it back up in the doorway. I wait on the opposite side of the road, following her through the steamy windows with my eyes to a seat in the corner where I can see the bright green of her coat.

I watch the waitress pouring coffee for Celia. Through the rain-streaked window, I see her watching the street like she's waiting for someone. She could just be taking a break from hospital visits, a moment to herself to unwind before catching a taxi home. Before listening to Ms. Pagan's message, this would've been my first conclusion, but now... Now I'm almost certain that she arranged to meet someone here, and I want to find out who.

Celia has already set the tone of playing dirty to keep Ruby away from me, so I'm not above playing her at her own game. *The winner takes it all.* Isn't that how the song goes?

Rain trickles inside my collar and down my spine, and I shiver. The buildings on either side of the narrow alleyway offer some shelter, but my hair is already plastered to my head. Fortunately, I don't have to wait long.

A familiar figure walks past the diner window, shoulders hunched inside his overcoat, chin jutting. Celia sits taller, her body subconsciously leaning towards the doorway as my father goes inside and joins her at her table-for-two.

It's several beats before my brain processes what I've just witnessed and starts functioning again. My gut had been right when Ruby and I walked into Charlie Trotter's and saw them together—they're colluding to stop Ruby from marrying me.

But I can still hear the PI's message left on my answerphone: *"Seems Mrs. Jackson might be suffering from a touch of insomnia. Either that, or she was enjoying a secret rendezvous with her lover."*

What else had she said though? *This one is different.*

Different how?

I can't put my finger on it, but I get the strong sense that she is right. Not lovers. But what then? This can't just be about me and Ruby, can it? *Forget what happened thirteen years ago, let's just make sure our kids don't get hitched.*

I've hardly slept in the past forty-eight hours, and this coupled with the alcohol consumed at the Plaza Hotel earlier in the day is making me drowsy, but I dare not get a takeout coffee from somewhere nearby in case I miss them leaving. Whatever is going on here, I want to hear it from my father's own mouth.

I tilt my face towards the rain and catch the icy drops on my tongue. It isn't caffeine, but it helps.

Loitering in the shadows, I'm grateful that the cold January weather keeps most folks inside. Which makes it easy for me to slip out onto the sidewalk when Celia and my dad leave the diner together and follow them back to the hospital.

Who are they visiting? Ruby or Graham? Has Celia persuaded my dad to make peace with my future father-in-law?

I grab a magazine from the table and take a seat in the main hospital entrance, where the heat hits me almost instantly. Skipping an article on improved healthcare packages, I settle instead on the personal story of a young woman who spent her childhood in the care system and went on to become a heart surgeon. My eyelids grow heavy...

I'm shaken awake by a rough hand on my shoulder.

I jump, drop the magazine onto the table, and blink furiously, trying to clear the sleep from my eyes and bring the world back into focus. "Dad? What are you doing here?"

Fuck! It hits me then that I was supposed to be trailing him and not the other way around. I have no idea how long I've been dozing, or where he has been.

"I could say the same to you." He straightens his spine stiffly. "Got nowhere to sleep for the night?"

"No... I..." I stand up and grab my carry-on, grateful to find it still there by my feet. One thing is for certain, I'll never make a private investigator. "I was waiting for you."

Realization crosses his face. "Let's walk. I could do with some fresh air."

His strides are wide and strong; he doesn't glance over his shoulder to see if I'm following him. He knows I will.

"Were you here to see Graham?" The nap hasn't done much to clear my head, and I'm thinking on my feet, trying to figure out how best to approach this conversation.

Karl Weiss has never been the kind of father who will sit down and discuss important matters, he'd rather bottle it up, wait for a solution to present itself, and move on. He's from an era when people believed that personal issues were supposed to stay that way—personal—and pushing him will only make him angry. When that happens, it's game over.

"What do you think?"

After the sauna-heat inside the hospital, the cold night air is like a slap in the face. I don't ask where we're going. "Ruby then?"

I match his stride, glancing at his profile, but he doesn't look at me, barely acknowledges my presence. To an outsider, he would appear to be a man minding his own business while I harass him for money to buy a coffee.

He stops at traffic signal and waits for the lights to change color. "Out with it, son. I didn't raise you to be a fucking coward."

I bristle, shoulders instinctively hunching up around my neck. I don't know why I expected anything less.

My father views kindness as weakness, an opening to allow someone to shoot an arrow straight through the heart and leave you broken. Things might've been different if he'd allowed himself time to grieve my mom, but instead, he donned his suit and went straight back to work, staying in the office until late, and making sure he was the first one there in the mornings.

Maybe that's why he doesn't want me to marry Ruby—he doesn't want to see me broken too. But I am nothing like him.

"You're right, Dad. You didn't. And you know what, I don't care what you and Celia are plotting together, because it isn't going to work. I'm not afraid of getting my heart broken. I love—"

I don't finish because he shoves me back across the sidewalk, my spine hitting the wall of the bank on the corner of the street. I drop my carry-on. His hand closes around my throat, the steam of his breath mingling with mine. He isn't strangling me. It's a warning: don't cross the line or else.

"You don't have a fucking clue about love." His spit hits me in the face as he hisses the words. "What would you do for her, huh?"

"I-what?"

"I want to know. What would you do for Ruby Jackson, this woman you claim to love so much?"

A young man, leather jacket, faded jeans, walks past, hesitates, and takes a couple of steps back. "What's going on here? You alright, buddy?" He aims this at me.

"It's cool." I widen my eyes at him, hoping that he'll move on. "Family stuff." I hear the snort of air leaving my dad's nostrils and ignore it. He deserves to be embarrassed.

The guy nods and keeps walking.

"I'd do anything for her."

My dad's eyes are slits in the yellow glow of the streetlamp above our heads. "Would you wait for her?"

"Of course I would."

"So, what's the fucking rush? Scared she won't feel the same way about you?"

"She does feel the same way." I don't understand what point he's trying to prove. "Love doesn't have to be a test. I don't need Ruby to pass some kind of initiation ceremony for me to believe that she loves me too."

He grabs my coat collar, pushes me against the wall one last time, and then releases me. I exhale deeply, unaware that I'd been holding it in my lungs, my knees trembling.

"How long would you wait for her?" he asks.

"What? I don't know, as long as it takes, I guess. But it's a moot point because we've already set the date."

"Cancel it. Tell her you've changed your mind. You want to wait a while, do it properly instead of rushing into it. Every woman dreams of a big white wedding. Tell her you'll make it worth the wait."

My brain is soaking up the words—more than he has ever said to me in one conversation before—and forming them into something I can make sense of. Is he buying him and Celia some time to turn me and Ruby against each other? Or is he truly hopeful that we'll realize what a huge mistake we're making?

"No. Ruby isn't like that. She doesn't want the big white wedding; she'd rather keep it simple." *It's not about the wedding, it's about the person you're marrying*, that's what she said.

"So, promise her whatever she fucking wants then." He swallows, looks away, like he's searching for the ace card on the wet sidewalk. "If she loves you, she'll wait."

"But I don't want to wait. Life's too short…"

A vision of glaring headlamps pops into my head, screeching tires, the volcanic sounds of metal-on-metal.

His shoulders slump inside his heavy coat, and he bows his head. "Maybe not as short as you think." He keeps walking, and I jog to catch up with him, my carry-on dragging behind me.

"What's that supposed to mean?"

He doesn't look at me.

"Dad! Talk to me. What the hell is going on here?"

"Go home, son." He crosses the road in front of an oncoming vehicle, and the driver hits the brakes, tires slipping across wet tarmac.

I raise a hand, yell, "Sorry!" to the driver, and chase after my dad.

He hears my footsteps, turns around, and grinds out between clenched jaws, "I said, go home, Harry. Go on. Fuck off!"

"Yeah, I know what you said, but I can be a stubborn bastard too."

He shakes his head, a half-smile tugging one corner of his mouth. "I got something right then."

My brain has been playing catch-up since he woke me up in the hospital, and now the reason I was there in the first place comes flooding back, sucking the air from my lungs. My dad and Celia Jackson. She called him from the telephone booth, and he came.

He came.

He wasn't there to visit Graham or Ruby; he was there because of Celia.

How long would you wait for Ruby?

"Thirteen years," I mumble under my breath, the truth crawling under my skin and squeezing my chest.

"Fucking bingo." His voice is thick with emotion.

"Celia Jackson?"

It doesn't sound right, the name on my tongue, not when I'm facing my dad. Talia Pagan said this one was different—not a case of the cheating wife. She'd seen something else, and she was trained to know what she was looking for.

"How long...?" Stupid question, I already know the answer. "I mean how did you... When did it start?"

My dad rubs the rain from his face with his hands and tilts his head towards the sky. "Wrong tense."

"What do you mean?"

He sighs heavily. "The question isn't, *when did it start*? The question is, *will it ever happen*?"

He walks away, and this time I let him go.

29

RUBY

After Karl leaves, my mom doesn't move for a long while like she's frozen in place by the window, something binding her there in case he comes back.

He doesn't.

I stay completely still. My pulse is racing, and my breathing is too shallow, but she doesn't approach the bed. I get an itch in my lower back, and I suck on my bottom lip, trying to ignore it as it spreads across my skin, clamoring for my attention. Just as I think I'm getting it under control, the pain flares in my abdomen again, and I pant through it, praying that she is too preoccupied to notice.

Once it has passed, I open my eyes, and she is gone.

First things first, I slide my hand beneath the covers and around to my back to scratch the tingling skin. The relief is almost instantaneous.

Then, I stare at the ceiling and replay their conversation in my head. Snippets of their voices fading in and out of my head, trying to hear what they were avoiding saying out loud.

They knew each other thirteen years ago, that much was obvious, only I never realized how well they'd known each other. My mom had always made it sound like the friction occurred between Karl Weiss and my dad—she totally downplayed her own role in their problems. And now, she wants to leave my dad for him... *That man!*

Tears sting my eyes when I think of them together. She doesn't even care how it will affect my dad because if I don't marry Harry, I'll be here to look after him.

Anger swirls around inside my chest, red-hot and bubbling at the way she dismissed my dad's feelings as if they counted for nothing. All these years she stayed with him when she really wanted to be with another man. I don't even recognize her anymore. The woman who stood in my room and promised Karl Weiss that she would leave my dad isn't my mom. She can't be.

But that isn't what's making my heart go slip-sliding around inside my chest. It's what she said before Karl left and after he issued his ultimatum: *"Ruby must never know that I married the wrong man. She must never find out that I'm in love with you."*

Why did she marry my dad if she didn't love him? Why live a lie all these years if she was that unhappy?

My thoughts start tumbling into a rabbit-hole that I might never be able to crawl out of. What else don't I know about her? How many other secrets has she been hiding from me and my dad? Did she know Karl before they even met?

But then, the final piece of the puzzle stabs me in the chest like a knife.

My dad's stroke wasn't caused by the stress of losing his business. It was the stress of finding out that his wife was in love with another man. She isn't trying to protect me with this secret, she's trying to protect herself.

I can't stay here and wait for her to come back in the morning. I won't be able to face her. I won't be able to look her in the eye ever again and pretend that everything is alright.

I push back the covers and sit up, swinging my legs over the side of the bed. The room spins, and I grip the edge of the mattress tightly to stop myself from toppling forwards. My hand stings, dragging me back to reality, and I wrench the cannula of the IV out, tossing it onto the floor. Blood wells on the back of my hand, but I ignore it.

I'm wearing the pajamas that I was wearing when mom brought me into the emergency room. I open the nightstand, hoping to find clothes that will make me look less conspicuous, but I only find clean panties. She didn't even bring my purse. My coat is on the back of the chair though—it will have to do.

Slipping my arms into it and fastening it over my pajamas, I pull on my boots and tiptoe to the door. I open it a crack, wincing at the clicking sound. Outside, the corridors are dimmed, the hospital dozing for the night.

I hold my breath, step outside, and close the door behind me. Hushed murmurs to my right, a chuckle followed by a question: "What are you wearing to Stacey's bachelorette party next week?" Must be the nurse's station.

Left it is.

I stick close to the wall, out of sight of the nurses, my heart hammering inside my chest. I've no idea where I'm going. All I know is, I'm not staying. I'm not going to be here when she comes back with her fake smiles and her perfect makeup and her, "I'll look after you, sweetie."

"Like fuck you will," I whisper to myself. My mom has only ever looked after one person: my mom.

Through the swing doors, and I'm in another corridor with a sign that points to the elevators. I can't risk using them in case a member of the staff gets in on a lower level. I head in the opposite direction to the stairwell, push open the heavy fire door and am greeted by a rush of cold air. It hits my face with a whump at the same time as pain flares inside my abdomen.

I let go of the door, watch it closing slowly, the stairs disappearing behind it. My escape route. Clutching my stomach, I bend double, holding the pain in, focusing on breathing through it. My knees hit the floor, and I don't even know how it happened, and then the world goes black.

"Ruby... Can you hear me, Ruby?"

A woman's voice. I push her away and open my eyes, my cheek on the cool tiled floor. "How did I..." I roll onto my knees, try to stand up, but my legs feel like Jell-O, and I lean against the wall for support.

"Ruby, I want to help you."

I move my eyes, waiting for my head to play ball, and look at the woman who owns the voice. I don't know her, but I recognize the blue uniform. She's a nurse. She's going to stop me from leaving.

"I can manage." I push myself away from the wall, sway giddily, and instinctively grab her warm hand to keep me upright. "I'm fine."

"Come with me." She keeps her voice low, and it seems strange, but I'm still wallowing in the dull ache that follows the pain, and my brain is screaming at me to get away from her.

"I'm not going back." I tug my hand from hers. "You can't make me go back."

She twists her mouth to one side as if preparing to debate that point, sucks in a deep breath, and places an arm around my shoulders before I can dodge her. "Look, I don't know what has happened tonight, but I won't take you back to your room. I promise."

"You w-won't?" Tears sting my eyes like I just found my guardian angel.

"I want to help you, Ruby."

"You know my name."

"Yes. Will you trust me?"

How can I trust her when I don't even know who she is? She could be a murderer disguised as a nurse. She might go around killing patients and making it look like they died of natural causes or complications with their condition. She might drag me into the stairwell and slit my throat.

But there's something familiar about her, and I guess she must've been looking after me since I was admitted. I'm not afraid of her. I don't know why, but I believe her.

"I trust you."

"Thank you." A glimmer of a familiar smile, gone before it's fully there. "My name is Melanie."

Realization spreads through me like a blackcurrant cordial spilt on a white tablecloth. Melanie. Harry's sister is called Melanie. The smile... It belongs to Harry, not this woman.

"Are you..."

"Shh." She raises a finger to her lips. "I'll explain everything later."

"Where are we going?" I follow her into the chilly stairwell, leaning on her for support, incredulous at how weak I feel.

"I'm taking you home with me."

MELANIE'S APARTMENT is small and cozy. She settles me on the sofa and covers me with a soft, fluffy blanket while she makes hot chocolate. I can see her from the sofa, fetching mugs from the wall cabinet in the kitchen, and spooning cocoa powder into them while the kettle chugs to life.

While she's busy, I peer around the room. It's filled with stuff. The sofa and armchair are piled high with cushions. The TV is on a stand filled with VHS tapes. The coffee table and every other available surface is littered with magazines and books, tiny porcelain dogs and cats, and dishes filled with shells and pebbles and sea glass. There's barely a space that isn't covered by something, but it also feels like a place in which to relax.

Melanie comes in with two cups, shoves some magazines aside to clear a space on the coffee table, and sets them down. Then she lights a cinnamon scented candle with a match and sits in the armchair, one leg curled underneath her.

It's quite surreal studying her face, which is Harry's face but with larger eyes and softer curves. Her hair is all soft waves that tumble over her shoulders now that she has set them free from their ponytail. I have so many questions, but she speaks first.

"Is Harry here? In Chicago, I mean?"

I wince. I remember hearing his voice, but so much of what has happened since I got sick has been nothing more than a hallucination, and I might've just imagined it.

"I don't know." I chew my bottom lip. How much do I tell her? "He has been looking for you."

She sips her hot chocolate, blinking as the scalding heat brings tears to her eyes. "He won't find me. I changed my name ... after I left."

"Why?"

She raises her eyebrows and smiles. "Now, there's the million-dollar question."

"We're getting married. Harry would love it if you came to the wedding."

She takes a deep breath. I don't know why she disappeared after their mom died, but there's a reason why she reached out to help me now, so perhaps I can convince her to come. I must at least try.

"I don't know." She shakes her head. "I haven't been back to New York since... Well, in a long while."

"How did you know me?" It's the question burning a hole in my tongue. I know that she could've checked the hospital records, but I sense that I was more than just a name to her, or I wouldn't be here now.

"I saw Harry after the accident. I wasn't on his ward, but I saw his name mentioned in the news report and I had to know that he was okay. You were there too. The blizzard?"

I blink. That's where I recognize her from. "The night nurse."

She laughs, and she sounds so much like Harry that I can't help smiling. "Damn! I thought I'd gotten away with it unnoticed." She pauses. "Call it sibling intuition, but I had a feeling that you were important to my brother. How did you meet?"

I tell her about the skating rink—it feels like years ago now—the party, and the car crash. "I had to know that he was alright too."

"And you ignored the weather warnings."

I wrinkle my nose. "I guess I wasn't going to let a bit of snow stand in the path of true love."

We talk about Edinburgh and Gretna Green and Harry's proposal, and I flash the diamond ring at her. "I can't believe I've only known him for a few weeks. It feels like he's always been in my life."

"I'm glad. He's a good boy."

"Spoken like a true big sis."

She laughs again, but I can't hear it through the pain. I see the way her eyes widen, and then she's on her knees on the floor beside the couch, and squeezing my hand, and I can hear her telling me to breathe. "That's it, Ruby, deep breath in through your nose. Good girl." I cling to her voice and her hand while my stomach feels like it's going to explode.

Finally, the pain ebbs, and she tells me to hold tight while she fetches a glass of water from the kitchen. I sip it slowly, hand trembling, tracking the chill as it goes down.

"How are you feeling?" Her eyes roam my face, noting the sweat on my forehead even though I'm shivering.

"Better."

Her expression doesn't alter. She knows I'm lying, she's a nurse.

"What's wrong with me?" My voice, laced with tears, sounds puny.

"I've seen your test results, Ruby. Looking out for you was the least I could do for my brother after leaving him behind," she explains.

When she doesn't elaborate, I ask, "Am I pregnant?"

"No." She reaches for my hand and nestles it between her own warm palms. "Your symptoms were a little like food poisoning. Can you remember eating something that might have triggered it?"

I rummage around inside my memories of the past couple of days, the meal that got scrapped, the hot dogs Harry and I picked up on our way back to his hotel. I can't even recall what I've eaten since then.

"Hot dogs. But we both ate them, and Harry didn't get sick."

Melanie shakes her head. "Not that. Have you drunk water that might've been contaminated? Or eaten rice or shellfish that wasn't washed properly?" When I say no, she continues, "What about pesticides? Have you come into contact with weedkillers or been inside a building that had been sprayed with some kind of insecticide?"

I shake my head, confused. "What are you saying?"

"I don't want you to panic, Ruby, but your test results came back showing traces of a compound linked to arsenic."

30

HARRY

I'VE ONLY BEEN asleep for an hour when the telephone in my hotel room wakes me up with an early-morning alarm call. I thank the receptionist and replace the handset, lying back on the pillow and groaning out loud. My head is fuzzy with tiredness, but I want to get to the hospital before any other visitors arrive.

Before Celia arrives.

My tired brain refused to switch off after my conversation with my father. Him and Celia Jackson. Ruby's mom and my dad. No matter which way I look at it, I can't quite slot the final pieces of the puzzle into place. Where does this even leave me and Ruby?

I want to speak to her alone before her mom arrives. I'm unsure how much I'm going to tell her, but my dad will have told Celia about our conversation, and I don't want her to manipulate Ruby further, especially while she's unwell and vulnerable.

I take a hot shower, grab some pancakes on my way to the hospital, and stop off at reception when I arrive to check that Ruby hasn't been moved to a different ward.

"Ms. Jackson left a message for you, sir." The woman hands me a sealed envelope.

I move away from the desk, open the envelope, and read the brief note contained inside.

Harry,

Come to E 65th Street, block 22, apartment 13.

I'll explain when you get here. Don't tell anyone else.

Ruby x

I peer all around the atrium as if I might find Ruby giggling behind a column, waiting for me to take her home. But she isn't there.

I go back to the desk. "When did Ms. Jackson leave this here for me?"

"I'm sorry, sir." The woman shakes her head. "I only started my shift a short while ago. This was left for me in the handover book."

I go to walk away and change my mind. "Can you please check which ward Ms. Jackson is in?"

She glances at the screen in front of her, eyelids flickering. "Ms. Jackson has been discharged."

I thank her and walk away, turning the letter over and checking to see if I haven't missed anything. The message might not have been left by Ruby but it's all I have right now, and I won't rest until I've checked it out.

E 65th is a long street lined on one side by low apartment buildings overlooking a school playing field. I find the right apartment, ring the buzzer, and wait for the external door to open.

When it does, Ruby appears in the doorway wearing her coat over pajama bottoms tucked inside fur-lined boots. Her face is still pale, but she throws her arms around my neck and holds me tightly. "Take me home, Harry."

"Home?" I hold her at arm's length and study her face.

"New York."

"Are you going to tell me what's going on?"

"Not until we're there."

We take a taxi to Ruby's house and I wait outside, standing sentinel, while she collects some clothes, her favorite teddy from when she was a little girl, and a photograph of her dad from his dancing competition days. Celia isn't there. Ruby doesn't mention her mom, doesn't even speculate on where she might be, and I don't press it. I suspect that she knows more than she is letting on.

When the taxi pulls away to take us to the Chicago airport, she doesn't even peer at the house through the passenger window.

It's early evening when we reach my apartment in New York. I order takeout noodles, and we eat them with chopsticks, sitting on the sofa overlooking the city skyline, the tartan blankets thrown across our legs. Ruby is still weak and nauseous, but the pains are gradually easing off, and she slept off the last remnants of the sedatives on the plane.

I wait for her to begin when she's ready.

"My mom is the reason my dad had his first stroke."

There's no emotion in her voice, and I wonder how long she has been protecting this information. Long enough to understand what she wants to do with it, I suspect.

"I overheard them in my hospital room. They thought I was asleep. Your dad gave her an ultimatum: leave my dad, or they're over." She faces me then, dry-eyed, and it breaks my heart that she had to deal with this alone. I'm doing a shit job of protecting her so far. "She made him promise never to let me find out."

Her eyes lock onto mine as if searching for something that only she knows about.

Finally, she says, "You already knew."

I feel her pulling away from me, and I move the noodle cartons onto the coffee table so that I can snuggle under her blanket, sharing my body heat with her. "I saw them together last night. I followed them to the hospital. I was going to confront them, but I fell asleep, and my dad woke me up. He was alone."

"He told you?"

I shake my head. "My dad doesn't know how to express his feelings. He asked me how long I would wait for you if I couldn't marry you now, and I said as long as it takes."

She sucks on her smile as a lone tear trickles from the corner of her eye.

"He told me to try thirteen years."

Ruby closes her eyes, her lashes thick and damp, and I know that she isn't crying for herself, she's crying for her dad.

"Ruby, do you want me to see if I can get your dad transferred to a hospital here in New York?"

"Can you do that?"

"I can try. We're in this together, remember. I promised to make you happy, Ruby. But I think you should talk to your mom."

"No." Her lips pinch together. "She lied to me my whole life. I could never do that to my children."

"Maybe she thought she was protecting you."

"You don't know her like I do, Harry. She was protecting herself. The night I met you, she'd set her sights on Alessandro Russo as her future son-in-law." A joyless laugh escapes her lips. "Even that was a lie. She wanted me to marry someone rich so that I would take my dad off her hands."

My heart swells with love for this woman sitting next to me. She's hurting right now, but I know I can make everything better. I can take her away from all this, build a new life for us on the foundations of love and honesty and trust, now that she has told me the truth.

"Then we'll give her what she wants."

Ruby blinks at me as if I've grown a second head.

"We'll take him off her hands, set her free if that's what she wants. You're all that matters to me. Your happiness. Your future. Your life."

"Harry..." Ruby scrunches up her face, psyching herself up for what she has to say next. "Alessandro... The night before..."

"Hey." I pull her against me and kiss her eyelids, her cheeks, her lips. "It's okay. I already know."

"You do? He told you?"

"It doesn't matter how I know. It will never happen to you again, Ruby. You're going to get better, I'll make sure of it, because you have lots to do."

She smiles then, and I'm reminded all over again of how beautiful she is. "Don't think I'm running errands for you while you sit in your nice cozy office."

"I think you might enjoy these errands."

"Hmm, I reserve the right to pass judgment until I know what they are."

"Okay, number one, you have a wedding to plan." I raise a finger in the air, and then a second. "Two, you have a honeymoon to buy clothes for, and three..."

"You haven't thought of three yet, have you?"

"Three..." I keep her waiting. "You have a new apartment to find."

Her smile is kind of wistful, not the full-on moonbeam smile I was expecting. "You know I'm not interested in a swanky apartment, right? You know I'll be happy living anywhere with you."

"I know. Call it a wedding gift."

"A wedding gift? You mean there's going to be more than one?"

"You'll have to wait and see, won't you?" I kiss the tip of her nose and go to clear up the cartons when she stops me with a hand on my arm.

"Harry, there's one more thing I haven't told you."

I sit back. "Whose apartment you were in this morning?"

Her eyes widen, and she stares out the window, at the city lights beyond. "No, that was just a friend from college. She works in the hospital. She found me when I was trying to sneak out in the night, took me home, and made me hot chocolate." She faces me then, not quite meeting my gaze. "She saw my test results."

My heart skips a beat and starts up again, gathering speed. I can't speak. I won't be able to bear it if there's something seriously wrong with Ruby.

"She said..." Ruby's bottom lip disappears behind her teeth. "She said I had arsenic poisoning."

The blanket is suddenly too hot. I shove it off my legs and stand up. I go to the window, turning the words over inside my head—*arsenic poisoning, arsenic poisoning, arsenic poisoning*—but the view is too busy, and I can't concentrate.

"What the fuck, Ruby?" I turn around to face her. "How does that even happen?"

"Turns out you can get it from contaminated water or by inhaling pesticides."

"But not in your case."

She shrugs. "I can't think of anything, but that doesn't mean—"

I'm on my knees in front of her, squeezing her hand. "Does she think someone was trying to poison you? Be honest with me, Ruby. Does she?"

My thoughts are spinning around while I wait for her to answer.

"Maybe. The hospital is investigating my results. According to Mel-my friend, my parents will be questioned."

I'm back on my feet, pacing the living room, hands balled into fists. Her parents will be questioned as a matter of procedure, investigating Ruby's lifestyle, recent activities, her mental health. But that will take time, and there's no guarantee that they'll find anything conclusive. Then what? What happens when they draw blanks all round?

I already know the answer. I vowed to protect Ruby, and that's exactly what I'm going to do. I'll find the fucker who poisoned her if it's the last thing I do.

"Who? Who would do such a thing? Why would anyone want to hurt you?"

"Harry, sit down." Ruby pats the cushion next to her. "I'm safe now. It'll take a little while to get out of my system, but I'll be okay."

"It could've killed you." The situation is magnified by a hundred times when I say the words out loud. "Whoever did this is not going to get away with it, Ruby. I swear I'll hunt them down and make them pay. They'll wish they'd picked on someone else by the time I'm finished with them."

"Please, Harry. Leave it. I'm not going back to Chicago."

But I'm not listening to her. Who would want to hurt Ruby? Why would someone try to poison her? Why poison? My thoughts are colliding like the bumper cars at Coney Island, crashing into each other and spinning off at tangents. I'll find them. I won't stop until I do, because no one hurts Ruby Jackson and gets away with it.

My dad's face, when he pinned me up against the wall with his hand around my throat, pops into my head. I pick up the phone and dial his home number. I expect it to go through to the answering machine and am surprised when he says hello.

"Dad, it's me, Harry." Silence. "Did you poison Ruby?"

More silence, the seconds ticking away with the beat of my heart. Ruby gasps from the sofa.

"Is that what you think of me?"

The adrenaline rush fades as quickly as it began, and I sit heavily on the edge of the sofa, the phone still pressed to my ear. "No."

"Glad to fucking hear it." The line goes dead.

"Harry, you don't really think your dad would do that, do you?" Ruby's arm snakes around me, and she rests her head on my shoulder.

"No." He can be intimidating, and rude, and ruthless when he wants to be, but is he a murderer? "I have to make another call."

"Now?" She sits back.

I'm on my feet and pacing the floor again. Carlos Russo answers his office phone on the third ring.

"How's Ruby?" he asks.

"Better than she was. She's here with me."

"Good, because I need to see you in the office tomorrow."

I don't know how I can even think about the new venture, but I agree to meet him anyway. "Carlos, I need your help with another matter. I promise this will be the last thing I ever ask you."

His laughter booms out of the telephone and bounces across the room. "You should never make promises you cannot keep. I'll see you in the morning, bright and early."

I hang up and pull Ruby into my arms, smoothing her hair away from her face. "Everything is going to be okay. I don't want you to worry about a thing."

She relaxes against me, and I allow my eyes to close, content in the knowledge that I never have to let her out of my sight again.

As I drift off, the lack of sleep finally catching up with me, I remember that I haven't been entirely honest with her. I'm keeping one tiny secret, just until our wedding day, but I know she's going to love it when she finds out.

31

RUBY

I watch Harry emerge from the steamy bathroom and stroll back into the bedroom, a bath towel wrapped around his waist, his chest still damp. He towel-dries his hair, flinging water across the room. Coconut scented shower gel wafts my way, and I can't help smiling at him from the bed. He's totally oblivious to his charm. Still.

Maybe that's part of it—Harry isn't one of those arrogant assholes who walk into a room and check out the women checking them out, knowing they can snap their fingers and take their pick.

"What?" He stops rubbing his hair and quirks his lips at me. "Did I cut myself shaving?" He touches his chin tentatively.

"Uh-huh." I push back the bedcovers and crawl across the bed towards him.

When I'm within touching distance, I slide my hand underneath the towel wrapped around his waist and stroke his cock which immediately springs to life.

"Right here." I lick my lips and release the towel, dropping it onto the floor before I take him into my mouth and tease him with my tongue. He's warm and silky smooth, and I find myself grabbing his hips and pulling him into me as far as I can take him.

If anyone had told me a year ago that I would meet a man who made me feel like this, I wouldn't have believed them. It's as if Harry has unlocked something deep inside me, an inner sex goddess I never knew existed, and now that I've tasted him, I can't get enough.

Harry's fingers entwine with my hair, holding me still while he moves his hips, sliding his cock out of my mouth, rubbing it across my lips, and back in again gently. Never too far. Giving me just enough to leave me wanting more. I cup his balls with my hands, massaging the tender skin behind them until I hear him groan out loud.

Then I suck harder. I squeeze the base of his cock with one hand, still stroking his balls with the other, and slide my hand up and down, growing faster in tune with Harry's panting breaths. I love that I can do this to him. It's like suddenly finding out that I possess a superpower that no one else has, singling me out from every other woman in the world and making me feel special.

I stop before I make him come.

Our bodies are so in tune with one another that I barely have a chance to release him before he pushes me back onto the bed, spreads my legs wide, and fucks me with his tongue and two fingers. My orgasm is quick and hard. Harry's tongue is relentless, waiting for me to explode again, my knees spread wide by his so that I can't wriggle away from him.

He keeps going, licking, nibbling, sucking.

My head reels. All sense of awareness deserts me as my orgasm chases his tongue, wanting it to end and wanting it to be all that I ever feel for the rest of my life. When Harry slides inside me, my brain is numb, every nerve ending in my body still tingling.

He smooths my hair away from my face, gripping it so tightly my eyes become slits. "I love you, Ruby. You're the fucking world to me."

I wrap my arms around his neck and hold onto him, kissing him while his body jerks, his groans swallowed by my mouth. Finally, I can't keep my feelings in check anymore as I proclaim, "I love you, Harry Weiss."

Harry smooths my hair away from my face, drinking me in with his eyes. His lips caress my eyelids, my cheekbones, the tip of my nose, my jawline down to the base of my throat. It's the most romantic, the most tender moment that we have ever shared, and my heart swells with love for this man. When his lips come back to meet mine, he murmurs, "Do you have any idea how much I love you and how happy you make me, Ruby Jackson?"

It doesn't need answering.

We lay together, Harry on top of me, my pussy clenching and unclenching, pushing him out of me slowly. A chuckle escapes my lips, and he rolls off me and onto his back on the bed.

"Morning." His smile is so filled with love that I wish I could capture it in a tiny precious box and bring it out whenever I'm feeling any less than I do in this perfect moment.

"Morning. I think you're going to be late for the office."

"Fuck the office." He plants a kiss on my lips and sinks

backward onto the bed again, and I know that he feels the same.

"Does that mean you're staying home today?"

"Do you want me to?"

I do, but I have plans for today that don't include Harry.

I've been living in his apartment for three weeks, and New York is already starting to feel like home. The barista in the coffee shop close to where we live already knows that I like my coffee extra-hot with a sprinkling of chocolate and cinnamon on top. The woman who lives on the first floor of Harry's building with a white fluffy dog called Pebbles always stops to say hi while I stroke behind the dog's ears, and the dog licks my hand in greeting.

I still gape in the windows of Tiffany's whenever I walk past, but that's something that will never change.

Harry managed to get my dad transferred to a private clinic in the city, where I can visit him every day between physio sessions. He has stopped asking what happened between me and Mom. He understands that it was bad enough for me to leave Chicago, but he also knows that I'll tell him when I'm ready.

I'm seeing him today, but Harry already knows this.

What he doesn't know is that Melanie is in New York for a couple of days, and I'm meeting up with her. She isn't ready for me to tell Harry yet, and I have to respect her wishes. I feel bad for keeping it a secret when he has been so honest right from the first time we met, but I have a plan, and if it works, I know that he'll forgive me.

I wrinkle my nose now and roll away from him. I stand, pick up the damp towels he dropped on the bedroom floor, and hold them at arm's length. "Not today. I'm busy."

He stands and retrieves a pair of boxers from the chest of drawers, turning his back while he pulls them up like I haven't seen him naked before. "Wedding stuff?"

"Uh-huh."

He takes out some black socks and pulls them on too. "You're not going to tell me what it is, are you?"

"Nu-huh."

Without warning, he tackles me onto the bed, tickling the tender spot on my sides until I curl up into a ball, giggling and begging him to stop.

"Not until you tell me what it is."

"No..." I choke out between bouts of laughter. "Stop, Harry. I can't breathe."

"Tell me."

His cast has been removed, and it feels as if he has eight arms like a spider rather than two. His fingers are everywhere, and I give into them, my body twitching of its own accord every time he hits the spot.

"I'm going wedding dress shopping," I blurt out.

He stops and sits on the bed beside me, offering his hand to help me upright. "Fuck. Sorry. I shouldn't have pressured you into telling me."

"It's fine, Harry."

I've left it a bit late, and who knows if I'll be able to find the dress I want and have it altered in time for the wedding which is only three weeks away, but I'm going to have fun trying. I didn't leave the apartment for the first week, and when I finally felt well enough to venture outside alone, I couldn't bring myself to think about it. Not after my mom's betrayal.

I know it's my dad who should feel betrayed, but she lied to me too. All these years, she didn't even want to be with us. I don't even know who she is anymore.

I should've been shopping for a wedding dress with my mom, but instead, I'm going with Melanie. I only met her briefly before I left Chicago, but we have spoken almost every day since, and she is already starting to feel like the sister I never had. Besides, I'm marrying her brother.

Harry kisses my lips. "I promise I won't ask again."

"It's fine," I repeat. "It feels kinda weird doing all this without you."

"I know I've been busy with work, but it will be worth it when we're on our honeymoon and you have me all to yourself. You'll be begging me to leave you alone after a few days."

"A few days?" I frown at him, lips tugged into a lopsided smile. "Two days, max."

He laughs out loud, pinching his thumb and forefinger together like pincers. "I'll tickle you again if you're not careful."

I watch him get dressed in an expensive gray suit, waiting for my favorite part of the morning ritual: fastening his tie. My dad taught me how to do it when I was a little girl, and I would rise early every morning just to help him fasten his tie in front of the full-length mirror in the bedroom he shared with my mom.

Now, Harry stands by the bed, and I kneel in front of him, tucking the tie beneath his collar, measuring the lengths on either side to make sure they're equal. I fold and tug until I've made a neat knot at the front and a perfect dimple just below, sitting back on my heels and surveying my handiwork.

"How do I look?" He spreads his arms wide and gives me a twirl.

"Ready." I allow my gaze to drift pointedly down to his pants. "Apart from one thing." I stroke the bulge of his erection through the material.

He smiles and pulls away. "Much more of that, and you'll be walking down the aisle naked."

Harry brings me coffee in bed before he leaves.

"You're spoiling me." I sip the steaming liquid and settle back against the pillows. I'm getting too used to this. I know that I'll have to get a job eventually, after the wedding, but it would be so easy to be a kept woman, easier than I could've ever imagined.

"I'm never going to stop spoiling you, Ruby Jackson." He leans closer and kisses the tip of my nose. "What do you want me to do if your mom calls again today?"

Mom has been calling Harry's office every day—multiple times a day—since I left Chicago. I haven't returned her calls or bothered listening to her messages. Lizzie said that my mom sounded angry when she discovered that my dad had been transferred, demanding that Harry or I return her calls.

I know that I'll have to face her at the wedding if she comes, but I'm not ready to listen to more of her lies. Not yet.

"Nothing." I smile at Harry. "I don't want you to do anything."

"Oh my God." Melanie covers her face with both hands, peeping out at me over the top of her fingertips. "You look ... beautiful, Ruby."

The wedding gown I'm wearing has a heart-shaped boned bodice and flares out at the waist into a huge ball gown, covered in layers of frothy white tulle sprinkled with tiny diamantes. It isn't the dress I would've chosen for myself, but I've tried on so many gowns now that my stomach is rumbling with hunger, and my legs are trembling.

I stare at my reflection in the mirror trying to suppress the memory of the terrible nightmare I suffered when I was sick. Seems I never really knew my own mind. This is the dress that Harry would've chosen for me given the opportunity, and now that I'm wearing it, I can see how utterly perfect it is. I feel ... beautiful. Special.

I feel worthy of marrying a man like Harry Weiss.

"What do you think?" Melanie dabs her eyes with a tissue. "I know it isn't what you were looking for." She exchanges a glance with the bridal assistant as she fusses around the skirt, teasing the layers out to make it even wider.

I suck on my bottom lip, turning from side to side to view it from every angle. I only get to do this once, and I want it to be perfect.

In Gretna Green, I told Donna and Bill that I wanted to get married in a forest, surrounded by trees and sunlight and a gurgling stream, wearing a floaty floral dress fit for a fairy. I still think that it would be a wedding to remember, but I understand more clearly now that it isn't only about me. As a child, I never pictured the groom who would be standing by my side, and now that I have Harry, I want to give him the wedding of his dreams. I want to walk down the aisle in a dress that makes me feel special and makes him proud.

Which is why we're getting married in a boutique Manhattan hotel overlooking the Rockefeller Center. The chandeliers are huge, the ballroom is elegant, and the salon will be the perfect setting for a dress like this.

"I…" I suck in a deep shaky breath. "I love it."

The assistant smiles. "I think this dress has been waiting for you. It doesn't even need any alterations."

I choose a long, floor-length veil and a sparkling tiara, and arrange to collect it on the eve of the wedding. When we step outside the bridal store, I feel as if the world has changed. It has suddenly become a brighter place where the sun always shines, and good things do happen.

Melanie and I grab lunch in a Japanese restaurant where our food is cooked on a grill at the table. We talk about the wedding and try to guess where Harry is taking me for our honeymoon.

"The Bahamas." I chew a mouthful of teriyaki salmon and swallow. "Or Mexico maybe."

Melanie shakes her head. "If I know my brother, he'll have booked the Seychelles or Bali or a private island that can only be reached by boat."

I sip my wine and try to get my head around it. This was always my mom's dream, to see me married to someone who had even heard of the Seychelles, whether I loved him or not, and I still can't believe that this is going to be my life now.

Melanie hesitates, her fork halfway to her mouth. "What are you wearing on your feet?"

I instinctively glance at the floor. "Boots?"

"No." She shakes her head. "On your wedding day."

I grimace. I hadn't thought of that.

"Right, next stop, every shoe store in town until we find a pair of shoes worthy of that dress. Call it my wedding gift to you."

32

HARRY

Ruby is so excited about the wedding that I haven't told her what Carlos and I have been up to. Carlos managed to get hold of Ruby's medical records from the hospital in Chicago —I didn't ask how—and has been trying to locate the source of the compound used to poison her. It seems that Arsenic hasn't been produced in the US since 1985, but Carlos knows a lot of people, the kind of people who know how to get hold of poison should they be in desperate need of bumping off someone unsavory.

So far, we've had no luck in tracing it to anyone with even a remote connection to either the Jacksons or my family. Whoever poisoned Ruby has covered their tracks well. Which, according to Carlos, suggests that we will know them when we find them.

I don't know what I'll do with the information when I eventually find it.

One thing I do know is that I will never allow anyone to hurt

Ruby again. It scares me sometimes, the intensity of my feelings for her.

I don't recall this kind of all-consuming love between my parents. Admittedly, my father has a real aversion to showing his emotions. But even in quiet moments at home during my childhood, the kind of moments when they would sit in the kitchen drinking coffee, my dad reading the newspaper, my mom either sewing or mending a hole in the knees of my school pants, I never saw them touch. Never saw them speak with their eyes or heard them share a private joke.

Knowing what I know now, I wonder if he ever loved her. Or perhaps he did in his own way, but that love paled in comparison to whatever he felt for Celia Jackson. I have to believe that he loved my mom. Because the alternative...

I can't imagine spending my life with the wrong person.

Now that I've found Ruby, I understand that I would kill for her. I would spend the rest of my life in jail if it meant that she could live her life unharmed. Just thinking about someone hurting her makes my fists clench and my pulse race.

Because what is the point of love if it isn't at the heart of everything you do?

At midday, I meet Carlos at the site of an old tenement block in a prime Manhattan location. With the joint venture preparing to take off, he is thinking of relocating, building another tower taller and sleeker than the first, and splitting it fifty-fifty between the two companies. Weiss Petroleum has outgrown the space it currently inhabits in Russo Tower, so it would make sense, and when I see the plans drawn up by the architect, excitement hums through my veins.

Everything that I want to give Ruby is within touching distance. This is everything I've ever dreamed of but bigger, grander, way beyond even my own expectations. I've never enjoyed extravagance, but I can already see Ruby surrounded by opulence, wearing designer labels, expensive perfume, getting her hair styled in celebrity salons; she's a gem, and she deserves the best setting. You wouldn't stick a diamond inside a plastic clasp.

I've already started making inquiries about buying a private plane too. No more busy airport lounges and economy class for my Ruby.

Wandering around the empty offices, I don't see the grimy flaking walls around me but the view from the windows overlooking the Chrysler Building, the Empire State Building, the Statue of Liberty and the World Trade Center. One day, perhaps, I'll grow bored with this skyline, but right now, it fills me with a sense of pride: this is what I've achieved since taking over the family business.

Peering outside, I scan the sidewalks for a man in a black overcoat loitering around and trying to appear inconspicuous. There's no one there. I haven't spotted him in a while, since Ruby came back to New York with me. Perhaps I've been too preoccupied to notice, but I've not even felt as if I were being followed. So, perhaps I did imagine it after all.

My thoughts instinctively drift back to my father. I haven't spoken to him since that night in Chicago. I don't even know if he is back in New York or if he and Celia have finally gotten what they wanted. Each other.

Part of me can't help wondering if reality will live up to their dream. Do they even really know each other after all these years spent apart, after everything that happened?

When I think of Ruby, I wholeheartedly believe that love will see us through a lifetime of ups and downs, of cold winters and baking summers, of children and grandchildren, vacations and Thanksgivings, chaos and peace. But when it comes to my dad and Ruby's mom, I think that they will get what they both deserve in the end.

On a whim, I ask the taxi driver to take me to my dad's house. He has already lost my sister; guilt will rest heavily on my shoulders for the rest of my life if I don't invite him to my wedding. I realize that I'm doing this as much for myself as for him, but it doesn't matter. I will have tried, and the rest will be down to him.

The house, when the taxi pulls up on the curb outside, appears lonely, sad windows overlooking an unloved porch. The trees are spindly and bare awaiting spring's revival, and the steps littered with mulchy leaves.

I pay the driver and watch him pull back into the traffic before I climb the steps and ring the doorbell. No answer. I try again, listening for the sound of my dad's footsteps and hearing only car horns, tires on the street, and raised voices from somewhere nearby.

I realize with a sharp pang of disappointment that this is the first time I've felt uncomfortable letting myself in with my key. It's almost as if I never fully moved out until I met Ruby. As if I'd left half of me behind in case I ever wanted to move back in, and now that I'm getting married, I no longer belong here.

Even the key feels strange in my hand.

I glance back at the street, at the silver-blond woman carrying a chihuahua on the opposite side of the road, watching me with narrowed eyes like I'm about to break in. Deep breath. I slot the key into the lock.

Inside, I close the door behind me, and stand in the narrow hallway, listening to the sound of the house breathing. "Dad?" He doesn't answer, but a sick feeling of dread starts to congeal in my stomach.

Pocketing the keys, I make my way through to the enormous living room, half expecting to find him slumped on the floor, one hand curled around an empty whisky glass. Now that I've got the vision in my head, I can't shake it, and I make my way through the house, opening doors and peering around rooms with my heart hammering inside my chest.

Eventually, I find myself standing outside my dad's study. It's the only room I haven't checked, and now that I'm here it makes sense that this is where he'll be.

I grip the handle and push the door open, the breath escaping my lungs with a whoosh when I find the study empty. I shake my head, scattering all sorts of grim images from my mind. He isn't here. From the deathly silence and icy chill, I guess that he didn't come back to New York after all.

With relief battling with pictures of him and Celia inside my head, I go to close the door when I spot the open file on his desk.

My dad has always been fastidious about keeping things tidy. He keeps every invoice he ever received in chronological order in a drawer in the filing cabinet. He could recite every transaction that passed through his bank account over the last three months. He can't even eat a slice of toast here without spreading napkins across the desk surface to catch crumbs.

Anywhere else, I'd have ignored the file because it's obviously personal, closed the door, and walked away without a backward glance. But because my dad has done something so out of character, I can't turn around and leave it there.

I step inside the study, recalling all the times I would come in here to show him school assignments at the end of the day when I was a kid. It was the only time he ever gave me his full attention, and even then, it was always followed by a comment like, "You could've done some more research," or "That was too easy, move onto the next level."

The document is typed. Official. But not something I recognize.

Peering more closely, I realize that it's a postmortem report. My mom's name is printed at the top of the sheet. I stare at her name, the individual letters dancing about in front of my eyes and making it hard to concentrate. I didn't know there had been a postmortem. She was sick—there was no need to determine cause of death. But here it is, so why did no one tell me about it?

I skip through the details of the coroner who carried out the postmortem, the measurements and weights, and get straight to the point of the report: why my mom died.

The word *arsenic* jumps out at me. Once I've seen it, everything else fades into insignificance; even the room has disappeared like I'm floating above the earth, anchored only by the document in my hand.

My mom was poisoned.

My mom ingested arsenic. It was the poison that killed her, according to the report, or rather heart complications and kidney failure arising from the poison.

"What does this even mean?" I mutter to myself.

It's going round and around inside my head: my mom was poisoned. Ruby was poisoned. My mom and Ruby. The two women I love most in the world apart from my sister Melanie. What are the chances of that...?

"Yeah, I thought it was a coincidence too."

I'm so absorbed in my thoughts that I didn't even hear my dad moving around inside the house. He looks rough. Disheveled. Tired. There's gray in his hair that I never noticed before, and the heavy pouches under his eyes swallow half his cheeks.

"You're here."

"Ha! Thought I'd run away, did you?"

"Celia..."

My brain is still five minutes behind real life, trying to wrap itself around the report in my hand. The house seemed so empty, abandoned, but looking at him now, I understand why. He isn't living here in the true sense of the word, he's existing. A man in limbo.

His eyes are bloodshot as he holds the name on his tongue and releases it again, his gaze drifting back to the document. "Needed to check it for myself."

"H-how long have you had this?" Dumb question. He must've requested it after Mom died.

"Wanted to be sure." He's holding his own conversation, not following mine.

"About what?" The word is still yelling at me.

Arsenic... Arsenic... *ARSENIC!*

Then it dawns on me like a river bursting its banks in a torrential downpour. He wanted to be with Celia. He doesn't want me to marry Ruby. He killed my mom so that he could be free.

"You did this?" My voice barely stumbles off my tongue. "You poisoned Mom?"

He blinks at me, the words penetrating his bubble of self-pity. "What? No. What kind of animal do you fucking take me for?"

The worst kind.

The *murdering* kind.

Before I know what I'm doing, I've crossed the room and shoved him in the chest so hard that he staggers backwards through the door. I'm already on him. I grab his jacket, drag him towards me, our noses almost touching, his stale breath making me feel nauseous.

"You fucking poisoned Mom, and then you tried to kill Ruby."

"No." His eyes flash a warning at me, but I'm too far gone to read it, too consumed by the overwhelming need to hurt him the way he hurt Ruby. "Harry—"

I throw him across the landing with a strength I never knew I possessed. He crashes into the balustrade at the top of the stairs, the wooden posts cracking with the force. He grabs hold of the banister, stops himself from hurtling backwards down the stairs, and crawls over the wooden splinters towards me.

One hand outstretched, he says, panting, "Hear me out, Harry."

My chest is heaving with rage. I barely even register how pathetic he looks on his hands and knees.

"I'm listening."

"How's Ruby?" The question catches me off-guard, completely out of the blue.

"She's... Why do you even fucking care?"

ARSENIC...

"That's what I'm trying to tell you." He touches the back of his head tentatively, testing the damage. "I needed to check the report for myself. To be sure."

"After you poisoned Ruby? You could've fucking killed her."

I can't even look at him. He did kill someone: my mom. And the thought of Ruby's cold lifeless body on a slab in the morgue is more than I can bear.

"I'll ignore the accusations after the way I spoke to Ruby." He swallows, his lips drawing away from his gums. "But I will not accept my own fucking son believing that I killed his mother."

"Who did then?"

"Not now. I'm not doing this now."

He clambers onto his feet and blunders past me, back into the study. He walks around the desk, opens a drawer and pulls out a half-full bottle of whisky and two glasses. He pours a large slug into each and hands one to me which I accept mechanically. My hand trembles as I raise it to my lips.

My dad downs his shot in one and refills his glass. "I was having you followed. I wanted to scare you; make you think twice about marrying into that family." This isn't his first drink of the day—his words are already slurred. "I'll hold my hands up when I'm wrong, and I was wrong about you and her."

"Her?" Hysteria gurgles in my throat and threatens to erupt. "Ruby?"

He shakes his head and rubs his hand across the week-old stubble on his chin. "Seems I was wrong about a lot of things. Your sister..."

"What about Melanie?"

"I know you instructed a PI to find her."

This is too much, too soon. What else has he been keeping from me? "How?"

"Bank transfers. You made it too easy." He takes another swig. "She'd have come back if that's what she wanted. Took you longer to figure it out than I anticipated. All those bum leads, and still you kept chasing them."

It takes me a beat too long to understand.

"Yep, that was me too." He slugs back his drink and refills the glass. "I never wanted to marry your mom."

My hackles are up. The fucking asshole is going to offload his shit onto me so that he can get a decent night's sleep, no more secrets weighing him down.

"You are some fucking piece of work," I growl.

He ignores me, lost in his memories. "I had no choice. I either married her or kissed goodbye to everything I'd worked so hard to build. They knew they had me over a fucking barrel—I could never have done it without them."

"Them?"

"*The family*. Our connections from back home in Ireland." A puff of mirthless air escapes his lips, and he turns damp eyes towards me. "I turned my back on love, devoted myself to my wife and our kids, and kept my head down. It's what's expected of a Mafia boss. I take over, I pass it on to you. I don't expect you to believe me, Harry, but I tried my best to love her. *I grew to love her.* She was ... a wonderful woman who deserved fucking better than she got. She deserved fucking better than a ruthless Mafia king."

That's the truest thing he's said so far.

I set the drink down on the desk. I need to get this straight, and I need to be able to think clearly. "Who poisoned Mom?"

Tears well in his eyes, and it's like a punch in the gut. I've never seen my dad cry, not even after Mom died. "Isn't it obvious?"

I stare at the report. I don't need to read it to see the words printed underneath the heading: *Cause of death*. I already know the answer. The common denominator between the two families, and the only person who could've poisoned Ruby and avoided having the finger pointed at her.

Her mom. Celia.

"No." I pick up my glass and swallow a mouthful of whisky—it burns as it goes down. "No. She wouldn't do that to her own daughter."

"That's what I thought till I heard it from the horse's mouth."

I gape at him. "She-she confessed?"

"Not in so many words. Thought she could get her away from you, keep her in Chicago to take care of Graham. She wouldn't have killed her."

I'm not listening. The whisky has added clarity to my thoughts, and I'm one step ahead, trying to figure out my next move.

33

RUBY

Two days before the wedding, I'm making pizza for dinner in Harry's apartment and singing along to a Fleetwood Mac song playing on the radio. "You can go your own waaaay." I fling an arm as I'm singing, tomato puree hurtling from the spatula across the marble wall tiles.

I'm getting clumsier by the day. Yesterday, I knocked the lamp off the nightstand in the bedroom with my elbow and broke it —I still haven't mentioned this to Harry—and this morning, I walked into the coffee table, spilled coffee all over the shaggy white rug underneath, and cut my knee.

Wedding jitters.

It's happening to both of us.

A couple of days ago I found Harry searching for his cufflinks in the refrigerator, and before he left for work this morning, he added salt to my coffee instead of sugar.

I wipe the tiles clean and finish adding the toppings to the pizza. Pepperoni, ham, red onion slices, red and green peppers, and chilis. I take a tin from the cupboard: pineapple. The finishing touch, a reminder of the night we had a picnic on the floor of the Drake Hotel in Chicago. Even though I still believe it's wrong, pineapple on pizza.

I want to see Harry smile again. I know it's only pre-wedding nerves, but he has been working so hard the last six weeks that I can barely remember the Harry who dragged me into a cave on a Scottish beach and turned it into a sexy memory. He has had a lot on his plate, but I can't wait to board the plane heading to our secret honeymoon destination and see him relax.

I open the tin and scrape my knuckle on the jagged metal. "Shit!" It stings like crazy, and as I squeeze my finger, a huge ruby droplet wells on the surface of my skin and drips onto the counter, barely missing the pizza. The sight of it there, so close to the food, makes me feel nauseous.

The dishcloth is close by, but as I reach for it, my fingers feel wet, and I instinctively lick the blood away. Big mistake. The instant I taste the tang of iron on my tongue, I start retching and I barely make it to the bathroom in time.

When the nausea passes, I sit back and rest my head against the cool tiles. Memories of being rushed to the hospital doubled up in pain come flooding back, making my pulse race, but I'm not in any pain right now. It's a weird sensation. And now that I've been sick, I realize how hungry I am.

I rinse my face with cold water, pat it dry with a fluffy towel, and peer at my reflection in the mirror. "You're fine," I tell myself. "You're not going to get sick again. You're getting married next week, and it's going to be perfect."

With a nod to myself in the mirror, I wrap a Band-Aid around my finger, my gaze turned away from the blood, and head back to the kitchen. The phone rings. Harry.

"What time will you be home?" I ask. "You're going to love what I've made you for dinner tonight."

Pause. My stomach twists.

"Damn! Will it keep till tomorrow? I have to fly to Vegas tonight with Carlos."

Tears well in my eyes like he just told me the wedding was cancelled. It isn't the first time he has had to stay away on business, and it has never bothered me before, but tonight, the news has tipped the scales into an emotional meltdown.

I wipe my damp face with my fingertips and sniff loudly.

"Ruby? What's wrong? Has something happened?"

"No." I shake my head even though he can't see me. "I cut my finger on a tin of pineapple."

I can almost see the smile at the other end of the line. "I can cancel my meeting, Ruby. It's fine."

It doesn't sound fine though; I can hear the reluctance in his voice, and I know how important this new project is to him, to the future of Weiss Petroleum.

"No, don't do that. I'm just being a wimp. When will you be back?"

"Tomorrow. I'll be back tomorrow no matter what."

In the kitchen, I scrape the uncooked pizza into the trash can. My blood clings to the jagged edge of the lid, and I toss that into the trash can too, catching a waft of pineapple juice from the open tin. I grab a fork from the drawer and spear a chunk of fruit.

Before I can stop and think about what I'm doing, I've eaten the whole tin. I'm still hungry though. I find a jar of pickled onions in the cupboard and eat them too, sitting on a stool at the breakfast bar with a block of cheese that has my name written all over it.

I think about the wedding.

I've organized flowers, the cake, the reception dinner, and champagne. I've sent out invitations, bought lingerie for our wedding night—white satin and lace, currently wrapped in tissue paper in the bottom drawer of the closet in our bedroom—and ordered rings. I've even arranged a surprise gift for Harry.

The only thing that neither of us has thought about is Harry's bachelor party. I don't want a bachelorette party—the only person I know in New York, aside from Harry, is Lizzie—and I think he is deliberately avoiding the topic because he feels bad getting one without me. Maybe we could do something together after the wedding rehearsal.

I don't care about it being bad luck spending the night together before the wedding—that bullshit is for superstitious people, not us. I pop a cube of cheese into my mouth and chew as Ronnie pops into my head. Ronnie was there the night I met Harry. He was there when we got snowed in at the hospital.

I think I know what to do.

"STOP RIGHT THERE." My dad beams at me from the seat in his room when I go in and raises a finger, warning me not to come any closer.

He has been moved to a stroke rehabilitation center, and although he's exhausted from all the physio treatment he's receiving, he also seems brighter than he has been in a long while. For as long as I can remember. Which makes me sad to think how unhappy he must've been.

He grabs the walking stick propped up against the wall, places it in front of him, and uses it to stand up. Then, smiling at me all the way, he crosses the room, using the cane for support, and links his free arm with mine.

"I promised I would walk you down the aisle."

I wrap my arms around him and hug him tightly, sniffing back tears.

"Hey, why so emotional?" He watches me closely when I release him. "They're happy tears, right?"

"Yes." I wipe my eyes with the back of my hand and try to laugh, which only makes me sound like a pig snuffling around for food in the mud. "I never doubted you would."

I wait for him to sit down and take the visitor seat next to him.

"I'm being fitted for my suit this afternoon," he says, propping the walking stick back up against the wall. I can hear in his voice that those few steps have drained his energy, but his smile is still in place, determined not to let it show. "Harry arranged it."

My chest swells with even more emotion than I'm already carrying around this morning. As busy as Harry has been, he still made time to sort my dad's wedding suit. "You could walk me down the aisle in a black sack, and I'd still be the proudest daughter in the world, Dad."

He blinks hard. "Now you're going to start me off."

Several moments of comfortable silence pass before we both say at the same time: "Have you heard from Mom?" She must be on both our minds.

"You first," Dad says.

"She tried calling Harry's office."

"But you haven't spoken to her?"

I shake my head. I know I'll have to eventually, but I can't bring myself to tell him what happened in Chicago. I just can't seem to find the right words. How do you tell your dad that his wife is in love with someone else?

"I've been thinking." He makes his right eyebrow dance comically. "About my wedding speech."

Wedding speech? Fuck!

"It's okay, Dad, you don't have to if you don't want to."

"I do want to. My daughter is only getting married once. I want to do this properly."

I can't help smiling at him. The bravest man I know. "Do you want me to help you write it?"

"I know what I want to say about my baby girl. But I need you to tell me about Harry. I don't even know his last name. I don't know where you met him, or how long you've known him. I..." He shrugs. "I keep trying, but the memories... They've gone."

My breath catches in my throat. My heart is doing funny things that are making me feel queasy again. The stroke. My dad doesn't know who Harry is. *Marry this Harry ... and be happy.* He doesn't know that Harry is a Weiss. He probably doesn't even remember Karl or what happened thirteen years ago.

Tears spill from my eyes. If he doesn't remember Harry, perhaps he has forgotten about Karl and Mom too.

Misinterpreting my tears, Dad reaches for my hand and squeezes it. "It's going to be okay, Ruby. You don't need to worry about me, you know."

I suck my bottom lip. "You might as well tell me to stop breathing or reading books."

The tears keep flowing. I feel like a walking bag of emotions today and they're going to get worse on our wedding day when Harry sees what I've planned for him.

"Sorry." Dad hands me a box of tissues. "I've really gone and done it now, haven't I?" He watches me dabbing my eyes, squeezing the tears out and trying to smile through it. "Everything okay, Ruby?"

I can't look at him. My dad has always been able to see right through me. "Dad, there's something I need to tell you about Harry. His last name is Weiss—he's the son of Karl Weiss."
"You're starting a new life with a wonderful man. It doesn't matter that he's Karl's son as long as you love him. He has proven how much he loves you by his actions. I'm not going to hold you back, not when there's a whole world out there just waiting to be discovered."

His tender words release the stress of my worries and I shudder in relief.

"You're feeling okay though?" He implores.

I don't tell him that I was sick again this morning. I skipped breakfast, and my stomach is growling, but I'll be fine once I've eaten.

After a deep breath I reply, "Now who's worrying for nothing?"

I change the subject and tell him about my plans for the eve of the wedding, but I can tell he isn't fooled.

ONCE I'VE HELPED him write his speech, I leave the center and pop to the grocery store to pick up more ingredients for pizza and to stock up on pickled onions and baby pickles. I hold my nose as I wander along the fresh produce aisle, and again when I reach the toiletries section. Someone has sprayed deodorant or cologne, and my head starts to pound the instant I get the first whiff. A woman wearing a paisley scarf wrapped around her neck and more layers than I can count without staring, eyes me up like I forgot to button my shirt.

Outside, I suck in great gulps of polluted air, open a family-sized packet of potato chips, and cram as many into my mouth as I can fit. Strolling along the street, my eyes are drawn to a baby boutique that I haven't noticed before. There's a crib mobile in the window in neutral colors with fluffy clouds, soft animals, and sparkly stars.

Closer, and I press my forehead to the storefront window. I watch it spinning around, mesmerized, and wonder what tune it's playing at the same time. What tunes do babies like to listen to?

Still stuffing potato chips into my mouth, my gaze drifts to a rocking crib trimmed with white broderie anglaise, two soft teddy bears in pastel shades of blue and pink strategically placed inside the basket. There are more soft toys: a long-necked giraffe, a Winnie the Pooh, and a black-eyed panda. Tiny outfits with coordinating bonnets and bootees. Dinky polka-dot wellington boots.

Another wave of nausea crashes through me, and I close my eyes waiting for it to pass.

Am I overdue? I frantically try thinking back to my last period... Was it before I was admitted to the hospital or after? Why can't I remember? It's as though my brain is refusing to settle the one thing I'm trying to figure out, but already I'm imagining all kinds of twinges and tenderness that were not there a few moments ago. Come to think of it, my breasts were sore when Harry groped them yesterday morning.

I head back home in a daze. The nausea, the tears, the craving for baby pickles—could I be...?

I stop off at the pharmacy. Back at the apartment, I tear the wrapper off the test I bought skim-reading the instructions which tell me the best time to do this is first thing in the morning, and pee on the plastic stick anyway.

Then I wait the obligatory two minutes, forcing myself not to look at the tiny screen before the time is up. "Come on," I mutter to myself, checking my watch for what must be the twenty-fifth time. Two minutes has never taken so long, and just when I'm starting to think that I've rewritten the theory of time, the two minutes are up.

I stare at the two lines in the center of the testing stick.

O-kay...

I go back to the instructions, study the *'How to read your result'* section three times, and then hold the stick so close to my eyes that everything blurs. Blink. Two lines. Blink again, harder this time. Still two lines.

I can't be pregnant. We both want children of course, it was one of the first things we talked about in Scotland, but we never discussed when. We didn't put a timeline on it. I kind of assumed that we would have some time alone together first, vacations, our first Christmas, impromptu trips to Vegas or Mexico or New Orleans. I didn't expect to meet the man of my dreams, get married, and give birth all in the same year.

I wander back to the kitchen, still clutching the stick tightly. I make coffee and then pour it down the sink when the smell makes me feel queasy. I sip a glass of cold water slowly, my brain reviving little by little.

How did this even happen?

My face grows hot, my heart skipping several beats in a row when I realize that I haven't taken the pill since I came to New York. I was so wrapped up in the Chicago drama that it hasn't even occurred to me until now.

Grabbing my coat, I dash back to the pharmacy and buy another test. To be sure. Fuck it. I buy five tests and run back to the apartment with them, my breasts feeling heavier and sorer by the second.

The second test is positive too.

And the third.

And every other test after that one.

By the time I've used them all up, a line of positive results staring back at me from the glass shelf in the bathroom, and I'm already thinking of baby names.

I'm going to have a baby!

I squeal at my reflection in the mirror and pop a baby pickle into my mouth.

34

HARRY

CELIA OPENS the door to her home in Chicago and goes to close it again when she sees me standing on the front step.

But my foot is already inside the door. "We need to talk, Celia."

"I have nothing to say to you." She grips the side of the door, hiding behind it, only her face visible. "If you don't move your foot, I'll call the police."

"Fine. Go ahead. I'm sure they'll be interested in what I have to say too."

Her face pales, her mouth chewing on words that don't quite make it. Several moments pass before she stands back and opens the door wide enough for me to enter. She doesn't wait around for me. I close the door and follow her to the kitchen, surprised to find that it's no longer the bright and sunny room that I remember from my previous visit with Graham.

I can't quite put my finger on what's different. There's no sunlight pouring through the window, but it isn't that.

The counter is littered with dirty dishes and stained mugs. A loaf of sliced bread is open on the side; an almost-empty jar, the lid sticky with dried jam; the apples in the fruit bowl turning brown and wrinkled. There's no welcoming aroma of freshly brewed coffee. Instead, a bottle of red wine is open on the side, several stained wine glasses lined up next to the sink.

Celia leans against the counter and folds her arms across her chest. "Go on then, say what you have to say and get this over with."

Looking at the woman standing in front of me, I struggle to find any resemblance to her daughter. She is all hard lines to Ruby's soft curves. Her lips are pinched together, an expression I've never seen on Ruby, her dislike obvious in her dark eyes and lowered brows. Her blond hair has been scraped back into a ponytail, and she isn't wearing any makeup, so what I'm seeing now is the real Celia, not the well-groomed woman she usually presents to the world outside this house.

"I know you poisoned Ruby."

I want to get out of this place Ruby used to call home, catch my flight back to New York, and wrap my arms around this woman's daughter. I hate lying to Ruby, but I needed to do this alone. I need to hear what she has to say, give her my proposition, and walk away from Celia Jackson without a backward glance.

"Ha!" she scoffs. "Is that it? Is that what you came all this way to say?"

"Are you denying it?"

"I don't have to deny anything to you, asshole. You think you can stroll into my house, accuse me of something like that, and expect me to wave my hands in the air and say, 'I did it.' You've got some fucking nerve. Get out." She turns away, fills a glass with red wine and takes a large gulp.

"You poisoned my mom too."

Now, she's listening. Her eyes are on the run, darting around the room like she's searching for something to stab me with. I'm grateful that I can't see a sharp knife anywhere.

"Fuck off, Harry. What shit has your dad been feeding you?"

"He never told me. I found my mom's postmortem report. She had traces of arsenic in her system the same as Ruby did. Only my mom had more severe complications that resulted in her death."

Celia swallows another mouthful of wine. She doesn't look at me. "So, now you're accusing me of murder." Her tone is dull, flat, matching the look in her eyes that are fixated on a spot in the middle of the floor.

"If she hadn't been given arsenic, she wouldn't have died."

A grim smile twists her lips to one side. "You're a fucking coward just like your father. You can't even say what you mean, can you?"

I ignore her. I'm not playing games—I'm here to say my piece and go home to my fiancée. I've spent the last couple of weeks getting my head around what Celia did. I can't bring my mom back, but I can make sure that this woman has no place in our future or the future of our children.

"What I want to know is, how you justified harming your daughter to yourself."

The twisted smile becomes a smirk. "You have no proof that it was me."

"True." I shrug. "But you didn't react to me telling you that Ruby had arsenic poisoning, and that's all I need to know." I pause, allowing this to sink in. "Oh, and just in case you're trying to scheme your way out of this and turn it around on me somehow, I can find proof that it was you."

"You're bluffing."

"Am I? I'm starting to wonder if you know my dad at all. You see, he has connections with some very dangerous people. They know where I am, and why I'm here, and I only have to say the word."

Celia wipes her mouth with the back of her hand. She pushes herself off the counter, refills her glass, and stares out the window. She's stalling, buying herself some time while she weighs her options.

Finally, she says without turning around, "Does Ruby know that you're here?"

"No. I don't want to keep secrets from her, but I figured it was kinder this way."

"Kinder for who? Ruby? Or you?"

"For everyone concerned."

"Such a fucking goody-two-shoes, huh? You've still got your father's blood running through your veins. You'll let her down eventually. It's only a matter of time."

"I will never let Ruby down. It's just a shame you won't be around to watch me prove you wrong."

She faces me now, sloshing wine over her wrist and down her legs. "You can't keep me away from my daughter forever. She'll come running back to me when she gets bored. That's the thing with Ruby, she—"

I cut her off. I'm not listening to any more lies. "Here's the deal. I promise that I will never mention this to Ruby, any of it, on one condition."

"Ruby is my daughter! You don't get to call the shots here." Her chest heaves with the effort of controlling her temper.

"I won't tell Ruby or the police, but my condition is this: you give us your blessing for the wedding, and then you disappear from our lives."

Her face crumples, her eyes large with tears. "Ruby will never forgive you for this..."

"Ruby will never know," I remind her. "You were going to leave with my father anyway. You were prepared to leave your husband in the care of your daughter so that you could live the life you wanted; I'm offering you the easy way out."

"You bastard."

"I take it that's a yes."

She turns back to face the window, but the set of her spine is proof that she knows she has lost.

"Don't try to contact Ruby. If I find out that she has even had a missed call from you, I'll find the evidence and I'll take it straight to the cops, and I promise you that Ruby will know exactly what you are."

I walk away from the Jackson house, filling my lungs with clean air and telling myself that I've done the right thing.

"Harry!" Ruby leaps off the sofa and runs into my arms,

wrapping her legs around my waist, and kissing me hard on the lips. "You're back."

"I promised ... I would be," I manage between kisses. "I should go away more often if this is the welcome I get."

She untangles herself, takes my hand, and leads me into the bedroom.

Then she undresses me slowly, her tongue poking out of the corner of her mouth as she unbuttons my shirt and tugs it out of my suit pants. Eying me mischievously, she sits on the edge of the bed, unzips my pants, and smiles when my erection springs free.

"I'm pleased to see you too." She licks it from the base upwards, slowly, dragging her tongue around the tip and teasing me with gentle nibbles.

Dragging my pants onto the floor, she doesn't wait for me to step out of them. She turns me around, my throbbing cock still in her mouth, and pushes me back onto the bed. Then she lifts her skirt, turns around, and straddles me backwards, her pussy in my face, and I realize that she wasn't wearing panties when I came in.

My cock twitches inside her mouth at the sight of her wet sex, spread wide for me, waiting to welcome me home. Gripping the inside of her thighs, I lower her onto my tongue, tasting her sweetness.

My good intentions to take this slowly vanish in an instant. I want her to come. I want to feel her gushing on my tongue. Sliding a finger inside her, I probe and push, finding the spot and licking until my tongue feels numb and she collapses onto my legs, panting, her swollen pussy still in my face because I won't let her go.

"Nu-huh, you're staying right where you are."

I pull back just enough for her to groan out loud, and then resume licking. This time, Ruby explodes in my mouth, and still I don't let go. The trip to Chicago has lifted a weight off my shoulders that I've been carrying around since I found the medical examiner's report on my mom, and I want to make Ruby feel like she has never felt before.

"Harry..."

"Do you want me to stop?" I grip her thighs tightly and lick my lips relishing the taste of her orgasm.

"Yes."

I drag my tongue across her pussy. "Sorry, I didn't hear you."

"Yes, I want you to stop."

I let her go and, in one fluid movement, slide out from under her and penetrate her from behind, raising her ass to meet my thrusts. My suit pants are still caught around my ankles, but I don't care. I need this. I've never needed this more and knowing that I have the rest of my life to enjoy this beautiful woman makes my own orgasm come hard and fast.

After, we lay on the bed, Ruby on her side, resting her head on one elbow so that she can see me.

"Hi," she says. "Good trip?"

I can't help smiling at her. "Very productive."

Her cheeks are flushed, her hair tumbling over her shoulder and caressing my bare chest. She looks different somehow, and I study her face, her eyebrows, the color of her hair to make sure I haven't missed a trip to the salon.

"Does this mean that you're all mine now until after the honeymoon?"

"Ruby, I've been all yours since the day I met you."

"You know what I mean."

"I do." I kiss her on the lips. Pause. I've been putting this off, but now I know I'm out of time. "Ruby, there's something I want to tell you," I say at the same time as Ruby says. "I have something I want to show you." We both smile.

"You go first, Harry." She chews her bottom lip, and I know she's up to something from the gleam in her eyes.

She rests her chin on my chest and peers at me like I'm some kind of demi-god. "I haven't told you about my family." Her eyes narrow, just enough for me to notice. "My family back in Ireland. They're not... Well, they're not just family. You've heard of the Mafia, right?"

Ruby nods.

"The Mafia doesn't only exist in Sicily like the movies would have you believe." Another nod. "My family... We have connections. My father... I'll take over from him someday." I wait. This might be the day that Ruby stands up and walks away from me, or it might be the first day of the rest of our lives without this hanging over my head.

"Wow," she says finally, and I release the breath I didn't realize I was holding. "Does that make me a future Mafia boss's wife?"

"How would you feel if I said yes?"

Ruby smiles, and I allow my heart to flood with more love than I ever thought I could contain. "Harry, I always knew there was something about you that was different to every other man I ever met. You'll look after me, won't you?"

I pull her over my chest and wrap my arms around her tightly. "With my life, Ruby. I promise."

"And our kids?" I feel her heart beating against mine.

"Goes without saying."

"Then I have something to show you." She pulls out of my embrace, stands, and offers me her hand.

I ditch my suit pants, pull up my boxers, and follow her to the bathroom where she stands in front of the mirror, and turns to face me, her expression suddenly serious.

"I can't get enough baby pickles."

I chuckle. "O-kay."

"I *hate* baby pickles. I always pick them out of my hamburgers because they make me cringe, they're so green and slimy." She shudders to prove the point.

"So, now you like them. Tastes change. It just means that, one day, we'll both have the same tastes. It'll make eating out a whole lot easier. No arguing over tacos or noodles."

"Harry, will you stop talking?"

I stop.

"This isn't about baby pickles. Well, it's not *just* about baby pickles." She takes a deep breath and moves away from the mirror.

I follow her gaze to the row of plastic sticks propped up against the glass like soldiers. I glance back at her, and her eyes are fixed on mine, hesitant, eager, waiting for a reaction.

"What are they?" I pick one up, spot the two faint lines across the middle of the tiny panel in the center, and turn it around to show her. "What does this mean?"

"I'm pregnant, Harry." She chews her bottom lip with her two front teeth. "We're going to have a baby."

"We're... You're..." My heart races as I stare at the other tests, each one showing the same double blue lines across the center.

"A baby." She nods.

The thumping inside my rib cage finally subsides long enough for me to process what this means. I toss the plastic stick into the basin and throw my arms around Ruby, spinning her around, her feet above the floor.

"We're going to have a baby." I set her back down, step back, and place my hand over her abdomen. "Oh my God. There's a baby in there. How far...? When...?"

She laughs out loud, and it will always be the most beautiful sound I have ever heard. "Not far. I'll make an appointment with the gynecologist when we're back from our honeymoon."

"Will it wait? I mean... Shouldn't you see them sooner?"

"Harry, it's fine. You might just have to call ahead and make sure we can get baby pickles wherever we're going."

"I'll have some shipped over if I must. I'll get you whatever you want, Ruby." I inhale deeply, trying to calm the thump-thump of my heart. "You're having my baby."

"Are you happy, Harry?"

"Do you really need to ask?"

"I thought you might've wanted to wait."

I pull her into my arms. "What for? You've honestly made me the happiest man alive. I'm so happy I could burst."

"Don't do that," she mumbles against my chest. "You'll spoil the next surprise."

I stand back and hold her at arm's length. "There's more? I'm not sure my heart could take it."

Her smile lights up her face. "I felt bad that you're not having a bachelor party, so I kinda arranged one for you."

"Ruby, you didn't have to do that."

"I'm coming too though. You'll need thick gloves and a warm hat."

I match her smile. "Do I get another clue?"

"You get more than that. Ronnie and Sumaira should be here any moment now. We're going ice skating at Rockefeller Plaza."

This time, when I pull her into my arms, I hold her there, breathing in the citrusy smell of her shampoo, and asking myself how I got so lucky. What did I do to deserve so much when so many people in the world have so little?

I only hope I never ever let her down.

35

RUBY

"You look beautiful, Ruby." My dad comes into the hotel room where I've been getting ready, his eyes gleaming with tears.

I face him in my wedding dress, feeling like his little princess all over again.

As a child, my dad always read books to me at bedtime. He would make a den in the corner of my room with cushions on the floor, blankets thrown across the backs of chairs, and tiny lanterns turning everything golden. This was where my love of books developed, during those evenings spent listening to my dad reading aloud fairy tales about glass slippers and fairy godmothers and charming princes.

Funny how the feel of the wedding gown swishing around my legs has taken me back to those special moments. I can still see the images in my favorite book, and now, here I am, playing the part of the princess in my own happy-ever-after.

"You look amazing too, Dad."

He stands still while I straighten his tie, his eyes on me, a smile tugging his lips upward. "I've missed this, Ruby, you fussing over my tie like a mother hen."

I stand back and check that it's straight and neat. "You loosened it on purpose, didn't you?"

"Am I that predictable?" He looks so forlorn, so wide-eyed and innocent like a child, that I throw my arms around him, careful not to make him lose his balance.

"Hey, what's that for? You'll crumple your dress."

"You're worth getting crumpled for, Dad."

"How can I argue with that?" I give him a twirl while he admires the wedding gown. "There were times when I never thought that I would get to do this for my little girl."

"No, Dad. No sad thoughts today. Only happy ones."

"That's probably the easiest thing anyone has ever asked me to do." He offers me his arm, and I take it. "Ready?"

"Ready."

We could've made a grand entrance down the sweeping staircase in the building, but I wanted to make it as comfortable as possible for my dad, so instead, we walk slowly to a wide door and take a deep breath. Harry is waiting on the other side for me. Our friends and families will have taken their seats, waiting for the door to open, handkerchiefs ready to dry their eyes if they're anything like me.

Only two people will be missing: my mom and Harry's dad.

My mom stopped calling the office a week ago. Karl went AWOL after his trip to Chicago when I overheard him talking to my mom in my hospital room. Harry doesn't think that they're together, but the past six weeks have been such a whirlwind that I haven't even had a chance to think about them.

I'm sad my mom won't get to see me in my dress, but I've come to terms with the fact that my mom isn't the person I thought she was, and the real Celia Jackson doesn't deserve to be the mother of this bride.

Music strikes up on the other side of the door, and I reach up to kiss my dad's cheek. "Love you."

"Love you too, sweetheart." He trembles as the door opens, and we step into the salon where I will shortly become Mrs. Weiss.

I never thought that I would be this nervous on my wedding day but seeing Harry in his tailored silver-gray suit at the front of the room with his best man Ronnie standing next to him, everything that we've done since we met flashes before my eyes like I'm drowning. The skating rink, Harry's hospital room, Edinburgh, the pizza picnic. It feels like I've only known him for a few minutes, and it feels like I've known him for a lifetime.

I walk on autopilot. I don't see the faces of the people in the seats on either side of the aisle. I'm waiting for the moment when Harry turns around to face me, and when he does, when I see his beautiful smile, my heart almost jumps out of my chest.

Without knowing how I got there, my dad hands me over to my soon-to-be-husband, kisses my cheek, and stands aside with Ronnie.

I glance at Harry, and our eyes meet. "Okay?" he mouths, and

I nod. I'm grinning and I know my cheeks are going to ache like crazy later, but I can't stop myself.

This is it.

We repeat our vows in front of the celebrant, and I don't remember a word of them. All I can feel is Harry's arm brushing mine. All I can hear is my heartbeat playing its own exciting tune.

Then, we're walking back down the aisle to the banquet hall where we'll greet our guests with glasses of champagne, and eat food that I won't taste, and dance to music that I won't hear. For a few minutes, we're alone in the hall, and Harry holds me close to his chest and kisses my lips. "I love you, Mrs. Weiss."

"I love you, Mr. Weiss."

"Did I tell you how beautiful you are?"

"Once or twice."

I lean against him, and I know that I never have to be nervous again because Harry is the rock that will hold me up, the sunshine on rainy days, the star that will never go out.

"You look pretty good too."

"Why thank you." He leans closer and whispers in my ear, "How's my baby?"

"She's doing just fine."

"She?" His eyebrows slide upwards. "What if it's a boy?"

"He'll look just like his dad, and I'll have two of you to keep on track."

The guests start filing into the banquet hall, and the day becomes a blur of speeches, toasts, and congratulations. I clap when I'm supposed to, kiss people's cheeks when they tell me what a beautiful couple we make and talk without thinking about what I'm saying. I feel dazed, like this is all a dream, and I'll wake up in my bedroom at home and realize that I fell on the skating rink in Chicago and imagined the whole thing.

"Breathe," my dad says. He's sitting next to me at the top table, and I realize that I've barely paid attention to him since he handed me over to Harry in the salon.

"Is it that obvious?"

"You're still my little girl, Ruby. No one knows you like I do."

Harry will, I think. Harry will know me better than my dad does in time, but then perhaps Harry sees a different Ruby to the one my dad sees. Perhaps I can be everything to both these men at the same time. This thought makes me feel even luckier than I already do.

Harry and I cut the cake together, his warm hand on mine.

Then we move through to the room where the band is already playing music to welcome our guests. Harry, still holding my hand, leads me onto the dance floor.

"Harry, what are you doing?" I whisper.

"It's our first dance."

"But..." I never thought about it. All the preparations I made over the past six weeks, all the choices I had to make for food, wine, flowers, and seating plans, I totally forgot to include the first dance on my many lists.

Harry stands in front of me, his eyes gleaming. "Do you trust me?"

"Ye-es."

"Then follow me, Ruby. I have it all under control."

The music plays, 'The Lady in Red' by Chris de Burgh, a song that we listened to together in a restaurant in Edinburgh, and Harry's hand slides around my waist. He whirls me around the dance floor, our eyes locked, and my body moves instinctively with his. I never knew he could dance like this, and by the time the song ends, I'm literally breathless.

We stop in front of my dad who is watching us with tears in his eyes, and I realize that Harry did this as much for him as for me.

"How did you...? You never said you could dance like that."

"I couldn't." Harry's smile is wider than I've ever seen it. "I've been having lessons."

"When? How did I not know about this?"

"Lunch breaks, after work some evenings. It's my wedding gift to you, Ruby. I know I'll never be as good as your dad, but, well, I tried."

I kiss Harry, and my dad is on his feet, pulling us both unsteadily into a hug. "You looked amazing on that dance floor, Ruby. Just like I always knew you would."

"Oh, Dad." Tears fill my eyes, and my dad catches them on his fingertip.

"No sad thoughts today, remember? Only happy ones."

"That's just it. They are happy ones."

There's only one more thing that I need to complete the day. I keep scanning the room, searching for a glimpse of a familiar face. I sent an invitation. I explained how much it would mean to Harry, but still, I don't know if it's going to happen, and I'll be gutted if it doesn't. What else do you give the man who has everything?

Especially when he learned to dance for me.

The evening is ticking by. I dance with Ronnie and Carlos and other friends of Harry's whose names I can barely remember. Donna and Bill flew from the UK specially for the wedding, and I squeal when I notice the swollen belly beneath Donna's dress. "You're pregnant!"

"Why do you think we ran away to Gretna to get married?"

We have so much to catch up on, but my dad joins us, and I can see how tired he is. I escort him outside and cling to him with the starry sky twinkling down on us, while we wait for the car to take him back to the rehabilitation center.

"See you when I get back from my honeymoon, Dad."

It feels like I'm leaving him for the first time. Like this is way harder and heavier than packing a bag and flying to the UK with a man I barely knew. It feels like goodbye, and suddenly, I don't feel ready.

The tears, once they start flowing, don't seem to want to stop. It's hormones, I know, but how do you stop them when every emotion is heightened a hundred times because your body is growing a baby?

"Don't forget to send a postcard." He climbs into the back of the car that Harry organized to take him and his caretaker back to the center.

I watch the vehicle disappear into the traffic. The night air chills my bare shoulders, pinching me back to reality, and I wave at a passing limo as it toots its horn at me, a young

Hispanic guy poking his head through the sunroof and blowing me kisses. I laugh at him as the car carries him away.

Will I ever get used to this crazy city and this surreal way of life that Harry is accustomed to? I feel like a fraud. I'm just a girl from Chicago standing outside a swanky building on a busy Manhattan street, wearing the kind of gown all little girls dream of wearing when they marry their prince.

I'm just Ruby Jackson.

"Hello, Ruby. I'm guessing I should call you Ruby Weiss now?"

I didn't realize that I said the words out loud until the voice catches me unawares. I turn around, and my heart performs somersaults. "You came."

"I wasn't going to." Melanie shrugs. "I didn't even pack my suitcase until this morning."

"What changed your mind?" I grab her hand, scared that she'll slip away again without Harry ever knowing that she was here.

"You did. You love my brother, and really, that's all I ever wanted for him. To be loved. And then I thought of all the years I've missed, and it made me realize that I was being selfish staying away all this time, no contact, no messages to let him know that I was still alive."

"No. I don't think you've been selfish."

Melanie's smile is all Harry. "I hope you never lose this ability to see the good in people, Ruby. I have been selfish. What happened between our parents wasn't Harry's fault, but I punished him anyway when I should've been looking out for him."

"You're here now. That's all that matters."

I go to walk back inside with her, but Melanie stops me. "How do you think he'll react?"

"Honestly? You'll make his day complete."

"There you go again, thinking the best of everyone, and forgetting about all the years of catching up I have to do."

"You're both different people now, Melanie. You can start fresh, draw a line under what passed before." I link my arm with hers. "Come on. Let's do this."

I spot Harry across the room when we enter, deep in conversation with Carlos Russo and his wife, the Italian's booming laughter rising above the music and turning the joyful atmosphere in the room up a notch. Harry has his back to us and doesn't see us approaching until we're standing right behind him. Carlos raises his eyebrows, nudging him in our direction.

My heart skips a beat when Harry turns around, his gaze hopping between me and his sister, and his wide smile tells me all I need to know.

Harry Weiss is the happiest man on the planet, and he's all mine.

EPILOGUE

"How's the most beautiful woman in the world?"

Harry comes into my room in the private clinic, leans over the bed, and kisses my forehead. Then he produces a bouquet of flowers in every shade of blue imaginable from behind his back.

I smile. "Harry, the room is already full of flowers."

I glance around at the vases overflowing with blossoms on every available surface, the petals catching the sunlight from the window. It doesn't even feel like a hospital room; it's like sleeping in a forest.

"Someone wise once said you can never give the woman in your life too many flowers."

"Someone wise?"

"My mom."

"Oh, Harry." I swallow the lump in my throat. "She knew what she was doing because she raised the best husband in the entire world." Hot tears well in my eyes and I sniff loudly. "Sorry, hormones."

"I'll take as many hormones as you want to throw my way, Ruby."

Setting the bouquet down on the mobile tray, he reaches into the bassinet and picks up the baby. Our baby. Our beautiful baby boy.

Cradling him in his arms, he sits on the edge of the bed and nuzzles the baby's nose. "I could stare at him all day."

I know how he feels. Every time I look at the baby, I can't help thinking that we created a little miracle when we were falling in love with each other. He's so perfect, so ... Harry.

"He looks just like you."

Harry shakes his head, still gazing at his son with wonder in his eyes. "He's going to have your eyes."

"How can you tell?"

"Because that's what I used to whisper to him every morning when he was inside your belly."

He kisses the tip of the baby's nose, and I can't help thinking that Harry is going to be the best father ever. He will protect him—protect both of us—with his life, but his son has already brought out a gentle side of Harry that I've never seen before.

I mean, he was gentle with me when I was pregnant, pre-empting my needs, rushing out in the middle of the night to find whatever crazy food I was craving, stroking my back whenever it was aching. But the way he is with the baby is another level.

And just when I think I couldn't love him more, I realize that my love for Harry is constantly growing, evolving, learning.

"It's true." Harry is watching me, a wide grin on his face. "You've made me the happiest man in the world, Ruby."

"You might not be saying that when he's screaming to be fed in the middle of the night, and you have to be up early for a meeting."

"I promise you that I will be saying it until I draw my last breath."

I study the baby's face, the tiny button nose, the eyelids that are almost transparent, crisscrossed with delicate veins, the perfect pink lips. "I've been thinking about what we should call him. I like Brandon." It's Harry's middle name.

"Brandon." Harry tries it out, caressing the sleeping baby's cheek with his fingertip.

The baby's eyes flicker open, his gaze settling on his dad as a smile twitches the corners of his mouth.

"He's smiling at me." Harry turns wide gleaming eyes my way, before directing them back to the baby.

"It's wind."

"No, it isn't wind, is it?" Harry kisses the baby's forehead. "You're smiling at your dad, aren't you?"

I chuckle. The two men in my life. How can it ever get better than this?

"I like it," Harry says. "Brandon Graham. What do you think?"

Fresh tears spill over my bottom lashes. "You want to name him after my dad?"

"I can't think of anyone better. Can you?"

Karl Weiss disappeared around the same time as my mom. I don't know if they're together; neither Harry nor I have heard from them since, and I've stopped trying to imagine them playing happy families in another city where no one knows them.

For a while, it made me sad to think that my mom would never be a part of our baby's life, but I've made peace with it now. Her loss, as Harry would say. My baby will have all the love that he needs from his parents. When he was placed in my arms shortly after he was born, I made a silent vow to make sure that he would never grow up to be like them. Brandon Weiss will fall in love one day and care for his family the way Harry cares for us.

I shake my head. "Brandon Graham Weiss. It's perfect."

Harry takes our son to the window. "You see this, Brandon Graham Weiss? This is New York city. That building over there—" I smile as Harry gestures to the skyline through the glass "—is the Chrysler Building. Impressive, huh?"

Harry glances over his shoulder and winks at me.

"This building—" he points somewhere right of the Chrysler Building "—is going to be Weiss Tower one day very soon. That's right," he adds as if the baby asked him a question, "Weiss is your name. And I'll tell you something else, Brandon: one day, this will all be yours. The entire city. The United States of America. The entire planet. There is nothing too big, or too grand, or too far for my son, and don't you ever forget it."

Harry looks at me with tears in his eyes.

"He's listening to every word I say."

I can't help smiling at my two beautiful men. "They say that babies are sponges." I read every baby book I could find while I was pregnant. "They soak up more information in their formative years than at any other point in their lives."

"I'll have to start teaching him about the business then. He'll be prepared when it's time for him to take over."

"What if he doesn't want to take over from you?" I arch an eyebrow at my husband. "What if he wants to be a teacher, or a journalist, or a dancer?"

"He's my son. He can do whatever he damn well pleases, so long as he does it from his office inside Weiss Tower." Harry chuckles to himself. "Oh, I almost forgot your mommy's gift," he murmurs to the baby.

"You bought me a gift?"

One thing I learned early on in our marriage: there's no point telling Harry that I don't want or need to be spoiled. He has made it his life's mission to do exactly that, spoil me, and if he gets it into his head that he wants to buy me a gift, or book a vacation, or buy an antique crib for the baby's nursery, nothing or no one will stop him.

"Over there, Brandon..." Harry gestures to the window again. "Is a place called Greenwich Village. You'd better get used to the name because that's where you're going to grow up. I've bought your mommy a townhouse in Greenwich Village with a courtyard out the back and a garden annex for your grandfather."

He turns around to face me, his eyes glistening with tears.

I push back the covers and swing my legs over the side of the bed. My movements are still slow following Brandon's birth, and I'm still adapting to my flat belly after months of not being able to see my feet, and Harry is there before I can stand up, ushering me back into bed.

"What are you doing, Ruby? I wouldn't have told you if I'd known you'd try to get out of bed."

"I'm fine." I peer up at him. "I've had a baby; I can still stand up and hug my husband."

Relenting, he helps me onto my feet and the three of us hug together, me, Harry and our son.

"Am I interrupting something?" The voice comes from the open doorway.

I whirl around to find my dad standing there with a bunch of vibrant wildflowers in his hand. "Dad!"

"I've come to meet my grandson." He enters the room, still supported by his cane, but looking stronger than I've seen him since his first stroke. "Although I don't think you need any more flowers."

"A wise woman once said, you can never give the woman in your life too many flowers," I say, welcoming my dad into our hug. "Meet Brandon Graham Weiss. Your grandson."

Dad sits down, stows his cane to one side, and Harry places the baby carefully into his arms. Tears stream down his cheeks as he peers into the green eyes of our baby.

"He looks just like you did when you were a baby, Ruby," Dad says, his voice filled with emotion. "Welcome to the world, baby Brandon. You've made all our lives complete."

He has.

You don't realize there is anything missing in your life until your baby comes along, and then you understand that you were simply biding your time, waiting for them to arrive and fill the invisible slot that belonged to them all along.

New baby. New home. New life.

It doesn't get any better than this.

Thank you for reading Ruby and Harry's story, I hope you enjoyed it, please leave me a review and share to help me grow.

Follow me on Amazon to receive exclusive news on deals and new releases.

Here is your next read featuring Ruby and Harry's son- Brandon and the beautiful Rose, he can't stop running into and falling for despite himself.

Read Fake Dark Vows Now Free With Kindle Unlimited and available on Paperback.

Brandon

My phone vibrates on my desk, my mom's face smiling at me like a cameo portrait inside a precious locket. She's wearing her favorite pearls in the image, her hair swept back Audrey-Hepburn style, her smile revealing perfect white teeth. I can almost imagine her hissing under her breath, *"Answer the damn phone, Brandon,"* while the photographer catches her still sharp cheekbones in exactly the right light.

I reject the call.

Again.

I hit redial on the landline telephone on my desk and get straight through to Julia, my personal assistant. "Has my mother tried calling today?"

"Wrong question."

"How many times?" I try.

"Ooh, at least a dozen, maybe more. I lost count shortly after I arrived." I can hear her chuckling to herself as I cut her off.

I swivel my leather seat and stare out of the penthouse window at the winking glass of the Chrysler Building in the sunlight. My mother wants to discuss my father's birthday arrangements even though she'll already have everything in hand with zero input from either me or my brother. It will be the same scenario as last year, and every other birthday before that: she'll run through the itinerary that she emailed to me a week ago, and wait for me to say, "I'll be there, Mom."

She knows I can't refuse. It's the big seven-oh, and she'll want everything to be perfect, because there's no room for anything less in Ruby Weiss's life. The decorations will be themed, the food will be gourmet, and the games will be competitive—just how my father likes it—and we'll all be expected to perform like circus animals, raising the bar a little higher with each turn.

I skim-read the email. A week on Ruby Island, the private island in the Keys my father bought for my mom to celebrate their fortieth wedding anniversary, dress casual, cocktails served at six, all arguments to be conducted behind closed doors.

Centuries ago, they'd have given me and my brother Damon pistols, instructed us to choose our seconds and meet at dawn to settle it like men. Winner takes all. Quicker and easier than the relentless tournaments we've been forced to endure all our lives in the name of competitiveness.

When my phone vibrates again, I close my eyes and inhale deeply. I stand, slide my suit jacket from the concealed closet in my office, and shrug it on, retrieving my phone as I pass my desk. Might as well take advantage of the fine spring weather and walk to my next meeting while I avoid her calls.

A glance at the Caller ID tells me that my mom has been shunted down the line—this is not a regular occurrence in Ruby Weiss's life. No doubt it will be noted in her silk-covered journal to be discussed with me when I finally pick up.

I hit the green button. "Sam."

I'm already exiting my office. Julia, my PA, glances up from her own conversation, eyes wide. She covers her cell phone with her hand, too late to hide the personal call.

"Eleven-thirty meeting," I say.

"Will you be back?"

I can't avoid my mother all day, and the anticipated conversation is already causing a headache to brew behind my eyes like I've been reading small print for hours. "Depends."

Julia's smile is fleeting and doesn't quite reach her eyes. She's immaculate in a dark-gray shift dress, her hair tied back on top in a coordinating bow, the kind a child of kindergarten age might wear. We've worked together for five years and in all that time, I've never seen her make a personal call, even discreetly, during office hours.

Her gaze drifts to the phone in my hand. Sam is still hanging on, but he can wait.

"My mother," I say, the lie slipping off my tongue easily. "I'll keep you posted."

My office is on the top floor of the tower that my father had commissioned when he made his first billion. I step into the elevator and glance back at Julia as the doors glide silently closed. She has her back to me, cell raised to her ear.

I follow suit. "You've got thirty seconds," I say to Sam.

"There might be a problem at the source."

I follow the levels on the display in front of me. "What kind of problem?"

"SEC is paying a little too much attention for my liking," Sam says.

"Do I need to step back?"

"No." Pause. "No, I can sort it."

"That's what I pay you for."

I end the call. The elevator stops smoothly, and the doors swish open.

One of my father's old associates is waiting to ride it back up, and I greet him with a wide smile and well-practiced handshake, firm enough to project confidence and control of the situation. Too limp, and you can kiss goodbye to any future business transactions; too heavy-handed and it implies a level of intimidation. It isn't something they teach at Harvard —it's a Weiss family thing. My father is a pro.

"Brandon, you'll be at the family celebrations."

"Of course." I incline my head and keep the smile fixed in place like the dutiful eldest son.

"See you there. My wife and I wouldn't miss it for the world."

Of course they wouldn't. It will provide a conversation starter for weeks after the event. *"Did you hear about Harry Weiss's birthday festivities? We were there by personal invitation."*

I turn away to cross the sleek marble-floored lobby and collide with a child.

The infant barely reaches my thighs—I know this because as she lands on her backside, her sticky fingerprints are left behind as evidence on my suit pants. The mouth opens, the chubby cheeks grow pink, and siren-strength wails fill the otherwise silent lobby.

A young woman comes running over clutching a plastic container filled with sandwiches, sliced salad vegetables, and a rosy, red apple. She hoists the child onto her hip, dropping the container in the process.

"I'm so sorry," she says, bouncing the child up and down, oblivious to the sound emitting from her. Her gaze immediately drops to the fingerprints on my pants, and she wrinkles her nose. "It'll wipe off. It's only watermelon juice. She was eating a slice of watermelon on the way here."

Sarah, the receptionist, joins us. She blinks slowly, her mouth a round 'O' of horror. "I'll fetch some tissues." She scurries back to the front desk.

"I'm on my way to a meeting." I'm still staring at the stains—there's no way they're wiping off with a tissue.

"It was an accident." The woman strokes the child's blonde curls and rubs noses with her until the tears dry up and the siren-shrieks morph into the occasional juddering sob. When she looks at me again, her eyes are accusing. "You should've been watching where you were going."

"You do realize this is a private office building, right?" I say.

Sarah is busy dealing with a client while the stains on my pants are drying up.

The woman with the child rolls her eyes around the high-ceilinged, glass and chrome lobby with its white leather couches and carefully chosen artwork. "My mistake, I thought this was preschool, but I can see now that it's far too clean and stuffy."

"Stuffy?" I don't even know why I'm getting drawn into this conversation. This is my building. I should be able to come and go without fear of sticky fingers and bawling kids.

"Yes, I bet there's zero fun to be had in this building."

A retort teeters on the tip of my tongue, the kind I might've spouted as a fourteen-year-old with raging hormones and giant footsteps to fill. Instead, I clench my fists and jut my jaw, the façade that works with everyone else in my life.

Sarah's gaze flits back and forth between the client and our conversation as if realizing she might've prioritized the wrong person.

The young woman's shoulders slump as the child rests her head on her chest and peers at me from beneath long wet eyelashes. "I'm sorry. Look, I'll pay for your pants to be dry-cleaned if it will help."

"Not really," I say. "I'm already late."

I see the hurt in her eyes and ignore it anyway. I don't know why the incident has me so rattled. Scratch that. I do know why it has me so rattled—it has nothing to do with the fingerprints that are already starting to fade, and everything to do with the young woman whose honey-blonde hair, if released from the ponytail secured at the nape of her neck, would curl the same way as Kelly's.

I go to walk around them and hesitate, bending to retrieve the plastic container from the floor. "You dropped this," I say, handing it over.

"Thank you. It's for my dad. It's his lunch; he forgot it this morning. He's careless like that. My mom always said that he'd forget his head if it wasn't—"

"Your dad works here?" I cut her off.

Most people tend to overshare. Ask a simple question, and they'll spill enough information to either incriminate themselves or gain a new friend. It's the reason why I stick to the questions that will give me the answers I'm looking for.

She nods. She has the same color eyes too... "He's the janitor."

I hear my own breath escaping and do nothing to stop it. I couldn't pick out the janitor in a police line-up, but I'd bet my lucky dollar that he looks nothing like his daughter.

"Tell him there's a café across the road if he forgets it in future." I walk away.

Sarah dashes around the desk waving a tissue at me like a flag. "Mr. Weiss. The tissues..."

"Forget it." I don't even glance behind me.

My phone rings again and, distracted, I answer without thinking.

"Brandon, honey," Mom's voice is silky-smooth. "I was starting to think that you were avoiding me."

"I've been busy, Mom," I say.

"Too busy to discuss your father's birthday party?"

"I'll have to call you back, Mom. I'm on my way to a meeting." I cut her off and locate Julia's direct line on my call log.

She picks up before the phone even rings. "What did you forget?"

"The janitor," I say.

I can almost hear her sliding closer to her desk and locating his personal details on the internal system. "What about him?"

"Who is he? Name, background, length of service."

"Jonathan Carter. Came to us from a local high school. References all checked out. Eleven years' service. Squeaky clean." Her tone is professional. "Was granted compassionate leave when his wife died four years ago. What's the problem?"

"His daughter and grandkid were in the lobby when I left. Make sure it doesn't happen again."

"Okay." Julia seems to want to say more, but I don't give her the opportunity.

A sleek black Bentley is parked outside the building, the rear passenger window rolling down as I approach. My mom's face appears, and she calls out, "Brandon!" At least she doesn't pretend that she was just passing by.

The passenger door opens—it's an order not an invitation.

I climb in beside my mother who is looking regal in an ivory Chanel two-piece, her legs crossed primly at the ankles, her favorite subtle perfume filling the back of the car. All that's needed to complete the queenly image is a gentle wave to her subjects through the window. I breathe in the familiar scent and my lips instinctively curl up at the corners. At thirty-five years old, I wonder if I will ever stop needing her praise and approval.

The Bentley joins the slow-moving traffic—it would be quicker to walk.

"Your father's birthday." She dives straight in—Ruby Weiss has never mastered the art of small talk. "You didn't respond to my email."

"I've been busy." I don't add that I knew she'd be angry if Julia replied on my behalf. "I'm not sure I can make it. I might have to fly out to Europe."

She fixes me with the gaze usually reserved for wealthy acquaintances who are about to donate a large sum of cash to whichever charity she's promoting at the time. "I already cleared your diary with Julia weeks ago, Brandon. I've managed to get hold of the Patek Philippe wristwatch your father has admired for so long. The Grandmaster Chime. And I want everyone to be there when he sees it."

"For the grand unveiling," I say.

For his sixtieth birthday, she had my father's portrait painted by a relatively unknown Baltimore artist highly recommended by a close friend. His reaction was somewhat anticlimactic, and the painting has never been seen since.

"You seem a little on edge." My mom's eyes narrow as she studies my face.

I glance at my phone. A message from Julia: *Done*.

I need to get out of the car, walk to the meeting, clear my head and release some of the tightness in my neck and shoulders. Perhaps I'll get Julia to arrange the masseuse for later this afternoon; weekly visits are no longer enough.

"I'm fine," I say tightly.

"You work too hard," she says without conviction. "You need someone to look after you."

"I have Julia."

"You know what I mean. Look how happy your brother is. All I ever wanted was to see you both happy and content."

"I know, Mom."

Satisfied that she has made her point, she sits back again. "I don't want the celebrations spoiled by business talk. I'm relying on you to steer the party the right way if your father is getting drawn into a serious conversation. You know what he's like."

I do, and so does she. If the chat turns to business, a bunch of wild horses won't drag him away.

"Kelly has been helping me with the theme. We're keeping it theatrical. Your father loved *Hamilton* when we saw it on Broadway..."

I tune out. My shirt collar feels two sizes too small, and the back of the car is starting to feel claustrophobic, my mom's perfume clinging to every available surface. Of course, Kelly has been helping her. She's the perfect daughter-in-law, a good mom, a loving wife, and never misses a family event.

"Stop the car." I'm already reaching for the handle as the Bentley draws to a smooth halt. "Sorry, Mom," I say. "But I'm running late."

I climb out and close the door behind me. My mother slides across the seat and peers out through the lowered window. "Brandon, next time you use an important meeting as an excuse to avoid talking to me, can you at least make sure your pants are clean?"

She sits back in her seat as the tinted window glides up and the car moves on.

Chapter 2

Rose

"Okay, this is beyond a joke." I toss my dinner plate into the frothy water in the sink and wipe bubbles from my cheek with the back of my arm.

I know where the instruction came from without waiting for my dad to elaborate.

Mr. Weiss.

The man in the gray silk suit.

The man who was horrified by a few fingerprints on his goddamned perfectly pressed pants. I'd bet his kids only get to speak to him from a safe distance. I can picture him standing in the doorway of their bedrooms and wishing them goodnight with a relieved smile at surviving another day without getting his hands dirty.

"He looked at Izzie like she was something I'd dragged in off the sidewalk," I grumble over my shoulder. Something smelly. Something that he would no doubt have his assistant remove from the soles of his shoes to save him from getting his fingers soiled.

No, scratch all the above—Mr. Weiss isn't the paternal type. I'd bet he never ate watermelon without a fork either.

I'm angry at myself for wasting any emotion on the guy, but seriously, who does he think he is? He could've asked me politely to take Izzie outside, but instead, he gets his assistant to suggest that Dad use the café across the street the next time he forgets his lunch.

"Hey, Rosie, it's okay," Dad says. "Mr. Weiss has an image to maintain. It's my fault. I shouldn't be so forgetful in the mornings."

"Don't apologize for him, Dad."

I inhale deeply and plunge my hands into the hot water. I don't like it when my dad bows down to his bosses like this. Running a corporation is one thing, and sure, the guy is probably under a lot of stress, but it doesn't give him the prerogative to treat people unkindly.

"He can't dictate what you eat, Dad," I say, swallowing my initial response. "Izzie wasn't even being noisy. Thirty seconds later, and we'd have been out of there, and Mr. Weiss would've been none the wiser."

"Bad timing, Rosie. That's all it was. You can't diss the man for doing his job." Dad cleans ketchup from Izzie's face with a baby wipe and gets her down from the table.

Maybe Dad's right. The guy probably didn't give the incident a second thought while he sat through his dull afternoon meetings, and scrolled through his emails, and added his illegible signature to a ream of classified documents. He probably doesn't even remember the call he asked his assistant to make.

Maybe this anger bubbling inside my chest isn't even about him.

The doorbell rings. I grab a towel to dry my hands and take it with me to the front door, Izzie almost tripping me up along the way.

It's Jess, Izzie's mom. "Sorry I'm so late," she says. She bends down, scoops her little girl into her arms, and smothers her face in kisses while Izzie squirms and tries to push her away. "Have you been a good girl for Auntie Rose?"

"Yes, Mommy." She wraps her arms around her mom's neck and rests her cheek on Jess's.

Jess and I have been friends since middle school.

As eleven-year-olds we became inseparable over our shared love of Fleetwood Mac songs, flared jeans and disco boots, *Scooby Doo* and *Ghostbusters*. As we grew older, Jess became more athletic and captained the high school basketball team, while I grew a pair of breasts the size of melons and realized that winning the 200-meter sprint was never going to happen.

We didn't hang around with the popular kids, but neither were we relegated to the bottom of the school hierarchy, floating along somewhere in the middle with our quirky obsessions and silly sense of humor. I always thought that we were tolerated by the jocks and the trendy girls because of Jess's love of sports, while she put it down to my breasts.

Whatever the reason, our friendship survived high school, relationships with boys, college, and everything else that life has thrown our way since.

"She's been an angel as always." I hold the door open wide to let her in.

"Hmm." Jess wrinkles her nose. "Will someone please explain to me why you get the angel and I get the demon?"

"I don't believe you," I say, tickling Izzie's waist and making her giggle. The child will break hearts when she's older.

"Okay." Jess sets her daughter down and eyes me suspiciously. "What's happened? And before you say 'nothing', I can feel the heat of your wrath from here."

Dad pokes his head around the kitchen doorway and calls out, "Come on in, Jess. I'll make coffee."

We go through to the kitchen where Dad already has the coffee brewing.

"Hi, Mr. Carter," Jess says. "I can't stay long. I need to get this little one into bed. Dave's on babysitting duties tonight, and I'm going out for a couple of drinks with my cousin."

"You should go with them, Rose." Dad's shameless when it comes to forcing my company onto others. "It'll do you good to get out."

Jess's gaze hops between the two of us. "Yes, come, Rose. You can tell me all about what's got you so rattled." Her eyebrows dance independently. "My guess is it's man related."

Dad chuckles, and I shoot him a glare that goes unnoticed. "It's not what you're thinking."

"Oh, sweetie, you tell yourself that if it makes you feel better."

"OKAY, I take it all back. Sounds like this guy wears his boxers too tight." Jess downs her glass of wine and asks the bartender for a refill after I recount the incident in the lobby of Weiss Tower.

The bar is busy, but not so noisy that we have to shout to hear ourselves speak; it's buzzing, and the urge to run home and hide behind a book in my pajamas is real.

"I just wish Dad would speak up for himself," I say, rubbing my thumb over the condensation on my glass.

She shakes her head. "Rose, your dad is a grown man. He has worked hard all his life, raised a quite spectacular daughter, and he doesn't need you to hold his hand."

I sip my drink, swallow, and feel the familiar sting behind my eyes. Dad meant well, suggesting that I get dressed up in something other than a T-shirt and faded jeans and spend some time with my best friend, but alcohol always produces the same result.

Jess's warm hand covers mine.

"I miss her so much," I say as the first tear trickles down my cheek. I catch it on the tip of my tongue and sniff loudly.

"I know." Jess nods. "You did everything you could for her, Rose. Your mom knew how much you loved her. You even dropped out of college to care for her."

"So, why do I feel so guilty?" I shake my head, swallow a larger mouthful of wine to blur the edges of what's going on in my head. But still the same old emotions drag up from somewhere deep inside like water being drawn from a well.

You go through life smiling at people, trying your best to be a good person, to be kind and thoughtful and compassionate, and it works. At least on the surface. No one sees what's going on beneath the bright smile because they have their own stuff to deal with, and that's okay. It's how it should be.

So, you keep going, tell yourself that you're coping, that finally, you've moved on from grief and guilt and loneliness, and then one glass of wine and wham! It all comes flooding back.

"She never got over it," I murmur. Jess has heard this all before, but she's the kind of friend who listens and doesn't tell me to let it go and move on.

"It isn't something you ever really get over, Rose, losing a baby. But you know what, your parents doted on the baby they did have—you! They poured double the amount of love into you, which makes you a very lucky person."

The bartender slides Jess's drink across the bar towards her, and she flashes him a grateful smile. He looks at my almost empty glass, raises an eyebrow, and I down it in one. He pours another without prompting.

He's good looking, dark hair, olive skin, high cheekbones, the kind of guy I'd be attracted to if my heart was in it. I turn around to face the room which is still filling up.

It's early evening. The place will be busy later, and that will be my cue to leave.

It isn't that I don't like crowds, I'm just out of touch with partying since Mom died and everything started sliding downhill. Robbie. My career. Marriage. Jess says it's because the universe is picking up on my negative energy, and maybe she's right, but I can't seem to drag myself out of it, and the bad news just keeps on coming.

"There she is!"

Jess points out her cousin Mindy who has just stepped through the doorway looking fabulous in an emerald-green pantsuit and strappy silver heels. Like Jess, she's tall and athletic with long raven-black curls that tumble over her shoulders and turn heads wherever she goes.

Even so, I'm not looking at her. I'm looking at the couple walking in behind her, holding hands, the huge diamond on the woman's wedding ring finger casting light signals around the room.

Robbie and his new fiancée.

I'd seen the engagement on our mutual friends' social media posts, but I'd buried that one deep too; in a city this size, you can go through life without ever bumping into someone you want to avoid.

"Rose?" Jess's voice penetrates my thoughts. "Are you okay?"

"Yeah, I'm fine." It's the standard response that spills out with minimal effort.

I have no right to feel jealous or bitter or any other kind of emotion now that Robbie has moved on with his life. I was the one who called off our engagement. There was too much going on at the time—my mom was sick, my grades were falling in college, Dad was a mess—at least that's what I told Robbie. The truth was, we'd been together since high school, and I always felt like something was missing, like I wasn't ready for marriage and kids and a home of our own. So, I handed back the ring and walked away.

I've spent the last few years convincing myself that I did what was right for me at the time, that I wanted all those things, but not with Robbie. Only now, I'm not so sure.

Blurry eyed with tears, I slide off my stool—I need to get away before Robbie spots me. My elbow connects with a glass. I gasp and hold my breath, watching the scene behind me play out in Jess's eyes and the way she flinches.

I whirl around, an apology on my lips, and realize that I'm face to face with the man in the gray suit from Dad's workplace.

Mr. Weiss.

He's still wearing the same clothes, but instead of mucky fingerprints, the front of his jacket is now wet and turning the same shade of red as the wine that was in his glass a moment ago. Recognition dances across his features.

"Do you ever watch where you're going?" I ask.

"Where *I'm* going?" He holds the glass away from him as if preventing the final few drips from landing on his jacket might somehow save it from being irreparably damaged.

Jess steps in and grabs my arm. "What my friend meant to say is she's sorry. She'll pay for your jacket to be dry-cleaned." She waggles her fingers in the general direction of his chest.

"That isn't what I meant." I straighten, facing him squarely.

Twice in one day—how is that even possible? Until this morning, I didn't even know this guy existed, and now he's everywhere, like a bad smell that refuses to blow away even when the windows are opened.

"This is the guy I was telling you about," I say, "the one who knocked Izzie over this morning."

"Okay." His jawline juts like he owns the place. Maybe he does own the place—it would just about sum up my luck right now. "Firstly, I didn't knock Izzie over this morning, she ran into me."

Jess is still clinging to my arm, but now she's watching him carefully, her expression unfathomable.

"Secondly, the kid shouldn't have even been inside the building."

Jess's eyebrows almost slide into her hairline, and I swallow the hysterical laughter that's threatening to spill out of my chest. I've seen that look before, and I wouldn't want to be on the receiving end of it, especially where it concerns Izzie. She's daring him to keep going.

And he does. "Thirdly, the suit is ruined, and I doubt she could afford to replace it, although I'm tempted to have another one made and send her the bill."

"Let's go," I say to Jess, turning around to leave. "It's not worth it."

Jess doesn't take her eyes off Mr. Weiss. When she speaks, her tone is cold. "Firstly, the kid, Izzie, you know the one who ran into you this morning, is mine. Secondly, if there's no sign on the front door saying NO CHILDREN ALLOWED, then she has as much right to be in that building as the next person."

"BEWARE THE OWNER would be more appropriate," I mutter under my breath.

"And thirdly..." Jess hesitates, a smile tugging the corners of her lips. "You should try buying washable suits, it makes life a lot easier."

I suck my lips in to smother my smile. I bet Mr. Weiss wishes he'd chosen any other bar to walk into tonight but this one.

The bartender has been lingering over the customer closest to us, following our interaction with a lopsided smile on his face. All around us, eager faces are turned our way, sensing the argument brewing.

"Hey, guys." Mindy, looking utterly gorgeous, appears next to Jess. "What's going on? What did I miss?"

"We're leaving," Jess says. "This bar is a little overcrowded."

"But I just got here." Mindy is still talking and glancing over her shoulder at Mr. Weiss as Jess leads her away.

I chance one final look at him before I follow them. Our eyes meet, only it isn't anger I see in them, it's something else. Pity perhaps? I walk away and I don't look back.

Read Fake Dark Vows Now Free With Kindle Unlimited and available on Paperback.

ABOUT THE AUTHOR

VIVY SKYS the author of Steamy Contemporary Romance novels, featuring smart, strong, sassy and witty female characters that command the attention of strong protective alpha males, from Off limits, age gap, bossy billionaires, single dads next door, royalty, dark mafia and beyond Vivy's pen will deliver.

Follow Vivy Skys on Amazon to be the first to know when her next book becomes available.

Printed in Great Britain
by Amazon